Madge Swinde  ~~~land.
As a teenager, ~~~~~~~~~~~~~~~~~~~~~~~~~~ here
she studied ar~~~~~~~~~~~~~~~~~~~~~~~~~ Cape
Town Universi~~~~~~~~~~~~~~~~~~~~~~~~~ Fleet
Street journalis~~~~~~~~~~~~~~~~~~~~~~ pub-
lishing company. ~~~~~~~~~~~~~~~~~~~~~~rvest,
*Song of the Wind, Shadows on the Snow, The Corsican
Woman, Edelweiss, The Sentinel* and *Harvesting the Past*
were international bestsellers and have been translated
into eight languages.

Snakes
and Ladders

Madge Swindells

WARNER BOOKS

A *Warner* Book

First published in Great Britain in 1997
by Little, Brown and Company

This edition published by Warner Books in 1997

Copyright © Madge Swindells 1997

The moral right of the author has been asserted.

A CIP catalogue record for this book
is available from the British Library.

ISBN 0 7515 1919 7

Typeset by Palimpsest Book Production Limited,
Polmont, Stirlingshire
Printed and bound in Great Britain by
Clays Ltd, St Ives plc

Warner Books
A Division of
Little, Brown and Company (UK)
Brettenham House
Lancaster Place
London WC2E 7EN

Acknowledgements to Jenni Swindells and Lawrie Mackintosh for their assistance, research and creative input, and to my editor, Hilary Hale, for her sympathetic and creative editing.

Prologue

——— ———

Long after Marjorie had left Dover the shrill cries of seagulls would always transport her home. She would be back in their cosy basement kitchen in Dover, where sycamore leaves waved in the breeze above the window well and blue gingham curtains shimmered at the open window. She would smell the herrings baking under the grill and bread toasting, and she would see Mum pushing her home-made quilted tea cosy over the willow pattern teapot and putting strawberry jam and a loaf of home-made bread on the table with her strong red hands.

Mum was a short, slender woman with good bone structure and eyes the deepest of blue. Her hair was grey, her face lined, but when she smiled, which was often, she reminded you of the girl she once was. It was something to do with her spontaneous grin and her air of delight. She was delighted with her husband, her daughter and her home. Most things pleased her. But there was another side to life, and Mum took care never to look at it. Her sense of denial always frightened Marjorie.

Funny, Marjorie thought, how her memories always took her back to tea-time. That was when Dad would walk in. He was a big, quiet man, with sea-green eyes and the softest voice imaginable. He would give her a quiet nod, and kiss Mum on the cheek, and moments later he'd be wrapping his fingers round a mug of strong tea. His mug was navy blue, with a big red heart on it, and white letters proclaiming: 'I love Dad'. Mum had bought it in Brighton on a day trip.

Marjorie was too proud to advertise her feelings. Instead she waited, weighing every word and glance, analysing each facial expression, *he loves me, he loves me not*, yearning for his love, but her father only had eyes for Mum. So there they were, the three of them, locked into their flawed triangle: Dad loved Mum, Mum loved her, she loved Dad. Full stop!

But then Robert came into her life and all the frustrated passion she had nurtured found its target.

Chapter 1
15 June 1972

There was pride and there was history, but little else. Looking towards Dover the observer's eyes would shift of their own accord to the castle on the cliffs, for it was larger than life and it dominated the town. Flags flying, its massive ramparts reaching for the clouds, it stood as a reminder of man's struggle for freedom and perfection, a trait that never abandoned him despite his many appalling failures.

Then there were the white cliffs of Dover, which looked more green than white when you stood below them. The cliffs were loved by the locals, a place to get away from tedious existence, nature's own garden. There was comfrey, wild thyme, purple orchids, harebells and banks of wild parsley.

To the casual traveller passing through (and there was little else you could do with Dover), the cliffs were nothing more than the sharp end of the chalk downs. In winter, the shrubs and grass that covered the slopes were washed away to expose sheer chalk, but the cliffs stood firm. They faced the storms and raging seas as if to say: 'thus far and no further'. The town's inhabitants were like the cliffs, sullen and strong, awesome in their patient strength.

So went the thoughts of a tall youth who stood on the pebbled beach gazing at the castle. He was trying to get to grips with the town and transpose his intuition into words, but he was struggling. After a while he sauntered over to the water's edge and gazed across the Channel. There was a glint of sun on the glittering water; a sparkling haze hung over the zooming hovercraft. It was mid-June and the sky was cloudless with the sun at its zenith, yet he could feel the thrilling sting of the east wind.

'In the midst of summer you can feel winter's breath,' he whispered, feeling the welcome surge of inspiration rising like sap through his limbs, but after several moments of frustrating blankness he thrust his notebook into his pocket and stripped down to his boxer shorts.

The sudden cold of the sea took his breath away and spurred him to action. He bellyflopped into knee-deep water and set out in a fast crawl towards the breakwater, pausing from time to time to float and tread water while he gazed back at the seafront. As usual the contrast of the castle against the scruffy town saddened him. He wondered whether or not the town deserved an epic poem. Pitman, his English teacher, was counting on him to produce a viable piece for the next college magazine.

His eyes stung with salty spray and he could taste the bitter brine as he sped on towards the breakwater. Then he noticed a small dinghy, sails flapping loose, bobbing over the swell, apparently with no one aboard. He changed course and swam towards it. Putting on a burst of speed, he kicked himself half out of the water to grasp the gunwale and haul himself onto the deck. He saw his mistake in a flash. A pretty, naked girl, who had been lying out of sight, grabbed a towel and tried to cover herself, but the wind was blowing up and her task was impossible. Mirth and lust surged simultaneously.

'Oops,' he said. 'My apologies. From back there this boat seemed abandoned. I mean, I couldn't see anyone . . .'

'Look away – or else . . .' she yelled.

From her voice he knew she was a local girl. Seething with sexual arousal, he was only too glad to turn away, but he hung on to her image. Her skin was light and flawless, her Titian hair hung in a long tangle of curls that glinted in the sunlight, her eyes were large and utterly beguiling. They were like the sea, both green and blue, and her mobile lips were made for kissing.

'Better hurry! You're too close to the breakwater.'

He heard her gasp. 'Wow! I fell asleep. I was getting a tan. You can turn round now. I'm decent.'

That was more than he was, but she was hauling in the anchor, and probably hadn't noticed.

'Coming about,' she called.

In faded denim shorts and an old grey jersey, she was still alluring and he wished he had something more concealing to wear. He decided it was time to introduce himself.

'My name's Robert MacLaren, and I'm in the Upper Sixth at Dover College.'

'That figures,' she muttered. She was crouched in the stern, holding the tiller, smiling as the boat planed lightly over the swells and troughs.

'Pretty good dinghy,' he said.

'She's a boat for all weathers. She enjoys a bit of fun on a nice day like this, but when the weather's bad, she's tough and as reliable as you could wish. My dad built her. D'you want to take a bit of a spin before we go back?' She pointed beyond the break-water.

'Why not?' he agreed.

She was a superb sailor, but a few minutes later he couldn't help wondering if she was getting her revenge on him. She hauled on the sheet until the boat was keeling over, almost touching the rough sea, and their speed was breath-taking. A sharp blustering wind was starting up. In next to no time they were racing through choppy waves. Her hair was drenched, her eyes red with salt spray, her wet jersey clinging to her full breasts, and she was smiling at the thrill of it. How lovely she was and how brave. Eventually she gave up trying to scare him and turned back.

'So what do you do when you're not sailing?' he asked when he could hear himself speak. He could sense that she was still resentful. 'Look, I'm sorry. The boat appeared to be abandoned and it was drifting onto the wall. What else could I have done? I'll swim back if you like.'

'No, it's all right. I'll take you in. I suppose I should be grateful, but the truth is, I was a bit peeved, being caught like that. Well, you know . . . sort of tanning a bit while I had the chance.'

She remained silent for a while. Was she sulking?

'How about tea and scones, just so we can get the tedious getting-to-know-you over and done with?' Robert suggested as they came into harbour. 'I have a longing to know all there is to know – when you were potty-trained, whether you floss your teeth every day, how many times you've been kissed, and that vital question every boy wants to know but is afraid to ask.' He paused long enough for that to sink in. Then said: 'Do you like cake?'

'If it's chocolate.' When she laughed her cheeks dimpled and her long sensuous neck throbbed. She had nothing on beneath her jersey and her full breasts shimmered. 'You're a cool one, I must say. The answer is "no". You don't have to buy cake to learn that. Have it for nothing.'

'But you will come?'

'Sure. And in case you're interested in my name, it's Marjorie Hardy,' she said firmly.

Part 1 – Robert
June 1972 – July 1973

Chapter 2

——— ———

Arms linked, two girls were sauntering home, carrying their tennis rackets, their school bags slung over their shoulders. Beside them the sea was softly swaying, glittering and mysterious. Like a woman, she was gentle and murmuring sweetly, hiding the passions of her fathomless depths, and the girls were like the sea. They looked ethereal in the twilight haze as they chattered.

Marjorie's lack of clothes was a sensitive subject which she tried to keep within the confines of the family, but Barbara, her friend and neighbour, persisted.

'Come on. Tell me. What're you wearing to the choir practice then?'

Marjorie flinched visibly. 'I guessed we were wearing school uniform.'

'No! Something quiet, teacher said, like a good suit with a clean white blouse.'

Her words brought a chill with them.

Marjorie had a navy school coat which made her look enormous, but who cared since it was for school? Then there was her shiny yellow mac and a bright orange coat bought three years back. It was too short by half and lately she'd had to give up breathing if she wanted to do up the buttons. Mum had put false hems on two of her skirts and her only pair of slacks, but the slacks were still too short and they looked downright silly. No matter how little she ate, her breasts kept on burgeoning and she didn't have a blouse that looked respectable.

Barbara was chatting on, but Marjorie wasn't listening. Then she felt a hand on her arm. 'Cat got your tongue then?' her friend asked anxiously.

'I'm sorry. What were you saying? I was thinking.'

'About that college boy you met, I bet.'

'Oh! I'd forgotten about him,' she lied.

The truth was, the image of him seldom left her thoughts. His hair was blue-black, thick and curly, his eyes dark brown and expressive. Most of the time he was smiling, but she'd seen his expression change like the wind and she reckoned he had a temper and that he was both moody and passionate. His skin was tanned; and he was tall and strong and altogether quite extraordinary. He should have been a gypsy, she mused, or perhaps he was half-Spanish, but there was a faint Scottish accent in his posh voice.

He'd kept her giggling for a solid hour over tea while he pumped every last detail out of her, but all she knew about him was his love of English. He'd gained a place at Oxford to read English, regardless of his A-level results, and he hoped to become a poet.

'Can you earn a living writing poetry?' she had asked him.

'I doubt it. I'll probably have to teach all my life to support my muse. Expensive whores, muses are.'

She'd never met anyone like him. When Robert said goodbye with a cheery wave outside the café, part of her seemed to stay with him. He hadn't said if he would see her again. Well, why should he? Since then she had dreamed about him nightly, but last night had been so real. He had swum naked to her boat, and clambered aboard when she was tanning. There they were, the two of them, as naked as babies and close together. What happened next made her blush with shame.

'Here! Look at your red cheeks. What is it with you?'

'Just a bit hot, that's all. The sun's hot.'

'Yeah! I bet it is, too, but it's down behind the horizon,' Barbara chortled. 'Reckon you've got the hots for him.' She burst into a raucous laugh and then put her arm around Marjorie to show there were no ill feelings.

The girls had reached Marjorie's house. Saying a quick goodbye to her friend, Marjorie slipped through the gate and went inside.

'Hi Mum,' she called and heard Mum's answering shout from their basement kitchen.

Now was as good a time as any to broach the subject of her wardrobe, she decided, still hovering by the stairs. Lately, she hadn't liked to ask for anything, what with Dad being so worried, but by now he'd have had his tea and would be halfway through a pint of bitter to wash down his bread and herring. At such times, the world was about as good as it could get for him. What's more, it was Wednesday – a good day.

Dad's life revolved around the football pools. The matches on Saturday afternoons brought the great let-down because he hadn't won the pools. Weekends were the pits and Monday wasn't much better, but around Tuesday hope was resurrected. Wednesday was a day of optimism. On Thursday hope soared and kept on soaring right through Friday until Saturday noon. And so it went.

It was a warm evening. He and Mum might take a

stroll along the seafront later and pop into the pub. Running downstairs, she saw she was right, they were going out.

'You're late for tea,' Mum said. 'I kept you a bite of something. It's under the cloth there.'

'Thanks,' she said. 'Oh, by the way, Mum, I'm going up to Dover College. We're going to sing Handel's *Messiah* with their Upper Sixth. There's a few practice sessions starting tomorrow night.'

Mum looked up sharply at her tone. 'So?'

'Mum, d'you think I could have a new coat? Mine's too tight. It hurts under the armpits and it's so short.'

'Silly idea,' Mum said. 'Like mixing oil and water. Don't you go setting your eyes on one of them college boys. Rich marry rich, my girl.'

'Oh, Mum! I'm only going to choir practice and you're talking of marriage.' She giggled.

'We can't afford to buy a new coat right now, dear. There's a recession starting up. Shipping is hit badly. Dad's hardly earned any overtime for weeks. We're really worried. But think, in a few weeks' time you'll be earning your own cash. You'll be quite the independent lady, won't you? If I were you, I'd bide my time until I had a bit of my own cash in my pocket.'

Marjorie tried to swallow her fear. What was Mum talking about – a holiday job? They both knew she was going to be a teacher. Mum was always conning everyone. Whatever was in Mum's best interest was always twisted round to make it seem as if it was best for the other person.

Dad was pretending to read the paper, but she knew he was listening. 'Dad,' she said, appealing to him. 'Won't you give me the cash?'

'She's going to sing in the choir up at Dover College,' Mum explained, as if Dad hadn't been listening.

Dad looked awkward. 'There's nothing wrong with your school coat,' he said. 'If it's good enough for school, it's good enough for the nobs.'

Dad's large green eyes gazed remotely at her and her problems. The contrast of his eyes with his square, lined face was shocking sometimes.

'It's mufti night,' she pointed out.

'Wear your orange coat, pet,' Mum suggested. 'It's really nice.'

'It's too short and too tight,' Marjorie snapped.

'Yes, it is. Looks silly,' Dad agreed.

'My skirts and slacks are too short and I don't know what to do,' she said, close to tears.

'I told you what to do. Wear your school uniform.' Dad returned to his newspaper.

'Nonsense,' Mum said. 'She can't wear school uniform if the others aren't. There's nothing wrong with a short coat. Short's fashionable.'

'Not that sort of short,' Dad grumbled.

Marjorie stood up, knocking her chair over, and rushed out of the room, but then paused outside the door, trying to think of a better plea.

'She gets more clumsy by the day,' she heard Dad grumble.

'Oh, she's all right. She's growing up. She'll be off our hands one of these days.'

Marjorie stumbled upstairs and sat on the bed aching with loneliness and the need to be loved.

Chapter 3

Marjorie's attic bedroom was filled with light from two skylights. It was a teenager's pad with posters of her heroes covering each square inch of wall and half the sloping ceiling. Marc Bolan, Rod Stewart, Donny Osmond and Elvis Presley jostled for space beside posters showing the frightened faces of a mother and child in Hue, South Vietnam, and protesting American Indians. There were books on art, music, the classics, poetry and fashion, gleaned from second-hand book stalls; fashion shots; a radio; cushions scattered on the floor.

Marjorie had borrowed a fashion magazine from the school library and she was lying on the floor under the window agonising over the pictures. There must be something she could improvise, she reasoned, but the models were killing her. Those long smooth legs, those perfect features, those haughty, self-confident expressions. She could die when she looked into the mirror. If only . . . Still, she reasoned, their hairdos didn't look like much – just long, straight, ragged locks. That shouldn't provide her with much of a problem. She had a brown eyeliner and some dark red lipstick, and that would have to do for make-up. But what about clothes?

She pored over the pages avidly, longing to be a

part of this glamorous world as she studied the words: 'The seventies are bringing realism to fashion. Fantasy fashions are vanishing, and the Modern Miss will have to cope with harsh economic realities.'

'Tell me something new,' she muttered.

Despair was sinking in. She had so little with which to experiment. Then she saw a shot of a model running down the pavement, arms flung up with joy, wearing, of all things, a pair of slacks that ended at knee length, but they were called *culottes*. She studied the picture closely and ran for Mum's sewing scissors.

How much hem did you need for the turn-ups? A lot, she discovered. Her heart was smashing against her ribs in time to the snip-snip of the scissors. She'd cop it from Dad if she ruined her slacks. She was still sewing the hem when Mum called out up the stairs. 'We're going down the pub, love.'

The money they spent in that pub would buy her fifty new outfits, but there was no point in griping about things that couldn't be cured. Running down to the kitchen, she pressed her culottes, then held them against her critically. Hm! Not bad.

Now for a blouse. Most of the models wore blouses unbuttoned to the waist. That was all very well for them, since everyone expected models to show all they'd got and most of them hadn't much to show except a lot of knobbly bones. If she could wear her blouse open to the waist no one would see how tight it was. Her eyes turned thoughtfully to her black school bathing suit. Grabbing some garments she ran downstairs and stripped off in front of Mum's long mirror.

It was not often she saw herself naked in a mirror. She stared long and hard, flushing at the sight of her breasts, which were fuller than the last time she'd looked, with dark circles around her nipples. Was this her? She looked . . . well, sort of strange. She was longer and thinner than she'd realised. After a while she reached up and cupped her breasts in her hands, feeling the firmness under the soft ivory skin. What if Robert's hands . . . ? At this wicked thought she flushed and felt her nipples become hard and swollen while a strange dampness was gathering between her thighs.

'Oh Robert,' she whispered.

'Enough of this nonsense,' she said aloud. Hopping into her bathing suit, she pulled the culottes over it, threaded her belt in and put on her school shirt, leaving it unbuttoned. Pretty smart, she could see. But what about shoes? She raced up the stairs two at a time and back again with the only pair of high-heeled shoes she possessed. They were white and bought for her cousin's wedding, but the chemist's shoe dye would soon fix that. Her outfit might have come straight out of the fashion pages.

The afternoon flew. At last she was done, but something was missing. Earrings! Half the girls had their ears pierced. Barbara's ears had been pierced for her birthday and Marjorie had her old studs, discarded when Barbara received her first gold loops. She took them out of the matchbox where they nestled in cotton wool and held them against her ears.

It couldn't hurt that much, could it? she mused, searching around for a large safety pin.

It did, she discovered when she made the first prick. The pain brought tears to her eyes. When she pushed harder it became agonising, so she hurried downstairs for some ice.

Back in her room with frozen ears, she glared at her reflection. 'Are you going to look like a fashion plate, Marjorie Hardy, or are you going to look like a ninny? It's only an ear when all's said and done.' She pushed the safety pin into a bottle of disinfectant, and got to work. Ten minutes later, her heart pounding, her eyes watering, her face as white as the cliffs, the studs were firmly in place.

Chapter 4

If only she had a rope ladder, Marjorie thought, poised at the top of the spiral staircase, trying to pluck up courage to make a dash for it. Propelled by the fear of being late, she began her descent. There must be a knack to walking downstairs in high heels, but she hadn't acquired it and each step sounded as if she were hammering a nail in. Clop, clop, clop! Damn! She bent to take off her shoes, but she was too late.

Dad emerged, his newspaper in one hand. He stared long and hard, exclaiming: 'Jesus! Mum. Come out here and take a look. Where does she think she's going in that get-up?'

Mum appeared looking harassed. 'It's a bit much, dear.'

'It's fine, believe me. I copied something in a maga-zine.'

Mum gasped as she realised the black slacks had been shortened to knee length. 'Well, I must say . . .'

The truth was she wasn't going to say anything in front of Dad, Marjorie realised and blessed her for it.

'Where did you get that lipstick?'

'I saved up for it.'

'Suits you. But why's your hair all swept over on one side like that? Look's like you're hiding something.'

Mum's hand reached towards her. Marjorie backed off and collided with the bannister and her hair fell back.

'Oh my goodness! Whatever have you done to your ear?'

'Nothing,' Marjorie replied sulkily.

'Idiot! It's badly infected. Must be very sore. Hang on while I get something for it. I think you look very nice.'

Tears stung Marjorie's eyes. She'd been ready to cope with censure, not with kindness.

Seconds later, her ears smarting from surgical spirit and Dad's caustic remarks, her eye make-up toned down with Mum's thumb and her lipstick wiped half off with a tissue, she clip-clopped her way towards the bus stop.

He wasn't there. A quick glance around the college hall assured her of that fact. Her disappointment was like a kick in the stomach.

The college choir master was moving them into position: girls on the right, boys on the left, soloists in front. Marjorie was one of them.

The choir master was looking apprehensive as he prepared for blast-off. Perhaps he thought they couldn't sing. Well, he was in for a surprise. Half the sixth form choir were Welsh. Their dads had moved down here when the Welsh mines started laying off men.

Moments later his face showed his shock and then amazed delight as the accumulated joy of a hundred young voices echoed round the old building. Once Marjorie began to sing she forgot her disappointment and her nervousness. Singing was one of the few things she could do really well. When her turn came to sing solo, her voice soared out: 'There were shepherds abiding in the field, keeping watch over their flocks by night.' She knew she'd done well when she came to the end. She'd got her voice from her dad's side, or so Mum always told her. Dad only sang when he was drunk, but she'd seen grown-up people spellbound, the tears running down their cheeks when Dad sang 'Danny Boy' in his clear, high-pitched yet soft voice.

The choir master was getting hot under the collar about his own choir. They weren't much good. Well, Welsh miners didn't send their kids to Dover College, did they? That was his bad luck, she reasoned with a secret smile.

She and the chorus were belting their way through the last bit: 'His yoke is easy and His burden is light.' Soon they were clattering down from the stage, pausing, bumping into each other, wondering where to find the refreshments they'd been promised. All this bother for nothing, she brooded, remembering her agonising efforts with the safety pin.

'Hello again.' *His voice!* She twisted round, gasping. There he was, all six foot two of him, smiling down at her.

'You came,' she sighed, but caught off-guard her eyes said much more. She looked away, but too late. His hand took her arm and pulled her close to him.

'Let's get out of here,' he whispered. 'I could do with a drink. I've been waiting for hours. What d'you say? Yes? It's stale biscuits and weak tea here.'

There wasn't much she could say since she'd lost her voice. It was like being on the big dipper at the fun fair. All her blood was racing around in the wrong direction, her breath wouldn't come and her feet weren't taking instructions, at least not from her, although they seemed to be following him meekly enough.

As she sank into the black leather upholstery of his car she realised she hadn't said goodbye to Barbara.

'I can't be too late or I'll cop it from Dad,' she managed to stammer.

'I was hoping you'd be in the choir.' He smiled at her and her stomach lurched. 'I was in the wings. I want to tell you something.' He was looking so serious. 'When I look at a really great painting, or when I read T.S. Eliot, or see a really good sunset, I come out in goose pimples. It's like an allergy to excellence. Feel my arm.'

She ran one finger tentatively over his skin, thrilling to the feel of the black hairs that covered his arm.

'The goose pimples are because of you and your voice. You sang beautifully and you are lovely.'

'Oh, go on with you,' she answered awkwardly.

'You mean you don't know?'

'Know what?'

'How lovely you are.'

His hand reached out and took hers. From then on she was hardly conscious of what they talked about, or where they went. The only true reality was the feel of his fingers pressing hers, and the summer storm making havoc of her stomach as lightning flashed this way and that way, piercing her entrails. She was only half-aware of sitting in a strange pub up River way. It was rather posh and someone was playing the piano. She drank a beer shandy and fell in love all over again as he dredged up his Scottish accent from childhood days and quoted Robbie Burns from memory.

At the stroke of midnight he parked outside her home.

'What about Sunday? Are you free? We could go out in the country. D'you ride?'

She shook her head.

'Would you like me to teach you?'

'Oh yes,' she murmured dreamily.

'All right. I'll fetch you elevenish.'

'See you,' she enthused recklessly, her mind on the problem of what to wear. After all, she'd worn it all tonight.

The prince and his coach rode away leaving her trembling at the open door, lingering and regretful. Eventually she stumbled in and found her mother waiting up for her.

Mum took one look at her and groaned 'Oh Gawd!'

Chapter 5

As Robert drove towards Marjorie's home on Sunday morning he was feeling strangely ambivalent towards his planned outing. He had half a mind to drive back to college, but finally he kept going. It was not so much Marjorie's beauty that drew him, but some deeper attraction. There was something here that he wanted. Something she had and he lacked, but he could not quite define the need.

He thought about her courage. It was staggering how well she had managed her small boat in the sudden squall. He suspected that she could cope with far more than this and come up smiling. She was like the blue harebells on the Dover cliffs, battered by cold winds, snow and ice, trampled by hostile feet, starved in meagre soil, yet stubbornly enduring, lending their fragile beauty to the world. She, too, had her roots deep down in British loam and the result was a girl of resilience and amazing beauty. He sensed her moral strength and her goodness. Something in her eyes said: I could take most things standing on my head and then some, and I wouldn't falter. No, not for a minute.

Robert felt that he had none of this strength. He had been reared in the exclusive world of money and breeding. His individuality was more fragile than hers. He could never endure the hardships that she would laugh off with hardly a second thought. She drew sustenance from the earth, and from her humour and her roots, and he longed to be strong like her, and to be filled with her raw passion for living.

As he approached her house he felt a spasm of panic. It was like the split second before high-diving or parachuting, or tumbling backwards off the boat at the start of a scuba-dive. He was about to free fall into the unknown. He accelerated and drove by, feeling reprieved. He could return to his exclusive friends, and his privileged life. And yet . . . He knew he had to experience Marjorie and her world to gain his manhood. After a while he slowed down, did a U-turn and parked at the kerb. Half a dozen neighbours came out to stare and a girl he vaguely remembered from somewhere called out 'Hello' to him.

It was a sunny morning and the front door was open. Robert tiptoed past a painted gnome, trying to pretend it wasn't there. Then he had to pretend that the net curtains weren't there and the large green mat with strawberries all over it, and the walnut whatnot standing in the hallway, filled with cheap ornaments, and with artificial flowers on top. Oh God! How awful.

A woman without the slightest resemblance to Marjorie hurried to answer his knock. 'Hello, you must be Robert. I'm Mrs Hardy, Marjorie's mother. Come in. She'll be down in a jiffy. Come out the back, Robert.' She was quite frail-looking and her face was pale and lined. She had dark eyebrows, blue eyes, greying hair cut in a bob, and a small mouth that was curiously youthful, but when she smiled, it was restrained and forced.

She led him through a small sitting room that had an

air of being seldom used to a back garden where her husband sat in his vest and braces under a sycamore tree. He was polishing his shoes and didn't look up as she introduced him as Mr Hardy. He could sense the baffled power of the man, and the air of discontent.

'How do you do, sir. My name's Robert MacLaren. I've invited your daughter for a drive in the country. We might go riding. It's a lovely day, don't you think?'

'If you say so,' Mr Hardy said heavily, by way of greeting, then went on in the same tone of voice, 'I think you're wasting your time around these parts. My daughter has been strictly brought up. She's never been out with a boy before. She's a good girl and you must respect her, or you'll have me to deal with, Robert.'

Suddenly he looked up and the message in his startling green eyes was loud and clear. It was of the utmost menace.

Oh God! How awful! His gauche warnings belonged with the gnomes and artificial flowers.

'Sir,' Robert cleared his throat. 'I have the utmost respect for your daughter.' Searching for a change of subject, he looked around desperately and saw a very large brown rabbit in a hutch by the back door. It was a great floppy, friendly thing, his ears falling forward, his nose twitching and his eyes benign as he gazed at them. Robert rubbed his finger against the furry cheek.

'It's a fine rabbit,' he ventured.

'Its name's Frank. Flemish Giant. They get a bit more flesh on their bones than the other varieties. We're fattening him up for next Sunday's lunch. Mrs Hardy makes a good rabbit pie.'

'Oh!' Robert sank into the nearest chair.

Head down, Mr Hardy polished harder while keeping

up a monologue on the weather, the crops and the roses that were particularly fine this year. His accent puzzled Robert. Each word was carefully pronounced with a slightly Irish lilt, but there was something else, Scottish perhaps, for he pronounced his 'h's in his wheres and whens.

Then Marjorie came running in, cheeks flushing, dimples dimpling, eyes sparkling, wearing her cut-off slacks and a turquoise jersey vest and scarf that matched her eyes. Her auburn hair sparkled in the sun, and a smattering of freckles had appeared on her nose.

'They're new,' he said, leaping to his feet.

'No, they're Mum's.'

'The freckles?'

She giggled.

'They weren't there last time I saw you.'

'As if you would remember!'

'But I do remember.'

'I've been gardening up at the allotment. We've got all sorts of things up there. I'll show you if you like. Come on, then. Let's not miss any more of the day.'

Chapter 6

As soon as they had driven out of sight of the house, Robert took her hand and the two of them sat in silence. It was a warm, lazy day with hardly a cloud in sight. Fields and small copses and little stone villages flew by. The grass was full of poppies and clumps of purple foxgloves; marigolds and dandelions dotted the fields with colour; and the hedgerows were bright with hawthorn.

'You'll finish school soon,' he ventured at last.

'Yes. It scares me.'

'And then?'

She frowned and stared away. He saw her bite her lip and he sensed her anxiety. 'I've gained a place at Bristol, subject to my marks in the exams I suppose, but I think I did all right. Trouble is, Mum's been throwing out hints about me earning my living soon. I don't know why. We talked it all out last year. I'm waiting until I'm sure about my results and then . . .' Her voice tailed off. 'But tell me about you,' she went on hurriedly, and he realised that she badly wanted to change the subject. 'You never talk about your home. Why choose Dover College? Funny place for a budding poet.'

He laughed. 'I suppose so. I'm the third son in the family. The eldest will run the family business. The second will take law and the third, that's me, should go into the Navy. That's our family tradition. Only I'm not going into the Navy. I want to write. When I left prep school I didn't know this, so the Navy seemed like a great idea. I changed. Of course we all do.'

He squeezed her hand. 'Promise me you'll never change. I wish you'd stay like this for ever.' What a crass thing to say, he thought, yet he meant it. He watched her flush.

'Wish in one hand, spit in the other and see which one fills up first. That's what my mum says.'

Her coarse words brought the whole sorry saga of her family back into sharp focus. With a twinge of revulsion, he dropped her hand, wondering if she was more like them than she seemed. Suddenly it was terribly important that he find out.

'Marjorie,' he said after a long silence. 'Does it ever worry you to keep something like a pet, I mean so friendly and so trusting as poor Frank, and then to eat it?'

'Oh!' When she flushed her whole body seemed to be a part of it. He almost veered off the road as he watched the white skin above her breasts change to a rosy hue.

'Well, the truth is, I take care not to look at them,' she stammered. 'When I was a kid I had a special pet rabbit. He was white with a black patch over one eye so I called him Nelson. I loved him, but I came back from school one afternoon and there he was, strung up by his feet outside the back door, split from top to bottom. So now I don't ever look at them. That way I can't get hurt, see?'

A part of Robert lamented for this sweet girl who sang divinely and who had once loved a rabbit. Yet another part of him still kept agonising, longing to be sure. 'Did you eat the rabbit? I mean your rabbit?'

'Give over, Robert,' she protested, suddenly cross with him. 'What are you after? Stop niggling at me. It's not fair. You're not being fair to my folks, either. Dad keeps the rabbits up at the allotment. Everything up there is for us to eat – cabbages, onions, lettuce, all sorts of things. It helps out with the housekeeping. There's never enough cash, you see. My folks aren't rich. Dad brings the rabbits down one at a time to fatten them.' She broke off and bit her lip. 'What's wrong with that? You're not a vegetarian, I assume. I bet you go hunting and watch the beagles drag those poor little foxes to pieces, don't you?'

She was right. He felt his cheeks flushing. What could he say?

'But the answer to your question, Robert, is no. I didn't feel hungry. Not for days, to tell the truth, but Dad vowed it was the best pie Mum had cooked in a long while. You know something? I blamed Mum more than Dad, for cooking it so well and for letting him kill Nelson. You see, she understood, but Dad never did, so that makes him blameless in a way.'

'You're not a bit like them,' he asserted, sorrowing for her mother's treachery.

'Here! What d'you mean? Who d'you think you're criticising with your highfalutin manner and your snobby accent? Don't look down your long nose at my folks, Robert, or you'll see the last of me.'

'I'm sorry,' he apologised stiffly.

He made a mighty effort to shrug off her awful family. They drove in silence for a while and when he reached out for her hand he felt her pull away. He braked gently and steered the car onto the grassy verge. Then he stopped and sat looking at her. She was glaring at him with wide, hostile eyes, her mouth pinched shut and her lips downturned.

'There's no law says I have to like the father of the girl I've fallen for. Or is there? And do you mind terribly if I don't? I like you so much.'

He pulled her close against him and the heat from her body shocked him. His sudden surge of passion jolted his thoughts. He was dazed, unable to think, agonisingly aware of the fire that had ignited deep inside him. His skin was scorching hot, and his lips felt a strange burning need to join with hers. He nudged her chin up and felt the soft, clinging sweetness of her lips merging with his. He shuddered and almost groaned with passion.

At last he straightened, but she was still clinging to him. 'Oh,' he sighed. 'I don't know how to handle this. I never felt like this. Let's get out of here. Let's walk.'

She stood uncertainly by the car door, but he took her hand and pulled her down the grassy bank and they walked along the ditch, arm in arm, moving awkwardly, both clumsy with sexual frustration, pent up and swollen, their legs stiff, two minds with one idea: where could they hide?

There was a gap in the hawthorne hedge and he pulled her through to a field of waving barley with purple patches of scabious here and there. He took off his coat and laid it on the grass.

'We could sit here if you like.'

She sat down reluctantly. 'Thought we were going riding. We didn't get far, did we?' She sounded resentful.

'We'll go. Soon. I couldn't drive, you see.' He tried to explain. 'It was like a forest fire. One spark and there we were, raging out of control. Did you feel like I felt?'

'I feel like that each time I think of you. I dream of you each night.' She looked at him so trustingly.

There was that courage again. It took guts to be so truthful, he decided. 'Me too,' he agreed. 'But back there. Well, it was something else. Scary! Have you ever?'

'No.'

'Me neither.'

'You mustn't think I ever will. I never will.' She sounded quaintly old-fashioned.

'I didn't bring you out to seduce you,' he insisted. 'This took me by surprise.'

He pulled up her top a few modest inches, revealing her bare midriff, and pressed his lips on her skin, tickling her with his tongue. He wondered if she would object, but she squirmed and giggled and somehow this made him feel much older than her. She was only a kid. He must look after her. It was sheer agony to break away.

'I've cooled down a bit. Let's go.'

She smiled up at him and tried to pull him back.

'Come on, come on. You want to learn to ride, don't you? If I kiss you again we'll never get there. I'll race you back.'

He'd always imagined girls were strictly for dating. He'd never had much to do with them, having no sisters, but Marjorie was great, he discovered. She learned the rudiments of riding without too much trouble, and when her horse galloped off with her and dumped her in the pond, she laughed and climbed right back on again. Her hair dried in the sun and he lent her his jersey. She was fun to be with.

Chapter 7

It was Saturday night and Rob was late. They were going dancing and Marjorie was anxious that the skirt borrowed from Barbara, and therefore too short, wasn't quite good enough. She'd been pacing up and down the hall for the past half-hour when Dad cornered her. He had a captive audience, she reckoned bitterly. It was unusual for him to say more than twenty words to her, but tonight he had plenty to say.

Earlier in the week, he'd received the news he'd been fearing for a long while: the shipyard was laying off most of its workforce, him included. He was too old to hope to get another job, so now he faced early retirement on an inadequate pension. The situation had brought all his resentment and bitterness to the surface.

'You've seen that Robert every night for three weeks,' he repeated now. 'You're asking for trouble, my girl. Rich marry rich. You can bet your life he'll marry into his class and it'll be someone as rich as he is, but not before he's broken your heart. I've been checking up on him. It seems he comes from an ancient Scots family – titled. His family won't want to be linked with the likes of us, even if he ever thought about it. I bet Robert's never even mentioned marriage.'

'Why should he? We're only good friends,' she repeated for the umpteenth time that evening.

'Since you say so I believe you, but how long can that last? Stop being a fool. Break it off with him now.'

A large, hiccuping sob spoiled her planned response. 'My friendship with Robert is the only precious thing in my life,' she choked out.

'Suit yourself,' he said grimly. 'But don't come crying to me when he scoots off leaving you in the family way. You'll be on your own.' He went down to the kitchen.

'Oh give over, Dad,' she muttered. 'You and your class-ridden claptrap's so gloomy I wonder you can get out of bed in the morning.'

It was true that they'd dated every night after that first special Sunday. They'd had so much fun, and both of them had been determined to keep their passions under control.

At first they'd seen all the local films and concerts and stuffed themselves with too much rich food night after night. Finally they'd admitted that they'd rather walk along the beachfront, or sit on a bench and talk, but Saturday, they both agreed, was dancing night. And this was probably going to be their last Saturday night together for some time, as Dover College was breaking up for the end of term that week. So where was he?

An hour later she began to think his car might have broken down. By midnight thoughts of accidents obsessed her. She wondered if she should call the hospital. By two a.m. she had come to the horrid conclusion that she'd been stood up. She spent a sleepless night examining the possible causes for his non-appearance.

As the next week passed with agonising slowness,

Marjorie was forced to admit that Robert had left for home without saying goodbye. She had gone over their last night together time and again, but could not think what she might have done wrong. Dark shadows appeared under her eyes and she walked around listlessly and would not eat. She could not come to grips with the Robert she knew and this other person who had cruelly abandoned her. She began to feel worthless.

As the end of term drew closer she had another problem to face – her future, but she was scared to broach the subject with her parents. Then Dad provided an opportunity when they were reading in the kitchen while Mum baked an apple pudding.

'You had your results yet?'

His soft voice disguised the underlying aggression that could be triggered off at any time, particularly since his redundancy, except perhaps when he was halfway through his first beer of the day, as he was now. This gave her courage.

'Miss Allington's expecting me to get As and Bs, but meantime I've been accepted at Bristol. You know there's a possibility I might make Oxbridge.' She knew she sounded tremulous, but she could not control her anxiety.

Dad pushed his glass aside and stood up. 'You're eighteen,' he growled. 'I was earning my living years before then. A-levels is as far as we can go, Marjorie. In fact it's further than we could properly afford. We're not rich, especially now that we're going to be living on my pension, and it's high time you paid towards your keep. There's plenty of good jobs around for young people despite the recession. You can feel thankful for that. I notice Alf's advertising for a girl to operate the till at his butcher's shop. He pays good money.'

Marjorie's cheeks burned with temper, but she hung on to her composure and quelled her rebellious impulse. Miss Allington had told her she was on the short list for the English and Modern Language prizes, but Dad couldn't care less. Had he ever? She could sit and gaze at sawn-up carcases and lungs and kidneys, and horrible gawping pigs' heads for the rest of her days for all he cared. In her mind's eye she saw the butcher's storeroom where she'd gone to have the beef minced last week and before she could prevent it she winced at the memory.

'Here we go again,' Dad grumbled. He stood up, grabbing his beer, ready to flee. 'I blame you,' he nagged, turning to her mother. 'You've spoiled her, giving her silly ideas about her future. She's got to get a job. You'd think she'd want to be self-supporting. I couldn't wait.'

'Why don't you go down the pub and have a nice game of darts.' Mum dug her hand into her tin. She would go to any lengths to avoid confrontations, even if it meant parting with her housekeeping money.

Dad pocketed the cash and left without a word, but, watching him, Marjorie sensed that he was only angry because he felt guilty. Well, that was that! She pushed her plate away.

'I'd always hoped you'd have things a bit better than I had,' Mum began. 'When I was fifteen . . .'

Marjorie switched off to avoid hearing the familiar saga of her Grandpa's disaster which had sent Mum to work as a maid until she'd met Dad. Tibby, their spoiled ginger cat, chose that moment to reach up with his front paws and pat her knee. He wanted his share of the herring. She picked up a bit and gave it to him.

'Heavens, child, we only get herring once a week now. Must you give it to the cat? It's you who taught him to beg at the table,' Mum grumbled.

Plucking up courage, Marjorie tackled her mother again. 'Listen, Mum, I know you've always expected me to . . . well . . . contribute towards the family . . .'

'No different to other families, Marjorie,' Mum said sternly. 'We've brought you up to the best of our ability, given you . . .' She was off down a familiar path. Marjorie let her have her say, then tried once again.

'Well, yes, Mum, I agree, but there's only me, you see. It stands to reason I'd make more money if I had some training – even a year would allow me to learn a trade. I mean, it wouldn't cost you anything. I went to the poly yesterday, and I found out that it's free. I can live very cheaply, I could walk there. I don't eat much, you know that.'

'You'll be glad when you're earning a bit,' Mum retorted. 'Look at all the lovely clothes you'll be able to buy. It's great to have your own cash and not be beholden to anyone. I know your teachers have been filling your head with ideas about University, but later on you'll thank us. What's the point of studying? You'll be married before you're any age. Make sure you make a good marriage . . . someone with a bit of cash who can help us a bit. Alf's a good lad. He's had his eye on you for a long time.'

'Alf's old and disgusting.'

'Don't be silly, he's still in his thirties.'

'That's old for me. How could you suggest something like that? When I marry it will be for love.'

'Well, remember this, Miss Hoity-Toity. It's as easy to fall in love with a rich man as a poor man.'

'You mean I should sell myself to the highest bidder, to keep you and Dad in beer and kippers?'

'That's a wicked thing to say.' Mum's eyes flashed with indignation and real temper. 'Sometimes I don't recognise you as my own daughter. I never heard of a daughter saying such a thing to her mother.'

Oh God! She'd blown it.

It was Dad who had been axed, but she was the real victim, Marjorie knew, for her dreams and plans had been severed as neatly as Anne Boleyn's poor head. And with them went her optimism and pride in her academic success, her belief, instilled in her by her teachers, that she deserved a university education, and even worse, her certainty that someone up there was looking after her.

Chapter 8

Marjorie's last day at school came all too soon – a day so gloomy that she expected a total eclipse of the sun, but in fact the weather was lovely. A warm south-west wind set the grass shimmering and the leaves fluttering, birds were singing, bees and insects filled the air with a sweet summer's hum, and the gardens were scented with roses, honeysuckle and wallflowers.

Barbara caught up with her and hung on to her arm. 'Here, what's it with you, love? You've been avoiding me for weeks.' She looked up half-mocking, half-sad, her huge eyes glowing with affection, and Marjorie felt guilty for neglecting her when Rob was around.

'Oh Barbara, nothing's wrong between us. I've just been a bit out of sorts lately. Writing the exams was a strain.'

'But you always do well, so you don't have to worry. Not like me – I'll be lucky if I scrape through.'

Barbara had always idolised Marjorie for her brains and for the future successes everyone had predicted for her. If only she knew. 'What will you do next, Barbara?' Marjorie asked. 'Are you still planning to be a cook?'

'Course I am. There's money in catering. You can run a canteen, or get a place in a big restaurant somewhere. The sky's the limit.'

Marjorie wondered why she hadn't thought of that. Mum was an inspired cook and she'd picked up most of it. Perhaps Mum would think again about a three-month course. 'How soon before you're earning your living then?'

'There's two years at poly. I'm looking forward to it.'

'Yes,' Marjorie muttered. 'That's great.' Even being a cook was out of reach for her. She couldn't come to grips with her new, lowly status. She'd been living so high in her dreams, egged on by her teachers.

Barbara chatted on and Marjorie tried to listen, but her mind was racing. There must be plenty of trades she could learn while earning a small wage. She'd have to find out. Suddenly she had a mental picture of herself sitting at a desk from nine to five, bored to tears. She cringed at the prospect.

'I haven't seen Robert around lately, Marjorie,' Barbara pointed out, jolting her thoughts from one disaster to another.

'Oh, Barbara. He's finished school now. He's gone home.' It wasn't in her nature to confide her woes to anyone.

'He'll be back,' Barbara predicted confidently. 'Bet you anything you like. He'll start missing you and he'll come visiting.'

The girls filed into the school hall for the last time, all of them happy and excited – except for Marjorie. For her this day marked the end of a dream.

Their headmistress, a staunch feminist, launched herself into her favourite topic.

'You girls are setting out into the world in difficult times. The juicy carrot of equality may seem to dangle before our eyes, but we soon find that it is seldom attainable.'

Marjorie loved their headmistress. She was a tall, good-looking woman with strong features and dark, almost black hair. She was stern, but just, and she always had time to listen, no matter how busy she was. She had never married, but her rumoured affair with the art master was of great interest to the Upper Sixth.

'The industrial revolution wiped out women's status,' she went on. 'Before then, our role was vital and we were revered for it: growing and cooking food, making soap, medicines, candles, looking after farm animals, weaving and making clothes. But most of these occupations have been taken over by men.

'Last of all women clung to the role of motherhood, but overpopulation means that none of us can look forward to a career of keeping the cradle full.

'So here we stand in the Seventies, girls, faced with a hazardous future, where things are stated one way, but in reality are the reverse. The male Establishment sees women as sex objects, even when married, and as second-class citizens. The vast majority of us work as "domestics" in the male Establishment, particularly in the role of "office wife".

'Many women opt for marriage as a career, but here they make a serious mistake. Legally, marriage is the most male-dominated institution of all.

'So what can you girls look forward to? Today we don't know who or what we are, or what society expects of us.

'The equality of the sexes won't come without a fight and you, my girls, will be at the forefront of the fight. So much depends upon you – so go for the best education you can possibly get. Never take second best and *never* let men reduce your status,' she added with heavy emphasis. 'Not even if you are married to them.'

She paused and smiled at them.

'That brings me to a most gratifying announcement. Four of our girls have won places at University, regardless of their examination results.'

To a round of applause, Marjorie heard her name read out. She wished she could fall down dead right there and then. She could not believe this was real. She seemed to be two people, one of whom hovered over her, watching the proceedings, like a fly on the ceiling. The unreality persisted as she twice mounted the steps to the platform to receive the English and the Modern Languages prizes. She wondered how she managed to keep smiling. Even when the headmistress shook her hand and told her that she was convinced that she, at least, would have no problem with status, Marjorie kept a fixed smile on her face.

At last it was over. 'I envy you, Marj,' Barbara said, throwing one arm around her as they blinked in the blazing sunlight outside.

'Do you? Whatever for?'

'I think everyone here does. You've got your future made.'

'Oh, I don't know. I'm not sure I'll take the place at Bristol,' Marjorie said casually. 'That's not what I want. I fancy something more exciting. Travelling, perhaps! I might get a post as a steward on a boat and see the world.'

She glanced over her shoulder to see how Barbara was taking this. Her friend was biting her lip, her eyes glittering.

She'd guessed! Shame was added to the complex mix of misery seething inside Marjorie. Thrusting her prizes into Barbara's arms, she waved her hand. 'Do us a favour, love. I'm going this way. See you,' she called. As soon as she turned the corner she began to run towards the cliffs. She had to get away from Barbara and her cloying sympathy.

Chapter 9

Robert stopped pacing the library floor and looked around in disgust. When Mother was alive, this room had been his favourite retreat, a place to nestle in roomy chairs while dogs snoozed around. Now it was sombre and claustrophobic, with black leather sofas carefully arranged on dark Persian carpets. Joy had fled in the face of order and no dog ever set foot in the house. Even the cat had been put down. Rhoda, his stepmother, always got her own way, and he reckoned her much publicised allergy to dogs and cats was mainly fiction, just another ploy to enable her to exercise control. She wasn't allergic to her damned fur coats.

Something inside Robert had stirred and almost woke from a long hibernation. There was a sullenness in him, a sense of anger, a groping towards inner steel, but he was not yet ready. He needed time to cross the bridge to this new life. Four days ago he had been a budding poet and writer, a boy with no responsibilities, a teenager hopelessly in love, but all this had been wiped away.

'Thank God it's all over,' Rhoda said, lighting a cigarette.

'It will never be over,' Robert countered. It was the closest he had ever come to contradicting her. He was always excessively polite, using good manners to hide his dislike of this woman who had slipped into his mother's bed six months after she died. And now his brothers, Duncan and George, had died, too, tragically, absurdly pranging the light aircraft George had coveted for years. They'd been drunk. It had come out at the inquest, although Rhoda had done her damnedest to cover up. Father had suffered a minor heart attack when the news came.

Robert was sad and angry and scared and he was not sure which emotion was uppermost. He'd loved his brothers and he could not get to grips with the fact that they were gone for good. But that appalling fact brought new terrors.

He was the heir to a title, to the MacLaren estates, to heading the clan, to running the plant and supporting the wider family of shareholders who lived on dividends from their holdings in the Glentirran distillery. He was also the heir to the biggest bloody mess imaginable.

Father was coping as best he could, but he was no financial wizard even if he did make the best whisky in the Highlands. Robert had borrowed enough to see them through several months while he learned the ropes. That was that for the time being.

'I'm taking a summer holiday,' he told his stepmother and watched her drop her eyes. 'I have loose ends to tie up. Besides, I have to think. This new status . . . well, it takes some getting used to.' He was not going to tell her about the girl he loved and had to see for one last time.

'A holiday is out of the question,' she snapped. 'I'm amazed you should suggest such a thing.'

Robert watched her thoughtfully and with distaste. Poor Father could never match her iron will, but if he was going to be here for the rest of his life he must learn to stand up to her, he decided. Now would be a good time to start.

'I'm not suggesting, Rhoda. I'm telling you what I've planned. Don't worry, I've told Father. He understands. Graeme Forbes runs the plant well enough and the bank won't pull any rugs from under us during the summer holidays.'

'What if your father needs you? she asked unemotionally.

'Father won't need me, he's fine now. I'll probably go sailing in the Med, but you can try to contact me through a girl called Marjorie Hardy, who lives at number eleven, Liverpool Street, Dover. She'll probably know where I am.'

'I might have known there was a girl involved. You're irresponsible like your brothers.' She was staring past and over him, as if an ancient enemy lurked on the wall behind him. It was a habit that had unnerved him as a child. Now she just seemed a little weird and he guessed that she was unable to cope with the trauma of being thwarted.

He shot her a look of sullen fury and stalked out. It took him ten minutes to throw some gear into a bag and then he was driving south, gulping the fresh air of freedom, wondering how to pack a lifetime of living into six precious weeks.

Marjorie was sitting on a grassy mound, gazing out to sea. She had been there for some time after she'd run away from Barbara's well-meant sympathy, sitting motionless, her hands clasped in her lap. She watched the waves breaking on the cliffs below, but she was thinking of Robert, remembering their last date and how he had kissed her so gently while his hands wandered from her back to her breasts. She had relived the evening so many times. His pent-up passion had come surging out and he had groaned involuntarily and thrust her against the wall, pushing his hips hard against her thighs, his lips bruising hers, his tongue pushing into her mouth. They had panted and writhed, but he had broken away suddenly.

'Shit!' He never swore, but suddenly he'd seemed to have spun out of control. 'I can't take this much longer. Either we make it, or we drop this petting business. I've got blue-balls. It's agony, I'm telling you.'

'I didn't ask you to kiss me,' she'd retorted, trembling with desire as much as he, but trying to hide her need.

'You're an iceberg. I can't take any more tonight. See you tomorrow. Usual time.' He'd driven off in a temper and that was the last time she'd seen him. How could he do this to her?

She was angry, but her body reacted to the memory of that last kiss. 'Oh Robert, I love you,' she whispered.

It was twilight and she was on her way home when she saw a familiar figure striding over the cliffs towards her. It couldn't be . . . Yet who else was so tall? Who else had that strange way of loping along? Who else had burnished black hair that grew in a thick, wild mop?

She started to run, but her legs turned to jelly, so she stood still. It was an illusion. She'd gone crazy. But it was truly him.

'Marj!' he called. He gave a loud, crude wolf whistle and ran towards her.

It was his silly grin that incensed her. How dare he smile as if nothing were wrong and take it for granted she'd come running to heel when he whistled?

She waited until he was close, then punched him hard in his stomach. 'That's for dumping me, Robert MacLaren,' she gasped. She burst into tears and began to run wildly and blindly until she fell. 'Oh damn, damn, damn . . .'

Robert was towering over her and the silly grin was entirely gone. She'd never seen such fury.

'That's a fine welcome,' he said quietly.

'Oh, Robert. How could you? You didn't even phone. Oh, these bloody nettles!'

He hauled her out, grabbed a handful of dock leaves and began to rub her arms and legs. 'Idiot!'

Suddenly there was no need for words. When Robert caught hold of her and pulled her close against him her joy obliterated the hurt. She did not need explanations. Robert was back and he loved her.

Violet shadows were creeping over the sea and the cliffs. There was a strange, ethereal light, like the echo of twilight, although it was almost dark, and still they sat on, obsessed with the nearness of each other.

Then she shivered and Robert seemed to break out of his trance. He wrapped his jacket round her shoulders. It felt warm and comforting and it smelled of him.

'Marj, listen. I love you, but it's all over between us. I had to come back to explain. You see, I had thought I was free, but something happened and now I'm not.' His voice was so hoarse she hardly recognised it.

He pulled her closer, feeling her shudder as he explained that the death of his two elder brothers, followed by his father's heart attack, had turned his world upside down.

'Oh Marj, I'm so sorry. I had other plans. Look, you're cold and so am I. Let's go. My car's not far from here.

We'll drive to a pub I know in Shepherd's Well. We can have dinner and talk.'

She felt out of place walking into that smart pub with no make-up and wearing her school dress and shoes, but Robert did not seem to notice. They found a table by the window and held hands while Robert tried to explain.

'I start work at the beginning of September. It's unbelievable, but I'll be running the show. Of course we have a manager. Dad's not much good at business, and to tell the truth I don't think Duncan was either.'

Marjorie listened in awe to his story. His father was titled, his stepmother was distantly related to the Queen, and their distillery made one of the best whiskies in Scotland. He was going to study business marketing and economics at night and learn to run the plant by day. For him, Oxford was out.

'So we have six weeks – that's all. We can either call it off now or pack a lifetime of living into a holiday. How about it? Some friends of mine are sailing in the Med. They might make Corsica and we're invited, but it's up to you, Marjorie. I don't know how you feel about it, knowing we part in September.'

Marjorie could feel terrible anger welling up inside her. She was not good enough for him. He'd stated that clearly enough. Why? He wasn't the bloody heir apparent. All he had was a distillery and a lot of silly, jumped-up notions about himself. She sensed that the snobbishness had been pumped into him at home and at school. Slowly a steely resolve was forming: Robert was her man and no one would ever mean so much to her again. He was wrong and she would show him.

'I'll take the six weeks,' she said flatly.

Chapter 10

Saturday dawned with a pang of fear. Marjorie lay staring at the shadows of leaves dancing on the wall. Time was passing and she felt torn in two. At home nothing had changed and yet everything was different, for she knew now that she loved Robert. The two of them had spent the last two weeks together and they planned to leave for a month's holiday soon, but she had not yet plucked up courage to tell her parents.

She moved restlessly under the blanket, smoothing her hands over her thighs and her belly. Her body had assumed a new status since every part of it was loved by Robert. She closed her eyes and remembered his lips on hers and his hands stroking her breasts. A hot wave of lust swept through her leaving her panting and guilt-ridden, cheeks burning.

Robert wanted her to go all the way. 'If you loved me enough you would put aside your prim, working-class inhibitions and give me your love whole-heartedly,' he had grumbled last night.

'Must we fight the class war each time we have a difference of opinion?' she had retorted, laughing at him. 'If you use that old line once more I'll go home.'

That had shut him up. But what if he were right? For whom was she saving herself? Would she ever love anyone as deeply as she loved Robert? So it stood to reason that her first time should be with him.

She got up and lingered in the bathroom, and eventually heard Mum calling her to breakfast. She could hardly eat as she tried to force out the words.

'Eat your porridge,' Mum murmured.

Dad pushed his chair back. 'I'll be getting along . . .'

It was now or never. 'Mum, Dad, it's like this . . .' Her words tumbled out without preparation. 'I feel I need a bit of a break and I've been invited to sail round the Med for a month. I reckon it's just what I need before I start work and you don't have to worry, Dad, because there's a group of us – about six in all – so please, relax.' She took a deep breath.

Dad's face turned ugly and Mum looked vaguely confused as her eyes moved from her daughter to her husband. Dad stood up, his hands gripping the edge of the table until his knuckles turned white as he glared at her.

'No, you're not. Not if I have anything to do with it.'

'Oh, I don't think you should worry at all,' Marjorie said soothingly. 'Everyone's going away for the summer.'

'It's about time she had a bit of fun,' Mum added.

'There's fun and fun.' Dad's voice began like a rumble of thunder, but she could see that the storm was passing.

'Look, I'm going and that's that,' Marjorie burst out. She stood up and placed her chair under the table. There was so much anger in her voice she hardly recognised herself. Dad shrugged and picked up his newspaper, while Mum followed her from the kitchen and up the stairs.

'It's only that you've never been away from home nights, so it's only natural that we should worry about you. I trust you, Marjorie. Of course I was married at your age . . .' She went on and on, until Marjorie caught her by her arm.

'Listen, Mum. I'll be fine,' she said firmly.

The *Columbus* turned out to be a magnificent two-masted schooner, berthed in the Marseilles yacht club. Robert and Marjorie walked past it twice without a glance, expecting something far more modest. When they finally identified it, Marjorie was filled with awe. Robert's friends must be millionaires. There was no one aboard, so they decided to go to the hotel where they were booked for the night. Robert had arranged to meet his friends there for breakfast, prior to sailing.

Eventually they found the right bus which carried them deep into the sun-baked countryside. Dusk was falling when they reached the old converted château where they were to stay. The gardens smelt of thyme and lavender, and there were flowers amongst the cyprus and olive trees growing on the steep fall of the stony hill.

'Oh Robert, it's totally enchanting here. Oh, thank you,' she whispered as they entered the tiled hallway under a high vaulted ceiling.

Robert had booked them into two single rooms, but sharing one bathroom. How daring it was to strip naked and walk into the shower. She had never done this before. She stepped into the warm steamy atmosphere and was transported to another world, a place of utter voluptuousness, as his lips melted on hers and the warm water cascaded over them, and his naked skin, wet and quivering, was pressed against her wet, slippery breasts and belly. They stood there, clasping each other, lost in the wonder of their own sensations, kissing, feeling, stroking. She took the soap and began to wash him, wondering at his powerful limbs, soaping her hands and feeling his manhood slip through her fingers, in and out, until he came in one agonised groan. 'I love you,' she whispered, pressing herself hard against him, needing something so badly, but not sure what, unable to move away.

Suddenly they were squealing and giggling as the water changed from hot to cold. It was so strange to be lifted from the shower, and dried lovingly with the towel, over her face and in her ears and tenderly in the soft flesh of her inner thighs. He dried her hair, holding her close against him, wrapping his arms around her, and she wanted nothing more than to stand there for ever, her lips and nose pressed hard against his chest.

'Have you done that before?' she asked sleepily.

He looked at her, amused. 'I don't know.'

'That's not an answer. Of course you know.'

'Come. Get dressed. We're late. I don't want to miss dinner, do you?'

They dined on the terrace overlooking the village, heads close together as they studied the menu, the lamp flickering in the soft breeze. There was a scent of lavender and jasmine, and a richer aroma of damp grass and earth. The lights of the village twinkled around them, an owl shrieked and, closer, the strains of a guitar drifted from a house nearby. For a while they sat in awed silence. Then Robert broke the spell.

'I can recommend the *Sauté de Lapin au Vin Blanc*,' he teased with a straight face.

'Oh you beast, you beast. Stop it now. You've had enough mileage out of one poor little rabbit. As a matter of fact, I never eat rabbit nowadays. I never shall.' She sighed. 'And I don't eat pork since Uncle Bert's piggery caught fire up at the allotments.'

Robert hoped she wasn't going to tell him that story, but she was. She recounted at length how her street woke to awful squealing as the wooden huts caught fire, then described the tragicomic sight of the fully-kitted and helmeted firemen chasing purple pigs up and down the street.

'Pork's out,' he insisted flatly at the end of that distressing story.

'I don't eat chicken if they're reared in batteries.'

'So what does that leave?' he asked with increasing dismay. '*Pâté de foie gras?*'

'Don't mention pâté to me. D'you know what they do to the geese . . . ?'

'I suppose veal's out.'

'Naturally.'

'Okay. How's this: *Soufflé au Fromage*, followed by *Darnes de Saumon Grillées au Beurre* and then pears in wine?'

As dinner progressed the moon rose over the olive grove, floating in a silvery haze across a sky that was never truly dark, but a strange midnight blue.

'Even the moon's better here,' she whispered.

Holding hands, they lingered over coffee for hours, neither of them wanting to break the spell of this magical night and their strange sense of bonding.

Chapter 11

A voice boomed: 'And who's this then? Introduce us, Rob.' The spell was broken.

There were four of them. Four enemies, Marjorie quickly learned. The girls wore Dior and Saint-Laurent shifts, with dainty diamond watches, the boys smartly cut shorts and shirts. They were from Rob's world and they quickly realised she was an outsider.

The boys, Clive Lawrence and Jean Mazel, ogled her quite openly, treating her as if she were an object Robert had bought in a bazaar. The girls, Claudia Wynne-Roberts and Diana Hamilton, were as catty as only plain girls can be, ignoring whatever Marjorie said and steering the conversation to areas beyond her reach. Diana, a blonde with pale blue eyes and witchlike features, seemed to be paired off with Jean, but that evidently did not prevent her from perceiving Marjorie as a threat.

Soon they were discussing the merits of the latest shorter skis and the new resorts they'd visited, a recent London party that had erred on the side of too much ostentation, Nureyev's performance in *Laborintus*, how the Japanese were snapping up English art treasures at the auctions, the failure of the British to win the single-handed transatlantic race, and why Mike McMullen only won on handicap.

With sailing Marjorie was on firm ground. 'If he'd

skippered one of the French trimarans he'd have won,' she said. 'He's the better sailor.'

Claudia, a tall brunette with a strong nose and too many teeth, gave a small tinkling snigger. '*Sigh-lor*. How quaint,' she said. 'I do love our regional accents. They enrich the English language immeasurably.'

'Tell me, do you *sighl*?' Diana echoed with obvious glee.

Marjorie took a long time folding her napkin into a small, precise square while the girls watched her in fascination. Then she stood up. 'Good night,' she enunciated. Robert's cheeks were scarlet. He couldn't look at her.

'Be right up,' he stammered.

When she reached the stairs she paused, suddenly wishing that she had not capitulated. Too late now, she decided.

She heard Claudia's voice saying, 'What an accent. Is it cockney, or what?'

'Don't be such a bitch, Claudia. She's utterly beautiful,' Jean chastised her in his sexy French accent.

'Totally wasted on her,' Diana added. 'How can you bear that terrible voice?' she asked Robert.

Looking over her shoulder, Marjorie saw that Claudia's arm was flung around Robert's shoulders. She was bending over him until her hair hung in his food and her breasts were clearly visible. She should wear a bra. It was indecent. She might have an English rose complexion, but her large nose and teeth gave her an unfortunate resemblance to a horse. Marjorie felt like marching back and telling her so. She had never had any reason to experience jealousy before, but right now she felt she could kill.

She unlocked the connecting door, undressed and snuggled into bed naked. She felt she had to do something momentous to make Robert forget the girls' gibes. But why was he taking so long? She closed her eyes and listened for footsteps. Gradually, she felt herself drifting off to sleep.

Robert returned to his room with curiously mixed emotions, part anger, part guilt. Marjorie was such a child. How ridiculous she had been rushing off like that. She should have fought back. She was worth ten of them. Bitches, both of them, and not very bright.

Most of the girls in his set were pushovers, but Marj never had been and lately he was glad of this because they'd had time to build a strong friendship.

Mainly he loved her for her beauty, but there were dozens of other reasons besides her looks. Were those reasons enough? This evening had shown him the perils of class prejudice. He suspected he had nothing to offer her in the long term — but did that matter? She was strait-laced, but that was mainly because of her narrow upbringing, and consequently her chastity both repelled and attracted him. And then there were her awful parents . . .

She had unlocked and opened their connecting door. He tiptoed over to her bed and stood gazing at her. A vague aroma of toothpaste, perfume and talcum powder rose from the bed and mingled with the scent of flowers outside the window. How beautiful she was. She was naked, one arm flung over the pillow, and the duvet was disarranged, revealing one perfect breast. Her mouth was open showing a glint of white teeth, her long lashes fanned her cheeks, her hair was damp and tousled and she was warm and highly desirable. He would love nothing more than to climb in beside her. But what then?

He sighed and thought of Claudia, who had been quick to assess Marjorie's virginity. 'When she goes to sleep come on up to me,' she had whispered, giggling. But he wouldn't do that either. He had the strangest sense of togetherness with Marjorie. Here in France, away from the endless reminders of their different backgrounds, he had felt uninhibited, but the evening had spoiled the holiday. Was he free to love her without regret? He wasn't sure. He pulled the duvet up to her neck and crept back to his room.

The next morning Jean drove them all to Marseilles and they boarded the *Columbus*. Soon after, they set sail, heading south-east and averaging a slow pace of five knots. They spent the day sprawling on deck, sunbathing, and at regular intervals Jean would drop anchor and let down the ladder so they could swim in the warm, translucent sea. A tough but courteous man of twenty-two, Jean Mazel was clearly spoiled, but had a healthy respect for his father and his father's property. He was Corsican, Marjorie learned, and his father owned the boat. He looked like a pirate of old with his dark, handsome looks and magnificent body. She could not imagine what he saw in Diana. At night, Jean played his guitar and sang strange, haunting Corsican shepherds' songs in a wailing, minor key that sounded more Arabic than French.

Despite their ample provisions, they dined mainly on the fish they caught, washed down with too much red wine. They talked far into the night, but Marjorie always felt excluded, although she was getting to like Jean.

Apart from the hotels, and the ski lodge in the Corsican mountains where they would stay, his father had many business interests in Marseilles, Jean told them, but he was vague about the nature of the businesses.

'Probably Corsican mafia,' Robert grumbled when they were alone. 'He's Clive's friend. I don't know his family at all.'

'Oh, go on with you. You don't like Jean, but I do. He's absolutely great.'

'That's because you're dazzled by his extravagant good looks. Diana will be sorry if she marries him,' Robert whispered. 'She'll find herself shut up in the mountains, wearing black and grinding chestnuts.'

'Well at least she'll be with him,' she snarled, but instantly regretted it. Robert withdrew to some private place inside himself and she couldn't reach him for the rest of the day.

Corsica appeared some days later, as oyster-grey mists fled before the rising sun. One minute sea and sky merged in a flat, featureless landscape, and then Corsica stood silhouetted against the dawn sky, a seemingly mystical island bathed in violet mists.

As Marjorie and Robert hung over the rails, Jean joined them, suddenly embarrassed. 'Look, it's not my business how you two act, but I notice you've slept in separate berths for the past two nights, so you won't have much trouble sticking to the rules. In my father's hotel you must keep your distance from each other, at least inside.'

'Wow!' Marjorie said to Robert when Jean had gone. 'So much for our planned month of sin.'

'The trouble with you is you're all talk and no action.'

Robert's mouth twisted into a crooked smile that didn't reach his eyes.

She looked up, smiling at him, but the smile froze when she saw how sad he looked. Suddenly she realised why he'd been so uptight for the past few days.

Chapter 12

As they entered Calvi harbour, Marjorie saw the chapel of Notre Dame de la Serra, set like a fortress amid huge granite boulders on a rock above the sea. The flaming sunset bathed the mountains with a purple glow, throwing great violet shadows across the cracks and chasms. By the time they had berthed the ship it was dark, but the water was brilliant with reflected lights from the cafés spread around the harbour. Roulette tables had been set up along the quaysides, and crowds thronged the pavements. It was good to stretch their legs as they wandered around in search of Jean's uncle, Pierre, who had come to drive them to the inn which was also the Mazels' summer home. They found him in a dockside café where they were greeted by the hostile stares of flashy men with gold rings and chains.

'We've got to be alone,' Robert whispered. When no one was looking he pushed her hand down hard on his swollen penis.

'Tell them I feel tired and you're taking me back to the yacht,' she replied softly. 'Jean will understand.' They walked back, arms entwined, thigh against thigh, a three-legged race.

'Why do you look so sad?' Robert demanded, tilting

her chin up with his hand, forcing her to gaze into his eyes that were bloodshot with frustrated longing.

'I'm not sad,' she lied. But she was. Her own special dilemma was never truly out of her mind because the two bitches, as she privately called Diana and Claudia, constantly reminded her of their separate worlds. How could she gatecrash Robert's world if she wasn't successful? And how could she be successful without any talent or training? Somehow she had to make Robert proud of her. She pushed her fears to the back of her mind.

'It's nothing, Robert. Look up there!' The lustrous moon was rising over jagged peaks and the wind was blowing softly from the mountains, filling the warm night air with the bitter-sweet fragrance of the *maquis*. 'What a night,' she murmured.

They had reached the schooner and Robert decided that the lifeboat, hoisted well above eye level, was the only really private place on board. So they made a bed of the tarpaulin, put a towel over it and lay beside each other.

Robert undressed her with clumsy, urgent fumblings. She, too, had to feel his skin against hers. His shorts and T-shirt were an unbearable barrier, so she wrenched them off. Panting, heaving, she pulled his hips hard against hers until, unashamed and naked like the moon, they lay stroking each other with smooth, subtle finger strokes, eyes locked, lips almost touching, caught up in the wonder of what they were about to do.

'Make love to me. I'll pull out,' Robert begged hoarsely. 'I promise! It's quite safe. I want to so badly.'

'So do I,' she gasped.

It hurt. That was the first shock. And the second was a sense of an infrangible bonding. When she pushed up her hips to meet his descending, she thrilled to the strange relief their incessant percussion brought. His sweet thrusts pierced her heart, but she sensed he was lunging into her soul.

Panting and drenched, fired with passion, they hammered their way to the final, sweet ecstasy. Later, they lay in each other's arms, murmuring endearments until the eastern sky lightened almost imperceptibly. Then they reluctantly parted and crept off to their lonely bunks.

Dawn found them dazed and tired. Jean and his uncle woke them and yelled for them to hurry. They gulped their coffee, piled into the truck and set off for the interior.

Marjorie fell asleep during the climb into the mountains and woke to find they were careering at an impossible speed due west, on a hazardous road overlooking perilous gorges.

'This is the only way to our village, Castiria,' Jean told them. 'It used to take days to get here by a mule track on steps cut into the cliffs. When the road came it was a lifeline to the people of the Niolo, but they still keep to themselves. The men leave home to make their fortunes, but their families stay behind.'

Marjorie gave Diana a hard nudge with her elbow. 'You listening?' she whispered.

She was subjected to a supercilious stare.

The truck rumbled around one last sharp corner, passing ancient rock formations, and they found themselves on an oval plateau entirely ringed by mountains, the peaks snow-streaked and sun-drenched, mysterious and inaccessible. Sunlight flooded over them, blue sky engulfed them. They had entered the Niolo, the core of the island. They drew up in front of a square stone building three storeys high, with a glaring red-tiled roof and high walls. Marjorie shivered in the mountain chill as they climbed out of the truck.

The door was flung open and a tall, thin woman emerged and rushed down the steps. She could not conceal her joy at seeing Jean. She was dressed entirely in black, which set off the pallor of her skin. Her blonde hair was pulled back into a harsh bun and she wore no make-up.

With a face like hers and skin like hers, make-up was entirely superfluous, Marjorie decided. Jean's mother was a rare beauty.

Madame Mazel looked calm and kind and her large eyes were of a strange dark shade of blue, like pewter, Marjorie thought. Her smile froze when she greeted Diana and she became as welcoming as the icy mountains. Clearly, she was not happy with her son's choice of a girlfriend.

'Come! I will show you to your rooms. Fortunately we have plenty of space here.' Although her French had a strong Corsican accent, Marjorie was able follow her, but curiously Diana and Claudia were battling. 'Six p.m. on the terrace for drinks,' Mariana Mazel told them.

Marjorie walked onto the terrace and down the steps to the garden, where fifteen men were seated around the table. Her appearance was the cue for two of them to stand, namely Robert and Jean.

A tall, older man with the breadth and strength of an ox tilted his chair and glanced off-handedly over his shoulder. Then his face lit up with amazed and absolute pleasure, there was no mistaking it. 'A goddess worthy of our devotion,' he bellowed in heavily accented English. 'You must be Diana.'

Oh God! What should she do? Pass out? What was he going to do when he found he'd waxed lyrical over a perfect stranger?

As he strode towards her she had to admit that he was superb in his black suit, with the open-neck white shirt, crimson bandanna and cummerbund to match. He gazed hard at her and waited for the old magic to do its job, as doubtless it had for the past half-century.

'I'm not Diana. I'm her friend, Marjorie Hardy,' she muttered in French.

'Ah. But what a relief,' he insisted. 'So you will never be calling me Papa. I like that.' He tucked her hand under his arm and led her to the table.

'So you are young Robert's friend. Well, I'm telling you now, he doesn't deserve you. You will come and sit next to me and be our guest of honour. Come.' She was propelled to the seat beside him, from which Jean was unceremoniously turfed out, while Monsieur Mazel fussed over her and poured her a glass of their best wine, spending a long time explaining to her exactly why it was superb.

Supper was set on trestle tables under the trees: hors-d'oeuvres of fish and goat's cheese and vegetables, with *charcuterie*, fresh salad, bowls of olives, fruit and pastries made from chestnut flour.

Madame Mazel and her two sisters-in-law, identically dressed in black, rushed in and out with the dishes and eventually joined them to eat. When the meal was finished they began to clear the table and Marjorie rose to help them, but she heard a bellow from behind her.

'Marjorie, come back here, my dear. The house is full of helpers. Come.'

'Go on then,' Madame Mazel said, nudging her. 'My husband loves to talk to strangers. Be patient, he means well.' She called out sharply to her husband in their Corsican language, with an imperious gesture towards Diana. Marjorie managed to grasp the words: 'Be kinder', 'duty' and 'insensitive'. Her husband dutifully called Diana to sit on his other side while he expounded on everything Corsican.

It was past midnight before the company broke up. Marjorie walked carefully up the steps to the terrace, her head spinning with legends and the strong, home-made liqueur.

'Well, you certainly made a hit.' She heard Robert's voice behind her and spun around.

'Oh, Robert.' At that moment she longed to clutch him tightly. His eyes were glowing with love and affection and she needed to hug him. As she lunged forward, he raised his hands and stepped back. 'Uh huh! Remember Jean's warning. You'll have to suffer.' He was laughing at her.

Absurdly he was right, she was suffering. 'I miss you,' she whispered regretfully.

'Wait half an hour and meet me in the garden,' he murmured.

How thrilling it was to lie on the warm ground, safely hidden in the dense *maquis*. How daring to strip naked in the dark and see Robert's head silhouetted against the moonlit sky. To Marjorie the act of sex seemed pure and awe-inspiring in its spirituality. Waves of love washed through them and back into the night. Love was holy. She knew that now, and that they were blessed because they loved.

Chapter 13

———— ————

It was almost dawn when Marjorie heard a soft knocking on her door. She opened it, expecting to see Robert, but it was Diana who stood there, her eyes puffy as if she had been crying. For a minute of stunned incredulity Marjorie listened to Diana's pleading.

'Marjorie, please. I can't sleep. I have to talk to someone. It's Jean and I . . . Well, the thing is, we'd hoped, but anyone can see that his parents are set against me. Oh God!' She sat heavily on the bed and covered her face with her hands.

'The trouble is, Jean would never go against his father's wishes, because there's too much at stake. They're quite wealthy.' Her voice trailed off. 'I don't care about that, but Jean does. I have to create a good impression. I'm sorry I've been a bitch. They like you and you speak French so well. If they thought we were friends . . . Please help me.'

Marjorie sat down abruptly. She longed to say: 'Sorry, I'm going *sigh-ling*,' but she had never been spiteful.

'Listen. If you really want to marry Jean you'd do better to ignore him and concentrate on his mother. She rules this home, not her husband, whatever they say about the MCP Corsicans. Work on her.'

'Are you sure?'

'Yes. You'll have to join their world, but do it better. Can you cook?'

'Hardly.'

'Watch me and you'll soon get the hang of it.'

'And you won't leave me alone with *them*. Promise?'

'I'll stick around for a couple of days, but only until you're more confident. Let's get some sleep.'

The next morning Robert was waiting with a borrowed car to take her to the beach. Reluctantly, Marjorie explained about her promise to Diana.

'Why bother? She's a bitch.'

'Well, I don't have to be a bitch too, do I?'

'Damn! Why did we come here?' he moaned. 'I want to be alone with you.' He ran his hand through his hair in despair.

The two girls presented themselves for work in the kitchen, while Diana explained in her halting French that two more pairs of hands would lighten the women's workload.

'Well, if you want to pull your weight, cook us some English dishes,' Mariana challenged Diana. Then they both smiled frigidly, but not at each other, Marjorie noticed.

Marjorie's promise bound her to the kitchen for most of that day and the next, as Diana sought to ingratiate herself with the Mazel women. Twenty guests for lunch or supper was the norm, and not the exception, they discovered.

Robert went hunting with the men and swaggered home with them at dusk. He drank too much wine and soon he was acting like the rest of the men in the family, but he lacked the locals' flamboyant acceptance of everything their women could give. When Robert was chauvinistic he was objectionable.

Marjorie had to have it out with him, so she cornered him after dinner on the second day. Robert was leaning back in his chair under a tree, half a bottle of red wine on the table in front of him. She could see he had drunk too much.

'There's no point in sulking and spoiling the time we have left. I know you think I'm wrong, but I promised.'

'Clearly you know what's going on in my mind better than I do. Our holiday is an enigma to me. Explain it to me, please, Marjorie, with your new-found psychological insight. Why is it we are spending our precious three weeks apart, when we had planned to spend the time together? Or perhaps I'm keeping you from your unlikely role?'

'I'm only helping Di to catch her man,' she argued.

'Oh, Di, is it? What about us?'

'Well, I'd like to catch you, too, while I'm at it.' She tried to sound light-hearted.

'Grow up, Marjorie. You know the score.'

What a cheek! He was playing Prince Regent again, but without the famous charm. She churned with fury, but bit back her retort.

By the end of the week the girls had befriended Madame Mazel with their lemon curd, wooed her with their brandy snaps, disarmed her with their pork and apple pie and seduced her with their cock-a-leekie soup. Finally, they crowned their success with cherry jam. Marjorie knew that she was no longer required.

Robert borrowed a car and from then on each morning they would career down the narrow winding roads to the

sea, or a lake, or the vast, beautiful indigenous forests, or
the *maquis*. They picnicked wherever they could find a
solitary place. Hidden from the world they would toast
naked in the sun, make love, drink wine, and wolf down
the delicious snacks Diana packed for them, and talk of
anything and everything – except the future.

On their last day, they decided to explore the mountain
slopes. They climbed for an hour, keeping to a deep
ravine where a stream of icy mountain water cascaded
over the rocks.

'I've got to rest,' Marjorie said later, collapsing on a
rock. 'Wow! Take a look at that view.'

It was a painted scene on a teacup: a vivid turquoise
sea, a misty purple horizon under a china blue sky, and
between them and the sea lay mile after mile of forests
and *maquis* glinting in every shade of green.

Robert stared out to sea, a sombre expression on
his face.

'We don't have to give up, Robert.' Suddenly Marjorie
was pleading with all the force of her longing. 'I love you.
All these divisions are in your mind.' She tried to explain,
but sensed she was not succeeding.

'I'm going to swim. Come on.' She climbed down the
rocks to the sand and stripped off her clothes, enjoying
the warmth of the sun on her bare skin. After a while
Robert followed.

'I love your breasts.' He pulled her down on the sandy
ground beside him and cradled her in his arms. 'I want
you so badly. It's become an obsession. You're driving me
mad. I can't bear the thought of being away from you.'

She looked into his eyes and knew that he told the
truth. 'I love you too,' she whispered.

He covered her naked body with his, and she felt his

sensuous flesh against her as he came into her. It was a
moment of absolute wonder, to feel his quivering penis
inside her, a part of her, lying still there, needful but
hesitant. She had only to move to drive him crazy. She
could kiss him and flick her tongue against his and at
once he would be groaning and lost, but she waited.

When waiting became too painful to be borne, she
squeezed him gently. 'Yes,' she whispered. 'Yes, yes,
yes. Do it . . . Oh, Robert.'

Soon she was panting and writhing, running out of
control . . . then they both jumped at the loud report
of a rifle being fired close by. Almost instantaneously,
Robert came inside her.

'Oh my God,' he said as he scrambled to his feet. They
had no time to move. She was frozen in horror as they
heard hoofs galloping down the rocky slopes, but Robert
pushed her behind a rock as Monsieur Mazel, Jean and
Pierre galloped into the clearing, then disappeared into
the *maquis*.

'Shit!' Robert swore. 'Shit, shit, shit! I'm sorry. Now
what?'

They sat on a rock for an hour, while the rays of the
setting sun reflected gold on the granite slopes and the
tips of the topmost leaves shone like burnished metal.
Aromatic shrubs – arbutus, myrtle, lentisk, cistus, rose-
mary, lavender and thyme – sent out their bitter-sweet
incense to soothe their fears.

'I expect it will be all right,' she ventured. 'People
don't always get pregnant. I guess we'd better go back.'

'No. Wait a bit,' Robert pleaded.

This is called fun, Marjorie told herself as they cruised
at eight knots towards Marseilles. Just in case you've

forgotten, my girl. Loosen up, snap out of it, join the
twentieth century. Marjorie Hardy, you're a real killjoy.
This is all that you've ever dreamed of and so much more.
Somnolent nights, balmy days, evenings spent dancing
under the stars, and a sense of wonder.

Her eyes had been opened; the world was so much
better a place than she had thought from her meagre
glimpses of it. So why couldn't she enjoy herself? she
wondered as she toasted herself to medium-rare and
guzzled ice-cold Portuguese wine.

All through the precious nights, after their love-
making, she wrapped her arms around Robert, tucked
her knees under his, and with her cheek hard against
his back, she hung on tightly, trying to keep her ugly
fears at bay. But they, like fearsome hounds, would not
let up. They harried her and pursued her, took hold
of the corners of her mind and shook hard until she
broke out in a cold sweat. They leaped out from every
shadow and polluted every waking moment with their
hot breath. They were called: '*He's-leaving-me-soon*' and
'*What-if-I'm-pregnant?*'

Before she'd even got to grips with quelling her fears
and enjoying the glorious here and now, it was over.
With waves and thanks and promises to meet up soon,
and heaps of forced gaiety, she and Robert parted from
the others in Marseilles harbour.

It was dawn on 1 September, and they had reached
Dover station. She got off the boat train, her mood as
heavy as the grey and drizzling dawn sky. Reality was as
hard as the paving beneath her feet. Gone was the soft
mattress of the sea, gone was the holiday spirit, and it
was raining.

She stood on the platform disconsolately. There was no need to say, What next? They'd discussed that enough times, particularly and exhaustively last night. Robert would return forthwith to home and hearth. He was taking the train through to London.

'Go on then, go,' she shouted, although he was standing right above her. 'Go and make whisky. Make it the best bloody whisky the Highlands ever tasted. Make a fortune. Go on, why don't you? But you'll always be in the debit column, and if you don't know why, then what was it all about? All that love, I mean . . .'

'Don't do this,' he muttered. 'I warned you.'

'But did you warn yourself?'

She ran away, blinded by tears or rain or both, murmuring 'God . . . God . . .'

Chapter 14

Utter misery descended on Marjorie, for she had lost something precious and irreplaceable. She was gripped by despair: life without her love stretched out like a barren track through a featureless desert. Nightly she was aware of her sexual deprivation, for Robert had left an open wound that could never be healed. Worse still, she had lost her friend. So she wept in the secret hours of the night, muffling the sound in her pillow. Yet in the morning she would bathe her eyes with cold water and summon her confidence. I'll win him back, she told herself firmly. The silly idiot! I'll join his world, since he thinks it's important.

The following Monday morning she woke thinking it was just another sad day. Then she remembered it was special and she leapt out of bed, propelled by joy and panic. She was reaching for the stars and today was launch day.

Because of her talent for English, her first choice was journalism. By nine a.m. she was sitting in the reception area of the local newspaper, hope shining out of her like a beacon as she surreptitiously wiped her sweaty hands on a tissue.

The female personnel officer, fired with self-importance, hardly bothered to look at Marjorie. She shook her glossy hair, fingered her necklace with long white fingers and gazed laughingly and longingly through glitzy glasses at a long succession of men who dropped into her office on any excuse.

'With your lack of qualifications you can forget journalism,' she explained between interruptions, taking off her glasses and blinking myopically. 'You need a University degree, plus typing and basic shorthand. Quite honestly, you aren't even qualified for office work.'

'I learn fast,' Marjorie snapped.

'Well, I have your address, Miss, er . . .' She peered ineffectually at Marjorie's CV. 'If and when . . .' she called as Marjorie stumbled to the door.

Crushed by her earlier failure, Marjorie was over-eager and tense as she pirouetted across the floor of a local modelling agency, watched anxiously by the owner, a tall, graceful ex-model who was past her prime but still stunning with her extraordinary violet eyes.

Marjorie tried not to see her reflection, but this was next to impossible since the mirror covered one entire wall. The occasional glimpse showed an awkward, untrained girl who should never have been there. She felt appalled that she'd had the gall to try. She smiled woodenly as the photographer clicked away for their files while, from some inner source of strength, she dredged up the courage to look failure in the face and maintain her dignity.

Violet eyes glowed with compassion. 'You'll never make it as a model, but you're pretty enough to land head and shoulder jobs from time to time. My dear, if and when . . .'

'Yes, that's me,' Marjorie said. 'Miss If and When.' She fled.

Her third appointment was in London with a casting director for a new show. It was a long shot, but the advertisement had read: 'We have a number of small roles available for pretty extras who will be coached.' Mum had parted with enough housekeeping for her return fare and a cup of coffee.

She emerged from the station at twenty past three and studied her map. In next to no time she had blundered into a world where the pedestrians were male and predatory, and tarts of all shades and accents lurked in doorways. Flinching, she pressed on, comforting herself with the thought that when she was a famous actress, Robert would come to his senses. If, that is, and when . . .

'Oh God! Now they've got me saying it.'

Surely this couldn't be the right place? The Global Theatre was a sleazy nightclub with sordid pictures of nude women in porno poses. Three swarthy clients gave her the once-over and walked inside beckoning as the doorman, resplendent in his gold braid, grabbed her elbow.

'Are you looking for Mr Martoli, young lady?' he said with a smile that didn't touch his eyes.

'Yes . . . no. I mean I was, but now I'm not sure.'

Could there be a mistake? 'Is there another Global Theatre?' she asked. And what about another Mr Martoli and another Wardour Street? Go home, you fool. But it was hard to let go of her dreams.

'Sooner or later you'll come to your senses and knuckle

down to what's available,' Mum said sternly. She had only half-listened to Marjorie's tale of woe and her last three visits to London employment agencies.

'Mum, it's awful. Without training there's only casual labour left,' she told her mother. Over the past depressing weeks, she had learned that a rigid class and qualification barrier lay between her and her dream of gate-crashing Robert's world, or any world come to that.

'Then get yourself some training. Study nights! The poly's got all sorts of evening classes. If I were you I'd take that job at Alf's. He closes early on Wednesdays. The likes of us can't be choosy.' Mum settled down with the crossword puzzle and that was that.

Marjorie took the evening paper and sat down with a cup of tea to study the situations vacant page, but as her eyes scanned the humble offers it seemed that Alf and his packaged offal were dangling over her head like the Sword of Damocles. She shivered. 'I'm tired out, Mum. I'm going to bed. Good night.'

Mum didn't look up. 'Night,' she murmured.

What a night! The bed seemed full of lumps, it was hot and stuffy and there was a raucous party going on down the street making a right old racket. At last she fell into a troubled sleep.

She found herself standing at the edge of a field, watching a vintage train approach. Somehow she had landed a job as a film extra. The hero of the film, Robert MacLaren, dressed as a nineteenth-century army officer, leaped from the train with his men and the firing began. The troops fell, real blood spurting from their real wounds. Marjorie rushed onto the set, waving her arms and shouting: 'Stop!

Stop! People are dying.' A bullet pierced her stomach and she fell to the ground. Strange that there was no pain, she thought as she was carried to a casualty tent at the side of the field.

A split second later she was watching the white-coated doctor pin the negatives of her X-rays onto a board. 'There is your womb,' he said, pointing with a baton, 'and there is the bullet. It has pierced your womb and nothing will dislodge it. I'm afraid it will have to stay there.'

She woke sweating with fright. The room was dark and quiet and the curtains were rustling in the draught. Switching on the light, she saw that it was two p.m. 'Crazy,' she muttered. 'Fancy getting upset about a silly dream. It's meaningless!' Yet the action kept on revolving in her mind and she sensed that the dream was meaningful. Was her subconscious warning her? She felt cold with dread. Around dawn she fell asleep clutching her teddy bear.

Chapter 15

———— ————

She had missed her period. 'I'm often late,' she explained
to Barbara in a flat, emotionless voice. 'Shouldn't wonder
if it wasn't all that pavement slogging I've been doing
lately. Silly to get upset by a dream. I'm not always
regular.'

'Sometimes you sound just like your mum.'

'Oh Barbara!' She clutched her friend and then pulled
herself together. Barbara would never be so silly.

'You don't have to worry,' Barbara told her. 'You go
to hospital for a couple of days and then you forget
about it.'

'Yes.' She spread her hands protectively over her
belly.

She eventually found work as a waitress at one of
the seafront hotels, from noon to eleven p.m., which
was fortunate, Marjorie considered, since her mornings
were spent throwing up. The tips were good and she
managed to save some money, but there was no time for
night classes.

It was Barbara who forced her out of her false com-
placency.

'You can't live in a dream world, love. You and
me are taking a trip to Folkestone. I've found out
there's a doctor who cares about these things. If you

have to go to hospital we'll spin some story for your parents.'

Marjorie had dreaded the examination, but the doctor turned out to be female and gentle. Her verdict was like a death sentence and Marjorie emerged white and shaken, amazing herself and Barbara with her vehemence. 'Little Robert is not going headfirst down any bloody toilet.'

In mid-November the doctor, Annabel Kruger, called her at home. 'Can I talk safely?' she asked. 'I've found a place for you at a convent in Wales. They take you in as soon as you feel you're showing signs. You earn your keep working in their laundry and they give afternoon lessons in shorthand and typing. By the time you leave you'll be qualified to get an office job. They arrange for the adoption. It's very efficient, very kind, so you're in luck. Now write down the details of how to get there.'

'How can I thank you?'

'It's my job. But don't leave it too late, please.'

From then on, Marjorie dreaded the day when she would lose her child. Her pregnancy was the only precious chance she would have to be with her baby and she vowed she would do all she could to make sure little Robert was healthy and happy until he was born. Her swollen body became a living cradle which she and he shared. She talked to her baby, ate little treats for him, and tried to go easy in her job, which was not difficult since it was off-season.

The morality of the situation bothered her. Robert had a right to know and to decide upon the future of his son, she reasoned. She had to tell him. She hardly dared to hope that Robert would find a way for her to keep their child.

Then a letter came out of the blue. The sight of

the envelope with the Glentirran crest on it filled her with joy.

Hi, Marjorie, a brief note to wave the flag. I'm still working like a dog at the distillery. Father's recovered, but retired, and I'm operating with a skeleton staff to get us through the next few famine years. I'm learning to blend the liquor and all the other details which I never thought would interest me but they do. I don't have time to think of anything else but work, starting at six a.m. and stopping around nine. One day you'll hear great things about Glentirran, but in the meantime I keep my head down and graft away, putting all dreams aside. How about dropping a line? How are you? Love, Robert

Love, Robert was the only personal touch. But it showed he hadn't forgotten her. She read the letter repeatedly and carried it around with her. She had to tell Robert what had happened, but she guessed it was the last thing he would want to hear, so she was dreading the coming ordeal.

She was cold and she felt demoralised after throwing up in the train lavatory, but she felt better as soon as her feet touched solid ground. She ate a bun and laced her coffee with sugar at the station café. There was no bus to West Linton, she discovered, so she was forced to pay for a taxi.

As she gazed stonily ahead, hardly noticing the pouring rain and the passing homes, she was remembering Robert the last time she'd seen him. She would never forget his expression. Remote was a vast understatement. He'd been engrossed in his problems and she'd become invisible.

And now? she wondered uneasily. Naturally he would be upset, as she was. Should she have come? But then she had never really had a choice: she didn't have the right to make this decision on her own. Despite her shame, she always came to the same conclusion: Robert should have a say in their son's fate, for the child was his as much as hers.

As the taxi turned into a driveway, her stomach lurched. *Tirran Lodge*. This was it! There was a small cottage behind the gate which gave her hope, but the taxi was speeding past it towards a house – or was it a castle? 'Oh God,' she whispered. It was huge. She paid the driver two days' precious tips and picked up her bag.

She felt so inadequate and alone standing in the porch. Then the door swung open and she was gazing up at a tall, stooped man dressed in a formal black suit. She forced a smile and said: 'I'm really pleased to meet you at last, Mr MacLaren,' and thrust out her hand.

The man stepped back. Without changing his expression one iota, he replied: 'Good morning, ma'am. Would you be here to see the young master or his father, Sir Duncan, who is indisposed? The doctor is with him. Shall I call Lady MacLaren?' His gaze flicked over her and seemed to hover significantly around the area of her midriff. 'Master Robert is away,' he added, and pursed his lips primly.

'I thought he was running the distillery. I mean, he wrote to me . . .' Her voice tailed off.

'The distillery, ma'am, is in the Highlands. I'll call Lady MacLaren. Please wait in the study. This way.'

Now would be a good time to leave, she reckoned, but without calling a taxi, how could she?

The study was intimidating, for it was bigger than their whole Dover house, but so cold and forbidding. 'Needs a bit of brightening up, that's for sure,' she muttered.

When Lady MacLaren swept in, Marjorie flinched. She brought warmth and colour into the room with her clinging, red woollen dress, the red scarf around her neck and matching lipstick. From her smart hairdo to her rings and necklaces, she shrieked rich. Once she had been a real beauty, but now she looked hard and her hair was too black for her pallid face. Not much real warmth about her, Marjorie guessed, watching her eyes. It's all an illusion.

Marjorie sighed, realising how gauche she looked in her school mackintosh, with galoshes over her shoes.

Lady MacLaren lit a cigarette and stared at her curiously. There was that look again. Marjorie folded her hands over her stomach.

'So you came to see Robert. I'm sorry that he's not here. In fact he's in America, but I'm not sure exactly where right now.'

Marjorie's heart sank. Suddenly she felt so tired. 'But he wrote to me,' she murmured.

'Did he mention that he's engaged to be married?' Lady MacLaren asked haughtily.

The shock came like a sword of ice thrust into Marjorie's belly. Every nerve end seemed to quiver and die. Her head was spinning and when she tried to speak she found her mouth was frozen. 'I've been foolish.' She shuddered with humiliation.

Finally, taking her courage in both hands she said:

'Robert and I went to Corsica in August and now I find I'm pregnant, and I'm not sure what he wants me to do. I've booked into a home for single girls who get in the family way,' she carried on gamely. 'They look after you and organise adoptions, but I have to ask Robert first. I couldn't give our baby away without asking him.'

'I think you're being very wise.' Lady MacLaren smiled, but something about the smile disturbed Marjorie.

'What a determined girl you are,' the older woman said. 'Perhaps I can help you to make your own decision. You see, Robert will inherit a title and eventually his wife will be Lady MacLaren. He is the head of the clan and the local squire around these parts. We have to lead very circumspect lives because we are looked up to. I entertain a great deal. Royalty stay here sometimes. Do you understand what I am saying, my dear? You are not equipped to fill this role.'

She was showing her claws and Marjorie watched her warily.

'Marriage to you would disgrace Robert,' she went on, as if she hadn't made herself clear enough. 'My husband would disinherit him. His life would be ruined. Of course, we should never allow it.'

'What makes you people so special that I could damage you so?' Marjorie blurted as she scuffed away a tear with her knuckles. 'He's not the Prince of Wales. You're not that important. You only run a distillery. Being pregnant isn't doing me much good either. And what about my baby?'

'I can see what sort of a girl you are,' the hateful voice went on. 'You took advantage of a lonely boy who was away from home. You assumed he would provide you with a cushy life so you got pregnant, thinking he'd have to marry you.'

She's like a snake, Marjorie despaired, watching her cold black eyes. And with as much feeling as a snake. And I'm acting like a rabbit. No wonder she thinks she's got me taped. The idea came to her that there were two kinds of women in this world: those who allowed their maternal generosity to guide their words and actions, and those who had repudiated all that was womanly and grew more cruel than men and maybe less than human.

'What proof do you have that he's the father?' There was so much menace there, Marjorie felt dazed. She could not think properly.

'I've had enough insults from you.' Marjorie rose, grasping for dignity. 'This is the twentieth century and I didn't come here for anything more than to ask Robert.' Clearly there was no point in staying. 'I'll be leaving, Lady MacLaren, but I'd be pleased if you would call a taxi for me.'

'No, wait! Perhaps I misjudged you and your motives. Please stay here a moment.' Abruptly, she left the room.

On the desk was a writing set and Marjorie wrote a short note for Robert, explaining why she had come and how his stepmother had mistaken her motives entirely. She left the address of the convent and added a post-script. 'I'm due around 15 May and if I haven't heard from you by then I'll assume you agree to the adoption.' She sealed the letter in an envelope and thrust it in her pocket.

A few minutes later Rhoda MacLaren hurried back.

'George,' she called into the intercom. 'Please bring the car round to take someone to the station.' She took a cheque book out of a drawer. 'This cheque is a gift from me to you. Nothing more. It in no way entitles you to think that my stepson has any commitment to you.'

The pen scribbled away as Marjorie waited, feeling wretched and dazed. Lady MacLaren had been calling her lawyer, she realised. How sad that she should feel it was necessary.

Five thousand pounds, Marjorie read from across the desk. Her first impulse was to tear up the cheque, but then she thought she'd give it to the convent. They could do with it.

'Your cruelty will bounce back on you, Lady MacLaren,' she said. 'It always does. Maybe one day you'll have to come begging me for kindness. Meantime, I'll wait on the porch for the car.'

She swept outside, trying to banish the vision of the woman's haughty amusement. 'Please give this letter to Robert,' she told the butler, or whoever he was.

It was only when she was safely in the car and they were driving out through the gates that she began to tremble.

Chapter 16

——— ———

It was Monday morning and still dark at eight a.m. Outside the wind was knocking the branches of the sycamore tree against the window frame and the rain was drumming on the roof. Liz Hardy had switched the light on in Marjorie's room and she was dusting. She would vacuum next, even though Tom was still sleeping. Funny how he could sleep late after thirty years of rising early, while she was a prisoner of habit.

Her daughter's many shelves and knick-knacks were a bind to keep clean. There was the striped tiger she'd won at a fair when she was six, her oldest teddy, called Poo, who still wore his spotted apron and bonnet, dolls and china animals, a printer's tray with glass and china toys which she'd bought bit by bit out of the housekeeping a right sod to dust it was, too – books on modern poetry, books in French, a lipstick and bra lying on top of a pile of old comics. How fast we all grow and change, she thought. Too fast! We're always a bit behind ourselves.

Before long a disquieting thought occurred to Liz. Why were there three packets of unopened towels in the cupboard? She bought Marjorie one packet a month down at the Co-op and it was never enough. Then came the sudden realisation that she hadn't had to bleach her daughter's underwear lately.

'Oh dear!' She began to feel ill as she worked.

By the time Dad got up the house was almost spotless. The washing machine cycle had reached 'spin', and the noise in the kitchen was like thunder.

'Can't you switch that bloody thing off until I've had my coffee?' Dad grumbled.

'Hang on a tic, love. It's three minutes off finished. Not like the old days, is it? D'you remember when you had to fill the copper and light the stove under it? You never missed once on Monday morning.' She buttered him up until the machine came to a shuddering halt.

'Can't do the washing much good,' he said.

'Neither did the copper.'

'When's Marjorie getting back?'

'Maybe tomorrow.'

'Hm. Funny they let her have all that time off when she's only just started work.'

'Oh I don't know,' Liz said vaguely, but she was thinking: Yes indeed, very odd that Marjorie should go up to Scotland in December of all times.

She was cooking, which was what Liz did when she wanted to escape life, when she heard Marjorie clattering down the stairs. She's back early. Something's gone wrong, Liz thought as her daughter walked in looking about as depressed as she'd ever seen her.

'Thought you were coming tomorrow, love,' Liz said.

'I came home early.' She closed her eyes wearily. 'I missed the last train and had to sleep in the woman's rest room. Hardly slept a wink and I didn't have enough cash to buy food. I took the first train this morning. I'm starving, Mum. You know what I've been longing for all the way home? Crumpets with treacle. Do we have any treacle?' She began to rifle the cupboards. 'Where's the treacle then, Mum?'

'Up there. But we don't have any crumpets. What about toast?'

'Oh, all right. I'll take my coat off and be right back.'

Liz put the bread in the toaster and wiped her damp brow with her apron. She looked up to the narrow strip of sky she could see behind the bare branches of the sycamore tree. The rain had stopped and the sky had a curious yellowish tinge. Could there be snow coming? In mid-December? And when had they gone to France? August, wasn't it? Four months! Too late to do anything about it now. So that was why she'd gone racing up to Robert. She shuddered when she remembered her daughter's expression of despair.

Liz got on with her chores, but she hardly knew what she was doing. She could feel her blood running thickly through her veins, swelling her feet and fingers, making her heart pound and her head feel funny and tight. Not that. Dear God, no! I couldn't face it. But I'm not going to meet troubles that haven't even crossed the bridge, she told herself in mixed but comforting metaphors.

Three weeks passed while Marjorie grew paler and sadder. Christmas came and went, followed by a particularly cold and blustering January. The Hardy family, gathered round the television each night, felt bewildered when Britain became a member of the EEC. Liz, in particular, feared change, but she was pleased when Phase 2 of the Pay and Prices Freeze was imposed, for Dad's meagre pension, plus Marjorie's contribution, was little enough to cover their living costs. They had been hit hard by inflation for the past six months. When, on 22 January, share prices fell by four thousand million pounds in one day, they reckoned life was going to get tougher.

'This is just the start,' Dad said ominously.

Marjorie turned nineteen on the twenty-ninth, so the family dug into their resources to buy her a new pair of high-heeled shoes which she chose from the best shop in the High Street. They were of black kid leather, with pointed, three-inch heels. When she showed them off that night Dad took one good look at her and said: 'Putting on a bit of weight, aren't you?' His daughter fled.

Liz put down her knitting firmly. 'It's about time I found out what's biting her,' she said.

What was she going to do? Marjorie crumpled on her bed. Why hadn't he written? Her anger was stronger than her fear. If he dumped her she would have to give up her baby. It was a terrible prospect, but without a proper home there was simply no way she could keep him, and he deserved the best. 'God help me,' she whispered. Dad had noticed she was thickening, so it was time to go.

There was a knock on the door. Mum stood hesitating in the doorway, her face twisted in anguish. She knows, Marjorie thought, but she doesn't want to accept the news. She's never been able to face up to things. Not her fault, it's just her way.

'Listen, Mum, I've got a six-month job and it means going away, but I'll be well looked after. Everything's all right. D'you know what I mean?'

Liz sat on the bed looking dazed. She needed reassurance badly, for she could no longer cope with her fears. 'If you promise me that everything's all right . . .' Her voice tailed off. 'You see I've been a bit worried that maybe you . . .'

'Everything's under control. Listen, Mum, you tell Dad I've got a live-in job. It's a laundry job in a convent, but I get the chance to take shorthand and typing classes every afternoon and to practise at night. I'll get a certificate. It's ideal, you see. It's just that I've been worried about leaving home. I won't be able to contribute for months, and with Dad being laid off and all . . .'

'Six months is nothing. You've always been a clever girl, Marj. I trust you to work things out properly.' Mum was almost too relieved to stand. 'So I won't worry any more,' she said with an explosive sigh of relief.

'Yes, Mum. Don't you worry now.'

Comforting her mother had made her feel better, too. It was all true, wasn't it? If she could just survive the next six months her troubles would be over. But what a crazy way to start her adult life. She'd had such big dreams, and she'd failed so badly. She felt like the lowest thing that crawled, but then she remembered what Mum used to say. 'When you're down there's only one way to go and that's up.'

She stared long and wistfully at her reflection in the mirror, noting her puffy face, the pallor of her skin and the deep smudges under her eyes. 'Marjorie Hardy, you're a fool,' she said sternly. 'When I think of all your plans, I could laugh my bloody head off. No more disasters. By next Christmas you'll be happy, getting rich and you'll know where you're going. Think positive, my girl, and that's an order.

'Okay, if you insist, I promise,' she answered herself with a wan smile.

Chapter 17

——— ———

Marjorie stood at the ironing board in the convent's laundry room, singing her heart out, hardly thinking about the shirt she was ironing – she could do that in her sleep – but keeping her mind on harmonising the song 'Waterloo' together with twenty other girls in various stages of pregnancy. She reckoned they had the best choir in the district. Not that they were likely to perform in public – picturing it made her smile – but singing helped pass the time. She had pressed hundreds of shirts in her five months at the shelter and she took a pride in being the fastest and the neatest. Profits from the laundry financed the shelter, so the girls felt self-sufficient, not charity cases, and this helped.

She would be leaving soon and she would leave many friends behind. The nuns were kind, and the girls were her friends. She knew all their lives and their disappointments and the mistakes that had brought them here.

Marjorie suffered, too, and there was the added bitterness that Robert had not contacted her. She tried to understand his unwillingness to be responsible for her and his child. With each day that passed the slow fuel of resentment was burning ever stronger.

Lately, she had become absorbed in the subtle communication growing between herself and her child, known as Little Rob, short for Robert, she had decided. The dragging weight was not a burden, but a joy. She had sailed through the second half of her pregnancy with the minimum of discomfort, filled with a sense of wonder and completeness. She was placid and content, longing to feel her child in her arms. Like the other girls, she dreaded the day when her baby would be given away and she spent hours agonising over her decision, but she always came to the same conclusion: she had no choice. How could she hope to bring up her baby properly when she had no training, no career and her parents were so poor?

The supervising nun came by, interrupting the singing. 'That's more than enough, Marjorie, dear. Time for a rest.'

She was feeling strangely energetic as she went to the canteen and drank a glass of milk before lying down.

'Hi, Rob. Exercise time,' she crooned. When she lay on her back Little Rob always liked to do his football exercises, but for the past fews days there had been no feet kicking out at the wall of her stomach and this was worrying her. She felt so restless. Her room was spotless, but she had to clean it again. She got up, fetched a bucket and a cloth, and began to wash out her shelves. It was a small room, hardly more than a cupboard, but she loved it and she kept it full of flowers. It was mid-May and she had roses, daisies, and irises, which she rearranged each morning.

She was halfway through scrubbing her cupboard when a deep, dragging pain began to creep up on her. It grew worse, until she crumpled on the floor and lay there panting. Could this be a labour pain? Surely it could never be this bad? She'd had enough tuition on giving birth, but no one had told her that the pains were unendurable.

Marjorie called Sister Agnes, who ran the hostel.

'It's only the first. No hurry,' she assured her.

'There'll be a long interval before the next pain and probably six hours or more before they get serious. Count the intervals between the pains and don't go out.'

She was able to finish the floor and put fresh water in her vases. She'd skip typing today.

'I don't think I could stand another pain like that,' she muttered.

'You will, don't worry, and afterwards you'll forget and perhaps you'll even get pregnant again,' Sister Agnes said crisply, leaving the room.

What did she know, when she'd never given birth herself? Marjorie sat on the bed and waited, feeling panicky.

The pain returned, as she had known it would, and this time it enveloped her totally. There was no other existence besides this agony. It was as if pain were the sea and she was drowning in it. Time seemed to stand still as she screamed and hung on to the bedrail.

It passed. She had to find someone to help her. She walked into the corridor feeling dizzy and light-headed, but otherwise normal. Footsteps came running and Sister Agnes came through the swing doors.

'Marjorie, dear, relax and lie down. You are hours away from giving birth. You must remember your lessons. Accept the pain. Don't tense up or you'll make it worse for your baby.'

'But no one told me how much it hurts,' she stammered.

'Perhaps because none of us have given birth,' the

nun ventured. 'Remember this, Marjorie. The pains
pass. Nature gives you time to recuperate between the
pains. You will survive it all and you will get the best
medical attention at the clinic, but right now it's too early
to go there. Try to be calm.'

'Oh God . . . Oh God . . . here it comes.' She tried
not to scream, but finally she succumbed, gripping the
nun's hands and writhing in agony. 'Is my baby in pain?'
she asked.

'If you tense up it will make it more difficult for the
child to emerge, I was told.'

Five hours later she was lying on a hard hospital bed
counting the seconds between the pains. Sister Agnes
had come with her to the clinic, held her hand in the
ambulance, and given her moral support all the way.
She wasn't so bad after all. Marjorie had endured the
indignity of an enema, and being shaved and poked at by
student nurses and doctors, but all this was unimportant
compared with the pain. Pain was her master and she
was its slave. She must obey and endure and not fight
it, for that made it worse. Her body had ceased to be
her own and become a pain-wracked shell over which
she had no control, and from which Little Rob would
eventually emerge, or so they kept promising. He was
taking his time.

A nurse came by and peered between her legs. 'Black
hair,' she called out in a matter of fact voice. 'And quite
a lot of it. I can see an inch of head. Keep going. You're
doing fine.'

'Fine?' she mumbled to Sister Agnes. 'Surely I'll die
soon. How is this possible in the twentieth century? Can't
they do something?'

'You'll be all right.'

She was too tired to do anything but lie and sometimes groan. Later, she did not know how much later, the nurse came and peered at her again. 'Right. Baby's on its way. Can you stand, dear?'

Marjorie heaved herself off the bed and between them, the nurse and Sister Agnes supported her to the delivery room. 'Call the doctor, get the sister. Be quick.'

By the time she was pushed onto the high delivery table Little Rob was on his way to being born.

'Push,' the doctor yelled. 'No, wait. The cord is round the baby's neck. Hold tight.'

'I can't . . . can't.'

'Don't throttle it. Wait.'

It took monumental willpower to resist her urge to convulse her muscles and push out the baby.

'Fine. I've had to cut the cord. Push with all your might. Heave away. You can do it. Push . . . More . . . Push for all you're worth. Come on. You must. Harder . . .'

Oh God, give me strength and save my child!

Grasped by the nurses, she summoned every muscle in her body to make that last supreme, mighty effort, as she heaved . . . and heaved . . . and grunted . . . until she felt the baby slipping out between her legs.

'Well done,' the doctor said. 'Now push some more. It's not over yet. There's the afterbirth to come.'

She was so tired. So very tired. She tried to do what they asked, but she was sinking into a deep lethargy. 'The baby's fine. Perfectly normal. A lovely, healthy child,' she heard the doctor say.

'A boy or a girl?' she muttered wonderingly. She seemed to be falling down into a deep lake.

'We can't tell you that, Marjorie. It's for your own good.'

'Let me see my child. Please, please,' she muttered.

'No, I'm sorry, dear. It's for your own peace of mind. If you see the baby, it will make it harder for you later.'

'He's mine. Give him to me. Please. I must hold him.'

She struggled into a sitting position, but already a nurse was carrying the baby out of the room. Marjorie sank back, desolate.

There was more agony to be endured with the after-birth, but by now Marjorie was almost beyond caring, overwhelmed with the grief of being parted from her baby.

Only later, when they'd wheeled her into a side ward and left her on her own, did she allow herself to weep, sobbing herself into a deep sleep.

Chapter 18

Marjorie hung grimly onto her composure as she faced the Mother Superior across her desk in her special sanctuary. Head throbbing, hands sweating and her stomach clenched, she tried to behave in a civil manner, but her breasts were so painfully swollen with unwanted milk she could hardly move her arms, and she was sad, so sad. She felt heavy with grief, even keeping her head up was a problem.

'I see you are back into your normal clothes. That's fortunate,' the nun said.

Marjorie cleared her throat, wishing they could talk about her child.

'I hope it hasn't been too difficult for you. You were a joy to everyone. My dear, I want to talk to you about the cheque you brought for five thousand pounds. I feel that the money belongs to you and you will need it.'

The saintly Mother Superior would never understand the fragile division between loving and whoring. 'I can't take it,' Marjorie said. 'I wish I could.'

'Very well. So once again, thank you. Here is your typing and shorthand certificate, my dear. You did well. And a reference. After all, you did help out with extra office work so I feel this is in order.' She slid an envelope across the desk. 'It will help you to find work. In addition, we pay a small bonus for laundry chores after deducting your board and lodging.'

Marjorie opened the envelope. Ten pounds a week, less deductions, left her a total of one hundred pounds in cash.

'That's really nice of you,' she muttered.

Wise old eyes were watching her anxiously as she wiped her damp forehead with a tissue.

'You must try to forget this episode. Make a success of your life, work hard and don't let your mind dwell on this loss. There will be other chances. With God's help you will marry a good man and have a family. We gave you no chance to bond with the baby and this was for your own good. I'm sorry, dear.' She was trying to be kind.

No chance to bond? Did nine months of sharing a body count for nothing then? But no one had forced her to come here. They were kind people helping others.

The adoption papers were pushed in front of her by the secretary. A pen found its way into her hand. After a while she put it down.

'I can't . . . You must think I'm so dumb, but I just can't . . . If I could just see him.'

'But I've already explained to you the reason why you may not. It's kinder for you,' the Mother Superior said gently.

'I just don't know,' she stammered. 'I want to do the right thing.'

'Oh, my dear, this is for your own good and for the sake of the baby's future. Trust me. Your child is going to a professional couple who can offer all the advantages of a prosperous, Catholic home. They've been waiting a long time.'

A bolt of jealousy tore through her, vicious as a tornado, leaving her gasping. It stood to reason that the best mother for her baby was herself.

Marjorie grabbed the pen and held it poised over the first page as her eyes skimmed the text. *A female child!*

'I had a daughter,' she gasped. Not far away in the convent nursery lay a little mite who was partly her and partly Robert. Her own daughter!

She felt dizzy as she flung down the pen and pushed the papers away. 'I won't sign. I want my baby,' she heard herself say. 'I'm sorry. I made a mistake. I can't give away my child. She needs me. And I must see her. Please . . . Please . . . I love her. Won't you help me?'

'But you're so young. You could never cope with rearing a child. You have no job. What will you do? Look, Marjorie. Go to your room and pray. I'll have lunch sent up to you and I'll call the social worker who helps out here. Her name is June Thornton and she's a very nice person. Perhaps you'd like to speak to the priest, too.' Anxiously, Mother Superior concluded: 'God be with you, whatever you decide.'

Four hours later Marjorie, the priest and June Thornton had reached a state of truce. The baby would remain in the convent's crèche until Marjorie found a job and a suitable home.

'You must understand that the moment you leave her, she becomes a ward of the court,' June explained. 'Later, if they find you are working long hours, welfare might take the baby away from you. It would be even worse then, Marjorie.'

'I can't give her up,' Marjorie repeated.

'Let's go and see your baby,' June said. 'You must

wonder why we tried so hard to persuade you to have your child adopted. I'm going to show you why.'

There was a house in the nearby village where fifteen youngsters lived in the care of a 'house mother'. One girl was almost sixteen. She was pretty with thick blonde plaits and freckles over her nose. She had been waiting for her mother to fetch her home since she was four years old. Then there was a dark-skinned girl of eleven, who had been placed in state care when she was three and who waited every weekend for her mother to come, but most times she was disappointed. The heartbreak stories went on and on.

'Most of them are waiting,' June ploughed on. 'And most of them will be disappointed. Sometimes their mothers visit them over the weekend and take them out, but generally only once or twice a year. Yet they always make these promises. At weekends the girls sit hopefully at the gate, although we try to keep them busy.'

'June,' Marjorie pleaded hopelessly. 'Stop twisting the knife. I get the message.'

'So let's go,' June said flatly.

When at last they reached the crèche, Marjorie did not have to be told which baby was hers. Instinctively she knew. As she bent down and picked up her child a hot wave of love raced through her.

She whispered 'God!' and lapsed into awed silence. She felt inadequate and incredibly sad and happy, both at the same time. She found she was laughing and crying. Her child was perfect in every way, so tiny, yet so beautiful. Her black hair was Robert's, her lips were hers, and when she opened her eyes they were dark and bluish, but she guessed they would turn brown like Robert's. Her little fingers were so long.

'Look at her tiny nails, so beautiful. I've never seen such a lovely baby.' Her tears were splashing her baby's hands. She sat down, cradling her child. She had the feeling she should snatch her baby and run for it. But where would she go? She bent over her and kissed her on the forehead, her eyes greedily taking in the sight of her, knowing it would have to last a while. Rocking her gently, she sat on dreaming of what might have been.

'I'm afraid we must go, Marjorie,' June told her eventually. 'The nuns may want to christen her in your absence. Do you have a name?'

'A name?' She had hundreds of boys' names. 'What about Lana? That's a lovely name, don't you think?'

'Lana it is,' June said.

Marjorie placed her baby gently back in the cot. 'Sometimes life can be so cruel,' she said wistfully. Lana began to wail and the last thing she heard were her cries.

'Remember the other children,' June said, as she dropped her off at the convent. 'If you can't make a go of it soon, you have to let her go.'

Marjorie spent a restless night worrying that her child was wailing in the cot with no one to comfort her. She woke early and took the first morning train to London. It was time to get to work.

The clickety-clack of the track seemed to echo June's words: 'If you can't make a go of it soon, you'll have to let her go . . . have to let her go . . . have to let her go.'

'I'll work like a dog. I'll be back for you soon, I promise. Hold tight, darling.'

But the grim reality was her dear little baby abandoned in the orphanage cot with no one to comfort her, being bottle-fed, while her own breasts were sore and swollen with unwanted milk.

Chapter 19

———— ————

Marjorie needed a home, a job and a crèche in that order and she needed them now.

The first accommodation agency she called on was staffed by a team of merciless women. 'No children,' they chorused. 'No one wants kids round these parts, especially if you're working.'

She tried another, but heard the same story. And another! Unwilling to give in, she kept pounding the pavements, but it was always the same answer: 'No babies'.

It was getting dark and starting to rain when she broke her heel outside a dingy rooming house in Swiss Cottage.

'Damn!' She hobbled in dismally and took the small room for five pounds a week. The landlady sounded doubtful about the baby, but she didn't refuse. Marjorie could see why. It was a slum: small, bare, damp and draughty. The only window was a French door leading onto a narrow, sooty balcony.

She was filled with tragic rage. How could they charge so much? How could it be so terrible? How could she rear a child in this cupboard with one gas cooker and a small heater for warmth? It was criminal.

She moved in, because it was late and dark and she had

broken her shoe. Despite the fact that it was summer the room was dark and chilly, and Marjorie spent the night shivering under the inadequate blanket the landlady had provided.

By the morning, she had a sore throat and a splitting headache.

The Tube was held up by a blockage on the line, so she strap-hung for two hours, feeling weak and claustrophobic. She arrived at the typing agency at ten where a cheerful Yorkshire girl went through her qualifications. The term 'office menial' had lodged in her mind ever since the headmistress's prize-giving speech, but this was not the time to be choosy. She had to cover her expenses and prevent herself from digging into her precious savings.

There was only one job available for beginners and that was in the typing pool of an insurance company. The pay was only twelve pounds a week, but she could start at once on a week's trial and soon she would be able to call herself experienced, the Yorkshire girl pointed out.

Maybe she and Lana could live on twelve pounds, but she could not bring up a baby in that awful room. She'd have to look further afield, but she was drained and still weak from giving birth and she didn't have the strength yet. She ate a bar of chocolate for supper and fell into a deep, exhausted sleep.

Boring, boring, boring. Was this to be her life? Despairingly she looked around the sanitised office, which was all in grey under the harsh fluorescent lighting. Dusty air was piped in, for the windows did not open. Four pale typists were getting to match the decor, she noticed, old before their time from living inside this tomb. One of them, Miss Annie Bates, had been working there for thirty-five years.

This was Marjorie's third week of working for the insurance company and as she sat down and plugged in her machine, she wondered just how long she could stick it out. Or would she learn to endure? The others were already hard at work, their earphones plugged in, with wrinkled brows, intent eyes, and racing fingers clicking keys. They were robots from nine to five, and probably they were getting to be robots in their free time, too, Marjorie thought bitterly.

What would become of her? All creativity and joy would be stifled soon, she knew. At the back of her mind she always carried the picture of her tiny baby crying in her cot. Would they hear her cries? Was she fed properly? Was she lonely? Did she know she had been abandoned? Oh, my darling. I'm trying, *trying*.

One of the women was married with two young children, so at tea break Marjorie asked her how she coped.

'When they get sick it's a right mess. My sister's got kids and she doesn't work, so she helps, or Mum comes to look after them. When they're healthy they go to the crèche, but it's damp and overcrowded and they catch everything going.'

She sighed. 'I get up at five to get here by eight. Lunchtimes I do my shopping and it's a real rush to get done, I can tell you. Then it's the Tube to the crèche and another Tube home and then a half-hour bus ride after that. Evenings I get the kids fed and bathed and put to bed and then I start the housework. I keep thinking, this can't be my life. I mean, not for ever, surely? Take my advice, Marj. Marry someone who can afford to look after you. Either that or don't have kids. One of these days they might get around to imposing standards on crèches, but right now it's just heartbreaking.'

The following morning Marjorie received two commission claims to type for the salesmen. They were both querying their pay cheques. She was staggered when she saw how much they earned. At eleven she rang through to the boss's secretary and insisted on speaking to the boss, Mr Petty.

'Okay, it's your funeral,' the secretary said. 'Come at noon when he has a short break.'

At twelve sharp she was shown in. The boss was a disappointment, Marjorie thought as she sat down. A grey man in a grey suit to match the decor. He was slightly bald, with horn-rimmed glasses and a tic in one eye.

'Strictly speaking you should not be here, Miss Hardy,' he said in a posh, Dover College-type voice. 'We do have a personnel officer for staff problems. However, since you're here, what exactly is your problem?'

'I want you to give me a chance to sell insurance, Mr Petty,' she began. 'I'm very hard-working and I think I'd be good at it. You don't know much about me, so I've just typed a few details. As you can see I did well in my A-levels and Maths is no problem . . .'

He cut short her spiel by gesturing with his hand.

'I'm sorry you wasted your time and mine, Miss Hardy. It's not a question of being brainy, you see, it's a matter of selling confidence. We sell our clients peace of mind. They have to trust us. Our salesmen have to have the right image. A slip of a girl just wouldn't do, don't you know.'

'No, I don't know,' she persisted and saw his eyes

narrow with annoyance. 'These men don't care about anything other than their commissions. I know that because I type their memos and letters, and your replies, Mr Petty.'

The posh accent was slipping as his temper got the better of him. She could see that and she realised she'd been silly.

'Listen, Miss Hardy. You're hard-working and clearly ambitious, but forget selling. You don't have the presence, the image, the voice. Now be a good girl and go back to your typing pool.'

Oh, to biff him between the eyes. She made one more impassioned plea.

'What about housewives, Mr Petty? I could sell to them. I'm on their level. I'd walk from door to door, I'd never give up. Trust me, Mr Petty. Give me a chance. I'd work for nothing the first month. I've got enough savings to do that. Just train me.'

'Listen carefully, Miss Hardy.' He glanced at his watch and then back to her. 'Most women are intellectually as well as economically dependent on their men. They leave things like insurance to their husbands, fathers or brothers. The men in question do not put their faith in women. You're the wrong sex altogether. Believe me, dear, I've made a science of selling. You're not the type.'

Her anger came bubbling up. You complacent, irritating, self-righteous man! she wanted to shriek. Instead she pulled herself together and said: 'You've never tried a saleswoman, have you? This is a clear-cut case of sex discrimination. Woman make up nearly forty per cent of the work force. They can make their own choices about buying their insurance.'

'Yes, Miss Hardy,' he said wearily. 'And I can make my own choice about whom I employ. You're sacked! I won't have troublemakers here.'

All of which turned out to be her lucky day, for when the agency demanded three months' notice and compensation, warning that if he failed to pay he ran the risk of a lawsuit, Mr Petty paid up. Marjorie gave up her room and fled to Dover with two hundred and forty-four pounds tucked into her bag.

It was the last Sunday in July. The sky was as blue as wild scabious, the sea a deeper shade. The warm wind wooed the flowers with whispered promises, coaxing them to submit to the murmuring advances of the bees, and Marjorie, who had also succumbed, wept for Robert and a home and father for Lana and a sense of permanency. She went to countless job interviews. For the rest, she wandered over the cliffs and fields, relishing a feeling of oneness with nature, pleased to be out of the typing pool, but fearing the future.

Then came the bombshell. Her dad's old stevedoring company went bust and with them went his pension. Mum told her the bad news at tea-time, when Dad had gone for a nap.

'Dad knows he's got to look for a job, Marj, but so far he can't pluck up the courage. He's been knocked for six, the more's the pity. I blame the war for his shot nerves. Of course jobs for men his age are hard to find. We'll have to rely on your earnings for a while. Please take Alf's job. He's always asking for you.'

'Well, how much is the least we could manage on?' Marjorie asked, sensing that it was now or never.

'Sixteen pounds a week is what he used to give me.

That means nothing over for Dad for the odd beer, but he could always start making those model boats he used to do so well.'

'Listen, Mum. I know I can earn the sixteen pounds. I'll pay the first week's cash right now. I've got enough to cover us for a while, but I need your help, too. You help me and I'll help you. Is that a deal?'

By the time Marjorie had finished her story, not forgetting what Rhoda MacLaren had said, Mum was crying at the ordeal she had gone through.

Dad laid down the law again, although Marjorie couldn't imagine what gave him the right to take over.

'She's got to be properly adopted by Mum and me,' he said. 'Otherwise we'll never see the end of those damned social workers who'll come sniffing around. They might even try to take away the baby if you're working. Besides, it wouldn't do your reputation much good either. You've got to think of finding a husband one day. Your mum and I will put out the story that we're helping out distant relatives. You and Mum had better go up to Wales and fetch her. The sooner the better, I should say. You shouldn't have left her there so long.'

'We must bring the poor little mite home at once,' Mum added.

'As for those bloody MacLarens,' Dad said. 'If they try to get their hands on your baby they'll get short shrift from me. That's yet another reason for adoption. They'll get their come-uppance one of these days. You mark my words,' he added darkly.

Marjorie went happily to pack an overnight bag, wondering how she could have misjudged her parents so.

Part 2 – Joe
August 1973 – June 1977

Chapter 20

Marjorie woke with a jolt, realising that the sun had risen. Her heart lurched with fright as she scrambled out of bed and peered into the cot, but a quick glance convinced her that her precious baby was alive and well and sleeping peacefully. How beautiful she was with her thick black hair and long eyelashes fanning her flushed cheeks. She had slept the night through, so for once Marjorie felt full of energy.

Racing down to the kitchen in her pyjamas, she mixed the formula and warmed the bottle, expecting to hear loud cries any moment. Returning to her bedroom, she pulled back the curtains and examined the eastern sky, which was a pale oyster grey with touches of violet.

'It's going to be a fine day, my love. Red sky at night is the shepherd's delight. Red sky at morning, the shepherd's warning,' she crooned. What a joy it was to teach her child the almost-forgotten rhymes and all the rituals and traditions that had enriched childhood. Admittedly, at three months, Lana was a little young, but she knew her baby listened to her.

As Marjorie bent over the cot and lifted Lana, she opened her brown eyes, Rob's eyes, and smiled for the first time. What a smile! It was all there, trust, love and togetherness.

'Oh, Lana. You recognised me.' The lump in her throat was threatening to choke her. 'Oh! How wonderful.'

She wrapped Lana in a shawl, thrust the teat into her mouth and carried her down to the kitchen where Mum was making coffee.

'Mum, she smiled at me,' Marjorie said, sitting at the table. 'Honest to God! It was a real smile of recognition. She loves me, Mum. Let's see if she'll do it again.'

She tickled her tiny chin and sure enough the baby gave a gurgling smile, stretching out her hands to grope at nothing, struggling for coordination and sensing the love.

Liz poured a cup of coffee for her daughter and pushed it towards her. 'Well, it's about time,' she said in a matter of fact voice. 'Three months is about right.' She tried not to show that she loved the little mite ferociously.

As Liz watched her daughter cooing over her baby she felt a sense of wonder and fear. Not for anything would she admit that Lana had been smiling at her for the past week while Marj was out job-hunting. How happy her daughter looked. Watching them, Liz felt like crying at the thought of the hardships ahead.

She made an effort to thrust off her negative thoughts. Babies were for the young, she thought. At her age you wondered when the next blow would fall. How could Marj manage to bring up this little child and help support them, too? It wasn't right. Perhaps she should get a job. She might well have to, but at least she should let Lana get a bit older first. She needed all the tender loving care she could get. And who would look after Dad? He wouldn't set foot outside the door nowadays, not even to go to the pub.

He was behaving as if the war had happened just a few days ago, for it had only just caught up with him. Like a bomb on a slow fuse. Funny that! Or like a plane when its wings couldn't take any more stress so they broke. What did they call it? Metal fatigue! Yes, that was what he'd got. And now her poor Marj was carrying so much on her slender shoulders. She wondered if she'd have the strength to cope. It was a joy to see her so happy, Liz thought, watching her daughter bath Lana in the kitchen where it was warmest.

'Help! I'm late. I must get dressed,' Marjorie called later. 'She's not quite asleep. Over to you, Mum.'

As Marjorie raced upstairs, Liz peered into the cradle, just to make sure everything was properly done.

Dad had made the rocking cradle which hung on two ropes from the beams so Liz could watch Lana while she worked in the kitchen. It had another advantage, for it kept the cat off the baby. Tibby disliked the rocking. It was always sneaking into the pram and the cot, but never the cradle. Instead it would sit absolutely motionless on top of the Welsh dresser, its wide yellow eyes fixed on the baby.

Marj rushed down to say goodbye.

'You look lovely, dear, but you should eat something.'

'I can't! I'm that het up. Really I am, Mum. Wish me luck.'

Liz watched her daughter twirl and make a last-minute adjustment to her hair. She looked so smart in the navy skirt with the Swiss lace blouse she'd treated herself to when she'd been paid out by the typing pool. If only she'd stayed with them. Every day she left so full of enthusiasm and each night she came home so dispirited.

A good husband is what she needs, Liz thought. Someone who can provide a good home for her and Lana.

She turned her attention to the washing machine and moments later Marj was gone.

Chapter 21

_____ _____

The day was perfect, Marjorie thought as she waited at
the bus stop. She had an appointment at eight-thirty
with the owner of a small printing shop who published
a local ad-rag. Although it was nothing much to look at,
it was brimful of small classified advertisements listing
hundreds of services, sales and jobs, and it covered the
southern half of Kent. Euphemistically called the *Kentish
Home News*, it came out fortnightly. The proprietor, a
Mr James, had advertised for a salesman, but she felt
confident that she would talk him into giving her a
chance. The printing works was situated in a warehouse
area behind the docks, but it was close to a bus stop and
that was handy. A cardboard sign pointed to an office
up some dirty wooden steps. She clattered up and stood
uncertainly at the top.

'Mr James,' she called.

'Over here,' a voice replied. She saw a figure bent over
a desk in a shadowy corner. What a scruff! When her
shock had passed, disapproval took its place. He hadn't
shaved for at least two days. His bushy brown hair was
uncombed, his skin veined, and when he looked up she
saw that his eyes were bloodshot and rather fierce. The
booze had got to him, she decided. As she moved forward
the dust spiralled in brave, scattered sunbeams.

She sat down unbidden, crossed her legs and hoped the dirty chair wouldn't soil her skirt. 'I'm here to apply for the job,' she said, trying not to look vulnerable.

'But I advertised for a man.' He seemed genuinely puzzled.

'Well, let's hope no one noticed,' she said, 'because the government's just brought out a report to stop this sort of thing. They're going to make a new law. You're out of date, Mr James. Have you heard of sex discrimination? You should be ashamed of yourself.'

The furnace in his eyes stoked up, but he smiled. A dangerous man, she decided, though she wasn't sure how she'd reached this conclusion. Intuition maybe? Suddenly he was full of apologies. 'You'd be out in all weathers, you see, tramping from door to door in the rain and snow.'

'I'm used to hard work.'

The telephone rang and Mr James was kept busy taking down details of a classified advertisement. That didn't look too hard, she thought.

Eventually he replaced the receiver. 'I expect my salesmen to do eight to ten calls a day, whatever the weather. I pay ten quid a week plus twenty per cent of gross earnings, not subject to extras like colour or special positions. Commission payable quarterly.'

The telephone rang again while she sat fretting.

When Mr James, 'call me Ernie', was on the telephone for the tenth time, she was still sitting there, waiting to hear if she had the job. By this stage, he'd taught her to fill in the contract, and how to charge. At an average price of 75p per column inch, a page brought in roughly £36. There were forty-eight pages in the latest issue, which totalled almost £1,700. If she sold half of this, she'd earn £172 commission twice a month. A fortune!

It was a pity she couldn't sit on the phone and take down the other half, too. Well, it stood to reason he would not want to pay commission on existing clients, she acceded grudgingly.

He replaced the receiver and turned back to her with a smile that revealed his crooked teeth. 'All right, you'll do fine.'

Just like that. She'd hardly managed to tell him more than her name and address between the calls.

He noticed her surprise. 'It's like this: I'm prepared to outlay a couple of tenners on you or anyone else who wants in. There's only one way to find out if you can sell or not and that's to let you get on with it. No cheating, mind you. I expect you to be on the beat between eight-thirty and four. Be in my office at eight a.m. sharp every morning, just so I can see you turned up for work. Make sure you hand in a report on calls once a week.'

'So when do I start?' she asked.

'No time like the present.'

Maybe her best patent leather shoes weren't made for pounding pavements, but she might as well get on with it.

'Thanks. I'll do just that.'

This was her lucky day all right. In her mind's eye she was seeing Dad's look of wonder when she brought home her first commission cheque. 'He'd be laughing on the other side of his face then,' she murmured. Behind her defiance was a deep yearning for acceptance. She had to prove herself. Dad had to realise just how wrong he'd been to doubt her.

Chapter 22

——— ———

Marjorie picked up the contract pad and a pile of printed tariff cards and fled. 'What a lark! About time I had a spot of luck.' As she made her way along the pavement, she seemed to be floating, light as air.

Their chemist, Mr Dodgen, seemed as good a place as any to start. He was always so friendly when she popped in for shampoo or headache pills for Mum.

'Hello, Marjorie dear,' he said. 'What can I do for you?'

'Well, I'm not buying today, I'm selling,' she said with her friendliest smile.

Something seemed to have gone wrong with Mr Dodgen's face. He looked stricken. Could it be stomach ache? she wondered, as she slid the *Home News* towards him.

'You can reach thirty-five thousand local homes for a few pounds . . .' She began to recite her sales lesson, but just then a customer hurried in trailing a whining child.

Dumping Marjorie without a word, Mr Dodgen was all smiles and sympathy again, his pain entirely gone.

'It's me! I'm the pain!' She felt astonished. Obviously he had one face for sellers and one for buyers.

She waited while he took five telephone calls and saw

four more customers and then at last there was a lull. A strange hiatus fell between them. Instinctively Marjorie decided to stick it out and say nothing. 'You still there, Marjorie?' he called eventually. 'You can see I don't need to advertise. I can't cope as it is.'

'But maybe . . .' She got no further, as another woman walked in and he turned away. She threw in the towel and walked out fuming.

Five calls later, she had to concede that Mr Dodgen wasn't the only two-faced shopkeeper round these parts. That was her friends wiped out. Now for the strangers! Five minutes later she was trembling after yet another unfriendly 'no'. Perhaps she should try a different area.

It was half-past three. Marjorie hadn't eaten all day and she was feeling faint. 'The way I'm going I can't afford to eat,' she muttered. As yet she hadn't sold one inch. She wandered down Snargate Street where a few small industries had become established. Joseph Segal Management Consultant, she read on a plaque by a doorway. And underneath, Channel Chandler's, Joe's Packaging Designs, Inventions Unlimited, Ltd, The Sportsman's Knockdown Mart – everything at wholesale prices.

'Well I never!' The window was full of paraphernalia for boats, fishermen and scuba divers. It was worth a try, since she was here. Plucking up courage, she walked inside.

A glamorous blonde with a milky complexion, baby blue eyes and a pert nose eyed her contemptuously. 'The both ith too bithy to thee you.'

'And I'm too busy to thee him, but I've managed to squeeze in a couple of minutes to give him some good news, so I expect he'd like to do the same,' she answered tartly.

'Then come in here,' a voice roared.

Venturing into the office, she saw a man bent over a cluttered desk. From the line of his cheeks and his long, sculptured neck she deduced that he was young, but when he looked up his dark eyes seemed old, although she couldn't think why, except that they seemed to have seen too much pain. He was graceful, tall and very dark, and his dark hair, streaked with gold by the sun, reached his shoulders. When he smiled his face lit up and his eyes glowed compassionately as if from some inner light. He was altogether beautiful, Marjorie judged, despite his nose which had been broken once or twice. He looked sensitive and kind, but she guessed he could be very tough indeed.

She glanced at the door where Joseph Segal MD, followed by a long line of letters, was painted in black on frosted glass.

'Yes,' he said. 'Fire away.' He had a strange voice, part cockney, part foreign, and the words came out like a rumble of far off thunder, but he was still smiling and that was encouraging.

'It's Mr Joseph Segal I want to see.'

'Your wish has been granted. You're seeing him, love.'

'Oh!' How come he was the managing director when he was so young? She sat down and smiled a little wanly. She was dead beat, but she hoped it didn't show. Moments later she was reciting her sales pitch.

Something was going horribly wrong, for the eyes that had been so full of warmth were getting very cold indeed. How hard he looked when he was cross.

But why was he reacting like this? She floundered gamely on.

Soon she began to sweat with the effort, and her hairdo, which had been threatening to slip all afternoon, chose that moment to slide down. She put up one hand and jerked it back into place, but the effort seemed to dislodge a pin, for it hung heavily in her hand.

Oh shit! She couldn't continue to talk with her hand holding up her hair, could she? Reluctantly she brought her hand down and felt her hair sag sideways. The end of her recital was in sight, but by now her 'prospect' was looking ferocious. Surely he'd known she was selling something? She came to a merciful end and took a deep breath.

'Not today thank you, miss,' he said perfectly pleasantly. Jumping up, he opened the door. Clearly he couldn't get rid of her fast enough.

Oh Christ! After a few seconds of stunned incredulity, she walked out.

'How could he do that?' she muttered as she reached the pavement. 'He was going to take an ad. I know he was. I blew it. I'd have done better to shut up entirely. I blew it with my own big mouth. But how?' She had the strangest conviction that she was to blame and she felt frantic with failure and too ashamed to go home.

Chapter 23

——— ———

Squirming with humiliation, she made her way towards a café at the end of the road. Once safely in the Ladies, she glanced in the mirror. 'Oh!' she gasped and burst out laughing. Her ponytail had somehow swivelled round and seemed to be hanging out of her ear. She splashed her face with cold water, unfastened her hair and combed it before returning to the restaurant.

I give up, she told herself as she pulled out a chair and sagged on it, feeling loathsome. Enough was enough! What a life, walking for hours, wearing down good shoe leather, getting drenched and cold, just so some bastard could put you down. And they did, too, in the meanest possible ways. If you wanted to see the seamy side of men, you had only to take up selling.

She ordered coffee and a sandwich and when it came she wolfed it down without caring how stale it was.

So what was left for her? The typing pool? But on a typist's pay the family would be living below the poverty line. Women hardly earned enough to keep themselves, let alone three others. The prospect appalled her. It couldn't happen, not to her own dear little Lana. She had to have the good things of life like other kids.

'Oh Lana. You're worth fighting for,' she whispered, close to tears. 'I'll try harder.'

Instinctively she knew she'd blown her last appointment. Joe Segal had been on her side, but she'd alienated him. So she hadn't been completely useless. *She'd sensed his thoughts*. For the first time in her life she was becoming aware of the value of her own perceptions.

Nerves jangling in time to her bracelets, she retraced her footsteps until she found herself mounting the steps to the showroom.

Luckily, the buxom blonde was nowhere around. Marjorie tiptoed to the MD's door and pushed it open.

Segal looked up and scowled. 'Did you leave something behind?'

'My self-confidence!' She sat down uninvited.

'You shouldn't have had any in the first place,' he retorted gloomily. 'Why did you come back?'

'This was my first day. I had ten appointments before you and every last one of them turned me down. I sort of knew they were going to do that right from the outset, but with you I saw that you were going to be my first "yes". I blew it. I want you to tell me where I went wrong. Please . . . It's important to me.'

'At least you're aware of it. That's important. It's something you can build on. I don't even know your name. That was your first terrible mistake.'

She tried to tell him, but he waved her down. 'It's too late now. So, Miss Nameless. As a salesman I resent people like you. Selling is an art, and like all arts it needs a great deal of studying and hard work. How would you like it if someone barged into your office and started to play the violin badly? Now you know how I was suffering.' As he warmed to his theme his cockney accent became more apparent.

'If you don't have any talent you could at least learn

the basics. You haven't read one book on the subject, have you? If you don't love what you do, you're
bound to fail.'

'How can anyone love selling? It's a horrible job.'

'It's an art form, but never mind. Give it up then.'

'I can't,' she said; trying to keep her temper. 'I have
financial commitments. But what is there to like about
it? It's just a job.'

'Sacrilege!' He jumped up and studied his bookcase.
'Tell me again why you want to sell?' he said.

'Honestly, Mr Segal, it's for the money. I'm the
breadwinner of our family.'

'Did you like those men you tried to sell to today?'

'Right lot of bastards, every man jack of them.'

'Wouldn't you like to beat them at their own game?
Imagine this. You throw down the gauntlet, take on your
adversary and win with your wits, which is a bit more
satisfying than using a sword, or a fast car, or your fists
encased in boxing gloves. I tell you, it's pure joy. Worth
a bit of effort, isn't it?' He smiled sadly. 'But like fencing
you have to learn how.'

'Yes, thank you. I'll pop off down the library and
get some books.' She was beginning to think he was
cuckoo.

'Borrow this one. It's very good. Read it tonight. You
can come here tomorrow evening and try again. When
you win fairly you'll get a contract out of me, but not
before.'

'Thank you,' she said, and bolted.

As she hurried to the bus stop, she glanced at her
watch and saw that it was past seven. Goodness, Mum
would be worried. She hoped Lana was still awake.

She was so exhausted she fell asleep on the bus.

'What a day,' she muttered as she trudged home. 'What a horrible day! Never mind! You, Mr Dodgen, and you, Mr Holman, and all you mean old shopkeepers will sign on the dotted line before I'm done with you.'

It was six p.m. and a blustering east wind was buffeting pedestrians with gusts of drizzle. It was rotten weather for August, Marjorie thought, wondering if summer would ever come. Dressed in her navy suit without a coat, she was frozen and wet through. She had a long list of 'nos' to show for her aching feet and exhaustion. Even worse, she had been put down at every call. She felt she'd reached an all-time low, but she was not yet ready to throw in the towel. She had one more appointment and that was to see Joe.

Joe had a new receptionist, as blonde, busty and dreamy-eyed as the last one. Where did he find them? The girl pointed towards his office. 'You may enter,' she said in a provincial French accent.

'Wonder how long she'll last?' Marjorie said loud enough for Joe to hear, then walked into his office.

He was messing around with a large black box and a screwdriver, and glanced briefly in her direction, raising an eyebrow. 'As long as she keeps out of my hair. I only have temps. It's safer!' His face hardened as he scanned her. 'One look at you tells me you've failed,' he snapped. 'Get out there and do your entrance bit again. This time convince me that you've sold every jerk you saw today.'

'How would I do that?' she asked, collapsing into his only easy chair and crossing her legs. She watched him scowling as he worked. I could fall for you, Joe, if I weren't in love with Robert, she mused.

'I dunno. How did I know you hadn't sold a darn thing? Off you go. Come in and act more confident.'

'I can't. I'm too depressed. Maybe tomorrow.'

'Not much good, are you?' He called out in French for two teas. 'Let me remind you,' he went on while he carried on working, 'that no one wants to make decisions. Your clients would feel more confident if they could see you were winning. Most people are like a lot of silly sheep.'

She sighed. 'You won't believe how rude people are. I can't take it much longer. I'll go back to typing, anything!'

'Well that's just typical, Miss Quitter. There's a war on in Israel, people are dying by the thousand. The world's tottering on the brink of disaster, US forces are on worldwide alert, the USSR is planning to send armed forces to the Middle East, there are serious rifts in NATO. To cut a long story short, the world has its back to the wall, but no one's quitting except Miss Hardy, who wants to give up a chance of future prosperity because a handful of Dover business louts have put her down.'

She looked up blankly. 'That puts it back in perspective. Thanks, Joe!' Her expression was impassive, but her anger was strengthening deep down like a banked-up fire. She'd show the bloody lot of them.

'It's a question of statistics. By the end of the month you may find you're averaging a contract for every eight calls. Then every *no* will be a step towards your next *yes*.'

She nodded and forced out a smile, but her expression was forlorn.

'Let's get on with it then. I haven't got all day.' He gave a deep theatrical sigh.

'You don't have to do this,' she said sharply.

'Listen to yourself! Your pride will be the ruin of you. You've got me on a long-term promise. I'm a sure thing simmering up. Don't ever let me slip through your fingers. Particularly not through pride. Sooner or later I'm going to have to sign the contract. Can't you see that?'

'That doesn't seem quite fair.'

'Ah! Now I realise why selling is such a neglected art in England. It doesn't live up to your ridiculous sense of fair play. Listen, Marjorie,' he said, suddenly serious. 'If that's your attitude you might as well give up now. So get the hell out of here and stop wasting my time. Here's another book, just in case you change your mind. Don't come back until you're ready to put selling first before any silly notions of fair play.'

'Jesus,' she whispered. 'Why are you talking to me like this? Do I have doormat printed all over me?'

'Yes, I think maybe you do,' he said thoughtfully.

Grabbing the book, she flounced outside feeling crushed. Joe followed her. 'I may come back tomorrow,' she called over her shoulder. 'On the other hand, I may not.'

'If you come back I'll take double whatever you've sold during the day. How's that for encouragement?'

She stopped in amazement, turned and walked back slowly despite the rain. 'You can shove your charity, Joe Segal.' She could hear how aggrieved she sounded, but what the hell.

'Sorry. I take that back. Good motives, wrong wording. Forgive me.'

She forced a smile and limped off to the bus stop.

Joe frowned as he watched her go. He had no idea why he was helping her. She was lovely, there was no denying that, but so were plenty of other girls who weren't half as prickly, including his secretary.

He wasn't trying to bed her or be her friend. The truth was, he was a loner. Sometimes he felt as if he didn't belong anywhere. He guessed this was partly due to his mismatched parents. His mother, Bertha Goldman, had been a pattern cutter in Golders Green. His father, Klaus Segal, had been a professor in mathematics in Berlin before the war forced him to flee to London, where he had met Bertha. Then he had been in turn a pilot, a salesman and a property developer. Later he had sold his business, divorced his wife and returned to Germany, where he had married a rabbi's daughter and devoted himself to writing mathematical books with a prospective readership of roughly one thousand throughout the world.

Joe could never understand why his parents had married in the first place. His father was intellectual and steeped in German culture, his mother cockney and streetwise. In strict rotation, Joe had been reared by his parents and his two grandmothers. One was Greta, a mad and melancholy Auschwitz survivor, who lived in Paris. The other one was Maude, who ran a barrow in Soho selling hot dogs and hot potatoes and who always had a laugh for everyone. The rabbi's daughter had done her best to whip him into shape, and so had his stepfather, a drag artist and pianist who did London's pubs, mainly in the East End.

Joe had learned to fit in everywhere, but underneath he fitted nowhere. He had no formal religion or culture, preferring to find his own path. He thought of himself as a 'quester'. He was after truth, but he doubted he'd find it in this lifetime.

Meanwhile he had his own code. He helped those who crossed his path, if they needed help, and if he could. He tried not to do too much harm to others and for the rest he kept his restless, questing, highly intelligent mind too busy to allow it to drive him crazy.

Marjorie had crossed his path and clearly she needed a push in the right direction. She was too young to have so much sadness clinging to her. Her desperation was real enough for him to sense. He guessed she was poised on the brink of survival. Now she was cross with him, she might never come back and in a way that might be a relief. She was distractingly sexy.

Joe began to plan his evening. He had found a recording of Korn's new violin concerto with Zina Schiff as soloist, which he was going to drool over Later he'd practise his clarinet for an hour and then meditate. If he had time he'd work on his inventions.

The bus came and Marjorie got on it. He waved, but she had no idea he'd been watching her. This was a dicey area in the evenings. Going inside, he locked up and switched on the telephone answering machine. He had an idea he had a dinner date, but what the hell, Korn was calling.

For five more wet days Marjorie slogged round Dover, getting very little for her trouble, but learning the hard way. She always sensed where she'd gone wrong, and talked it out with Joe at night. 'Sold anything?' was the question that struck shame, or cowardice, or anger, depending upon her mood.

'Give over, Joe. Look! It's Friday. I've had enough put-downs for one week. I've clocked out in my mind. I wouldn't say no to a cup of tea.'

'Not one inch?'

She scowled at him. 'I got a lot of empty promises.'

'They're not promises, they're future sales. Play your cards right and the promisers will find themselves committed. If the promisee is smart enough, that is. Now listen! When Joe Bloggs keeps you waiting, use the time to visualise yourself walking out with a signed contract.'

'You're a weirdo. D'you know that, Joe?'

'You're prevaricating. Get on with it.'

'Mr Segal, I wonder if I could interest you . . .'

'God! Can't you be a bit original?'

'Damn you, Joe. I've had enough of this.' She bounded to her feet in a rush of nervous temper and raced outside, longing to punch someone hard and work off days of pent-up fury. Down the road was a second-hand car dealer and in his window was a large poster of himself, on his hands and knees with three predatory kids on his back. '*Put your trust in Uncle Jim for a reconditioned used car*,' the caption read. Every time she saw it, she wanted to puke.

She stalked in, dry-mouthed with anger.

'So you're Uncle Jim, are you?' she snarled. 'Have you ever asked yourself how many people walk down this back street? Have you ever thought to widen the scope of your shop window? Do yourself a favour –

take the poster to the people with this . . .' She flung her paper on his desk.

'I sold him!' She burst into Joe's office. 'Half a page an issue for a whole year. My God! I sold a contract. I'm in shock. Truly I am.'

She flung herself at Joe and hugged him.

'Thanks, Joe. Sorry for the tantrum.' She flapped the contract under his nose. 'Signed and sealed and it didn't take five minutes. What do you think of that?'

'A good start,' he said, smiling his funny sad smile. 'So now sell me.'

'You? Come on, Joe, I shouldn't have to sell you and you know it. You're losing sales while you're teasing me. You sit here in your burrow like a silly rabbit and you never go out to sell anyone anything. This little rag can do twenty thousand calls for you. If you don't want to get off your butt, then let this rag do it for you.' She hadn't noticed she was shouting with the force of her conviction.

'Now you're selling! I'll take the back page every issue for a year.'

She gaped at him. She could feel a flush rising from her feet to her cheeks until she was burning all over.

'No you won't, you can't afford that much.'

'Yes, I will and I can,' he bellowed.

'It's too much for you.'

'Listen. I want it. If you won't take it, I'll call your nasty Mr James and give it to him. Look here!' He flung some old copies towards her. 'I always took the back cover. You should have gone through past issues to find out who'd dropped out. That's something you didn't think of, Miss Clever Guts. By some strange coincidence,

I was just about to phone your Ernie James when you pitched and massacred your chances.'

'You bastard! You'll never know how close you are to being biffed.'

'You wanna try? Come on, try me. Come on. Punch here.' He pointed his finger at his chin. 'Let it all out. Hit as hard as you can.' His face leered over her. 'You haven't got the nerve, have you?'

Quick as a flash of rage her fist shot out towards his jaw, and kept on going as she followed it through the air. Joe caught her before she hit the carpet.

'I'll teach you how to fight when I've taught you how to sell,' he said. 'Maybe this time you'll show some talent.'

Chapter 25

What a glorious day. Black clouds hovered above the chimney pots and the driving rain was freezing, but this did nothing to dampen Marjorie's mood. It was the last day of October, commission payday, and she was owed a massive four hundred pounds – a fortune! She had been window shopping for days, and her needs were endless: baby clothes, toys, a pushchair, a chest deepfreeze for Mum, perfume for Barbara. They were selling boxes of cheap frozen herrings down the docks and she would buy one and a case of beer. Four hundred pounds! Wow! She felt dazzled by her choices. She had spent the cash many times over in her mind as she thrilled to her new rich status.

'Good morning, Mr James,' she trilled, as she ran up the stairs two at a time.

'Watch out for those slippery steps. How many times must I warn you?'

The office was much improved nowadays and smelled of disinfectant and polish with a vase of flowers on her desk. Marjorie cleaned up on Friday afternoons and Monday mornings, times when absolutely no one wanted a salesman hanging around.

'D'you realise the latest issue is full of my advertisements? There's hardly anything else!' She grinned happily at her boss, who scowled and looked away.

'Don't take it to heart,' she gloated. 'That's what you hired me for, isn't it?'

'I have absolutely no complaints about your enthusiasm, Miss Hardy,' he said in a gruff voice.

Well, today was not his day, that was for sure. It was probably the thought of paying her commission that was riling him. She pulled out a contract with Mr Dodgen, the chemist, and slid it across the desk.

'This one cost me,' she told him. 'Mean old skinflint. It took four calls, but he finally signed on the dotted line like a good boy. They all do eventually. A year's contract. Not bad, eh?'

'Very good,' he grunted.

'It's payday, so I'll be on my way. Can I have my cheque now, please?'

Squinting slyly at her he slid an envelope over the desk.

'My first commission. I'm so excited,' Marjorie said. She opened the envelope and out slid a ten pound note and two fifties. 'What's this then?' She dropped the money as if it were burning.

'Your week's pay, ten pounds, plus your bonus.'

'But I'm not working for a bonus, Mr James. I'm on a twenty per cent commission rate.'

'Who said so?'

'You did. You know you did. We've discussed it dozens of times since that first day.'

'Look here, Marjorie, be reasonable. I can't pay you that much and that's all there is to it.'

'You must. You owe me the money. That was the basis of my contract.'

'I don't make that much profit. I didn't mind for the

first few ads, just to get you going, but now . . . well, to be honest, you sold two-thirds of the latest issue. There isn't that much profit in it for me.'

'That's not the point. You made the rules. Do you think I'd slog my guts out for a lousy . . .' She broke off, quickly calculating. 'This brings me up to two pounds a week more than what I earned in the typing pool. And what about my bus fares, phone calls, shoe leather and the wear and tear on me, out in all weathers all hours, and the rudeness and the put-downs . . . Oh! You can't do this to me,' she wailed. 'Pay me what you owe me or I'll go to the police.'

'Calm down, Marjorie. I've given you a generous bonus. I owe you nothing.'

'We have a contract.'

'Show it to me.'

She gasped. She'd been had. As the truth sank in she wiped her contracts and layouts off her desk and thrust them in her briefcase.

'Hey, those are mine.' He lunged too late as she fled, clattering down the stairs.

'Oh dear, oh dear, what shall I do,' she mumbled as she hurried along the street. All that boasting at home, all their plans, all the lovely things she had promised Mum, and now she had a lousy hundred pounds. She owed Mum over half of it. The mean, cruel, spiteful, two-timing crook. She'd get him!

She went into the police station and told them what had happened, but they explained it was a civil matter, so then she visited the only lawyer she knew, Mr Lockyer, who was handling Lana's adoption.

Sitting in his office, she poured out her story. 'Oh Mr Lockyer, please make him pay me what he owes me,' she implored as she ran out of steam. She was halfway to panic, her heart pounding, her eyes burning.

'Calm down, Marjorie. Would you like a cup of tea?'

'Not really, thanks. Just the money. I'd counted on it. We need it at home.'

He patted her hand. 'Steel yourself, Marjorie. Next time you get any sort of a selling job on commission, or bonus, ask for a written contract and bring it to me. It's his word against yours and there's nothing you can do about it. If you go back get a contract for future services.'

'I'll never work for him again,' she vowed in a fury.

'I'm sorry, Marjorie. I'll try to talk some sense into him, but you'll just have to write the loss down to experience. I'm sure you'll never make this mistake again. At least it was only three months. It could have been longer. You were learning, too.'

He kept trying to soften the blow, but nothing could compensate her for all those lovely things that Lana and Mum weren't going to have. She felt such a failure. What on earth was she going to tell the family? She was a fool. Her heart was pounding, she could feel the blood rushing round her body and she was beginning to feel sick.

She left and wandered along the beachfront, too ashamed to go home without the cash. How could anyone be so selfish? He knew how hard she'd worked. Was business always like this? She'd been so sure she was halfway up the ladder to success.

I bet he's lying – I bet the mean old crook can afford to pay me every penny he owes me, she thought mutinously. After all, it couldn't cost much to print that miserable rag – he used cheap paper and it only had one extra colour. She had a good mind to find out, but who would know?

Perhaps Joe. He had a small printing press for churning out his own direct mail leaflets. That was how he did his business, she'd discovered recently.

'Mr James, robbing me was the stupidest thing you ever did,' she muttered as she strode along the beachfront to Joe's office.

Chapter 26

The shop door was closed. Marjorie pressed the bell and waited, shivering with anxiety. 'Be here, Joe,' she muttered. On her third ring Joe's voice snarled through the intercom.

'Joe, it's me . . . I wasn't sure . . . are you working?'

'Stop stammering and get to the point.'

He wouldn't win any prizes for manners.

'I need your help.'

'What, now?'

'Yes, if you can.'

There was a pause long enough for a sigh.

'Come on up to the top floor and walk in. Don't ring the bell, I can't stand the noise.'

As she mounted the last stairs she heard the strains of a clarinet playing something fierce and wild – no melody, but sounds like the wind made on a stormy night. She paused in the doorway to glance around curiously. The room was one big empty space, white walls and ceiling and bare wooden floors. There were two chairs like canvas seats, but made of black leather on an aluminium frame, and perspex tables that were close to invisible until you fell over them. The only picture was as weird as the music. *Kokoschka*, she read.

Joe, wearing black shorts and a sweater, was standing

in front of a music stand holding a clarinet. His legs were muscled and tanned dark brown. Pretty nice, she thought, despite the odd scar. He nodded coldly, switched on his tape deck and repeated the mournful dirge, playing against a professional, trying to keep pace. As he swayed backwards and forwards the sinews rippled in his legs and shoulders. How did he get that body and that tan? she mused lustfully. Not sitting in an office all day, that was for sure. Was he one of those narcissistic types who worked out in a gym? Somehow she didn't think so. The music made more sense with the orchestral background, but it was still freaky. Joe was so intent, hardly aware of her, lips pursed, frowning, his slanting eyes glaring at nothing, hair falling over his shoulders. His hands were strong and beautiful. She longed to feel those hands touching her, and his lips on hers.

There was a sudden halt as he switched off the tape deck. His head swivelled to peer at her. 'You're putting me off. Stop staring.'

That was a bad start. 'Where did you get those muscles, Joe, and your Mediterranean tan?'

'In Israel. I was in the army for a while.'

'Why did you leave?'

'Invalided out. Now quit probing and sit down,' he snarled. 'Don't clatter.'

'I wasn't. You couldn't have heard me anyway with that racket on.'

'Racket? Is that your considered opinion? That was Nielsen. D'you mind waiting while I have another shot at it?'

'I'm in no hurry.' She put on her best smile, but Joe wasn't looking. He was alone in his own world.

Somehow she had to get through to him. He had to

teach her more about business. Help her to get the paper costed and find the right printer. Would he help her? She leaned back and closed her eyes.

What an awful day. What if Joe didn't want to help? What would she do then? Then she remembered what Joe had taught her. Switch off, blank your mind, imagine a silver chord snaking out of you and binding the other person to you. Visualise them signing on the dotted line. It was a pity she hadn't visualised that old sneak writing out her commission cheque. And here she was using Joe's methods on him. She quietened her mind and began to visualise Joe and herself working on her plan. 'I need you, Joe,' she muttered.

The next thing she knew Joe was shaking her shoulder.

'These chairs don't look like much,' she said, blinking up at him, 'but they rock you to sleep.'

'They're my own patented design and they don't look so bad either.' He seemed more at peace with himself now.

'Got it right at last,' he explained.

'I didn't know you played.'

'I used to have my own jazz band, but I like classical best. Want to have a look around?'

'Mm, yes.' Joe showed off his pad with obvious pride. The place was not exactly cosy, but that didn't seem to worry him. He'd spread himself over the entire top floor, and there was plenty of open space, if you liked open spaces, but not much furniture. The bedroom had a bed, and that was that. One long room was filled with shelves, drawing tables, big arc lights and drawing paraphernalia.

'You see this?' He held up a small black box with a cord hanging out of it. 'It emits a high-pitched sonic whistle indiscernible to human ears, but it's enough to drive away every rat within a half-mile radius.'

'That should make a fortune.' She felt startled. Maybe he wasn't such a fool after all. 'Have you patented the idea?'

'No,' he grimaced. 'The damned cats got earache and left home, too. But I'm working on it. 'This is my latest – a model of a circular parking garage. I sold that to a London architect.'

'No kidding? You sometimes make money with your inventions?'

'Enough to cover the cost of my world patents.'

'You might check some of the ideas with me,' she told him. 'Then I could tell you if you're being clever or just plain silly. Now if you'd invented something that could wash, dry and polish a floor you'd be talking. Or what about a remote-controlled vacuum cleaner that rolls around the floor all night? Or an automatic potato peeler, then you'd be doing something useful. I can't work out if you're for real, or just a regular nut.'

'I taught you to sell, didn't I?'

'Yes,' she admitted. 'But you just learned bits out of books and repeated them to me. I know because you lent me the selfsame books.'

'True. But I made it real for you.'

'Yes and thanks. What are all those dirty old bricks and lumps of sooty cement doing here?'

'Top secret. Don't ask. Forget you saw them.'

'That'll be easy,' she said.

Marjorie's head was soon spinning with mad and clever ideas from a brain that seemed to have no boundaries or any idea of what was smart and what was dumb.

'So what's your problem? But let's have a drink first,' he said, when they were back in the big space. 'Sake. It's strong, just so you know. Okay, get on with it.'

She explained how she'd been cheated and how much she was owed, spreading the contracts on the floor to prove her point, repeating what the lawyer had said. 'So you see,' she concluded, 'I'm going to publish his damned ads in my own newspaper and I will write my own editorial, too, but I need a bit of advice on how to set it up. What do you think the printing costs would be?'

Joe shrugged. 'One's thing's sure, he makes a bit out of it or he wouldn't waste his time, but I can't suck these figures out of my thumb. I'll need a day at least.

'Listen, Marjorie, switch off now. It's only money. Mr James is going to get what he deserves. It's you I'm worried about. You're hooked on all the wrong things: owning things, having money. The secret of contentment is not getting hooked on your desires. It's great to be free. Try it sometime. I bet you haven't a clue what you're going to do with all that money when you've made it.'

'Are you mad? I don't *need* it. I have to have it.'

'I'd really like to know why, before I go to all the trouble of helping you.'

She wondered if it were the sake that loosened her tongue, but she couldn't stop talking as her dreams came pouring out. Dreams for Lana: she had to win back her birthright. Dreams for Dad and dreams for Mum. And then there was her special dream, of showing Robert that she was as good as he was.

Listening to her, Joe wondered if he should ration the sake. She was on her fourth. Poor kid! She'd had a bad start and hardly out of school, too. But she was gutsy and hard-working and there wasn't an ounce of self-pity in her. He made a snap decision. He'd keep an eye on her. Someone had to.

'Tell you what,' he said. 'We'll go into partnership on this thing. You do all the work and I'll get half the profits. How's that for a deal?'

'Does that seem fair to you?' She wrinkled her brow.

'What's fair got to do with it? That's the deal! Take it or leave it. I do all the worrying, don't forget, while you only have to sell. I'll cover initial costs and make sure you get your basic sixteen quid a week until we rake in the money.'

'I'll take it,' she said happily.

'Okay, that's enough of that. Business has to be kept in its place or it takes over. It's boring and then you become boring. Be in my office eight sharp the day after tomorrow. Tomorrow you're on holiday. Let's celebrate our partnership and I'll play you some of my favourites.' He poured some more sake and before she knew where she was, she was flowing way out over the rooftops with his weird but compelling music, which was somehow like him: frighteningly free, full of surprises with hidden passions skilfully concealed.

Chapter 27

She'd never seen Dad so angry, or Mum so scared.

'Her vanity will destroy us,' Dad said, addressing himself to Mum, his lips quivering with rage. 'We can't pay her debts and she'll run into trouble, I promise you that. There's a recession starting, but what does she care? She's been nothing but trouble from the word go. She wasn't content with a normal job, or a decent boy, oh no. Instead she got in the family way with that college boy and saddled us with her brat.'

'Shame on you,' Mum managed to say. 'Where would we be without our little Lana?'

'Much better off,' Dad said. 'And then she boasted about all the money she was making, but she wasn't making a damn thing. Alf would have paid her more.

'You're all talk, my girl,' he said rounding on Marjorie. 'But nothing ever comes of big talk except shame.'

'Oh . . .' She clapped her hands over her ears and ran for her bedroom as she had always done, but this time she paused midway and slowly turned back. For the first time in her life she had someone to fight for.

'Dad, in your mind there will never be a good time for me to start a business or anything else, because you'll always be scared. But don't you worry, I intend to keep my bargain with you. I'll earn the cash for all of us, but

I'm telling you this now, if you ever put Lana down, like you've been putting me down all my life, I'll take her away and you'll never see either of us again. No one's going to put her down *ever*. You got that, Dad?' She ran upstairs gasping with tension.

Bending over the cot, she gloated over her sleeping baby. Lana would never have to listen to that sort of trash. She'd have the best schools and the best chances. 'You'll get your birthright back, my girl,' she whispered. 'I'll grab it for you. Promise!'

'Off you go then!' Joe sounded preoccupied as he parked in a loading zone and picked up his book.

Majorie stared dismally at the rain pounding the windscreen driven by a gusting, gale-force wind. She'd tried so hard to look exactly right. She was wearing her best navy tailored suit with a white silk blouse tying at the neck. Her hair was pulled up in a chignon, and pearl earrings borrowed from Barbara, court shoes and a briefcase completed the image of a successful businesswoman, she felt sure. But right now all this was hidden under her old yellow plastic mac and sou'wester, which she would leave at reception.

She had to walk into Ted Little's office looking trim and businesslike. This was her first selling call for their new magazine, *The Handy Home Guide*. She had a superb dummy, rate cards and a contract pad. She knew it was important that her first call was successful and she was trembling.

'Hurry up and get your licence,' Jo said. 'I'll die of boredom waiting all day.'

'I'm scared.'

'You're scared of everything: selling, getting rich,

living. You need a burrow to hide in. Or better still a typing pool.'

'That's what I told myself all night long. If I don't do this, I'll be sitting in someone's typing pool for the rest of my life. Like poor old Annie at the insurance company. She's sat there for thirty-five years. Makes you want to weep, doesn't it?'

'Or sell?'

'Okay, clever stick.'

The rain and wind blasted her as she ran across the pavement and rushed through the swing doors, barging into Mr Little himself, who was standing at reception. Oh hell!

'Hi, Marjorie. You look drenched. Come over to the counter. I can't take you into my office as I've got a buyer there. Have you come about our ad? Carry on as usual. Don't take your coat off, girl. I've only got a minute.'

'Mr Little,' she began, wondering why everything had to go so horribly wrong. 'I now represent the opposition. There's a new publication coming out. Look at this dummy! Isn't it lovely?' She thrust it under his nose. 'Higher circulation for less money, and on better paper.'

Mr Little was backing away. 'Oh I don't know, Marjorie,' he muttered. 'I'll have a look at it when you've brought out the first issue.'

Oh God! What could she do? He had to say yes.

'Mr Little,' she persisted, desperation making her brave. 'I came to you first because you're a business leader in this town.' She tried to steady her voice. 'The rest of the local businessmen will follow your lead and that's a huge responsibility, sir, if you don't mind my saying so. Don't just knock this idea into the bin. I deserve your considered decision, because it counts. You must see that. If you're too busy I'd rather come back later when you have time.'

He laughed deprecatingly. Then he stood back and scanned her face, but she gazed at him steadfastly.

'Yes, you're right. I have responsibilities. Let's have a good look at it,' he muttered. 'Who owns it?'

'I own half of it, and I have an established business backer for the other half. The full audited details are here, if you'd like . . .' She fumbled in her bag for her various guarantees.

The minutes passed like aeons while he studied her information. 'I suppose I should have the best position.' He looked so pompous she almost laughed.

'I had this position – front page column – in mind for you, sir.' She pointed to the space ringed with red.

'Can I write on your dummy?'

'Please do.'

'Right! Reserved for Little and Hampton Sports,' he mumbled as he wrote. 'That's every issue, of course. Come back later for the copy. Oh, and good luck, Marjorie.'

'Thank you, sir.'

She got in the car feeling frenzied. She was on an impossible high, hands shaking, lips dry.

'Drive on, drive on,' she muttered. 'Drive somewhere I can relax.' She hung on to her composure until they were out of sight and then she crumpled, burying her head in her hands and trembling like a leaf.

'He said *no*?'

'He said *yes*.'

'So what's up with you?'

'Nothing.'

'Come on. Out with it.'

'I'm getting to dislike myself,' she said. 'The truth is, I conned him.'

'You can't do that, Marj,' Joe said, suddenly serious. 'Business has to be absolutely above board.'

'Selling isn't. You see, I know what they all long for, so I tag it onto the product I'm selling. That's how I succeed.'

'So what does he want?'

'He wants to be like his father – a respected leader in the community, someone who's looked up to, a man who built up a chain of stores from nothing. He wants to be important, so that's what I sell him.'

'So?'

'He's not his old man and he never will be. He's the laughing stock of the sports industry since his wife ran off with a copper, and his business, which he inherited, is losing money daily. They've already closed down three branches.'

'I see. Well, look at it this way, Marj. Perhaps some of what you implied will rub off on him and he'll grow to be nearer the man he'd like to be.'

She shook off her gloom with a laugh. 'Reckon he'll have to lay off the booze and the women, but who knows?'

She began to giggle. Suddenly she couldn't stop laughing. It was something to do with losing the tension. If she could sell one, she could sell them all. She was made.

Chapter 28

By six p.m. Marjorie had nine signed contracts.

'Publishing's a piece of cake,' Joe said. 'I must study it further.'

'It's just that I know these people.'

'Don't kid yourself. You have a natural born talent for selling. I realised that the second time I saw you.'

She sat pondering this, knowing that it was not the whole truth. 'I'll tell you what selling's like, Joe. Imagine a big dark lake full of lovely fish and you go down there scuba diving and get to know all the fish and their habits and their likes and dislikes and then maybe you feed them a bit. Then one day, when you've got them eating out of your hand, you harpoon them one at a time with swift sharp thrusts, right at the opportune moment. You've got to hide in the shadows of friendship and then, bang! They're dead!'

'Just remember that your customers are very much alive.' Joe parked the car outside a pub. 'We're going to celebrate. Come on.'

She followed him in dutifully. Anything to wipe the day's conning out of her mind.

She sipped her gin and tonic, warming herself by the fire, lulled by the murmur of happy voices and the ping of the darts on the board. Familiar sounds, happy sounds.

Joe was smiling his beautiful, compassionate smile, the one that made her feel safe and special, the one that inspired her to bring out all her secret fears and lay them on the table for Joe to see and soothe and kiss better. Only he never kissed her. She wondered what it would be like. Sensational, she decided, feasting her eyes on his sensuous lips and his beautiful, desirable face. His strong brown fingers were lying on the table beside his glass. She reached over and put her hand over his. They had to start some time. Joe placed his other hand over hers, squeezed hard and removed both of his.

'That's my girl,' he said, contriving to sound paternal. 'Listen, Marj. If you feel that selling is damaging you, then we must stop before it's too late. Money's not worth that.'

Oh, but it is, she thought, and I don't want to stop.

'I was being over-fanciful,' she retorted. There and then she decided not to confide in Joe again. He was such a nut for morality. She had to succeed. For Lana she was prepared to harpoon every big fish in Dover.

'Get a grip on yourself, Marj. All you have to do is ask yourself a question: will the advertisers get a better deal?'

'That goes without saying.'

'Then I wouldn't worry if you have to bulldoze them into signing. It's for their own good.' He was laughing at her.

She hung on to Joe's comforting words over the next two weeks while she signed up more businesses, selling twice as many advertisements as Ernie James ever had.

The atmosphere was frenzied as they waited in the print and layout room in Joe's Snargate Street premises for the first sheets to roll off the press. Joe had bought a second-hand litho machine and employed a commercial artist, Mike Valentine, a short, clever, freckled boy with dark curly hair and brown eyes that were always crinkled in a smile. He was newly qualified and ready to try his hand at anything, so they persuaded him to double as a printer, but they had put out the typesetting to a local firm. Joe opened the bottle of champagne and solemnly filled three glasses.

'Here's to us,' he said. 'We've had our bad moments, but it's worked out all right. After your commission, Marj, plus salaries and expenses, we've made five hundred pounds clear profit on this first issue.'

Marjorie's eyes locked with Joe's while she sent him a subtle message and saw it hit home. He could pretend all he liked, but he was not inviolate. And she? What exactly were her feelings? She still loved Robert, she always would, but Joe was the sexiest man she'd ever met. Right now his eyes were signalling a warning to her, so she wrenched her mind from silly imaginings.

There was a sudden loud knocking on the door downstairs.

'I'll go,' she said.

Who on earth would come here at this time of night? One of Joe's girls? Dismay flooded through her as she drew back the bolts. The door smashed open, throwing her against the wall. Momentarily she lost her balance and sprawled over the mat as two thugs with batons leaped over her and raced up the stairs. She heard the first thuds, followed by tinkling glass and crashes, but by this time she was on her feet and screaming blue murder.

'Joe, look out, Joe! Muggers!' She raced after them.

Oh God! This was Ernie James' evil work. She'd been expecting something like this, but how had they got their timing so right?

Reaching the doorway of the printing room she saw one of them float as if in slow motion across the room towards Joe. As his baton swung down on Joe's face, he seemed to take off again, bouncing over the layout table, to crash headfirst into the wall. And Joe was floating after him. He took hold of the baton and swung it in a wide arc to descend on the thug's head.

The sound of the crack brought time back into something she could recognise. The other intruder was grappling with Mike, but Joe caught hold of him, swung him round and smashed his face into the wall. Suddenly the only victims were the thugs and they were groaning on the floor. There was blood all over them. I'll have to mop it up, she thought, or the cement will be stained for ever. Joe disappeared and returned holding a revolver.

'Fuck off, you two,' he said. 'Tell Ernie James to look out or I might be tempted to come and see him.'

'Where d'you learn to fight, Joe?' she asked as she mopped up the final pink soapy suds ten minutes later.

Joe was sticking plaster on Mike's cut forehead.

'I didn't learn to fight,' he grunted. 'Fighting was thrust upon me. I was the only Jew amongst three hundred gentiles in a Berlin school. It's funny how quickly you learn under those circumstances. Then, of course, there was my army training.'

Berlin? That was a new one. Joe's character and past appeared bit by bit like a jigsaw puzzle, but most of the bits were missing from the box. They pitched up now and then, when you least expected it.

*   *   *

Things were looking up. She would soon have her driving licence and the business was buying her a car. She had plans to extend her sales to take in several neighbouring towns. Her surprise came at the end of the month when she got her pay. Her weekly wage was upped to eighteen pounds a week plus a bonus of one hundred pounds.

'But Joe . . .' she protested, hoping he wasn't overdoing things. 'The magazine hasn't come out yet, and the advertisers pay ages afterwards.'

'Currently, we're not short of cash flow. I put it there. I finance, you sell, remember? That was the deal. I thought at the time you seemed to think I was conning you. This is your commission, earned by you and payable monthly on your contracts. Should you get any cancellations it will be deducted from the next payment.'

Joe could be bloody pompous when the mood took him, she thought. She knew he liked her, yet he was holding back and deliberately creating barriers. Perhaps it was because she'd spent so much time talking to him about Robert.

'How about I take you out for dinner to celebrate?' She tried out her most alluring smile.

'I have a date,' Joe said. 'I can manage a quick drink and that's all.'

She watched him curiously. Joe was an enigma. One of these days she'd suss him out, too, like all the other fish, but she wasn't yet able to swim that deep. Like the Loch Ness Monster he belonged to the unfathomed depths.

She brought herself up short, feeling guilty. Love had no place in her life nowadays. She intended to devote her life to bringing up Lana. She'd learned the hard way, hadn't she? She would use men, but never again would she lower her defences. That way she'd never get hurt.

Chapter 29

——— ———

It had been dark at six-thirty a.m. when Robert left the town of Keith, but after half an hour's drive towards the north-west a soft light appeared from nowhere as if the snow itself was glowing incandescently, yet the sky was still as dark. At last he could see the road ahead, a black ribbon of ice cutting through snowfields. He put his foot down on the accelerator and moments later he was skidding out of control as the road fell away down a steep embankment. As the car slipped sidelong into a bank of snow he tensed for the impact which never came. Instead there was a series of soft, muffled thuds.

'Oh shit!' He had tunnelled into a snowdrift. There was a spade in the boot but how was he to reach it? Repeated slammings forced the door open enough for him to slither out. Minutes later he was shovelling, and fighting against a numbing sleepiness. Damn! He'd grown soft and careless in the south. He'd be late at the plant unless a vehicle came this way, which he reckoned was unlikely.

It took him three hours to free the car and fifteen minutes to finish his journey. At eleven-ten, over two hours late, he walked into Glentirran Distillery.

'I was about to send a car out to look for you,' Graeme Forbes, the manager said, his tone unconcerned. He was a thin, wiry man in his mid-sixties. Crow's-feet at the corners of his eyes and thinning hair were the only signs of age. For the rest he might have been forty or fifty with his pale smooth skin, his light blue eyes and sandy hair. He ran the distillery well and Robert valued him highly.

'I'll have a glass of the best, Mr Forbes,' he said, hoping it would warm him. There was a roaring fire at the end of the long office and Robert was grateful for it. He stood on the hearth, trying to thaw out, unable to stop shivering.

'This is the real stuff. Your father put it down in nineteen fifty,' Forbes said, pouring two glasses. 'Your health, sir. To my mind this is the finest whisky in the country.'

'Of course,' Robert said as he felt the fiery liquid warming his veins, making his sluggish blood move and bringing his frozen feet and hands back to life.

'You're blue with cold, Mr MacLaren. Reckon your blood has thinned with easy living in the south.'

'Yes, perhaps,' Robert said. 'I ploughed into a snow-drift three hours ago and I've been digging myself out ever since.'

'Aye. It was a bad night. The snow was melting for days but then it froze. Black ice can be hard to manoeuvre.'

From his expression Robert gathered that he was at fault.

'I'll get used to it,' Robert said, smiling at him, but Forbes looked away, unable to conceal his anger. This saddened Robert. Apart from being his father's friend, Graeme Forbes was the best blender in Scotland. He'd never left Glentirran, not even when Father and Duncan had decided to sell their entire production of three-year-old malt to a Lowlands English-owned brewery. There wasn't much blending left for Forbes, other than their own private stocks, but he'd stayed on.

As Robert toured the works and smelt the familiar rough odour of steaming raw whisky, passing the water tanks, the furnace and the rows of copper stills looking like onion domes, he was reminded of his childhood holidays. He and his brothers had played here when Father was working and later they had learned how to make themselves useful around the place. Today there was a big difference. The men were resentful; he could see it in their eyes, and sense their anxiety. It hurt when they looked away with curt nods, unwilling to look him straight in the face or shake his hand. A pep talk would help the mood, he reckoned, as he walked back to the office.

'Mr Forbes, I think it's time for a small celebration. Get out a keg of our best seventeen-year-old malt and some glasses. How many are we?'

'Thirty-two, plus the cleaner.' Forbes looked reluctant. 'And the auditor is waiting to see you.'

'Ask him to join us and tell them to provide thirty-four glasses, if you please,' Robert insisted.

He stood warming himself by the fire until the first of the men filed in awkwardly. He nodded, but kept quiet while the glasses were filled and handed round. Then he lifted his: 'To the finest malt in the Highlands and my congratulations to you all.' From their expressions he saw that he was considered as the local clown who was bringing them to ruin.

He had returned to the Highlands just in time to prevent his father from selling out to an English brewery and distiller's group called Selbies. Privately Robert blamed Rhoda for persuading Father to take the easy way out years back, and Duncan for backing him and agreeing to downgrade their family heritage by selling their entire production for blending with low-grade Lowlands' spirit. It had been a messy, lengthy fight during which his father had been laid low by constant heart problems. Robert had returned to find himself in charge and had broken off all negotiations with Selbies. Now Glentirran was living on borrowed cash and borrowed time. The men knew this and resented it. They felt that he had gambled with their jobs, perhaps recklessly so.

'Well, men,' he began. 'It's not the first time we've found ourselves at war with the English through trying to hang on to our whisky. I feel that our ancestors would be proud of us. It was they who made the first Glentirran Scotch back in the Middle Ages, first noted in writing for its fiery strength and superior flavour at the wake of Ian MacLaren in 1483. We've had many a battle over it since then. In 1644, we hid our whisky underground to avoid punishing English taxes. Those old vaults are under our feet right now. In 1707, we fought for our survival against the terrible malt tax imposed by the English, and once again we went underground. Still later, when Parliament increased malt taxes to an absurd degree, it was back to the cellars and to defying the English. Harsher penalties followed, but the English couldn't wipe us out. Eventually they came to accept that Scotch whisky was here to stay.

'We were laid low again by the First World War, Prohibition in America, and World War Two which restricted whisky production, for our barley was needed for food. But there's no keeping a good Scotsman down and at last prosperity came to the Highlands in the Sixties. We'd earned it. We deserved it. And we deserve the fruits of centuries of labour.

'Today whisky has become the world's favourite drink. Naturally, the English want to control it and as you know they've bought many of our Scottish distilleries.

'In our case the distillers played dirty and tried to trick us. They called up the loans they had invested and they refused to buy our year's production of maturing malt unless we handed over control.

'I ask you, men, should we have capitulated?

'I thought about this – and then I sent my reply: No thanks. Find another sucker. This is ours. We'll bide our time and make more sacrifices and we'll show you damned gin distillers that it takes more than cash and acquisitions, and buying up peaty bogs and pure fresh mineral water, to make the best whisky. In my opinion, the making of a truly fine Scotch whisky has most to do with the people who make it. So here's to all of us,' he said as Forbes refilled their glasses.

'Aye, it does indeed,' he heard muttered around the room.

'We have the financial resources to win, I promise you that. I know I can count on all of you.'

The men clapped him on the back and one and all declared that he was a true son of Ian MacLaren after all. Unwilling to leave, they burst into a song. There were more toasts until the keg was empty, but eventually they went back to work looking considerably happier than when they'd arrived.

'You have a way with words,' his auditor, Bart Shaw, said, when at last they were alone. Shaw was in his mid-thirties, a tough, ambitious accountant who never gave an inch. He was a bull of a man with a shock of brown hair and rosy cheeks, but his shrewd eyes left no doubt of his business acumen. 'Writing was to have been your vocation, I've heard.'

Robert cleared his throat and nodded. 'Let's get on with it,' he muttered. It was still too painful to talk about what might have been, for that included Marjorie, too, and he still missed her more than he could bear.

Chapter 30

———— ————

'Now the rhetoric's over let's get on with the real cost. Money, my boy!' Bart said gloomily in a broad Scottish accent. 'On behalf of yourself and your father, you have signed away what I consider to be your heritage to the bank. That is, your family's paintings and heirlooms, including rare manuscripts and the library – which is almost priceless by the way – the various cars, your fine Highland cattle, your distillery and all the new warehouses. The farms and two homes are tied up in a trust, so you can't touch them.

'You know the score. I won't bore you further. I was about to warn you of the implications, but from your talk I realise you are a very clever young man. Now just give me a minute to find the papers.'

Their two homes! Robert was thoughtful as he sat in silence. He had forgotten their modest place in Keith.

'What happened to the cottage in Keith?' he asked.

'It's empty. Your father used to stay there when he visited the Highlands. A neighbour looks after the place.'

While Bart delved into his briefcase, Robert's thoughts turned to Marjorie, who was seldom out of his mind since he'd returned home. He missed her badly. What he had thought was a teenage romance had all the appearance of deep love. He wanted her by his side helping him fight his battles. He wanted her as the mother of his children. Lately he thought a great deal about starting a family. Their old home was so empty and he missed his brothers. Father was slowly dying and he needed a family to sustain him. It would be years before Rhoda vacated Tirran Lodge. By then Marjorie would be able to cope. He hadn't written to her lately because he was torn both ways, not wanting to make false promises, and needing time to sort himself out.

He was brought back to reality by Bart who was pushing papers in front of him. 'Sign here . . . and here . . . and here . . .'

There was no end to it. 'Will I ever get out of hock?' he asked Bart wistfully.

'I have the utmost faith in you. I told Grampian Bank the same thing.

'One last matter before I go. I have no doubt her Ladyship will be peeved with me for mentioning it to you, but I must. On December the sixteenth, last year, a cash cheque for five thousand pounds was drawn on the business account. At first I added this amount to the personal drawings of her Ladyship, but she objected, claiming that the amount was paid on your behalf. Do you know anything about it?'

'No, but I'll sort it out.'

'Let me know as soon you can.'

'Tomorrow,' Robert said. 'I'm driving back in the morning.' Since his father remarried he had never been able to call the lodge 'home'.

Robert stood at the study window gazing out over his mother's garden, now overgrown and tatty, but once a mass of fragrant flowering shrubs. He had the strangest feeling that he could turn back the clock and find the room just as it once had been, full to overflowing with joy and colour and warmth. The Scot in him rebelled at Rhoda's paraphernalia, installed two weeks after her marriage to his father, when their home had been stripped of its former comfortable furniture. Now they lived amongst quasi-antiques, overstuffed velvet settees, tasselled cushions and delicate porcelain that was completely out of place in a raw Scottish castle.

He found himself reluctantly reliving scenes which had traumatised him for years: his mother balanced precariously at the top of a ladder leaning over a Christmas tree, floating down as time stood still, his own feeble efforts to move forward and break her fall, the sound of the ambulance that came too late, the red-faced housekeeper who took over when his father quit their house for six months, and his return with their hated English stepmother, Rhoda, who systematically and savagely erased all traces of her ghostly rival. In this room, too, he had said goodbye to his brothers and his father before being banished to Dover College for 'persistent and unforgivable rudeness to your stepmother' – his father's own words.

The door swung open and Rhoda came in. She was wearing high-heeled leather boots and a sensible tweed suit, an image she disliked, but affected for visiting local wives.

'Robert, dear,' she said in the deep, grating voice which he detested.

Living here had aged her, he thought dispassionately. Whatever she had expected or searched for, she had not found it in his father's arms and hearth.

'How's Father?'

'Holding up. Why don't you go up and see for yourself?'

'I shall, soon.'

She was always so sure of herself, but today there was a change. She was fumbling for a cigarette and lighting it with concentration, as if her life depended upon a quick, hard puff, like a junkie.

Robert turned and opened the French window. 'That filthy habit will kill you.'

The roots of her hair were white, he noticed for the first time. She was getting careless and the once dark brown tresses were dyed black, which was too harsh for her age. She had a passion for dressing in brilliant colours, and now that he saw her in tweed, he realised why. She looked old and drab and the suit made a harsh contrast of her scarlet fingernails and lipstick. Her eyes had always looked hard, but today they were watery with bags beneath them. That was new, he thought. She peered up at him malevolently, matching his dislike, glance by glance.

'Have the men walked out on you yet?' she asked contemptuously, for she was set against his long-term programme. Her influence, more than anything else, had led them to this crisis, Robert knew.

There was a moment's silence before he gave a puzzled laugh. 'Heavens, no. God forbid! I wanted to see you about a silly matter – a cash cheque for five thousand pounds which was taken off my allowance. Naturally I should like to know what it's all about.'

'Let me see,' she pondered, while a nervous tic pulled at the corner of her right eye. She seemed to come to a decision. 'If you must know, I paid it to that common

Dover slut of yours to shut her up and get her off your back.'

He tried not to show his shock and dismay. 'Marjorie?' he said incredulously. 'When did you see her?'

A sly tinge of amusement shone in her eyes, while her lips curled, and Robert cursed himself for showing his emotions.

'I think it was late last year.' She looked on the desk for her diary and began to fumble with the pages.

Robert took the cheque out of his pocket and smoothed it on the table, keeping his eyes downcast, unwilling to look up and reveal the hatred and the panic he was feeling.

'The date on the cheque was December the sixteenth,' he said quietly, 'so get to the point.'

'She was obviously pregnant – about four months, I think. She told me that she had arranged to have the child adopted. She actually admitted that she had *sold* it. This is quite prevalent, I've heard. She came here to threaten you – she wanted ten thousand pounds or she would go to the press with her story of being seduced and dumped.' She broke off to cough. She had been coughing that same cough for years, he remembered.

'Naturally, she couldn't ask for child support, since the child was already bespoke, so to speak, but she said she would make such a scandal she'd ruin all of us. I was afraid your father would take a turn for the worst so I fobbed her off with half the amount and threats. I never heard from her again.'

'You had no business . . . I had a right to decide about my child. But surely she came to see me,' Robert said, sounding calmer than he felt. 'Why should she want to see you?'

'She had a man with her, a rough-looking youth. Perhaps that's why she didn't want to see you.'

'Did she ask for me?' Robert insisted, sensing Rhoda's evasiveness.

'No.'

'Don't ever meddle in my business again,' he said angrily.

'Look. You're young, Robert. You made a terrible mistake. She's not the girl you thought she was. She's a shrewd, hard, money-grabbing slut. Besides, you never could have married her. There are too many things against her.'

'Such as?' he asked quietly.

'Her voice, her upbringing, her education, the way she dresses, even the way she sits.'

'You're half a century out of date, Rhoda. That's because you're old,' he added to watch her flinch. 'Your stupid, archaic class sentiments are dead.'

'So how about this? She sold your child without asking you, and then she came to blackmail me. Is that the right mother for your children?'

What had happened to the girl he loved? Was she really the cruel, greedy woman Rhoda described? He could not believe that Marjorie would sell their child.

Unable to bear Rhoda's shrewd, malicious smile any longer, he turned on his heel and left the room. Going outside, he paced the grounds restlessly, wondering what he should do next. He didn't trust Rhoda. He decided to check on her story without involving either woman.

The Mother Superior of St Mary's Convent kept him waiting for half an hour, and as Robert sat in a draughty passage, he gained the impression that she was conferring with lawyers about what to say to him.

It was mid-December, two weeks since Robert had been told of Marjorie's pregnancy, and since then Bart had been busy checking birth records. He had discovered that Marjorie's baby girl had been born at St Mary's Convent on 15 May. She was seven months old and that was all Robert knew about his firstborn. Did she have Marjorie's red hair or his own colouring? He felt tormented because he did not know. When he traced his child he would find a way to adopt her.

At last he was shown into the nun's office, an austere but pleasant room with stained-glass windows set high in the white walls under a domed ceiling. The Mother Superior joined him with a swish of starched petticoats and a strong scent of talcum powder. Her cheeks looked freshly scrubbed; her blue eyes gleamed through her rimless glasses. A shrewd and formidable woman, Robert deduced.

'Mr MacLaren, I am sorry to have kept you waiting so long,' she said in a deep voice with a trace of an Irish accent. 'The truth is I was checking with our legal advisor. You already know that Marjorie Hardy's baby was born here. She remained in our crèche for two months prior to adoption.' She looked pained as she told him this. 'We are definitely not at liberty to divulge the whereabouts or the name of the baby, or of her adoptive parents. I'm sorry, but I have to remind you that you have no legal claims on this child at all. As the law stands there is nothing you can do to find the baby. I'm sorry, but I must ask you to leave and not to try to find your child, if indeed it is yours.'

She stood up and held out her hand. Robert hesitated,

but good manners forced him to stand and touch hers briefly. 'I hope that God will give you the strength to sustain this grief and the wisdom to marry before you commit further carnal sins that might lead to a recurrence of this tragedy. Good day to you, Mr MacLaren.'

That was that. After waiting so long, how could the meeting be so brief? 'I have some questions,' he stammered.

'I'm sorry. I have nothing further to say to you.' She left by another door.

Well, there was no point in standing there like a fool. He stumbled into the convent's garden, gulping in pure fresh air. He walked until he was out of sight. Then he crumpled on a garden bench and mourned for his lost girl, his lost dreams, and his firstborn, who was filling some stranger's life and cradle. Would they be kind to her? Would she be happy? His bitterness made him feel nauseous. He still loved Marjorie, but he despised her, too. He knew it was only a matter of time before his love was entirely corroded.

As he sat there, he came to a sudden decision. He would engage a first-class business manager and move to New York where he could spend the next few years marketing his whisky. There was nothing left for him here. Despite this resolution he stayed where he was, lost in memories.

Softly the day fled and sadness came stealthily with the night. Something beautiful had been destroyed for ever.

Chapter 31

It was the best Christmas by far, Marjorie decided. They had a tree so high it curled at the ceiling and the angel dangling from the tip seemed to be parachuting to earth. Lights lit up, gewgaws jingled, and Lana's eyes were bright with wonder as she crawled around. She was nearing eight months old and she spent most of her time trying to stand and toppling over. She was drawn to the presents like a moth to a light, and most of them were for her.

They had moved the presents from the base of the tree because Lana was determined to open each one of them. Now they were out of reach, but Lana was learning to pull herself up and shake the bottom branch until she dislodged one. Then her little fingers would be tearing at the pretty paper while she laughed delightedly and her eyes lit up with glee.

'There she goes again,' Mum called. 'She's got another one. She's going to be a right tartar, I'm telling you.'

She did seem unusually bright, Marjorie thought, watching her carefully. She couldn't wait for Lana to see her toys. If only Joe would come.

Mum was ecstatic about the deepfreeze she'd already received two days ago, but there was more to come: chocolates, perfume and a new dress. Then there was

a beer tankard, a bottle of good cognac and a tie for
Dad; and new socks, a book and some tapes for Joe.
Not forgetting a packet of dried minnows and a table
tennis ball for Tibby.

But why was Joe so late?

Marjorie picked up the receiver and dialled his number.
Eventually someone picked up the phone. She could hear
loud music in the background.

'Joe,' she queried, 'is that you? Say something. Why
are you late? You're holding up dinner.'

'I'm not coming,' he said in his flat, business voice.

Oh no, he was in one of his moods. 'Why not? You
promised! We're expecting you. Besides, Mum cooked
for you and she bought you a present herself. We'd all
be disappointed. Please, Joe. And hurry up.'

'The truth is I don't want to gate-crash your Christmas.'

'Our Christmas? Christmas is for everyone, but here,
in this house, it's your Christmas specifically. You, more
than anyone, made it happen, Joe.' She was almost in
tears, her voice rising to a squeak.

'I've never celebrated an English Christmas in my
life. Besides, I'm a born Jew and a practising Zen
Buddhist.'

'*Please*, Joe, just come. Hurry up.'

'But I'm vegetarian.'

'You're a bloody nutcase. Now come, or else.'

'That's an invitation I can't refuse.' She could hear
the laughter in his voice, so that was all right.

She flung down the receiver and raced upstairs to fix
her hair and spray on more perfume. She was wearing
black woollen slacks that showed off her figure and an
emerald green cashmere jersey that did a lot for her eyes.

Satisfied that she looked her best, she ran downstairs in time to hear his car being parked outside. Moments later he walked in, carrying a load of presents.

'How could you even think of staying away? You're one of the family, Joe, aren't you?' Mum asked.

'Well, I don't know about that.' He looked embarrassed as he shook hands with her parents and wished them Merry Christmas and handed over his gifts.

He had a passion for Lana. He picked her up and snuggled her, and talked to her in French, as he always did, and sang French songs to her, waltzing her round in his arms. Then they settled down on the floor together to unwrap her presents.

'The child's going to be that confused,' Mum called.

Joe climbed off his high horse after a couple of glasses of Dad's cognac. He could be so sweet at times. There was a recklessness about him that was exciting and sexy. Every time Marjorie glanced at him, she caught his penetrating eyes on her. She had a sudden, irrepressible urge to feel those sensuous lips against hers. She'd never dared before, something about him still scared her, but the wine gave her courage. When Joe lingered in the doorway under the mistletoe she flung her arms around his neck and stood on tiptoe to push her mouth against his.

'Merry Christmas, Joe,' she whispered.

As always, Joe was unpredictable. His left hand was instantly pressed against the small of her back, holding her tightly against him. She could feel his hard body, it was solid muscle. She gasped. She'd never realised how strong he was. His eyes compelled her to look up at him. At such close quarters he was intensely exciting.

As he pulled her closer, she smelled the musky male

scent of his skin, mingled with his aftershave. When his lips were gently touching hers, and his tongue caressed her mouth, she knew that nothing would ever be the same again. She felt as if she'd lit a bonfire, only to watch it running wildly out of control to burn a forest down.

They heard footsteps and he released her.

It was three p.m. and they'd eaten their way to the mince pies with brandy sauce, pulled their crackers, dutifully put on their silly paper hats, and Marjorie was hovering over the table, removing some of the debris. Lana was in her highchair laughing delightedly at her newly opened present – a mouse that jumped when you pulled its tail – Dad was reading the rhyme in his cracker and Mum was sipping her wine, a dreamy look on her face, when Joe dropped his bombshell.

'Here's to our new magazine.' He lifted his glass of wine.

He looked a little drunk, Marjorie thought. 'What new magazine is this?' she asked laughing.

'Our new management magazine. I've thought of a good name, too, *Leadership*. How does that strike you? I'm sure that you will be supremely successful in selling it.'

Marjorie felt her knees weakening. She sat down abruptly. 'I don't want a new magazine. I'm perfectly happy as we are. We're making good profits, so why change?'

'Business can't stand still, Marjorie.' Joe looked regretful. 'We're riding on the crest of a wave, but we must move with it. We have to go national.'

'You're crazy. There are no local advertisers for a management magazine. They're spread over England

and Europe. So who . . . ? Oh no! Forget it!' Fear dried her mouth and ruined the day. 'Besides, I can't leave Lana.'

'This silly rag we publish could go under at any time.'

'How could it when we have so much advertising?'

'Listen, Marjorie, we give our rag away free. The local newspaper has a large, paid circulation, and they could wipe us out in a couple of months if they brought out an insert like this. They certainly will when they find out how much we're making.'

She crumpled with dread. Around her were the results of all her commission cheques. Could all this be wiped out? She almost panicked, but then she thought: Joe's playing on my fears. 'I have far too much work to take on more,' she said firmly.

'Are women always this short-sighted?' he countered.

'You two are always fighting hammer and tongs. I wonder what you see in each other since you can't be together five minutes without quarrelling. What exactly is it that you like about my daughter, Joe? There must be something.'

'Oh, Mum. How can you say things like that?' Marjorie was hot with embarrassment. 'We're business partners.'

For once in his life, Joe was floored. The question was one that he asked himself often enough. Their brief physical contact today had shocked him and left him feeling vulnerable. He loved Marjorie's pragmatic approach to life, her courage and her humour. He had to admit that he found her highly seductive and with his obsessive love of beauty, it was natural that he would enjoy looking at her. Sometimes, on a lonely evening, he would lust after her. But Joe never confused love and lust, nor would he ever marry for either one of those misleading feelings.

There were things about Marjorie that he intensely disliked, such as her short-sighted view of business, her ridiculous obsession with Lana's father, whoever he was, her resistance to change, and the way she closed her mind to all matters that she considered weren't her territory. The truth was, she was an intellectual peasant.

'Mrs Hardy, I miss my sister,' he lied, inventing a non-existent sibling. 'Marjorie is taking her place.' He stood up. 'Think about the new magazine, Marjorie. It's time I was off. Mrs Hardy, thank you for a wonderful Christmas lunch, er, that is, dinner.'

Liz could hardly disguise her disappointment as she showed Joe out.

Marjorie felt shocked by Joe's dream of a national magazine. She sat on a pouffe by the fire, feeling chilled. He had frightened her, too, with his predictions of doom. When Barbara arrived a few minutes later, she was still sitting there.

'Cooey, Merry Christmas everyone,' her friend called from the doorway. She was maturing into a warm, capable, attractive young woman, with a naturally buoyant, cheerful nature. She had taken to wearing platform soles with five-inch heels to give her the height she felt she needed and she had acquired a poised and confident air.

'Here! It's Christmas, love,' she said to Marjorie. 'Season of joy – remember? What's up with you?'

She had brought more toys for Lana, some chocolates for Mum and a new scarf for Marjorie.

Marjorie tried hard to recapture Christmas as she delved into the tree for Barbara's presents.

'I saw Joe leave. I'm surprised he came.'

For some reason Barbara did not like Joe. Marjorie knew that she thought he was too clever by half, but she guessed the real reason was that Joe didn't much like her.

'Bet he didn't buy you anything.'

'No, he didn't,' Marjorie admitted. 'But he bought dozens of presents for Lana and that's what counts.'

'Still, I would have thought . . .'

'You see, I still feel for Robert and Joe knows that.'

'It's time you did something about it then,' Barbara pronounced decisively. 'Go get him, or forget him.'

How could she forget Robert? His eyes gazed up at her from her baby's face, and his lips curled with delight at each and every new toy.

'Look at her,' she said, picking up Lana, 'and you'll see why I can't.'

'Well, then. Let's think. Robert's grown up a bit since you last saw him, I bet. You must contact him. Phone him now, why don't you? Wish him Merry Christmas. Try to make a date. I can see you sitting here wasting your life for the next ten years, Marj. Go on. What's his number? He's bound to be at home. I'll get him on the line for you.'

A few seconds later, still in a daze, Marjorie listened to Robert's father explaining that his son had never been engaged and was living permanently in New York where he had set up a marketing company.

Replacing the receiver, she burst into tears.

'Why didn't he write? Why didn't he tell me? How could he leave without letting me know? Oh, Barbara, this reinforces my view of men. Use them, but never love them. That way leads to disaster.' She tried to laugh, but the tears were streaming down her cheeks.

'Any guy who dumps you isn't worth crying over, that's for sure, love,' Barbara said loyally.

'I forgot this. I'm sorry to intrude.' They heard a gruff voice from the passage and both of them looked up to see Joe standing there, his face a picture of embarrassed misery. He put a box on the table and fled for the second time.

Marjorie opened the present with the minimum of enthusiasm. Beneath the wrapping was a long, navy box which looked expensive. Opening it, she gasped, for there lay an exquisite bracelet of emeralds and sapphires, set into a plain gold band.

'Sister, my eye,' Dad muttered, coming into the room and eyeing the gift.

Barbara was full of questions. Were they going steady? Did he dance? And had they made it?

'It's like this,' Marjorie struggled to explain. 'When I first met Joe I told him I loved someone else and later, when he found out about Lana, I told him about Rob. We started off as business partners, nothing more, and it's stayed like that. I guess it always will.' Particularly now, she thought, since she had seen the hurt in his eyes.

Chapter 32

——— ———

Marjorie passed through January in a daze of misery. She had always hoped that Robert would one day be hers. Now she felt bereft. However much she tried to tell herself that New York was only a short flight away, it felt as if a door had been slammed in her face, particularly because he had not even written to say goodbye. To add to her loneliness Joe had become strangely remote.

At the month's end, an artist's airbrushed dummy of Joe's *Leadership* magazine appeared on her desk. It was beautifully designed, full of fake editorials yet to be written, and fake advertisements for typewriters, desks, accounting and dictating systems, still to be sold.

How she hated offices! Marjorie leafed through it with a feeling of dread. She could not believe Joe would go to all this trouble when he knew she was set against it. She decided to have it out with him. She made two coffees and walked into his office, the dummy poised on the tray.

'Careful with that,' he said.

'Joe, it's brilliant,' she said. 'I've been thinking that you're right, we should expand one day, but I fancy a fashion magazine. I think that's more my style.'

'I fancy a Porsche,' Joe mused. 'That's more my style, too, but we can't afford either.'

'I just don't feel confident enough to sell office equipment, at least, not right now.'

'You only fight when your back's against the wall.
Consequently it will always be there,' Joe said gloomily.

After that brief conversation, Joe became even more
remote. He spent hours each day tinkering around with
bits of dirty brick and he seemed uninterested in their
publishing venture, although he never failed to visit Lana
every second day and bring her little gifts. Nevertheless,
the advertisements rolled in and so did the profits.

Money did nothing to alleviate the pain of Robert's
rejection, Marjorie discovered. She dreaded the nights,
but having Lana to love helped her through them. And
while money might not soothe the pain, it was undeniably
satisfying to know that she had plenty to lavish on her
family. Whatever they needed, Marjorie bought. Lana
was a joy and Marjorie spoiled her with gifts and toys.
The larder and the deepfreeze were stocked to capacity
and new clothes created new problems – not enough
cupboard space. The fortnightly deadlines raced by, each
one traumatic with the need to gather the advertisements
in time, and Marjorie lost herself in her work.

It was Mr Dodgen, the chemist, who shattered her
security. He wanted a new advertisement and Marjorie
went along to fetch the copy. He usually looked pained
at the prospect of spending money, but today his eyes
were gleaming. With what? she wondered. Compassion?
Amusement? How odd! She puzzled about it as she
signed him up for the next six months.

'Listen, Marjorie,' he began. 'Some young girl in a
mini up to her thighs and blonde hair down to her
waist (know what I mean?) came in here from the local

newspaper. It seems they're going into competition with
you. Same sort of thing as your magazine, but it will
come out weekly as a loose insert. Of course, they offer
paid circulation and a bigger print bill than you can. The
point is, they're undercutting you. Reckon they're aiming
to put you out of business. I thought I'd best tell you.'

She returned to the office with her head pounding
and her breath coming in short, panicky gasps. It was
a cold late February and snowing, but she was burning
hot. It felt as if an invisible hand was choking the life
out of her.

'We'll be ruined,' she muttered to herself as she
went in search of Joe. She found him in his research
room, as he liked to call it. As usual he was spraying
a thick white liquid onto lumps of sooty bricks. He was
obsessed with this idea, whatever it was. He looked up,
smiling coldly as she repeated what old Dodgen had
told her.

'So what are you going to do about it?' He did not say
I told you so, and she blessed him for that.

'Can we have a board meeting please, now,' she
demanded.

'Go ahead, I'm listening.'

'Away from these filthy bits of brick.'

'This is my future, since you don't like my publishing ideas.'

'Oh for goodness sake!'

'Look here, Marjorie, if it's back to the wall time, why
don't you pick any prospective advertiser from the list in
the top right drawer of my desk and try to sign him up?
If you succeed, you could take it as a pointer that you're
on to a good thing.'

Something was very wrong. Why was he so distant

and uninterested? And why had it taken her so long to tackle the problem head on?

'Joe,' she said. 'There's something I must tell you. D'you remember Christmas, when you came back with my present and found me crying? You see, I'd always hoped that things might work out with Robert and me. I mean, he's Lana's father, after all, and she needs a father. But it's over. He . . . well, he left for New York. He lives there permanently and he didn't even say goodbye, so that puts the lid on our friendship.' She flushed as she remembered Joe's expression that day.

'And Lana?'

'When I was pregnant I wrote to him and begged him to come. I told him I'd have the baby adopted if he didn't want us. Well, clearly he didn't.' She almost gagged on the words.

'Then he's a fool and you're better off without him.'

So I'm free, Joe. Doesn't that mean anything to you? Remember the mistletoe? She longed to bellow the words in his ear, but what was the point, since he knew it all anyway? She put one hand lightly on his shoulder, feeling the strength of him. His back was like a steel board. Then she ran her fingers playfully through his thick, dark hair. She bent over and kissed his cheekbone, letting her lips slide down to his ear. His head lifted slowly and he stared at her looking strangely offended.

'You'll get dirty. Mind! This stuff will spoil your clothes. You'd better take your pick of that list. You'll have to start selling soon. If you want you can have it all. I'm easy. After all, I have my inventions. Oh, and Marjorie, you might still be able to sell out *The Handy Home Guide* to the local newspaper. I'd tackle that next if I were you.'

'Am I hearing you right?' she asked, grabbing his hand. 'Why are you so obsessed with your dirty bricks?' After a long silence she added: 'I thought we were a partnership?'

'So did I. It seems I was wrong.' He gently took his hand back.

Now she was spoiling for a fight, but underneath was a deep hurt.

'You're sulking because I didn't like your idea of a management magazine.'

'On the contrary, I was only trying to help. I have plenty of other interests to keep me busy.'

'So publishing's to be cast off, is it, Joe? You have a new toy. Out with the old, on with the new, with no time for regrets or explanations.'

'That about sums it up,' he said.

'And what if I don't want to go it alone?'

'The choice is entirely yours, my dear. I'm here for you as usual.'

'So nothing's changed, I mean, with us?' she said with a sob in her voice.

'If you say so. I don't really follow you.'

And that was that. She was deeply hurt, but she didn't intend to prolong her suffering.

'I'll be getting along then.'

She had plenty of time to consider her mistakes as she walked home. What a fool she had been imagining she was secure and that the money would keep on rolling in for ever. Or that Joe was waiting on the sidelines for when she recovered from her hurt. Did life have to be this hard?

As for business – she hated it. Had men invented the system because they missed the old cut and thrust of personal warfare? she mused. The local newspaper was making a fortune. Everyone knew that. Yet they had to grab her little bit of security as well. Joe had known they would. Why? Because he thought like they did?

What was it Joe had said: 'If you're on to a good thing it stands to reason someone will try to get it off you.' She couldn't see the logic behind that at all. She wanted to be secure, and her family to be looked after, and all the families in the world should have enough, too. If someone else had more than she, good luck to them. But this wasn't the way the business world was run.

Mum had tea ready. It was special tonight: herrings, sausages, some home-made plum jam, and fresh bread just out of the oven. Scrumptious, she thought, until she remembered that their cash would soon run out. Suddenly it all turned sour.

'Life's exactly like Snakes and Ladders, Mum.' She looked up imploringly, longing to be able to confide and to be understood. 'You work like a dog and up you go, right up where you wanted so badly to be, and then life clobbers you. Maybe someone up there sees you're getting along just fine, feeling pretty good, so then he clouts you back in the mire – undeserved and unexpected. And it doesn't just happen once, believe you me.'

Moodily she warmed to her theme. 'Sometimes it seems to me that life is as meaningful as the throw of a dice. You don't even know you've reached a peak until you're on the chute. If you'd only known, you might have taken time off to enjoy it, instead of striving for more. Suddenly you're sliding back to where you started. So you summon up what's left of your courage to start the long climb – and what do you find? You can't even get a foot on the ladder. You have to throw six to move.'

'I don't want to listen to this sort of talk,' Mum said. 'It's a lovely evening. Dad and I thought we might go down the pub for a while. Are you staying home?'

'Yes, as usual.'

'Well, it's not your night, that's for sure. Remember this, Marjorie. Just when you think you're down and out, life has a habit of finding the solution, like a rabbit out of a hat at a kid's party. It's not all doom and gloom. We've always been lucky. Something turns up.'

We're lucky because I work my butt off, Marjorie decided with a surge of temper. If I had Mum's attitude I'd be happier, but at the same time I might be a lot poorer.

She went to bed early that night but she could not sleep. Instead she thought of Lana relying on her to provide a safe life, and poor Dad who was shell-shocked by delayed reaction, and Mum who couldn't look trouble straight in the face at all. Were they all to become life's victims?

For the first time it dawned on her that there was no Big Daddy to put things right, not in the clouds, nor in the government, nor in the police station. There was no referee to make sure everyone played fair, either. All these snobbish men in their smart tailor-made suits, with their silk shirts and manicured hands, were no better than pirates. They grabbed whatever you had – business, wealth, youth, sex – and when they'd got what they wanted you walked the plank, or lived out your life in poverty-stricken desperation, which was worse. And who cared? Absolutely no one.

Could she join their world and be as predatory as

they were? Could she stifle compassion and learn to win without a qualm? Could she drive the opposition into bankruptcy and push forward without regrets? If not, she might as well give up now.

She could and she bloody would.

'Shiver me timbers, I'll do it,' she whispered, smiling to herself. At last she was able to sleep.

Chapter 33

———— ————

Marjorie's new navy gabardine suit, leather sling bag and court shoes helped her feel the part of the competent businesswoman, but when she arrived for her appointment with the managing editor of the local newspaper she found her confidence slipping. In no time she found herself sitting at the end of a boardroom table surrounded by middle-aged businessmen – not journalists, that was for sure. Nothing but the best for this lot: Glentirran noses, steak tartar stomachs, Armani suits and Gucci aftershave. She was introduced to the chairman, the company secretary, their lawyer and the managing editor. They must want something to do with their time, she thought. Surely one person would have been enough to deal with her?

'Well, Miss Hardy . . .' The managing editor cleared his throat and his pale eyes began to glitter behind his gold-rimmed spectacles while his long, pale face turned slightly pink. 'We've discussed this matter and quite honestly we've decided that *The Handy Home Guide*,' he paused for a sarcastic laugh, 'has very little goodwill and really contains nothing that we would want to buy.'

Who were they kidding? They could have told her that on the telephone, she reasoned. She glanced around, feeling intimidated by their maleness, their status, their posh voices and their self-assured manners.

'Now look here,' she began, wincing at her own inexperience and her obviously local accent. 'You'll have to buy us or fight us. Either way it'll cost you, but I think the former will be cheaper. You see, we own our own printing press and we have hardly any costs, so if you undercut us, we'll undercut you. Finally you may win, but it will take time. Later, you'll have trouble putting up the rates to a proper level.'

She smiled at each of them in turn, trying to gauge their thoughts from their expressions.

'If you buy us out, you'll find our rates just about as high as the market can take for this type of advertising, and furthermore we have enormous goodwill with everyone. Undercutting us would spoil that goodwill. Look at it this way – a David versus Goliath-type battle wouldn't do you any good at all. It might even affect your normal daily advertising. So it stands to reason you will have to make a generous offer.'

She was all too aware that she was flushing and flustered. She took a deep breath.

A smart-looking woman was approaching her with a tray laden with cups and a silver coffee pot. Oh no, Marjorie thought, panicking. She's coming towards me. She wouldn't ask me to pour out, would she? I don't know the posh way to do it. Help!

The tray was placed right next to her. The woman was leaving.

Marjorie stood up. 'You lot seem to have all day to do nothing in, but I have a few contracts to get signed. I'll be on my way. Think about what I said and send me an offer in writing. Here's my card.'

She flung it down and fled, leaving the astonished men gaping.

'Why did you chicken out?' Joe demanded furiously. 'You should have stayed put and pressed home your advantage. You could have had the cheque in your pocket by now. Know what I've been thinking? Possibly they're scared someone else might buy us and use our paper to go into competition with them.'

Well, at least he was showing an interest in their joint venture now. Marjorie's decision to approach the local paper might not have paid off, but it had certainly shaken Joe's detachment. However, they still weren't thinking along the same lines.

'Joe, I'm sorry. I've been thinking hard about your *Leadership*, but it isn't going to work.'

'Why not?'

'Your magazine is too posh. You see, I'm not and it showed badly at that meeting. I can't walk in on those sorts and expect them to talk on my level and give me advertising. You should have seen how patronising they were. I could've crawled under the table with mortification. My courage was seeping away. I couldn't take another minute of it. I almost ran. I was *that* intimidated.'

'But why?' He stared at her, genuinely perplexed. Surely it should be as plain as the nose on his face.

She tried to explain: 'Their la-di-da accents, their posh ways, their clothes, their way of acting like they owned the ruddy world, not just their local rag. They acted like they owned me too.'

'Is that all? Just their voices?'

'And their confidence.'

'If you're so scared of la-di-da accents, get one your-self. And hurry up about it. You must start selling in the spring – with the right clothes, the right voice and the right manner. I know, take yourself off to a modelling school, too. Confidence will follow along. The business will pay.'

'Just like that?'

'Yes. Just like that, you silly nut. Most of the problem is inside your head and no one else's.'

'Sometimes I think you're crazy. I don't know, Joe. I really don't know. I suppose I'll have to give it a try, because we have to publish something.'

'If I've told you once, I've told you a dozen times. You can't make a silk purse out of a sow's ear.'

The scene in the Hardy kitchen that evening was cosy: the coal stove glowing with warmth, the percolator bubbling on it, Lana crawling after Tibby. She loved to pull his tail and Tibby never scratched her. It was so ordinary, so homely. Marjorie had a sudden longing for an ordinary husband and a regular, secure income, and nothing more scary to face than to make ends meet with the housekeeping. Mum was busy at the sink and Marjorie could sense the fear and disapproval surging out of her.

'Aren't we good enough for you, Marjorie? How come you're turning up your nose at what we represent and the way we talk?'

'Oh Mum. I'm talking about money, not preferences. I have to be able to sell to these snobs, take them to lunch, discuss their problems, and so on. That's how you sell. Have you any idea how much I know about the local shopkeepers? I know which ones are having trouble with their wives or their kids, I know if they've got arthritis or suffer from migraines, I know their hopes and dreams and dreads. I even know about their bits on the side. They talk to me almost as if I'm not there.

'Now I'm faced with a real problem. I can't talk on the same level as these men I met today. It's not that I want to, it's that I have to.' That wasn't entirely truthful and she flushed.

'Nor will you ever. Like I told you . . .'

'Oh, not again, Mum, please.'

Marjorie picked up Lana and put her in her high chair. Mum had her tea ready and Marjorie spooned it in. Lana was a joy to feed. She opened her mouth like a baby bird, chortling with fun. Marjorie couldn't decide whether or not she'd be pretty. She was quite unusual-looking with her wide, square face, her thick eyebrows and large brown eyes set wide apart. Her mouth was wide, too, almost too large, and with her tiny turned up nose and pointed ears she looked like a changeling child. Perhaps she was, for at ten months she was as bright as a penny.

'I'm going to give it a go, Lana, my pet,' she whispered. 'You and me are going to reach for the stars.'

'You know what happened last time you reached for the stars,' Mum snapped.

Marjorie couldn't understand her mother's attitude. She was working for all of them, wasn't she, so why should Mum begrudge her success?

Miss de Putron was a real shock. A tall, broad woman, half-crippled with arthritis, she had thick white hair cut in a pudding-basin style, fierce blue eyes and a ruddy, mannish look about her. Once she had skied, played lacrosse and ridden for England, but she had fallen upon hard times and now she gave lessons in etiquette. She lived in a tatty, rambling house with a lot of smelly, ancient, cooty King Charles spaniels and a paid companion, Miss Smith, who hovered around looking anxious and dabbing at her eyes. There must be something wrong with her tear ducts, Marjorie decided.

Joe had found Miss de Putron and Joe was in for it when she got her hands on him, Marjorie promised herself as she brushed a flea off her leg.

'I'm told you had difficulty in coping with a coffee tray, so I thought we'd deal with that one first,' said Miss de Putron with an imperious wave at poor Miss Smith.

The blasted traitor! Marjorie thought indignantly. 'Well, yes,' she admitted.

'Well, yes! Not *wall, yass,*' Miss de Putron snarled. Her mangy dogs, who took their cue from their mistress, snarled in unison. She began to show off her photographs and trophies around the wall.

Here came the tray. Well, she wasn't scared of these old scarecrows, Marjorie told herself. She took hold of the coffee pot in one hand and the cup in the other and began to pour.

'This cup,' Miss de Putron was saying, 'was given to me by the Queen Mother in 1930. This picture was taken when it was presented to me.'

Marjorie glanced up at the picture and froze in dismay at the image of a young, slender and very beautiful girl. How could it be? She glanced at the picture and back to Miss de Putron, and back at the picture again. Could time be this devastating? How horrible! She began to tremble. Had she remembered to put on her face cream last night? She wasn't sure.

'Well now,' said Miss de Putron crossly. 'I can see you have a problem since you've poured most of the coffee on the mat. You will notice how I accept this with cool equanimity. That's how it's done. Naturally the dry-cleaning will be added to your account. More coffee, Miss Smith. We'll try again.'

'I beg your pardon,' Marjorie said, in as posh a voice as she could.

'Pardon!' The woman seemed to explode in wrath, spitting all over her. 'I'd rather you ruined a hundred mats than said pardon.'

'Oooh!' Marjorie stood up in a panic. She had to get out of there. 'Can I go to the loo, please?' She felt as if she was back in school.

'Don't whine, don't beg and if you mean the lavatory, say so.'

'Oooh, but I thought . . .'

'Don't bring your vulgar euphemisms into this house, young lady. Call a spade a spade.'

Grabbing her bag, Marjorie moved backwards towards the hall and collided with a large ornamental pot which toppled in slow motion and smashed on the floor.

Marjorie gawped at Miss de Putron.

'I see we have a great deal of work ahead of us, that is, when you have relieved yourself in the *lavatory*. I suggest you start by looking where you are going. You don't have to back out of rooms, by the way. I'm not Genghis Khan.'

Shit! Shit! Shit!

'I like ice cream,' she said for the fiftieth time that morning, and this was her fifth visit. Right now she could hardly stand the pain in the back of her throat

and the root of her tongue. Her long-suffering tutor, Mr
Denbigh-Jones, tall, elegant and even poorer than Miss
de Putron, switched on the tape recorder.

'Oy loik oice craim,' she heard.

'Listen . . . listen to me,' he said with a touch of
desperation. 'I like ice cream. Can you hear the difference
in the sound?'

'I'm not bloody deaf,' she said sulkily, 'but I can't do
it. That's the truth of the matter. I just can't.'

'So would you like to give up?'

'No!'

He sighed. 'Seriously, Miss Hardy, why go to all this
trouble? Don't you think you're a trifle behind the times?
Your accent is fashionable. Your idioms and expressions
are imaginative and virile . . .'

'Cut the crap. I want to speak Queen's English. Let's
get on with it,' she snarled.

His eyebrows shot up. 'I thought we'd dispensed with
that particular expression. No?' He sighed. 'Let me tell
you something. Pronunciation begins in childhood. Different muscles control different types of sounds. Some
foreigners can never get the sounds right simply because
their muscles aren't developed the right way. You don't
have the muscles to say "I" correctly.'

'Now you tell me, after I've blown a hundred pounds
at least on you.'

'However,' he went on, ignoring her outburst, 'all
muscles can be developed with enough practice. It will
hurt,' he said, watching her rubbing her throat. 'Of
course it will, but just keep on forcing yourself to make
that sound.'

'Do you think there's any improvement yet?'

'No, not yet.'

'Maybe I'll never make it.'

He turned and laughed at her. It was an unkind laugh and she sensed his antagonism. 'You, my dear young lady, will succeed in anything you put your mind to. I have no doubt about that whatsoever. You're one of life's winners.'

His words, spoken more in spite than anything else, cheered Marjorie as she walked home.

The modelling school was the least of her problems. Even shedding ten pounds had been easier than shedding her Dover accent. Nevertheless, things were moving in the right direction, she thought, feeling optimistic.

The newspaper management had finally come up with an acceptable offer on their third try and she and Joe were richer by five thousands pounds – quite a sum to help launch *Leadership*. She was taking Barbara to dinner to celebrate. It was almost time to get to work again.

Chapter 34

——— ———

Springtime. Leafy buds unfurled, the fields were dotted with frisky lambs and brave flowers, birds soared and swooped for sheer joy, and Marjorie emerged shyly from her crysalis, ready and able to sell space to the world's élite.

A new plaque, Segal and Hardy Publishers Ltd, had been added to the plates by Joe's office door and they'd hired painters to decorate the first floor. Soon it would be time to hire some staff – if she sold the required amount of advertisements, that was.

A shiver of fear went through Marjorie at the thought of all the expenses they were about to incur, to say nothing of their newest joint endeavour, their overdraft, which was still an infant at ten thousand pounds, but growing lustily.

Oh God! What had she done? But she was committed now. They'd spent a bomb on her new image and her new wardrobe, and her little red mini, which she loved. Last Sunday she'd taken the family for a spin around River and they'd had a picnic at Ewell Minnis. Lana had been entranced with the bluebells and swans.

That reminded her why she was doing it all. She was determined to give Lana the best, and for that she needed an income, so it stood to reason that she had to sell the space. The more she thought about it, the more apprehensive she became.

'Well, today's the big day,' she said, walking into Joe's office.

'You'll have to work here until your office is painted,' he said gloomily. 'Look! I've put your desk there.'

So he had. 'Damn,' she muttered. She felt more confident selling on the phone when she was alone. Never mind. It was only temporary.

She picked up the list of prospects, but her hand was shaking so badly that she put it down again.

'Like my outfit?' she asked, pirouetting. She was wearing a powder-blue tailored suit with a flared skirt and fitted bodice, and a white blouse tying at the neck, with navy shoes, gloves and briefcase. Her hair had been cut into a chic bouffant style which suited her.

Joe examined her dispassionately. 'You'll do,' he said eventually.

She rang through to their newly acquired general factotum and asked for coffee, which arrived promptly on a silver tray. All very swish, but it had to be paid for and she was the only one bringing in the income. She began to shake visibly.

'I'd better get started,' she said nervously.

Moments later she was on the telephone to the boss of a workshop that welded and spray-painted steel desks. He sounded busy but interested. 'Come whenever you like,' he replied. 'I'm always here.'

'Sounds foreign,' she said to Joe as she replaced the telephone receiver.

'Who?'

'Mr Kubis from Atomic Sheet Metals Works.'

'With a name like that I should think he would sound foreign. Why pick him first?'

'I'm starting with the lowest of the low. He has a humble workshop in the Old Kent Road.'

Joe scowled. 'Go for the big ones first. The rest will follow.'

'I need to practise so I'm going for the small ones. If they say no it's not the end of the world.'

'Suit yourself!' He frowned at her. She knew what he was thinking and he was right, but positive thinking was something that evaded her quite often, particularly when she needed it.

Mr Jan Kubis was a shock, the opposite to what she had expected. Admittedly he was wearing overalls, but beneath them was a smart white collar and tie, and his mohair jacket hung on the back of his office door. He had penetrating black eyes that scanned her from behind his glasses.

Funny-looking cove, she thought, then mentally corrected herself to quite unusual-looking. He dusted a chair for her and complimented her on her appearance, thanked her for coming and then subjected her to the third degree about the magazine.

'I have the feeling you're onto a real winner here. I'll take the front page for a full year, subject of course to my advertising agency's approval. Here's their address. Please contact them.'

Mr Kubis's account executive, Kevin O'Connor, handled three other prospects on her list, so she invited him to lunch and put her presentation to him.

'Quite honestly, I couldn't possibly recommend your

proposed magazine to any of my clients,' he said, smashing her hopes. His pale blue eyes glinted at her through rimless glasses, and his double chin wobbled over his collar. 'It takes a great deal of cash to launch a magazine, my dear. More than you've got, I'm sure.

'You can't expect the agencies to care whether or not you succeed. There's plenty of media available. If and when you produce a good product, and succeed in achieving a minimum of 50,000 paid subscribers, we'll be happy to put you on our list of recommended media, but even then we spread the clients' budgets very thin.'

'Then how can we ever get started?' she burst out, trying to conceal her instinctive dislike for him. How does anyone get started? I need advertising to bring out the magazine.'

'That's your problem. I don't think you have the vaguest hope of succeeding and I shall have to tell that to my clients.'

He gobbled his way through twelve oysters, pâté, *filet mignon* and *crème brûlée*, while she made do with a bowl of soup, pretending that she was slimming.

'Personally I'm not in favour of trade publications at all,' he admitted, becoming talkative with the wine he had guzzled. 'For the same outlay and trouble we can hit both the retailers and the end-users. Besides, we charge a higher commission for consumer ads. In fact,' he confided, 'we make much more out of TV, radio and newspapers. If I never saw another trade magazine I'd be happy.'

Damn him and damn them all, she thought as she paid the exorbitant bill.

Her next thirty visits brought negative responses. Each

time, she was that much less confident at her next call
and her prospects sensed this and withdrew. It was like
a vortex and she was being sucked down. They all had
so many excuses: they'd consider advertising when the
first issue was printed; their advertising budgets were
spent until the next financial year; they'd wait until she
built up paid circulation.

How could they get paid circulation without producing the magazine? She agonised over this with Joe.
He had dozens of ideas for building sales, but he needed
to have the first issue published before he could start
operating his direct mail campaign. And to produce the
first issue, they needed advertising. It seemed to be a
vicious circle.

Despite their debts there was no stopping Joe's spending spree. He ordered a word processor, desks, chairs,
an intercom, a drawing board, dictating equipment, tape
recorders, – the list was endless. When she taxed him
with it, he simply said: 'You'll sell them, Marjorie. I
know you will. I have the greatest faith in you.'

After fifty 'maybe laters' she began to think about
throwing in the towel, but that was impossible because
now they jointly owed the bank thirteen thousand
pounds. They had reached the point of no return,
Marjorie knew, and she had sold a miserable total
of ten pages of advertising. She was tossed into a
permanent state of painful tension as she faced the
prospect of personal bankruptcy and no income.

Chapter 35

———— ————

Over the next month their joint debt approached fifteen thousand pounds, and this was only the start of it. Marjorie knew that if they ever managed to produce the first issue there would be weekly and monthly salaries to pay, freelance fees for feature writers, artists and photographers, plus her car and travelling expenses, to say nothing of feeding greedy advertising executives with oysters and caviar.

Her fear had become a permanent physical pain in her guts, her neck and her stomach. She began to suspect she had developed an ulcer. By the end of August she had ten per cent of the advertisements they needed, and they had promised to publish the first issue by the year's end.

From then on, austerity ruled her days. To save on petrol she took a dilapidated room in a scruffy Chalk Farm tenement, sharing a basement kitchen and bathroom, and stayed there during the week. She went by Tube to her appointments. After a hard day slogging round workshops and offices she would buy a pie and a tomato, half a loaf of bread and some milk, and walk home, her mouth watering longingly as she passed the fish and chip restaurant. Once she was back in her lousy room she would wolf down her food and go to bed early.

She was lonely and scared and she missed her baby all the time. By day, thoughts of Robert were banished from her mind, but at night her subconscious would drag him up from the depths and she would find herself entwined with him on a Corsican beach. It was bitter to wake, but worse was to follow, for her business problems would come zooming in with sickening intensity. She had been tossed into a new and scary world where only survival counted.

As summer fled and autumn set in, her room became damp and she shivered rather than waste cash on heating. She was getting to know the industry well, for she was on first-name terms with the advertising managers and the managing directors, she knew all their products, and she had files of information that each of them would like to have published in the columns of *Leadership*, should it ever see the light of day. Yet she hardly ever closed a sale. She reckoned she had enough promises of future advertising to fill fifty issues. They all wanted the same thing – to see the issue in print. If they had enough cash, Marjorie mused, they could give free advertisements for three months, but even then they had no guarantees.

All the time their joint debt was mounting but Marjorie kept on trying. Not a company in England escaped, she saw them all, and consequently her travelling expenses were astronomical.

Christmas approached and Marjorie reluctantly packed up and went home for three weeks. What was the point in staying? No one wanted to see her right now.

She tried to help around the house, but even playing with Lana made her sad. She had promised her daughter so much, but was unable to deliver.

'It will be a meagre Christmas this year,' she warned

Mum as they did the cards together. 'Next year it will be different,' she promised. 'We just have to get the first issue out.'

She tried to relax and recuperate, but she couldn't put their overdraft of twenty thousand pounds out of her mind.

'Business is a game,' Joe told her one morning when he found her in the offices moping over future layouts. 'You win some, you lose some, but you learn all the time.'

'It's the debts. I can't stand being in debt,' she said.

'That's what banks are for. Lending and borrowing. They expect to lose out some of the time.'

He smiled cheerfully and watching him Marjorie could not help admiring him. The bank manager had told her that his building stood security for their loans, but Joe thought she didn't know that.

'So the bank takes a knock,' he said cheerily. 'Who cares? When you feel you've had enough say so and we'll find something else to do. If the worst comes to the worst you'll always have a job as my secretary.'

'That would really be the bloody worst,' she snarled.

Yet at the back of her mind was the thought that Joe had put his building on the line to help her get established. She couldn't ruin him. She couldn't give up. She'd have to make it work – somehow.

With further generosity, Joe insisted that she draw a full month's salary as a Christmas bonus. She almost cried, but somehow she forced herself to spend Joe's money so that the family could have a decent Christmas. At last the holiday was over and she returned to London to do battle again.

On the third Friday of January, Marjorie surfaced from

sleep around six a.m. and immediately felt the familiar surge of dread. Trying to take her mind off her debts, now standing at twenty-three thousand, she got out of bed, switched on the kettle and wrote up her appointments for the day.

She was about to have her bath when she heard the water running. 'Damn!' One of the Jamaicans was up early. She would have to queue or she wouldn't get in at all. She stood shivering outside the door with her towel and wash things until the man came out, leaving behind him a dark rim round the bath, plenty of scum, and pools of water on the floor. And the place was steamed up as usual. She opened the window and cleaned up. Five minutes later she was soaking in lukewarm water.

Someone began to hammer on the door. 'Get knotted, I've just got in,' she yelled.

Breakfast was a roll and a second cup of coffee. By eight she was pushing her way through the crowded Tube station; by nine-thirty, she was getting her first rejection. And so it went.

Her last appointment was at three-thirty and she broke her heel as she arrived.

Frank Ambrose could have walked straight out of a Dickens novel. He was pale and stooped, and looked undernourished. He wore a black suit, a stiff white collar, a conservative tie and a waistcoat, although it was a hot day. His secretary brought Marjorie a cup of strong, sweet tea and a digestive biscuit.

'You look as if you need that,' he said, smiling softly. He picked up her dog-eared dummy magazine and peered myopically at it, while his black hair fell forward over his forehead.

She knew that he had recently inherited his stationery manufacturing business and that he was very conservative and very rich. When he asked her how *Leadership* was selling, something about his straight grey eyes gleaming with concern prompted her to tell the truth.

'I can't get it past the advertising agencies,' she admitted. 'I've sold about fifteen contracts so far, but all of them to smaller companies. The agencies don't want to be bothered with us.

'Quite honestly, I can see their point,' she went on earnestly. 'If they recommend us and we fail, they land up with egg all over their faces. It's safer not to. Besides, it doesn't pay them to advertise in trade journals. And the clients themselves are holding back, waiting to see what the others do. I know the industry needs this magazine, but people are taking some convincing. We could do such a worthwhile job.' She swallowed hard and shrugged.

'And when is the fee for advertising normally payable?' he asked. She sensed that this question was important to him.

'Thirty days after publication is the norm, I've learned. The agencies pay at forty-five days. Long before then we shall supply audited certificates to back our claims regarding the amount printed and posted.'

'I see.' Now he was smiling slightly. 'I'd like to help you, Miss Hardy. I'm secretary of the committee running our office equipment and computer associations. Perhaps I could find out what the majority view is about your magazine. If you'd like me to, that is. Let me know if there's anything else I could do to help.'

Other than taking a full year's contract, she couldn't

think of a thing, but once again he was waiting to see what the others did, as they all were.

Marjorie spent a dismal weekend at home. Mum had been nagging her to buy a pushchair which was badly needed, but she was unwilling to spend a penny. She couldn't bring herself to tell her mother about her plight and she agonised at not being able to give Lana the basic necessities.

'You're obsessed with business nowadays,' Mum said crossly. 'You can't even take off time to do the shopping. If you're so busy, give me the cash and I'll buy it. She's too big for her pram.'

Oh God help me! If I go bust how will I pay off the debts? How will I keep my family going if I'm out of work?

Watching Lana play made Marjorie feel even more guilty. Lana deserved the good life her father should have given her and she would have it, somehow. There must be a way to turn this disaster into a triumph. She just had to make those timid entrepreneurs take their courage in both hands and back her. It wasn't too late; she still had a chance.

Mum was talking to her, but she didn't hear a word. 'Sorry, Mum, I'm thinking,' she muttered.

On impulse she suddenly went to the telephone and called Frank Ambrose. To her surprise, he was in the office although it was late on Saturday afternoon.

'Listen,' she implored him. 'You said you'd help me. Well, get me into one of your regular meetings. I want to talk to the members. It's no good everyone hanging back and not wanting to make a decision; they must decide as a group. Can you do that for me?'

'It's worth a try,' he said.

Mum took up her theme again when Marjorie returned to the kitchen.

'If you ask me, you're getting obsessed with making money,' she said. 'And when are we going to see your first issue? You keep talking about it, but I never see a sign of it.'

'Soon,' Marjorie said. 'And, Mum, thanks for offering to get the pushchair. I'll pop up and get the money.'

From now on it was positive thinking all the way. No more doom and gloom, thank you. Those damned businessmen were going to sign on the dotted line if she had to pull a gun on them.

Chapter 36

――――― ―――――

Marjorie awoke early on the following Friday morning feeling nervous. It was the day of the Association's dinner and in less than twelve hours she would be facing a room full of businessmen, much like those she had sold *The Handy Home Guide* to, only this time there would be more of them.

She had returned to Dover the night before, and spent most of that morning writing and rehearsing her talk, and choosing what to wear. Finally a plain black suit with a white silk blouse seemed to be her safest bet since she hadn't the faintest idea what to expect.

She gave Lana a big hug. 'Wish me luck, darling,' she whispered. 'You'll have to put her to bed, please, Mum.'

'You don't have much time for your family any more,' Mum grumbled in her familiar way. 'You're far too engrossed in yourself and business. This little mite deserves more from you.'

'Sorry, Mum.' She turned away. Not for anything would she admit that she had brought them to the very brink of disaster, that all four of them were hanging on to the cliff edge by their fingernails.

It was a clear, crisp winter evening and Marjorie tried to think positive as she drove towards London, but the negative thoughts kept creeping in. What would happen if they went bankrupt? It didn't bear thinking about. Perhaps she should have employed a professional speaker, someone in public relations? But it was too late to change her mind, she reminded herself.

She hung around outside the conference entrance of the Dorchester, smelling the perfume, watching the well-dressed patrons walk inside. Well, she wasn't Orphan Annie, was she? Her suit had cost a fortune and so had Denbigh-Jones. 'Your inferiority is all inside your head,' he'd told her when he'd signed off with obvious relief. 'You need therapy, not speech training.' To hell with Denbigh-Jones – but thinking about him made her feel more confident.

When she walked into the conference centre she was taken aback to find that the hall could seat five hundred people, and that it was rapidly filling with members and their wives. The wives wore evening dresses and jewels, and Marjorie, in her plain black suit worn over a simple white blouse, felt that her outfit was all wrong.

Frank Ambrose was hovering by the door. He grabbed her elbow and pulled her towards the nearest group, where he introduced her to the chairman of a typewriter company and an importer of Japanese office equipment. She knew many of the guests, but she could hardly say two words to them before Frank had grabbed her again and whisked her off to see the owner of a firm producing dictating equipment and an industrial designer who had just won a prize for his revolutionary office chair.

Heavens! How would she ever remember all these new faces? She felt scared to death.

She kept an eye on her magazine dummy and a pile of rate cards which Frank had put on a table by the door.

Occasionally someone would pause and look at it, but no one picked up a rate card. Marjorie felt as if she was on display and she had failed. She longed to run away, but Frank had her in tow and he was determined she should meet the men who counted, all those bigwigs whose secretaries had fobbed her off, the very ones who had hired all those admen who had so enjoyed putting her down.

They were all tanked up and in a jovial mood, but she sensed that now was not the time to try to say one word about her magazine. Instead she found herself listening to a variety of industry woes.

Marjorie began to feel dizzy. How would she cope with trying to communicate with five hundred people? How could they possibly hear her voice? When she saw a young man carrying in the microphone and cords she almost fainted with fright.

Dinner was a nightmare. The food arrived and she toyed with it, and then it was taken away: pâté and sherry, fish and white wine, braised duck and red wine. She couldn't swallow a thing, so she just pretended to eat.

She began to feel very strange. It was as if she was swelling up like a toad, a sledgehammer was bashing against her ribs and her cheeks were burning red. Could she pretend to go to the lavatory and never come back? One more course and then she'd be in for it.

Suddenly she knew that she had to get out of there. She could not do it. Even though they faced ruin, she just could not stand up in front of all those people and speak.

At that moment Frank stood up and caught her eye. 'Ladies and gentlemen, I suggest we take a break and listen to Marjorie Hardy who has something to tell us all. Come up here, please, Marjorie,' he called.

Oh God help me! She stood up and walked to the microphone, and stood there while it was adjusted, which seemed to take several hours, and tried to pretend she was real and this was real, but of course it wasn't. She tried out her voice. It was still there. Strange, she thought.

'I have to thank you all for a really enjoyable and interesting evening,' she began. Her nervousness had fled. It belonged to the real Marjorie who had faded away. She tried out a smile, and that worked, too. She fumbled for her talk and realised too late that it was in her handbag by her chair. Oh God! She took a deep breath.

'When I arrived here an hour ago I did not realise that we were facing a revolution in small electronic calculators and that the silliest thing a retailer could do was to stock up with items that will be obsolete in six months' time, or maybe sooner. I didn't even know that computers were helping bus drivers to keep their timetables, or that the blind could read and write with computers, or that new programmes could help pilots to prevent crashes, or that computers could now operate security access doors. I guess a lot of people here didn't know that either, or else you wouldn't have been talking about these new developments.

'I suppose that it's only by meeting together once a month that you can all keep abreast of industry news, and not just the advances I've been hearing about, but vital news on marketing, inflation, and finance. I can't help thinking that it's a pity you can't get together with your customers, just as you suppliers have done tonight. Of course with fifty-odd thousand of them this would be a physical impossibility.'

She broke off for a moment and gazed around anxiously. Frank gave her a broad wink and the thumbs up sign, so she ploughed on.

'Your customers probably rely on your sales staff to keep them informed, but it would take hours to get over all the information I've heard here tonight. Your whole industry and your customers need to hear for themselves the buzz, the hum, the heart of what's making the industry tick right now. What are the hazards? Where is the future?'

She took a deep breath. The room was quiet. The diners appeared to be listening and that was a miracle.

'So you see, ladies and gentlemen, that's where *Leadership* can be such a valuable marketing tool for you all. Informed customers sell more, they become more viable, they buy more from you. This magazine will provide a vital link between you and your customers.

'Most of you employ advertising agencies to plan your advertising. It's not their job to take business risks for you. They cannot in all fairness give *Leadership* their advertising at this stage, although they all will when we have sufficient paid circulation. Meantime we need your support. If *Leadership* is ever to be born we need you as a body, as an association, to make a decision jointly and severally, to back it. And I need that decision now. You must decide if you need a trade magazine linking you with your customers.

'I'm not going to keep you sitting listening to me for much longer. You've all had the chance to see our dummy and hear about the project which I'm trying to get off the ground. I just want to say this to you – make a decision to turn this magazine into reality. You will all benefit from it.

'Now, if you don't mind, I'd like to throw the whole matter up for debate. How about you, Frank? What are your views?'

She sat down feeling truly strange. Time had altered its pace: every second was vital and significant and she felt a strange power flowing through her as she listened to Frank explaining why he felt the magazine was vital to the industry. His vote was definitely yes, he said.

The chairman of a leading computer company stood up and asked what guarantees she could give them to publish editorials on new products. She nodded nervously, intending to say 'yes' to everything.

Her head was spinning. If they voted 'no' that would be the end of it. And then what would she do? Crawl out of there? And after that? She'd have to face the music. Oh God! Perhaps Dad had been right.

Frank was taking a quick vote by a show of hands, aided by the waiters.

The tension was killing her. It began in her legs and moved up to her back. She felt like a puppet with the strings pulled too taut. Why was Frank looking so serious as he muttered to committee members around the table? She took a gulp of wine. She should never have come here.

Then Frank returned to his place and said: 'All right, ladies and gentlemen, let's drink to the birth of a new magazine, *Leadership*, and to the very tough fight put up by a certain young lady here. Four hundred and fifty "yeses" to twenty-three abstentions, Marjorie. But there's a rider in almost every case. You have to agree to a section of editorial news that features new products. Call it whatever you like, but subject to this, we agree to make *Leadership* the official journal of our various associations and we shall all support you. And it better be good, Marjorie, I'm telling you now.'

She hardly remembered the drive back to Dover. Afterwards she was sure she must have floated there in her lovely little red mini. She tried not to think of Joe and what he would say when she told him that eight pages of product news would be inserted in his precious editorial.

What did it matter? They were going to survive.

Chapter 37

Triumph surged in her blood, vibrating to her fingertips and bringing a flush to her cheeks as the very first bound copy slid across the binder's desk towards her. There was her magazine in all its silvery blue glory, with *Leadership* in white letters and a glossy typewriter set into a square window in the middle of the cover. Marjorie caught her breath, feeling entranced.

Everyone wanted the first issue. Garth Clark, their editor, an introverted, clever man with a biting sense of humour and too much talent for this job, was hovering, longing to grab it. Over six foot and skinny, with a mop of dark red hair, he resembled a scarecrow. He knew this and consequently he was always immaculate. Mike was trembling. Even their willowy blonde production editor had lost her usual bored expression.

It was one of those special moments. There it lay, their baby. Soon other copies were skimming across the table. Joe picked up the first one and handed it to her. 'You made it happen, Marjorie. You get to keep it,' he said.

She hugged it, knowing she would treasure it for ever. Here was a monument to the most extraordinary effort she had ever made in her life – a total of eighty pages of advertising that represented three months of solid grind, including evenings and weekends. She thought back to all those visits, endless conversations, promises, enforced listening to confidences, hundreds of cups of lousy coffee, at least eighty invites out, twenty propositions, a handful of lewd attempts to blackmail her, dozens of lunches and dinners. Here lay her future hopes, Lana's education, her parents' pension and her security. It was a good feeling. She'd done it!

Needing to be alone, she found a stool in a corner and leafed through her issue, remembering. Every page told a story. Here was Ace Office Machinery's advertisement. She flinched as she recalled this particular disaster. Daniel Moore, Jr, the chairman's nephew, a spoiled, handsome man with over-candid blue eyes, had been kicked up the ladder to marketing manager only two years after he'd graduated. Somehow he had discovered her London address, a carefully guarded secret since it was a real slum, and he'd arrived at the door at ten p.m. when she was watching TV in her pyjamas. She had opened it unthinkingly, and Daniel had forced his way in and taken a running jump at her. For the next five minutes they had fought their way around the room until her yells brought her neighbour, Johnson, a six-foot Jamaican, to her rescue.

'What on earth . . . ? Whatever did you think . . . ? Why . . . ?' she had asked, when she could talk.

Gasping for breath, she saw that Johnson was roughing him up. 'Don't hurt him, he's one of my business prospects,' she had called out.

'Shit, lady. What sort of business are you in?' Johnson had asked. 'Want me to call the police?'

'Yes, I think I have a black eye,' she'd said, feeling the flesh with her index finger. It hurt!

'Hey, wait a minute,' Daniel had begged. 'For God's sake, don't. Please! I read your signals all wrong. I thought you wanted . . . well . . . I mean to say . . . you have to reach your target, don't you?'

'Not this way,' she had told him icily.

'Hey, listen. If you're sensible you'll forget this happened. I promise . . .'

'Don't promise anything,' she'd snapped. 'Throw the idiot out,' she'd told Johnson, knowing that she could not afford the bad publicity. Exactly three days later, Daniel's advertising agency had called Joe to place a full-page, full-colour, year's contract. Daniel's uncle was retiring, she'd heard, and Daniel was about to run the show. She felt sorry for the female staff.

She turned over a few more pages.

'Oh God. Him!' she murmured. Sir Baldwin had told her that his working hours were divided amongst attending the boards of various companies of which he was honorary chairman, and environmental duties, which was where his heart lay. He ran the marketing of his fountain pen manufacturers from his home, so if she wanted a contract, Saturday afternoon was the only available time.

So Marjorie had driven up to Pothwick Manor, Oxford, feeling delighted by the summer afternoon, to find herself in paradise – a beautiful Queen Anne home set in gardens so immaculate, hedges and lawns so manicured, flowers so brilliantly arranged that it left her breathless.

Sir Baldwin Pothwick, squarish, brutish and very strong, his red face topped with a mane of thick white hair, had been widowed for exactly a year, he had explained as he showed her round with obvious pride. She'd felt sad for him and she admired him for his self-imposed year's mourning, which he explained at length.

Sir Baldwin had marched her to his stables where he bred Shire carthorses. 'How'd you like that?' he'd exclaimed as his groom led out a massive stallion. 'Feel its haunches!' She got a crick in her neck admiring the beast.

They passed on to the kennels where he kept his Irish wolfhounds. They were penned, he explained, because they were too valuable to run around loose. 'How'd you like that?' He'd tossed a massive, six-week-old puppy into her arms. 'Feel the weight of it!'

He took her to the rose garden, where she was shown each prize-winning, massive bloom. 'This is the Pothwick crimson.' He plucked one and pushed it into her cleavage, with a great deal of unnecessary fumbling. Marjorie began to get the message.

They were moving into the immaculate vegetable garden where marrows, tomatoes and cucumbers grew to the proportions that were expected of them at Pothwick Manor. He thrust a tomato, a cucumber, and the prize-winning Pothwick runner bean into her hands. She slid them into her handbag.

'How'd you like that?' he exclaimed. 'The Pothwick chilli. Have one.' He handed her a massively long red chilli. 'Feel it! You won't find another chilli like it anywhere in the world. Go on, squeeze it.'

She pinched it, squeezed it, rubbed it and gripped it in her clenched fist. Thank goodness they were approaching the house, past another immaculate courtyard shielded on four sides by a tall yew hedge where a fountain played into a pond full of koi fish.

'I knew it,' she groaned inwardly as they paused to admire the size of the fish.

A French door led into the house and Sir Baldwin flung it open. Clearly this was his den. There was a TV set, a bar, cosy rugs on the floor, the head of a massive red deer and a Bengal tiger mounted on the walls, amongst other paraphernalia.

Now we're going to admire the bloody heads, she guessed.

She was wrong! Sir Baldwin unzipped his trousers and produced the longest, thickest member she'd ever seen.

'How'd you like that?' he asked as he showed off the high point of his achievements. 'And it's been resting for three hundred and sixty-five days.'

And she was the fool who had wandered into Pothwick Manor on the 366th day. Clearly the beast was not intending to rest much longer – it was moving, pulsating and turning purplish blue as she stared, mesmerised.

'Go on. Feel it! Touch it! Hold it!' he commanded.

She did, rubbing her hand over the skin, feeling the tip, pulling back the foreskin and pressing all that prize chilli juice into the Pothwick prize member.

Sir Baldwin let out an ear-piercing scream of pure agony. Moments later he was spread-eagled over the fishpond, wiggling his big fat member amongst his big fat fish and letting out whimpers like his big fat wolfhounds. She left him there.

Marjorie had never expected to see Pothwick fountain pen advertisements in her magazine, but she'd been wrong, for his agency had sent a full-page full-colour contract a week later. Sir Baldwin was a good loser after all. She wasn't surprised when they had to reduce the transparencies to fit their page.

Most of the advertisers were her friends, she thought, turning the pages, remembering lunches, drinks, and so many shared confidences. She had made only one bad enemy, namely Alfred Cave, media manager of a large advertising agency.

Nondescript would describe Cave well, for he was short, thin and mild of appearance, except for the glint of power mania in his grey eyes. It was his job to examine the media presented to him for its effectiveness in various marketing areas and to pass on his skilled evaluation to account executives and ultimately to their clients. He'd propositioned her on her very first visit.

'Look here, Miss Hardy, your facts and figures sound good as you've put them to me, but one can be very creative with statistics – know what I mean?'

She had frowned at him, not understanding.

'We can put dozens of contracts your way. Big clients, big money. It all depends on how I present your facts to our top brass. You be nice to me and I'll be nice to you. Know what I mean?'

'Nice in what way?' She'd brought her tape recorder as a matter of course, and now she fumbled in her bag to switch it on.

'Don't be naive, Marjorie. Play ball with me and dozens of contracts will come your way.'

'Well, how would I do that?' she had stammered.

'The usual way, Marjorie. Like you sell most of your space, on your back.'

'I've heard of men like you,' she had murmured. 'It's

a power game, isn't it? You just want to put me down. You're a horrible person.'

'Horrible or not, I'd hop up on that table if I were you. Think about it, love, all those pages of ads, some in full colour. You're on commission, I suppose. I'll lock the door.'

'Don't bother,' she'd said. 'I'm leaving.'

The tape had been copied and delivered to his MD the following morning. Alfred Cave was now pounding the pavements, but the agency had vetoed her magazine and no one there would see her – an example of men sticking together.

But was she really such a virtuous person herself? Wasn't she selling her soul daily? While Barbara was continually congratulating her on her new image, her wonderful figure, her hair styling, her straightforward, no-nonsense accent, and her superb selling ability, she herself was getting quite a different image: one of expediency, an opportunist, a conniving, manipulative, ruthless saleswoman who could gaff the fish without a moment's compunction whenever her quarry left themselves off-guard. And they always did. There was always that moment. Admittedly at times she had to wait a while, but sooner or later they would let down their defences and then, snap, they'd be wiggling on her hook.

'Come on, Marj. Snap out of it,' Joe called. 'We're celebrating.'

She tried to find a quick excuse for her gloom. 'How much do we owe?' she asked.

'God! Marjorie, you can spoil anything. Fifty thousand pounds, but we made five thousand clear on the first issue, taking in one month's normal expenses and the interest on the overdraft. We'll be out of debt in a year, so cheer up.'

'Our expenses will soar,' she said gloomily. 'For starters I need an assistant and I need a secretary in London, and an office. Better still, we should all move to London.'

'How should we set about getting another sales-woman?' Joe asked. 'If they can't sell like you, we'd be throwing away good contacts.'

'I shall employ only divorced, widowed or unmar-ried women with children,' she said in a moment of sudden insight. 'Flexible timing, low wages and high commission. They are the true desperadoes of this world. They won't let anyone slip through their fingers. They have too much at stake.'

Feeling slightly tipsy, she leaned back imagining her flock, like anxious mother pigeons, circling London, quick to alight on a juicy worm and not neglecting any crumbs, for in some Camden Town attic, or Chalk Farm basement, or Notting Hill Gate tenement, or smelly, overcrowded crèche, the nation's single mums hid their nests. And their precious offspring were clamouring for more and more of the better things of life.

'I'm off. Goodbye,' she called out. 'See you in ten days' time.'

'Don't go. The fun's just starting.' Joe had his arm around their new secretary.

'I want to get back to Lana. And I want to show this to Mum. For me, that is what it's all about,' she said.

She had neglected her child, she knew, but from now on she would make up for it, starting with a holiday in Devon for the two of them. They deserved it and Mum deserved the break, too.

Chapter 38

After their launch late in June 1975, Marjorie was on a high, climbing up the ladder of success until it seemed that she had her head in the clouds. She was a person of some account now, the co-director of a renowned national magazine. Her clients put out the red carpet when she appeared and locked their baser instincts in the filing cabinets until she left. Rampant willies, crude suggestions and downright blackmail were a thing of the past. Marjorie was happily aware of both her sexual and her business power.

At the end of their first year she moved from Chalk Farm to Hampstead, where she leased a basement flat leading onto the Heath, which saved her sanity in the evenings. She began to plot how she could move her parents close to London so that she could spend more time with Lana.

When, in January the following year, Marjorie was featured in a prominent social magazine as Britain's marketing woman of the year, it seemed to be just another step on this magic ladder leading to the stars, and as they climbed fate smiled on them and showered them with booty.

Surrounded with love, Lana grew vigorously and joyously. At three she could speak well and she was sturdy and clever. There was no 'dad' in her vocabulary, but 'Joe' made up for it. When Marjorie was away, Barbara helped out.

Each Friday, Marjorie drove home from London, arriving by five in time to bath and feed Lana and play with her until she put her to bed. How bitter it was to tear herself away from her baby on Sunday evenings.

In July 1976, a group of five trade magazines folded and Joe went out and bought them lock, stock and barrel from the liquidators. Garth Clark took over as managing editor of the group, with a ten per cent share of the company. He persuaded a former colleague and friend to take his place as editor of *Leadership*.

These were new areas for Marjorie, but this time she was not daunted by her ignorance of the subjects: jewellery, hotels, plastics, textiles and transport. She took a few days off to learn about the industries and to find premises. She was lucky to get a sub-lease on three offices situated in a shopping complex in Finchley.

It was time to set about turning her dream of creating a specialised sales team into reality. She advertised for, interviewed and appointed her flock of homing pigeons: anxious, ambitious mums with too much responsibility and too little training. She handed them a lifeline and as she had predicted, the benefits she offered turned the women into her devoted assistants. She gave them flexible timing, a company-sponsored crèche which was clean and reliable with qualified nurses in charge, a clothes allowance, travel subsidies and a generous time-off arrangement enabling them to nurse their children when they were sick. When she set about training them she was amazed to find how much she had learned and could pass on.

The Dover building was rapidly filling as the new team took over the second and third floors. It was absurd trying to run the editorial department by remote control. Joe would have to leave Dover, but moving him out of his building was worse than prising a limpet off a rock.

By the end of 1976 the company was so profitable that Marjorie was able to purchase a lovely apartment overlooking the Thames in Chelsea. For Marjorie, this was a dream come true. She took a week off to plan the decor and furnishing of her new pad and then Joe arrived and they fought long and furiously over her ideas. The result was a compromise: plain wood floors with bright Afghan rugs, modern Swedish furniture, plenty of uncluttered space and a few good paintings.

She gave a housewarming party and was delighted to find how many people she knew – half of London by the look of things, she thought, watching the throng spilling into every available room and crowding onto the roof garden.

Soon it was time to fly to Europe where she would spend a month launching their new European supplement to *Leadership*, which if successful would appear quarterly. As usual sales beat their target by a long head. The supplement became an advertisement-packed quarterly and Marjorie kept this magazine and the travelling for herself.

It was amazing how quickly she had become used to being rich. Suddenly she was tossed into a jet-set world where she had to learn the art of travelling light and keeping a suitcase packed, ready for instant flight. She stayed in five-star hotels and met the glitzy élite. She was famous, beautiful and young.

Only she knew how false was the winning personality

she had built. Inside was someone else. Who? She was not sure, but she knew herself to be a failure: a woman who had not succeeded in winning the man she loved, who had deprived her daughter of her birthright, a woman who had forgotten how to love. So while she held herself in low esteem, she took refuge behind the glorious façade of Marjorie Hardy.

Chapter 39

——— ———

Marjorie emerged with the first-class passengers and walked briskly towards the airport, enjoying the warm wind that touched her bare shoulders and fanned her cheeks. It was good to get out of England, which was enduring a cold spell. She threw back her head, letting the wind play with her hair, enjoying the sensation of her thin silk suit moulding against her body. She felt at one with the morning.

A man was waving from behind the distant fence. 'Marjorie, Marjorie, darling . . .' she could hear faintly. But who was he? And where was she? Momentarily she couldn't remember.

Blind panic stopped her dead in her tracks. She fumbled in her bag for her itinerary – Italy . . . Ah, Milan, and if it was Milan it must be Angelo. Dear Angelo, who was so good in the sack, but a little temperamental. Very possessive, too. She waved and moments later she had resumed her usual brisk walk towards the airport building, customs, Angelo's welcoming arms and his four-poster bed.

She had booked to spend five days here, but it would be no punishment. Angelo, with his Roman profile, his full, sensuous lips, deeply hooded expressive brown eyes and his jet black curly hair, was about the best specimen *homo sapiens* was capable of producing. To top it all, he was six foot plus, strong, sexy and a superb dancer. He was also a madly talented, fiercely possessive, fun-loving artist, and she loved him to bits.

Nowadays Marjorie looked for friends in areas far removed from her business. She had learned the hard way. Most of her advertisers tried to date her, and a handful were very eligible, but to date a client was to say goodbye to his advertising. The affair could only end one of three ways – she dumped them, they dumped her, or they married. Whatever, she'd be bound to lose out.

She began shuffling towards passport control, pushing her suitcase with her foot, her white leather briefcase slung over her shoulder.

Her life was becoming complicated, she knew. In Brussels she had Frans, a lovable South African expatriate who published books in his home language for other expatriates and dreamed of returning home. He was warm, patient and very strong and she loved him for his unselfish ways and his common sense. She usually stayed in his town house and they went flying, which was his hobby, when she wasn't busy seeing to her large circle of local office suppliers.

In Paris she had Pierre, a writer, who needed an undemanding woman who would cost him nothing and supply an occasional interlude of passion. Yet lately he, too, had become jealous and possessive. Her love for Pierre was tinged with anguish, for he was a difficult man, affected by black moods of despair, although he was also an inspired lover.

In Hamburg, Helmut would be waiting for her. Dreamily she considered why she loved him. Perhaps it was his endless striving towards perfection in everything he did – including his love-making. He was so serious and so clever, and he was making pots of money with his engineering business. Or perhaps it was because he was so vulnerable. Behind the stern blue eyes, immaculate blond hair and courteous façade, a lost boy lurked.

Oh God! The queue was taking for ever.

She had gleaned a fair amount of business around Milan – office equipment, furniture, clothing – but she could get more, she considered. A leading advertising agency had promised to place their car, liqueur and fashion advertisements in *Leadership*'s European supplement, which came out quarterly and which made a huge profit.

Her last stopover would be Malta, where some crazy expatriate Brit wanted to push his conference centre and holiday villas. She had never been to Malta and she was looking forward to the luxury of being alone and getting a tan.

The trip had come at a bad time. For months she had been nagging Joe to move their offices to London. Then suddenly, inexplicably, he had agreed to move and sell off his Dover-based interests, including the ship's chandler's. Why now? she wondered. Perhaps it was because she was away, which meant that he would be free to find his own premises. She was aware that Joe was losing interest in publishing, but it did not matter so much because he was no longer indispensable. The fact that he took all their spare cash for commodity broking worried her greatly, on the other hand. She had everything she wanted, but so far she had never seen a penny of their profits.

Ah. At last! She flicked her passport at the official and he waved her through.

Suddenly she was in Angelo's arms. As always she was caught off-guard by his blatant sex appeal, the scent of his skin and the sheer joy of gazing into his laughing brown eyes. At this moment he was the only man in the world and she felt happy in the here and now.

When they reached his apartment they made love with the urgency of two people in love who have been long parted, ripping their clothes off in feverish haste, clutching and panting and reaching a peak, only to scale another.

'I love you,' Angelo said as she lay on his shoulder feeling happy and dreamy.

'Silly boy. You lust after me.'

'That, too. I dream of you always. Why don't you believe me when I say that I love you? Do you love me?'

She took hold of his beautiful hand and ran her tongue over his long fingers, licking the palm, stroking the hairs on his arm. 'Love doesn't exist, or if it does it's pure agony. Don't talk to me about love. Talk about lust. You're so beautiful, Angelo. Just looking at you turns me on. Don't ask for words. Don't actions count louder than words? Just feel how I lust after you.'

She lay over him, cupping his face between her hands, straddling her legs over his thighs, while she smothered him with light little kisses, pressing her lips over his, tickling his tongue with the tip of hers.

He groaned softly, so she bent lower and sucked his nipples, writhing her body over his belly.

'Insatiable bitch,' he whispered, drawing her down onto the pillow. 'I've never met anyone like you. I want you all the time, always. I love you.'

There was that silly expression again. How could

he love her when she knew herself to be unlovable? She wondered vaguely what he meant by it, and then stopped conscious thought, giving herself up to voluptuous delight as Angelo began all over again.

Like Cinderella, her dream exploded exactly at midnight.

She was lying on Angelo's shoulder, replete and content, laughing uncontrollably at the cruel gossip he was relating about his friends, who were Roman aristocrats, politicians and artists.

He stopped talking, sipped his wine and folded his arms around her, nuzzling his nose against hers.

'Darling,' he said. 'I have a wonderful surprise for you.'

'Oh yes?' She yawned.

'My aunt died.'

'Shame on you! How can that be wonderful?'

'She was very old and now I am very rich.'

'Oh, Angelo, I'm happy for you, but I hope you won't give up painting. You'll be famous soon.'

'Naturally not. But I am planning to get married.'

'I shall miss you,' she whispered, feeling a deep and genuine sense of loss. There were tears in her eyes as she clutched him. 'Darling, Angelo. You're the best,' she whispered, meaning it.

'But you don't understand? I am going to marry you.'

Sleepiness fled. She sat up, eyes wide, her heart hammering. 'Marry me?' she whispered. 'But Pierre, I can't marry you.'

'Who the fuck is Pierre?'

'I mean Helmut . . . I mean Angelo. Oh hell!' She

climbed out of bed, grabbed her wine, and swallowed it in a gulp.

He glared at her, one eyebrow raised as his eyes reproached her. 'I have often wondered about you and all your trips,' he said sulkily. 'This time I am coming with you. We shall be married in London.'

Marjorie refilled their glasses and got back into bed. Propped on one elbow she tried to explain about her life. At home she was the dedicated career woman and mother to her fatherless child. There was no place for a man in her life. She had to live it up on her European trips, packing a few weeks' joy into the odd snatched hour.

'Then I shall follow you round on your trips, like your little dog, and I'll pay my own air fares.'

'But you can't. You see, this is your territory. You can't come to Munich, or Brussels . . .'

She didn't make a very good job of explaining. Angelo turned away with a gesture of exasperation. 'You are perfidious, like all the British. You have a man in every airport, just like your proverbial British sailor.'

'What's British got to do with it?' she snarled. 'Don't tell me I'm the only woman in your life.'

Angelo, she learned for the first time, was a practised sulker, and she spent as little time with him as possible during the rest of her stay in Milan. It was a relief when she left for Hamburg, but he waylaid her at the door. 'Give up this silly life and find yourself some happiness,' he muttered. 'You think you're winning, but you're wrong. Find a man and marry him. What good is your career to you? Can it hug you in bed? Can it make you feel warm and loved and happy? A woman without a husband is only half of what she could be.'

'Grow up and join the twentieth century, Angelo,'

she yelled as she pushed her way past him, lugging her suitcase.

'I won't offer to carry your things to the taxi. I wouldn't like to insult you,' he said, watching her struggle.

She wept in the taxi, but for the life of her, she couldn't work out why.

Chapter 40

As soon as she saw Joe waiting behind the barriers at Heathrow panic surged. 'Why are you here? What's wrong? It's Lana, isn't it?' She grabbed his arm.

'Hey! Nothing's wrong. Calm down,' he said.

'So why *are* you here?'

'Don't you like being met?'

'Sure. Don't you like answering questions?' Her alarm had fled and she was able to grin at him and notice how good he looked. His eyes and teeth glittered from his darkly tanned face. Deep grooves lined his cheeks nowadays, but his dark curly hair still hung to his shoulders. As always, she regretted whatever it was that had flipped their relationship into a brother-sister affair. She hugged him affectionately.

He grinned. 'I have a surprise for you. I've bought a building for us.'

Stunned, she stepped back and shot him a look of pure fury. It was funny how her intuition was always right, so why did she consistently ignore it?

'Damn you, Joe,' she managed to stammer. 'I knew you'd wait until I was out of the way. Don't you think I might have wanted to have some say in deciding where I'm going to work?'

'Even better news.' He shot her a sidelong look with

a hint of a shame-faced smile, pointedly ignoring her anger. 'We've moved. That's why I'm here.'

'You've moved in a month? You couldn't take transfer that fast.'

'True! That's why we're paying rent.'

She lapsed into sulky silence as he led her to the car. On the way to London she decided she was acting like a fool and wasting valuable time. It was done now, so she put aside her bad temper and recounted the many instructions, requests, new contracts and editorial ideas that she had picked up in Europe.

An hour later she was only halfway through her news when Joe parked his Jaguar in a leafy Knightsbridge square, where tall, austere terraced houses faced onto a pretty railed private park. It looked very quiet, very exclusive, very rich.

Hans Place, she read in shock. 'What did this cost us?' She almost choked with fear.

'A hundred thousand pounds.'

'A fortune! We'll be in debt for the rest of our lives.'

'I've told you before, leave the finance to me.'

'Oh,' she gasped. Joe could be infuriating. Now his mouth was pressed into a thin, tight line and he was giving her that odd sidelong look she hated so. He parked in a private residents' bay and she followed him up the steps and into the house, admiring its grey and white tiled floors, the pale blue and white decor, the paintings of birds around the walls, and the Swedish furniture. A new receptionist sat behind a large L-shaped desk. She was exceptionally lovely, with huge blue eyes, perfect features and an amazing figure. Her cool appraisal and dismissal of Marjorie as competition hurt.

'This is my partner, Marjorie. Marjorie, meet Helga from Sweden,' he said.

Marjorie waved and tried to smile. 'My, you have been busy. How much does she cost?' she whispered spitefully as they moved towards the passage.

Marjorie inspected the house in grim silence, starting with the reception on the ground floor and the sales offices behind it, with a separate room for her office. It was a light and airy room with a high ceiling and it overlooked a tree at the back. On the first floor Garth Clark presided over the *Leadership* team. Editorial staff of the trade magazines took up the third and fourth floors and Joe had kept the top floor for his private use. That was where he gambled all their money away. Something would have to be done about it.

'Aren't you forgetting to say something?' Joe grumbled when they were back where they had started.

'What's in the basement?'

'Circulation and accounts. There's something else you forgot.'

'Like what?'

'Like thanks.'

'We'll probably go bust paying off the mortgage,' she muttered gloomily. 'It's far too smart. You should have waited for me. Besides, even if it's perfect, even if it cost next to nothing, you had no right.' She didn't want to look at him. Fighting with Joe always hurt her. Instead she moodily played with her fingers.

'You always behave as if we're married and you hold the purse strings,' she went on. 'It's not like that at all, Joe. I think you have some explaining to do.'

When she did shoot a glance his way she saw how fury had twisted his mouth and hurt had narrowed his eyes. How well she knew him. Too well, she decided.

'Listen, Marjorie, my pet, I've created a property company that owns this building and I own the controlling interest in this company, so I do hold the purse strings. That's because I put in more cash than you. Understood? I sold the Dover building and a warehouse I owned near the docks, and last month I found a buyer for my ship's chandler's business.'

'What!' She rounded on him in a fury. 'All that in a month? Pull the other one, Joe.'

'But Marjorie, listen to me, I've been working towards this for the past year. I knew we'd have to make this move, but it took me longer than I expected to get my price. Let's face it, you've been nagging me silly.'

She ignored his rebuke. 'So how much of all this do I own? Half of the half?'

'You personally, nothing, but our publishing company owns forty-nine per cent and I personally own fifty-one per cent. We shall jointly pay off the bond over a twenty-year period. Satisfied?'

'I would have liked to have been involved. You don't understand me at all. It's not the money, it's the fun.' She was still hurting.

'Perhaps I do. Perhaps I want you to stick to sales, since that's an area where you excel,' he said softly.

'Insinuating what exactly?'

'That I happen to have a flair for property and finance.'

'How much am I worth, Joe? I mean, it would be nice to know.'

'Hard to say. Let's wait a bit. The auditors will be with

us soon. Let's hear what they have to say.' As usual, he was neatly side-stepping the confrontation.

It was funny how Joe's voice got lower when he was depressed. Right now it was little more than a bear's growl. Perhaps he'd made a couple of mistakes and he needed time to cover up. She decided to give it a break for a while, but not too long.

Marjorie decided to pressurise Joe for a little information. She invited him to lunch at her special nook, the Verbenella restaurant in Beauchamp Place, which was just around the corner from her office and the scene of many of her more important sales. Something about the intimate atmosphere and the food, which was sheer artistry, never failed to soften up her clients. 'Bring all the figures, Joe. I want to know what's going on,' she insisted.

She could not help feeling worried. According to Joe her savings continued to multiply, but all she ever saw were lists of profits resulting from commodity deals. She had no idea what she was worth, other than her share of the publishing company, and as for cash, she seldom saw it. They lived on credit and every last penny was confiscated by Joe. Was he a gambler? Were they in trouble? If so, she had to know. She knew she would back Joe with every penny she owned, but she had to put a stop to this.

'Joe,' she began as tactfully as she could, somewhere between the calves' liver and the *crème brûlée*, specialities of the house, 'what am I worth?'

'Your weight in gold, Marjorie, and I've told you so often enough.' Arguing with Joe was as bad as playing chess with him. You lost!

'How much money do I own?' she persisted. 'I mean, apart from the publishing company, are you actually making profits with all this frenetic activity?'

'I should hope so. I'd hate to waste so many years for nothing.'

'But Joe, where are all our publishing profits?'

'Invested. Where did you expect to find them? In gold nuggets under the bed?'

He was looking stony-faced and his eyes challenged her to persist.

She persisted. 'Come on, Joe.' She snapped her fingers under his nose. 'Give! What am I worth? Where's the cash? I need to buy my parents a house. Join the twentieth century. Women run their own affairs, hadn't you heard? Besides, we're not married.'

'Financially speaking, being fifty-fifty partners is worse than being married,' Joe said gloomily.

She would try another tack. 'Joe, I'm twenty-three. I want to spend some of my cash and have fun before it's too late.'

'What would you call too late?'

'Thirty!'

'Okay, I promise before you're thirty I'll wind up the investment company.'

She'd fallen into that trap neatly. Foolish Marjorie. She gave up and devoted herself to her dessert.

Silence seemed to work better than nagging, she noticed with surprise. Joe squirmed and fidgeted and cleared his throat and behaved rather like her advertisers who faced a long and dismal silence after she had popped the vital question.

'Listen,' he began. 'You own a fifty per cent stake in the investment company. That's because I started

240 *Madge Swindells*

off by using our cash, which means you get fifty per cent of all the profits, so I don't know what you're moaning about.'

Silently she turned her attention to sipping her coffee.

'I know you think you're smart, Marjorie, since they made you Marketing Woman of the Year, but you succeeded on my ideas,' Joe persisted. 'Now, Miss Grasping . . .'

He fumbled in his briefcase and thumped some papers on the table between them. 'Here's the details of every one of my, or rather *our*, deals. It will take you a while to work this lot out. These papers are your copies. Take them to your accountant, if you have one. The bottom line is here.' He flipped the pages over and she noticed that his fingers were as agile as a card sharp's. 'Your share . . .' He pointed to a figure: £1.2 million.

'Wow! Can't I spend some of it?'

'This figure is on paper only. The cash is in shares and commodities, all sorts of things. It's not easy to get hold of hard cash when the money's out working for us. If we suddenly sold our holdings we might not realise that much.'

'My God! I thought you were ruining us. Why do you have to play so close to the cuff?' She smiled with relief. 'Big oaks from little acorns . . .' Then she flushed and closed her mouth. Mother's clichés lurked in her genes, in remission, but always there, waiting for a weak moment to burst out.

'I'm a millionaire,' she said. It took some getting used to. Strangely, there was no joy, and it took her a minute or two to work out why this was.

'Joe,' she began gently. 'I don't want you to think that I'm not grateful, but really I long to be the captain of my own ship. I've worked hard to build this publishing company. I'm proud of what I've accomplished. I don't feel proud about this at all.' She pointed to the papers on the table. 'You see, you did it all. I didn't even know, let alone help. Well, thanks, but Joe, I want to take charge of my own life. I'm sure you understand me. I'm just not the little woman type. Maybe once I might have been, but not any more. I learned to stand on my own feet and that's the way I like it. One of these days, at your convenience, I want out.'

Joe was hurting, she knew, but she had only told the truth. He left shortly afterwards and Marjorie went on to her next appointment wondering if she were wrong. Perhaps being the little woman had its own unique advantages. She could not help remembering Angelo's warning.

Part 3 – Hamish
June 1977 – December 1978

Chapter 41

————— ———

Marjorie's first meeting with Hamish Cameron was memorable, but for all the wrong reasons, she was to decide later. Her temper erupted, something that rarely happened, and she behaved as if she'd never left Dover's dockside. 'Screw you,' she told the astonished man. 'And screw this company and your damn feature.' So saying, she had tipped her notes and the layout into the nearest bin and stalked out.

Later she came about as close as she ever had to an apology. 'So I lost control, but it only lasted a minute.'

'So does an earthquake,' Hamish had retorted.

She had first got on to a slow boil on Wednesday morning at exactly ten a.m., when she was lying in bed in her Chelsea flat enjoying a cup of coffee and a book. London was experiencing a warm and balmy June, and Marjorie was about to shower, dress and saunter off to meet Lana and Mum at the station. They were going shopping and later they would return to Dover together. Marjorie was looking forward to a short break with Lana. What bliss. She wondered what to wear as she stretched and lay back, smiling at nothing in particular.

Then the telephone shattered her good humour. It was Garth, at his most neurotic.

'David's hurt his back and there's absolutely no one

available to fly up to Inverness at short notice,' he explained. 'It's an important survey; several thousand pounds are involved. What difference does it make if you shop next week instead of this week?'

The difference was not something Garth Clark would understand, she decided gloomily, replacing the receiver. He had no children.

That was yesterday, a spoiled day, with Mum asking her pointedly who worked for whom at her office and Lana crying with disappointment. And after all that she'd wasted this entire morning waiting in the draughty reception area of Glenaird Distillery.

Marjorie scowled and glanced at her watch briefly. Seeing that it was almost one, her irritation mounted, driving away sleepiness. She had flown up from Heathrow, via Glasgow, to Inverness, carrying her camera and tape recorder, to start pre-planning a supplement on the 100th Anniversary of Glenaird Distillery. Her appointment had been for eleven and she was furious.

She never waited longer than half an hour for anyone, not even in the old days, and least of all for John Erskine, MD, a man to whom she had taken an intense dislike although she had not yet met him. How can he do this? she wondered. The days of waiting around and begging for appointments were ancient history as far as she was concerned. Nowadays red carpet treatment was the norm. She felt affronted, yet a part of her could not help laughing at her newly acquired arrogance. After another fifteen minutes had dragged by, she stood up.

'Okay, he wins, I'm leaving,' she told the receptionist with a sigh.

She turned as she heard a deep voice say: 'Mr Erskine's

been unexpectedly called out. Maybe I can help you. What's the problem? Why are you here?'

She was surprised to find that this deep, attractive voice belonged to the caretaker or repairman. Not the type you'd expect to see in these prim offices, she considered, quickly noticing his rough corduroy trousers and checked short-sleeved shirt, and his kind, but subservient manner. It was then that she lost her temper. How dare they fob her off with him!

It was only when she was striding across the car park that she recovered enough to remember that she had come by taxi. She would have to walk the five miles to Inverness, or hitch, or crawl back foolishly and ask to use the telephone, so it was a relief to hear footsteps running behind her.

'Don't be like that,' she heard. 'At least have some coffee. Look here, I rescued your layout from the bin.'

It was him again and he looked both amused and concerned. His was the first friendly face she had seen that morning, so she smiled back gratefully.

'Okay, I suppose coffee is exactly what I need the most.'

Taking her arm, he guided her back to the receptionist. 'Tell Mr Erskine that I've taken Miss . . . ?' he glanced enquiringly at her.

'Marjorie Hardy.'

'Miss Hardy to the canteen.' He led her along the passage to a large canteen with a self-service bar at the end.

'Sit here, Miss Hardy.' He pulled back a chair. 'What would you like? I'm afraid the menu is limited to fish, hamburgers or chicken and chips. Or perhaps you would prefer a toasted sandwich?'

'Oh, thanks. A sandwich would be fine. And coffee, please, but let me come with you. I must pay for my food.'

'No, no, it's on the house.'

As her rescuer moved along the queue, sweet and apologetic, smiling at everyone, she studied his oriental eyes, high cheekbones, delicate nose, and the shock of straight black hair that kept tumbling over his face, only to be swept back again. No one so beautiful should be so damned humble, she decided.

When he returned he hovered as if he was afraid to sit with her. 'Oh, please, join me. Where's your coffee?'

'Yes, maybe I will. I don't usually eat here.' He returned to the queue.

Ah! she sighed inwardly. The cheese was exactly right, soft and melting Gouda, and the toast was crisp and smothered with real butter. She began to feel better.

'I'm grateful to you,' she said as her rescuer returned with his tray and another coffee for her.

He shrugged. 'I saw you sitting there once or twice as I passed. You were getting so pale and so angry.'

'And it showed?'

He laughed.

She decided to explain. 'You see, I came here in place of someone else. It was a last-minute arrangement. I was supposed to be on holiday, and Lana . . .' She flushed. 'My parents have adopted a little girl who's four and I . . . well, I love her very much. She was so looking forward to the holiday. She cried and that upset me. It's awful to disappoint children. D'you have any?'

He shook his head. 'I'm not married.'

'Well, neither am I.' She felt herself blushing. 'Anyway, after all that, it was too much to feel that I'd wasted the morning. Though it's my own fault really ... I antagonised your MD when I called.

'My company are publishing a supplement on Glenaird's hundredth birthday and when I realised I'd have to come, I called to say that I'd also like to meet your chairman, Hamish Cameron, and feature him on the cover of our magazine, *Leadership*. I always plan the covers, you see,' she explained. 'Mr Erskine warned me that Hamish Cameron would be hard to find, somewhere amongst the Alps and dead drunk to boot. He hinted that he'd do instead and I sort of turned him down. So here I am.'

She broke off. 'I shouldn't be gossiping like this. Let's talk about you. I don't even know your name. What do you do here?'

'As little as possible, actually. Sometimes I check the place is clean and take a look around.'

So he was the caretaker, although with all those rippling muscles and his strong, sinewy neck, he could also be the stockman. She could not help stealing glances at his strong tanned hands. Only his voice was wrong.

'So where did you get that posh English accent of yours?' she asked.

His face showed his shock. He was deeply offended, and the temperature was rapidly reaching minus zero. Suddenly she realised that he'd assumed she was referring to his oriental appearance. Hastily, she set about putting things right.

'I mean a brawny Scot like you should have a Highland accent, shouldn't you?' She smiled brightly, refusing to look embarrassed, outfacing him. 'I bet you toss those cabers all over the place.'

She was reprieved from death by freezing, but only just.

'Och aye, lassie, I can talk like that if you want, but I went to an English school, although it was based in Edinburgh.'

He wasn't sure that he had forgiven her, she could see. She suspected he was ultra-sensitive to slights and always on his guard, so she set about putting him at ease. It wasn't very difficult. He just wanted to be a true Scot, so they talked about the Highland Games and she discovered he could play the bagpipes.

She was on her third cup of coffee when a tall grey man with predatory eyes and a mean mouth hurried towards them.

'Miss Hardy,' he called out. 'I'll see you now.'

She pushed back her chair, but her companion put his hand on her arm. 'Join us, if you like, John,' he snapped without a tinge of subservience. 'Have some coffee. All Miss Hardy wants is me. She's got me, so there's no need for her to hurry away.'

Marjorie felt flustered. Could he be . . . ? Was he . . . ? 'Are you . . . ?' she murmured.

Hamish Cameron winked.

'Well, since you've met our chairman I'll leave you to make your arrangements, but as I explained on the telephone, Hamish has very little to do with the running of this business. He's chairman in name only.'

She glanced sidelong at Hamish, who was nodding his affirmation. She wondered why this made her feel so angry.

'As a matter of fact, I hate business,' he muttered, looking shame-faced. 'Perhaps you should feature Mr Erskine on your cover after all. I'm not really suitable.'

Why was he so damned craven? She wanted to shake him.

'On the contrary, Mr Cameron, you are exactly what we want.' She was ad-libbing, groping for inspiration. 'I've been looking at some of your Glenaird advertisements. Being a rugged outdoor Scot is synonymous with drinking scotch, or so your advertising team would have us believe. They use fancy models and props to create an image that they already have. I mean, they have you. Ironic, isn't it? That's one of the things we want to write about.'

The idea appealed to her. She was unwilling to let Hamish fade out of her life; he intrigued her. Besides, he was kind, and how many men were kind? Moreover, even his modest manner could not disguise the underlying passion of his nature, or quell the beam of sexual attraction in his slanting black eyes.

'When are you returning to London?' he wanted to know.

'Tomorrow night.'

'Are you busy tonight, or would you have dinner with me? We could talk business if you insist.'

Afterwards Marjorie often thought about the extraordinary twist of fate that had allowed her to meet Hamish. He seldom went to the plant, but on this occasion the accountant had required his signature. And on her side, David, their features editor, was back at work the following day, his back much improved. When Garth called to tell her she could come back and enjoy the rest of her holiday, she pointed out that she might as well finish the job she'd started and she would be staying on until the end of the week.

Chapter 42

It was Marjorie's last night in Inverness and they were dining in a small exclusive pub near the river. Hamish was toying with his food, clearly upset that she was leaving in the morning, and she had to admit she would be sorry to leave, too. Hamish was fun to be with and he was a superb dancer. He liked music, but most of all he loved climbing and he told her about it at length, but she was never bored. She sensed that he would make a passionate and caring lover, but she would never become involved with a customer, or anyone connected with their magazine. She watched the lamplight flickering on his sensuous, mobile lips as he tried to persuade her to stay another day.

'Tell me about you,' she commanded. 'It's my last chance. I want to know all there is to know.'

He smiled sadly at her. 'Where shall I start?'

'Start at the end, of course, and move slowly backwards.'

'All right. If you really want this sordid story. Here I am, having dinner with the most beautiful woman in the world, and she's clever, too. And I can't for the life of me work out how I got so lucky, and whether or not she'll come again, particularly when I tell her that the chances are I won't be chairman of Glenaird for much longer.'

'Why ever not?' She was disturbed by the despair in his voice.

'Glentirran Distillers are making a bid for Glenaird and I think they'll win . . .'

She sat up in shock. Did he mean Robert's Glentirran? 'What is it? What's the matter?'

'No, it's nothing. I was wondering if you meant Glentirran of Edinburgh, owned by the MacLaren family. I mean, they sometimes advertise . . .' She was lying badly, but Hamish did not notice.

'Yes, but I don't want to bore you. I shouldn't have brought it up.'

'Bore me,' she commanded.

'My family want me out, particularly Andrew Cameron, my uncle, who is in league with Glentirran management. He's helping them in their takeover bid. I have a strong suspicion that John Erskine is with them, too.'

His story came in fragments throughout dinner while she laboriously fitted the pieces together.

Robert and his stepmother, Rhoda MacLaren, were heavily involved in a takeover bid of Glenaird Distillery, which, she had already learned, produced a superior pure malt whisky. Glenaird, she gathered now, was badly run. It was a private company and the shares were mainly owned by the Cameron family.

'I should fight them, but I have the feeling they'll win anyway. Besides, I don't have the power to win, and even if I did, I wouldn't have the cash to revitalise Glenaird. This is probably better for shareholders, since I have no talent for business,' he wound up, looking sad.

'Stop putting yourself down,' she begged him. She could not help identifying with Hamish. They were both Robert's victims and this was a kind of bond, she reasoned.

Suddenly Marjorie did not want to leave Inverness. She was intrigued by the possibilities this confrontation presented.

'I'm longing to know all there is to know about you. For starters, why do you have such an abysmal self-image?'

He smiled sleepily and tenderly at her. 'Perhaps because I am the most unlikable and unlikely boy ever to inherit a distillery and a stately home, or so I was told. Whoever heard of an Asiatic coolie heading the clan?'

'Stop it! Don't put yourself down so.' She placed one hand over his and squeezed hard as she realised how incredibly satisfying it would be to provoke Hamish into beating Robert.

'Start again. Start at the beginning this time,' she said firmly.

It was a sad story that emerged. Hamish's father, Simon, found himself head of the family at an early age, and since his father had gambled away most of the family's wealth in gaming and bad business ventures, Simon left home at twenty-one to try to recoup the family fortune. His plan was to resurrect their almost defunct Hong Kong trading house.

He soon fell in love with his Japanese business advisor, Hamish's mother, and married her, but after one trip home to introduce her to the family, they agreed never to return. They both died in a car crash when Hamish was eight and he was sent back to Scotland.

'To say that I was unwelcome would be a gross understatement,' Hamish confided. 'If it weren't for me, Ian, my cousin, would have been in direct line for the farmlands, the cattle, the home and the distillery. I was a pariah, an oriental cuckoo defiling the clan, a yellow belly, as I was called by Ian's friends. I was too young to understand that I had cost them a fortune, simply by being alive. It was well and truly drummed into me that I had no right to my name, my home or my heritage.'

'But you fought back?' She grabbed his hand and pressed it, trying to instil some of her own fierce aggression into him by force of will.

'At eight years old? With little English? Sadly, no, Marjorie. I learned to sublimate my feelings, to turn anger to depression, aggression to passivity, and I kept to myself. I couldn't get back to Hong Kong, but I could go up into the mountains, and I did, for days at a time.'

'I should have been there to fight for you.'

She longed to erase the hurt in his eyes, so she leaned forward and kissed his eyelids, then brought his hand up and pressed it hard against her cheek. 'Oh Hamish,' she whispered.

His hand lifted her chin and very gently he brushed his lips over hers. Then he pulled away.

She wondered why one kiss could be so extraordinarily encompassing. She looked around nervously, but no one was watching. Then she realised she was still clinging to his hand, and Hamish was still talking.

'So I may not be the chairman for that much longer. I'm sorry, Marjorie.'

But why was he apologising to her?

'I think we'd better leave. Feel like a walk?' he asked. 'There's a lovely path along by the river below. We can go down in the lift.'

'Yes, let's,' she agreed.

Something about the loneliness of the night and the bright moonlight seemed to bond them in a strange intimacy. She found herself telling him about her life – how she had longed to go to university and her bitter disappointment when she realised she couldn't do so. Then she told him about Corsica and Lana and how she had taken herself to Wales.

'Don't ever ask who her father is or where he comes from because I shall never tell anyone,' she confided. 'Lana has no father and that's the way it will always be. People think she's adopted – well, she is, so that's the truth. I don't know why I told you this. I'm sorry.'

'Perhaps you feel as I feel.' He stopped and leaned against the wall and pulled her close to him. She gasped as she felt the strength of his arms and his back. Her hands moved up to his neck and that was hard and muscled, too. She gazed at him, taking in all of him. His eyes were so expressive she could read every expression: there was hope, there was a lurking smile and there was a strong passivity that contrasted strangely with his physical prowess. He was expecting and accepting defeat, she realised.

On impulse she ran her hands through his thick black hair. Her hands slid down to those beautiful, wide cheeks and pulled his face towards her. She watched him carefully, her eyes wide open as he closed his eyes. Softly she placed her lips against his. She felt his body tense, and his arms were like a steel trap around her, but his lips were soft and melting against hers, his tongue was touching and feeling. Then she felt his penis throbbing hot and hard against her.

'Oh,' she gasped. 'Oh, Hamish.' Her desire was so

intense she almost fell. He steadied her and pushed her gently away.

'Why are you so devastatingly sexy?' she sighed, when she had pulled herself together.

'Perhaps because I am so hideously ugly.'

'Is that what you think?' Her voice emerged like a high-pitched squeak and they both laughed. 'Oh Hamish, if only you knew.'

Later, when she returned to her lonely hotel bed, she felt obsessed with strange regrets. Hamish had begged her to stay on for the weekend, but she had refused. Should she have stayed? No! she told herself firmly. It would have been totally wrong, because she missed Lana so much and her daughter was always longing for the weekends. Eventually she fell asleep and slept restlessly, waking often, murmuring Hamish's name.

Chapter 43

————— ——— ———

Fresh flowers arrived at Marjorie's office daily and Hamish called whenever he could from his Peruvian base, where he was leading a team of British climbers up the Huascaran Mountain. He loved her, he said, but Marjorie was full of doubts. It was not her he loved, but the image of himself that he saw in her eyes. He should not be so trusting. Surely he was naïve for his twenty-eight years? She wondered how she would handle the situation when he returned.

After two weeks of indecision, she went to seek help from Joe. Pausing in the doorway, she asked herself wryly why she was expecting Joe to be any help, when he was such a huge source of anxiety to her himself. He appeared to have lost interest in publishing. Even his inventions were taking a back seat. Now he sat surrounded with charts and graphs listing every company on the London Stock Exchange. One wall was devoted to commodity trading and this was the section he was currently engrossed in. Then he beamed up at her, and she remembered how very fond of him she was.

'I want to talk to you about Hamish Cameron.' She sat down at his desk and crossed her legs. She was pleased that at last she was able to participate actively in Joe's other interests.

'Robert MacLaren of Glentirran is heavily involved in a takeover bid of his biggest rival, Glenaird Distillery. I stumbled on this by chance because David hurt his back and I had to fly up to plan Glenaird's anniversary feature. There's dirty work at the crossroads, I can tell you.'

She paused, waiting for a response, but Joe made no comment. She wondered if he resented her intrusion into an area that had been exclusively his own. 'I thought you'd be interested,' she persisted. 'Surely this is the type of opportunity you're always looking out for, a chance to make a quick profit? That's what we do, isn't it?'

Joe sighed. 'True, but . . . okay, who owns Glenaird?'

'Well, it's complicated. A trust company, actually. Of course, they hold the shares, land, stately home, et cetera, on behalf of the first male heir, namely Hamish Cameron. He's more interested in climbing mountains than running the distillery. He hates business, but he's agreed to be featured on our cover when we publish the survey.

'The distillery is a private company, and the shares were originally owned exclusively by the Cameron family, but years back about half were parcelled off in small lots to various children, and are now mainly owned by their progeny.

'Hamish's problem is that he only owns twenty-six per cent of the company (or the trust does), and family shareholders control the rest, except for those bought by Glentirran recently. So although Hamish is the biggest single shareholder, he can be outvoted if the great-aunts and others get together. Actually, they're scattered all over the place and some of them are abroad, but it seems that Glentirran are trying to pick them off, one by one. They've joined up with Hamish's Uncle Andrew, who owns a small parcel of shares, and they're offering to buy out other family members. They're picking up the shares for a song. I'd love to thwart them – as long as we're not harming Hamish, or putting him out of business,' she added hastily.

'You should know me better than that.' Joe scowled at her.

'So I've been thinking that we could buy up some of the shares and put a spoke in Robert MacLaren's wheel. What d'you think?'

'Off the cuff, I don't know. I'll get busy on it. Oh, and thanks for the idea.'

'Since we're fifty-fifty partners in this investment business, I should come up with some of the ideas, shouldn't I?'

Joe controlled his annoyance with an obvious effort. 'Come on. I'll buy you lunch. Let's go.'

Joe's enthusiasm was sadly lacking until some days later when he bounded into her office, just as she was on the telephone to Hamish. She grinned and waved him into a chair.

'Phew!' She replaced the receiver. 'It must be costing him to call so often.'

'Was that Hamish?'

She nodded. 'He's flying back from Peru today.'

'Poor bloke! Managing that distillery must be like running the gauntlet between two rows of greedy great-aunts armed with steel-tipped brollies. You'll be pleased to hear that we've acquired a small part of the action, hopefully enough to put a spoke in Glentirran's wheel. I have other ideas, but I have to speak to Hamish first.'

'Such as?'

'Oh, nothing that I would like him to know right now, since I haven't made up my mind, but one possibility is to lend him cash secured by malt maturing in barrels. Glentirran are playing dirty, although it's rumoured that the real villains are Andrew, Hamish's uncle, and his son, Ian. It was they who appointed John Erskine as MD and he's definitely playing the game their way. It's rumoured that he reports to Rhoda MacLaren, Robert's stepmother.'

'Is that possible?' she queried. 'That's wicked. I must say I didn't like him.'

'Hamish's problem is that he inherited the distillery when he was eight and his Uncle Andrew was running the show, so he's never been able to regain proper control. That's if he ever tried.

'Apparently Andrew Cameron has a deal with Glentirran that they will form a new subsidiary to market the best malt from both subsidiaries and he will run it, until his son, Ian, takes over.'

'Heavens! How d'you know all this?'

'Believe it or not, in cases where shares prices are involved, I commission the services of an industrial intelligence investigator.'

'That's a long word for a spy!'

'He wouldn't like that,' Joe chuckled. 'Ex-Cambridge, doctorate in economics, huge fees, that sort.'

'A spy's a spy.'

'Have it your own way.'

'I don't understand why Hamish is chairman, since he only owns twenty-six per cent of the action.'

'Wrong! He doesn't own anything. The trust does, and the trust is controlled by trustees who act for the benefit of the male heir, namely Hamish. Grampian

Bank hold twenty-five per cent of the shares, pledged
by the trustees on the request of Hamish's father, and
not redeemed within the stipulated time.

'It's the bank that have the power. They would shift
their allegiance if a sufficient number of shareholders
wished them to do that and if the shareholders could
prove that a change of ownership would benefit the
distillery. So far they have not been able to persuade
the bank to transfer their loyalties.'

'It's complicated. Poor Hamish. So how much have
we got?'

'So far, about three per cent.'

'One last point, whatever we do can't harm Hamish,
can it?'

'Perhaps it might, in a way. We'll be prolonging the
agony by helping him to hang in there. Anyway, before
going further, I'd like to talk to him, so hang on until
we've purchased a few more shares. It's difficult with a
private company, but friends are looking out for me.'

'Be quick. I've got Hamish dangling at the end of a
line.'

'He's used to that. At least he's not freezing to
death.'

'He will soon, I'm feeling the strain,' she countered.

'It's not as if he's an ogre,' Joe argued. 'I saw the cover
proofs. He's beautiful.'

'Yes,' she admitted, 'if you accept him as he is, but
in his eyes he's the ugliest man in Scotland.'

'Why?'

'Because his coal black eyes slant the wrong way for
him, because his skin is golden instead of raw pink,
because his hair is jet black, thick and luxuriant, instead
of mousy and balding . . .'

'Okay, I get it. I'm almost ready to talk to him. I'm working on a second cousin and a great-aunt. It won't be very difficult to persuade them to let go because profits have been minimal. Most of the shareholders aren't well off and depend upon their Glenaird profits.'

'Oh!' That hurt a little and she wondered why. 'Are you still playing around with sooty bricks?' she teased, changing the subject.

'Not any more. The research is finished. I've taken out world patents. So far I've sold dozens of franchises to builders anxious to clean up Britain's buildings. Receipts to date amount to more than a million. I stand to make a real fortune when I launch the system in America. My method's cheaper, easier and more effective than any other known system to date.'

Marjorie gasped and felt a painful pang. What was it – jealousy? No, she reasoned, only grief that their togetherness was crumbling more as each day passed. Joe and she would never be a team if he were a multi-millionaire.

'You sound like an advertising brochure,' she faltered, trying to hide her dismay.

'Possibly, since I was studying the one Garth's written only half an hour ago.' How remote he was.

'Want some coffee?' she asked.

'No thanks, Marjorie. I've got too much on.'

She watched him leave the room, feeling vaguely fearful of the future and more lonely than she had been for years.

Two days later she received a call from Joe. 'I'm ready. Ask Hamish for dinner – we'll make it a foursome – ostensibly a social evening.'

'It better bloody be a social evening. And remember your promise. We aren't pulling the plug on Hamish.'

'Yes, yes, we've been through all that.' He dismissed her fears impatiently. 'And Marjorie, I'm not entirely without morality or subtlety, in case you hadn't noticed.'

'Point taken. But Joe, who can you bring?'

'Possibly Véronique?'

'So who's Véronique?' she asked, feeling strangely shut out of Joe's life.

'You might have seen her face decorating those new French Primitif cosmetics.'

'*That* Véronique?'

'Why not? Even famous models eat.'

'Smugness, thy name is Joe Segal.' She flung down the receiver. Fancy Joe knowing a famous model. And why was he so studiously casual? She puzzled over this as she dialled Hamish's number.

Chapter 44

——— ———

Joe was in love. It was painful to watch his cool urbane manner crumple while his eyes glowed with spaniel devotion. Marjorie had never seen him look like this and it was strangely shocking. Once she had fancied he loved her, but she had been wrong, she knew that now. Joe in love was a man obsessed. She felt hurt, although she had to admit this was absurd. But why had he been so damned secretive? She had never heard about Véronique before yesterday.

Véronique was even lovelier in the flesh than on the labels of face cream, but she was the antithesis to the description Joe had always given of his ideal wife: warm, placid, hard-working, supportive, cultured, intelligent and preferably Jewish. Well, maybe she was clever, Marjorie conceded, but for the rest, forget it. Her looks were extraordinary. It stunned you just to look at her. She was too lovely to be real, with long, gleaming, platinum-blonde hair, dazzling violet eyes, perfect features and a flawless white skin. She looked Nordic, but she was French and even her accent was sexy.

As the evening wore on, it became obvious that Véronique was totally dedicated to her own well-being, and, to Marjorie's mind, she was pure ice. She became bored and impatient if anyone talked of anything other than her career, her looks or Joe's money. When she flickered her long talons around the table, Marjorie belatedly saw a sparkling diamond and emerald ring on her third finger.

'Oh my! What a magnificent ring. Are you, I mean . . . ?'

'We're engaged,' Joe murmured coolly.

'Didn't Joe tell you?' Véronique giggled triumphantly. 'It was all so sudden, wasn't it, Joe?'

Marjorie gulped. 'We must celebrate,' she declared through frozen lips.

'You order,' Joe retorted dismissively.

Marjorie beckoned the wine waiter and chose a good, dry champagne.

'I much prefer a sweet champagne if no one minds. How about my favourite, Joe, Laurent Perrier Crémant?' Véronique simpered, pouting prettily.

'Can't stand the stuff,' Joe growled, 'but if it makes you happy, sweetie.' His hand had been resting on her shoulder for most of the evening and clearly it was staying there.

Why not piss on her, if you must demonstrate your ownership? Marjorie screamed in silence.

Joe leaned forward and favoured Hamish with his best rendering of Simple Simon.

'Hamish, I'm dabbling a bit in shares and a little commodity broking, very amateurish, of course. I have a few Glenaird shares, and I hear your opposition are buying them. Any idea what they're paying? Have they made you an offer?'

Hamish shook his head and looked painfully awkward.

Joe was breaking his promise not to talk business to Hamish. And why hadn't he told her about Véronique?

Marjorie agonised. Clearly the bond between them was an illusion on her part. Who was she to Joe? she wondered. Was she merely someone who could sell? Someone whom Joe needed around? Their many recent fights whirled around in her head. What had he told her when she came back from Europe? 'Why don't you stick to selling? That's what you do best.'

Was that what their friendship was all about? she wondered glumly, nagged by memories and premonitions. She was useful to Joe, but that seemed to be the extent of it. She couldn't remember when they had last shared an evening together. How come she hadn't noticed that lately business was their only tie? She might as well be a carthorse. She had been labelled 'seller' and she was stuck with it. At that moment the years seemed to stretch ahead with horrid and predictable monotony.

Under the table, Hamish was pinching her knee, and Véronique's choice of champagne turned out to be sickly sweet.

They danced, and in between Joe told unfunny stories, and mercilessly probed Hamish for information, but Hamish mulishly resisted.

This was not the place to bring Hamish, Marjorie discovered. He hated it. He drank steadily, with the obvious target of getting as drunk as he could, just as soon as he could. As far as Marjorie was concerned the evening would go into her book of records as the worst ever.

When Hamish began to slur his words and knocked his glass over, Joe and Véronique stood up as one. Joe's arm was still locked firmly around her. 'I think I'd better take Véronique home. I'll leave you to cope with Hamish. Better get the waiters to help you. Sort out the bill, love. I'll settle with you in the office on Monday.'

She reeled with shock, unable to believe that he would leave her alone to cope with one very drunk guest, but he had. She kicked that around in her head and came to some more hurtful conclusions.

Oh well, she couldn't sit there all night. She called the manager, paid the bill and explained her predicament.

Discreetly and immediately two waiters hustled Hamish to a taxi as she hovered behind. No one had even noticed.

She took him home. What else could she do, she rationalised, since she had no idea where he was staying? Marjorie was an honest woman and she never conned herself. She was aware that her feelings for Hamish were highly conflicting. There was lust, and a genuine liking; and there was the knowledge that Hamish offered the means to thwart Robert, or maybe one day to hurt him badly. That idea came like a thunderclap and she shuddered as her arms came out in goose pimples. Why, Marjorie Hardy, whatever are you thinking? she chided herself. There was also the suspicion that Hamish needed her. But not love, never love. She had turned her back on that sort of nonsense.

Chapter 45

Marjorie woke at nine to find the sunlight streaming through the bedroom windows. She'd overslept. Damn! She sat up with a pang of guilt and then remembered it was Sunday. She sank back on the pillows and wondered why she was in London on a Sunday morning. A split second later memory returned and she scrambled out of bed and quickly threw some clothes on.

Peeping into her second bedroom she saw that Hamish was still asleep. He had kicked off the blankets, revealing his naked body, and the beauty of it took her breath way. A bolt of lust raced through her as she gazed at the dusky, golden softness of his skin. His limbs were lithe, sinewy, ultra muscular, his neck was long and strong. In sleep his face had lost his defensive, guarded expression and she saw the sensuousness of his full lips and flared nostrils. She couldn't resist bending forward and tracing the line of his high cheekbone with her index finger.

A hand shot out and caught hers and suddenly she was sprawled over him and he was laughing up at her.

'Caught you peeping,' he laughed. 'Now for the punishment,' but he merely kissed her, then rested her head on his shoulder. Wrapping his arms around her, he snuggled her close.

Lying next to Hamish in her blue cotton dress, with

his arms locked around her, lust surged and with it a sense of anxiety.

Last night she had wondered if she should marry him, but last night was last night and she had drunk too much champagne. Was she to squander all the love she bore Robert upon this man, and use him to punish the one she truly loved? Was that fair?

Hamish would never know, she reasoned. He'd never guess. She'd make him happy. Arranged marriages were as old as time and they worked. It was just that she was arranging it. So why did she feel like a whore? As Hamish tenderly stroked her breasts she began to get a glimpse of the road she had chosen. But it wasn't to be quite as simple as she had imagined. When she tried to pull Hamish onto her, he pushed her back.

'What good is sex without love and tenderness?' he asked gloomily. 'You don't feel that love for me, I sense it. I know it. You feel only lust.'

She felt so sad. She couldn't feel the sort of love he wanted from her. Not any more. She had loved Lana's father passionately, but she'd blocked off that side of herself. She used men: for selling, or for business, or quite simply for lust, and she would take good care never to love again. Yet she didn't want to hurt him.

But this was her secret. 'We've just met. Give me time,' she coaxed him. 'I feel so much for you already.'

'And in the meantime what do you have in mind for me?' he asked and she sensed he was very serious.

'Lots of good, healthy lust,' she answered, laughing.

Propping his weight on his elbows, he began kissing her face and her eyelids and her lips with light, tender kisses.

'Perhaps I have enough love for both of us.' He sighed

and stroked her cheek softly. Then he bent over her swiftly and kissed her and she felt his tongue probing her lips and caressing her tongue, thrusting into her mouth. He pulled back and began to tug at her dress with clumsy movements and she could feel his hot, panting breath on her neck. She reached back for the zip and her dress fell away as Hamish fumbled behind her and removed her bra. Throwing it aside, he pushed his lips over her nipples, each in turn, sucking and licking and tantalising her. She could feel his swollen flesh against the soft skin of her thighs, hot and throbbing, leaving a moist patch there. She gasped and writhed, pushing up at him. 'Please, please, oh please,' she implored him.

The air was charged with the musky scent of his sex. She shuddered at the immense strength of him as he lifted her with one hand and slid off her panties. Then he ran his tongue up the inside of her thighs, nuzzling, kissing, licking until he reached her cleft. When she felt his tongue caressing, flicking, moving, she cried out. The sensation was shocking; she could hardly breathe.

'Oh God! I didn't know . . . I never felt . . . Please . . .'

He kissed her gently on her belly button, moving his mouth over her body, exploring, searching, finding those special places that might drive her crazy. He turned her over and ran his hands over her back, nibbling her skin all over. His hot breath made her shudder.

Slowly he kissed the back of her thighs and let his tongue move down to her feet, flicking over her toes. When, at last, he turned her onto her back she was beyond caring. She lay abandoned and swollen, taking sharp little intakes of breath, throbbing with innumerable intense sensations. When his lips again reached her cleft she began to groan softly. She felt herself falling into a trough of sexuality.

'I want you.' She forced the words out of suffocated lungs. 'I need you. Do it, Hamish.'

'To erase the past?'

'You . . . you . . . I just want you. Please . . . Hamish,' she urged him in a long drawn out groan of agony.

It was like nothing she had ever experienced. He wooed her with his body, filling her with strange sensations, holding her hands pinned above her, clasped in his.

'I can't hang on much longer,' he whispered.

He tensed and groaned and rolled his hips, arching his back, pushing up into her belly, thrusting deep and hard, and she felt him throbbing and moving inside her, while his mouth was joined with hers. She let go and gave herself up to the sheer pleasure of passively participating.

'Oh my God!' she whispered. 'Don't stop, please, please, don't stop.' The strangest feeling was growing inside her. It was like every nerve end throbbing together in magnificent ecstasy. She began to groan as the pleasure intensified. She was held helpless in the grip of it. She screamed long and hard. Clutching hold of Hamish, she burst out sobbing and laughing. The words came bubbling out of her: 'God! What was that? It was something wonderful. Oh Hamish. You won't believe what happened to me.' She lay spread-eagled, languid and replete.

'You never came before?' he asked incredulously when she had stopped sobbing and shaking.

'I was sure I had, but I was wrong. Is that coming? It seemed like an earthquake.'

'I can do it again whenever you wish, now that I know what you like,' he boasted, looking smug.

He opened his arms and she fell into them and snuggled onto his shoulder. She had found her special place, her head on his shoulder, one knee flung over his belly, her throbbing navel warmed by his hot thigh.

She woke an hour later and jumped out of bed. 'I'm going to make you breakfast. You need your strength. It's important, and not just for business,' she added, teasing him.

Chapter 46

Hamish Cameron, the seasoned loser, sat patiently at the kitchen table staring at the back of the girl he loved as she stood at the stove, knowing that he was foolishly entering into her charade just to prolong the dream. He felt incapable of letting go, for the dream had lasted for weeks and for the first time in his life he had been happy and proud, not just of her, but of himself. She had a knack of doing this and he knew that she used it mercilessly in her business. Well, he was her business, too, wasn't he?

Why had he not declared himself to be totally in possession of all his senses and all his brains, and not the cretin she took him to be? And why had he drunk himself senseless? He knew the answer to that: because he could not stand the pain of his despair. Everyone in the world, it seemed, wanted what he had, and God knows he didn't have much. Not any more.

He listened again to her murmured advice as she spooned the sizzling fat over the eggs with one hand while tossing the bacon with a fork in the other. Not many people could do that. How sexy she looked. Was it her long, graceful neck, or her square shoulders, or her slender waist flaring to tightly muscled buttocks? Her blue cotton mini-shift was highly provocative. He wanted her all over again. She had been wonderful to make love to, but the suspicion that she had loved him with ulterior motives hurt like hell. And what did that make her? Was that why she had come to Inverness?

'Fight back, Hamish,' she was saying so casually that at first he hardly concentrated. 'They're out to get what you've got. You've been a fool. You had no right to opt out.

'Erskine's trying to downgrade profits and performance so that shareholders sell out to Glentirran. Then at last they'll have control and you'll be out. Is that what you want?'

'Why not?' he retorted in his most detached voice, trying vaguely to defend his failure. Here came the sting. He braced himself. He was about to discover what exactly it was that Joe and Marjorie wanted.

'Oh, well, I'm glad you don't care,' Marjorie said cheerfully. 'That way you won't be hurt. But Hamish, I'm telling you now, I care. I want you to fight back. Don't I count for anything?'

'So what is Joe's solution?' he asked with studied nonchalance.

She paused, thinking that it was wrong to blame Joe for their ploy, but did it really matter, since she had come to a momentous decision?

'Joe's always out for a fast profit — well, so am I — and he can see which way you're going. He's not a cruel man, and he would never actually destroy anyone, but he doesn't mind making a fortune out of you while you destroy yourself. He's been buying up some of your shares on behalf of both of us — beating Glentirran to it. I don't know how he does it, but he's done it. He's got about eight per cent so far, I believe, but he wants more of

the action. His plan is to offer you a considerable amount
of cash which would be secured by your maturing whisky
stocks in the casks, at the value quoted in your balance
sheet. I don't suppose you realise that it's hopelessly
underquoted pricewise. Another little ploy by dear John
Erskine.

'The cash will keep the wolf from the door for
another few months until you are inexorably sucked
into your self-made whirlpool. Eventually, the enemy
will be forced to pay Joe handsomely, at the matured
whisky price, in order to gain control of their stocks.
Furthermore, Joe reckons his eight per cent will be
worth double to Glentirran's and he aims to make them
pay handsomely. That is, once they find they can't get
any more shares. It's a very good plan.'

'For me?' he ventured.

'No! Idiot! For Joe and me. That's why it isn't going
to happen.'

Hamish took a deep breath. He wondered if she could
hear his heart knocking against his ribs. She was on his
side. Or was she? He could hardly hear for the pounding
in his ears.

'I don't understand what you are saying. What is it
that you want me to do, Marjorie?'

'I want you to struggle. I want you to win. I want you
to get off your backside – or perhaps I should say your
slippery Alpine mountains – and take *real* risks.'

'Real risks!' He held his breath again. Here came the
sting after all. 'Okay, explain. How do I take these
real risks? What would you have me place on the line,
Marjorie?' He was trying to lighten the tension that had
sprung up between them.

'Your reputation, your morale,' she said. 'By opting

out and pretending you don't care, you save face. That's what the Japanese do, isn't it? They save face. I thought you wanted to be Scottish.'

'Do you really care?'

'Care? Of course I care. I care about those expressive black oriental eyes of yours. I care about your finely shaped, strong hands, your high cheekbones, your strength and incredible physical bravery which probably stems from Samurai ancestors – but I'd like to see a bit of dirty, Anglo-Saxon in-fighting grafted on to this oh-so-beautiful man.

'Eat,' she commanded, pushing crispy eggs and bacon onto a plate. 'And then we'll make a plan. Listen, I'm offering my help. Don't turn me down, Hamish. I'm good at business; I'll show you how to fight. Give me a job – I'll take any sort of a title: secretary, sales manager . . . I want to help you.'

'Wife!' he answered without hesitation. 'Since you offered.'

She turned away to hide her face and stood there frozen, unable to move, her mind racing round.

This is what it's all about, isn't it? This is what I was angling for. But can I marry a man to use him as a tool? I'm not in love with him, but I've got a lot of love going begging and I'll shovel it all on him. I swear I'll never hurt him and I know I can make him happy. That's a good bargain, isn't it? I'll get his bloody family off his back and make him famous. And when I've built him up, I'll take on Robert and his bloody family, too.

'Well,' he asked impatiently. 'Will that position do?'

She turned and took his face in her hands, and gazed at him long and earnestly. 'The answer, Hamish, is yes.'

Chapter 47

———— ————

It was two p.m. on Monday afternoon and Marjorie felt as tense as a caged beast and twice as dangerous as she stalked back from her lawyer to see Joe. She knew she had to be calm: no one, but no one, fought with Joe and won. She had to reason, but she only had resentment on offer.

Her secretary had a long list of queries. 'Later,' she muttered. 'Where's Joe?' As usual, he was in his office.

She paused outside Joe's door for two minutes, listening to him speak on the telephone. When he replaced the receiver, she leaned against the wall, hiding her face in her hands and shutting her eyes. 'Be calm,' she whispered. She walked in hesitantly, but the sight of Joe looking so cool and complacent brought the whole sorry spectacle of Hamish's disgrace back into focus, and all her intentions crumbled away.

'Bastard,' she yelled. 'Sometimes I really hate you.' She slammed the door behind her.

'Is something wrong?' he asked without looking up.

Clenching her fists, Marjorie sank into the nearest chair.

'You promised, you absolutely promised not to talk business, not to put him down, not to humiliate him, but you talked business and worse, you talked down to him and rammed his silly mess down his throat. You put on your Simple Simon act which fools no one, least of all Hamish, and you treated him like an imbecile. Next you pumped him for information, which he didn't want to divulge, and then when he drank himself into a coma, because he was so damned embarrassed and hurt, you calmly walked out leaving me to cope. What's so special about that money-digging limpet that she can't be allowed to see a drunk? How could you do that to me?'

'I knew you could cope. So what happened?'

'I took him home. I didn't know where else to take him.'

'Has he recovered yet?'

'Yes. He doesn't suffer from hangovers.'

'Drunks seldom do. I hope he apologised.'

'No, he proposed.'

'Is he very cut up about it?'

'He's delighted.'

'That you said no?'

'That I said yes. You can congratulate me. I'm engaged to Hamish. And Joe – I want my money. All of it! You see, I need cash for the distillery. I want to be bought out of this place – the publishing and the building and my share of the commodity trading – and I want it done now. Part of my payment can be those Glenaird shares we hold.'

The silence was definitely pregnant, Marjorie surmised. Joe's lips tightened, his eyes narrowed, he went pale and then turned very red. The tantrum that finally erupted was like nothing Marjorie had seen before. Her knowledge of French swearing wasn't up to a good translation, although she caught the words con and traitor. She walked out and made two cups of coffee. When she returned Joe had his back turned and he seemed to be staring out of the window.

'Got yourself under control, have you?' she asked. 'Good, because we have business to discuss. First there's something I want to know. Why didn't you tell me that you were engaged?'

'I suppose I was scared of your reaction. Now I'm more scared. You don't have to copy me with the first available man who comes along.'

'Marrying Hamish is not a reaction. Don't flatter yourself.' She tried to stop pacing his office and sank into a chair.

'A woman scorned . . .' He sighed.

She decided to ignore this. 'I've always told you everything.'

'Except when you cried to Barbara about how much you loved Robert and that you intended to use men, but never again to love one.'

'That was years ago. We weren't so close then.'

'I imagined we were. After that silly mistletoe episode I felt that we were very close.'

What a strange, introverted guy he was. Was that why he had switched off her? She voiced her question: 'Did you care?'

'Water under the bridge, my dear Marjorie.'

'Oh Joe! Are you really going to marry that gold-digger? Can't you see that she wouldn't be interested if it weren't for your superb money-making ability?'

'Are you saying that no one could love me for myself?'

'Of course not, but it's pretty obvious she's after money. She spent most of the evening trying to pinpoint your worth.'

'She happens to be the sexiest woman in Europe. That's why I want her.'

'Well, I want my own share of the cash in order to invest in my husband's business. I think that's a reasonable request. I've worked hard for years.'

'We have no cash available, so you'll have to wait. Possibly for years. This will save you from yourself and Hamish, and protect you from bankruptcy.'

'Joe, I've been to a lawyer. That's where I was all morning. Now you're not up against me, you're up against Enzo Amarti. Name mean anything?'

This time Joe was really shattered. His eyes filled with tears and he went very pale.

'So you're deadly serious. Tell me, why did you choose the nastiest divorce lawyer in the city?'

'You once told me that a fifty-fifty partnership was worse than a marriage.'

Joe was drumming his fingers on the desk. He looked up speculatively. 'Is there anything I can say that will talk you out of this absurd plan?' he asked.

'Nothing.'

'Hamish is a loser. Don't be a fool, Marjorie. You'll be keeping him for the rest of his life. How will you manage that, plus your family, if you don't have the publishing company to fall back on? What will you do when you've lost all your money?'

'His distillery will keep us all. I just have to work at it.'

'Are you mad? You can't possibly succeed. It's all a question of cash. The market wants a prestigious drink: eight-year-old blended malt is a minimum quality requirement nowadays. Twelve-year-old pure malt is what the future is all about, with classy presentation and all the trimmings, plus a costly agency to establish and maintain the brand.

'You can imagine what a massive investment that entails. That's why the Seventies is proving to be a decade of consolidation and takeovers for the whisky industry. The sheer economics of this kind of operation are separating the men from the boys, and most of the traditional distillers haven't had the chance to recover from the war years. Huge, well-established English brewers and distillers are moving in and grabbing whatever they can. Some of the Scots are trying to consolidate and keep whisky in Scottish hands, and one of them is your old friend, Robert MacLaren, which is why he's making a takeover bid for Glenaird.

'Glenaird is finished. Washed up. You can't possibly succeed. You must understand what you're up against, Marjorie.'

Joe was shaking with emotion as he rummaged in his drawer for a file. He looked stricken and at that moment she almost weakened.

'Surely you realise that you'll lose all your money? You aren't strong enough to fight the family. Class barriers in Scotland are even worse than in England and in this family they've got pettiness down to a fine art.'

'I'll work my butt off, and one million is quite an investment,' Marjorie retorted.

'It's peanuts! Even Hamish has more sense than you. He found out the hard way that he can never crash that invisible barrier based on class, race and Scottish nationalism. The bank and the shareholders will support their own kind, namely Uncle Andrew and his son, Ian, who have cooked up this merger with Glentirran.'

'If they succeed I can still sell my shares – that was

your idea in the first place.' She broke off abruptly. Why was she pleading for Joe's approval?

'Dear Marjorie, you forgot that the entire takeover bid depends upon timing. If you delay, or make it tough for the buyers, they'll give up and leave Hamish to sink into bankruptcy. Then they'll pick up the pieces for next to nothing. You'll lose your capital. All of it!'

'I'm giving it a go. You see, I have to, Joc. I might apply for a ninety per cent bond on my flat, as well. Now buy me out.'

'The publishing was for you,' he argued moodily. 'To make you secure. I have my own interests.'

'Oh Joe!' She caught hold of his shoulder, but he brushed her hand off. 'I never wanted to be looked after,' she wailed, trying to get a grip on herself.

'Remember this, Marjorie. You'll be gambling for very big stakes. I would never take this kind of risk. You're crazy and your motives are wrong. I know what it's all about – teaching Robert a lesson. You want to show him you're as good as he is.'

'No, no.' She answered too swiftly, knowing that she was lying.

'You're debasing yourself if you marry for any other reason than love, and you're cheating Hamish of the love he should have. It will boomerang back to you, and finally it's you who will be cheated of love.'

His words seemed like a prophecy and Marjorie shivered. 'Thank you for your vote of confidence,' she said, trying to keep her voice steady.

'Oh Marjorie, you stupid, stupid bitch,' he mourned as she walked out, and that more than anything unnerved her.

Chapter 48

The once stately Inveraird Lodge lay derelict and empty. Its intricate stonework was filthy, the windows were broken, and somewhere a door was slamming in the wind, the only sound to break the sad silence. Marjorie looked at the stout old door's iron bolts falling to rust, studied the rusty key in her hand, and for the first time in her life courage fled altogether.

Little wonder that Hamish had insisted she should see his home before they married. He should have come with her, she brooded resentfully, but he'd refused: pressure of business, he'd insisted, but he was lying. He'd chickened out. She was getting to know him. When he felt guilty he suffered from intolerable tension, and heavy drinking or violent exercise were the only ways he knew to alleviate the pain.

Given time, she'd change all that. What choice did she have, since she had well and truly burned her bridges? That thought brought painful thrusts of fear through her stomach. Just when everything had been going so well, too. She was risking their hard-won security by throwing all her capital into this decrepit ruin and the ailing distillery. Joe was right. She was a fool.

She knew what Mum would say: 'Your vain pretensions

will be our downfall, my girl. I've warned you enough times, you can't make a silk purse . . .'

She backed away from the house, too scared to venture inside, and wandered off through the knee-deep grass of Hamish's neglected park. The field sloped gently towards a distant lake. Perhaps it had once been a lawn, for she saw some stone benches overgrown with grass and weeds. Wild flowers grew around in colourful patches: red poppies, the flimsy white sheen of wild parsley, clumps of teasels, ragged robins peeping through the grass, forget-me-nots just about everywhere, and yellow flags gone wild round the borders which perhaps were once flower beds.

As she pushed ahead, the wonderful tang of baking earth and wild herbs rose around her and sweethearts caught onto her coat and skirt. She stopped and peered around as her stockings caught on thorns. She was walking through a neglected rose garden. There were even some blooms, although most of the bushes had run wild. It occurred to her that Dad could fix this place, if only he would.

The field bordered a small wood of oaks, beech and elm trees. Squirrels fled as she approached, and doves cooed. The wood reverberated with birdsong and the hum of summer insects.

'Oh how lovely,' she murmured, recovering her nerve. 'Lana will love it here.'

Beyond the small wood was a broken-down cottage, Hamish had told her. She emerged from the wood and there it stood beside a willow tree, a postcard scene, with a thatched roof, rambling roses and clumps of lavender round the door.

None of the keys fitted, she discovered, two broken

fingernails later. She felt peeved as she smeared the dust off with a tissue to peer through the windows. There was some furniture covered in dirty sheets and piles of dirt and rubbish. There seemed to be two bedrooms upstairs, so perhaps Lana could stay here with Mum, at least until the house was habitable?

Feeling braver, she hurried back to the main house and pushed the key into the lock. The door swung open with enough creaks and groans to satisfy Alfred Hitchcock and she found herself in a grand hall, her feet clattering on a floor that might be stone or marble: it was impossible to tell under the layer of grime. The furniture was covered in sheets which were black with soot and dirt. Pulling one off, she discovered an ancient monks' bench, barely visible through all the dust.

A dozen girls armed with commercial vacuums would do for starters, she reckoned. She wandered from room to room until she lost her bearings. There weren't any damp patches on the ceiling, and that was a relief. When she found the kitchen, she gasped with pleasure. It was quite splendid, she discovered when she had ripped off the dust sheets, with a long kitchen table of dark oak and two dark Welsh dressers, and a massive old stove. She began to poke through the drawers and cupboards, gloating over the copper pots and pans and the amazing selection of antique cups and saucers and utensils, some cracked and with nothing matching, but full of surprises. She found a pantry, a scullery and another back room full of pegs with some old discarded boots. Once again, the floor was black and hard under her feet.

Whatever was it? She had to know.

Eventually she found a pail and a bottle half-full of

ammonia on the windowsill of the scullery and an old scrubbing brush with half the bristles missing.

'You'll do,' she muttered aloud to cheer herself. Returning to the hall, she took off her coat and put it in her car. Then she got down on her knees and scrubbed away at a small patch of floor near the front door. After a few minutes of vigorous exercise, the top of the blackness dissolved away, revealing itself to be nothing more than compressed and polished common-or-garden dirt.

'Lord love a duck,' she exclaimed. She kept going as if her life depended upon it. More dirt rolled away, but soon there weren't many bristles left. Perhaps a knife . . .

Five minutes later she was chipping away at the black mess. She was getting there. 'Just like archaeology,' she whispered, for she was half an inch down. A last careless splash of ammonia set her nose burning and her eyes streaming, but when she'd wiped them dry she saw beneath her a portion of intricate mosaic tiles in shades of pink, cerise, blue and mauve. She gazed in disbelief as a last swipe of the cloth revealed the exquisite colours. It would take days to clean it all, but it would be done in time.

She stood up, feeling overwhelmed by the treasure she had uncovered. A sudden surge of intense feeling brought more tears to her eyes. She wasn't sure what the feeling was: relief, joy, or just a sense of being thankful that there were lovely things amongst the dirt and cobwebs and neglect of the years.

She went outside and stood on the steps, staring at the clouds, which was where she considered God was likely to be.

'Dear God,' she prayed. 'I reckon I'm going to do the

wrong thing in marrying a man I don't love, and for what he's got, rather than what he is, so I'm asking you to forgive me, now, in advance, so to speak. I promise I'll look after him. I'll build up his distillery and make him as happy as I can.'

She paused to think. She hadn't really reached the kernel of what she was trying to express. 'Okay, so Mum says you can't make a silk purse out of a sow's ear, but what about Lana? She should have a home like this, and since her dad doesn't want us, and Hamish does, here I am. I won't do him any harm, I swear I won't. I'll just scrub away at everything, at this house and the distillery and the farm and even Hamish himself. I'll clean away the debris and the pollution that's been hurled all over him until the real beauty of him shines out just like this floor. I swear I will, so help me, God. Yes, that's what I'm trying to say. Help me, God.'

Suddenly she felt more cheerful. She whistled a happy tune as she put the bucket back. She couldn't wait to get her hands on this lot. 'It'll take an army,' she muttered to herself. 'Or at least a bus load of cleaners. And it'll cost a packet – just the broken windows alone, and the wallpaper. We'll have to get in a small building firm. Perhaps I should do a part of it and lock the rest up for the time being. I wonder if the central heating works? Come to think of it, I haven't seen any central heating, have I?'

She stood in the doorway, staring down at the small patch of mosaic tiles. 'You hold tight, love. I'll be back here one of these days, and then I'll get all this rubbishy dirt off you,' she told the floor. 'You'll be as good as new by the time I'm finished. I have a few ordeals to get through before I'll see you again.'

She locked up and got into her car, her mind already dwelling on those coming ordeals and how to cope with them.

Keeping Hamish sober enough to say 'I do' was one of them. She wasn't looking forward to the ceremony. Getting her cash out of Joe was another. Well, let the lawyer fret about that.

Her parents would resent being uprooted from Dover, and having to move here. Come to think of it, there wasn't a pub within walking distance. Her heart sank.

Then somehow the distillery must be pulled out of its slide into ruin. She'd get the best business brains money could buy. That was Joe, of course, but maybe he wouldn't want to help her. Okay, so then she'd make do with second best.

She reached the main gate and drove through it, parking to lock the rusty old gate. It needed replacing like everything else. She hovered there, gazing back in awe. From a distance, Inveraird Lodge looked enchanting.

She waved goodbye. 'I'll be back,' she promised aloud. 'Trust me.'

Chapter 49

'I'm in shock,' Marjorie muttered to herself. 'That's why life doesn't seem real – not even those distant mountains, or the road, or the rooftops of the village I can see over there amongst the trees. It's all like a dream. So why bother to drive to Inveraird Lodge? I could float there, couldn't I?'

She lapsed into silence and tried to concentrate on negotiating the winding road moving north from Edderton. Talking aloud to herself had not dimished her dreamlike state. The trouble was, her plan had run wild, like an unbroken horse, and she, like a fool, was riding it, hanging on for dear life. There was no point kidding herself that she was in control: she feared falling, for the crazy beast would run roughshod over her.

So here she was, Mrs Marjorie Cameron, heading up a convoy of two minibuses containing ten Filipinos from an industrial cleaning agency, plus their supervisors and cleaning gear. There were several vans behind them and she guessed they formed part of the army of tradesmen who were due at the lodge this morning: plumbers, electricians, carpet and upholstery cleaners; a laundryman who would remove and wash the dust sheets; curtain cleaners; mini movers, to shift the furniture around; a roofing expert; a small building firm who would check the gutters, mend the windows and patch things up; painters; the grocer; and even a firm of caterers who were going to run a canteen for the workers. There wasn't a thing she had forgotten. Or was there?

Unbelievably, it had taken only a few weeks to accomplish all those onerous legal details, including marrying Hamish, and here she was.

Her parents had been shocked, dismayed and finally downright angry when she had put her foot down. She bit her lip as she remembered that awful scene.

'Since you're forcing us to move, I suppose we have no choice,' Dad had muttered, looking murderous.

'But Marjorie,' Mum had wailed. 'We always promised to look after Lana and we've kept our promise, as you've kept yours, but we're settled here. We have some good friends. Dad runs the local darts team.'

'Don't suppose those damned Scots ever play darts,' Dad grumbled. 'Besides, I don't believe there's a pub within walking distance. I've been looking at the map.'

'But there's one within cycling distance, or you could take the car.' Dad had never learned to drive and she knew he never would. 'You could get your licence, Mum.'

'What! At my time of life? Don't be daft.'

'It's not as silly as you might think. It would change your whole life. You could have your own car.'

'I reckon you should give it a go, Liz,' Dad agreed, shocking both women. 'We'll need transport if we're to be dumped in the back of beyond. How's Lana going to get to nursery school? Bet you hadn't thought of that.'

'I don't want to leave my friends,' Lana had grumbled as she hugged her dog, a scruffy cross-Irish terrier, called in turn Paddy, and Paddywonks. Lana seldom cried. She was a strangely self-possessed little girl, far in advance of her age. Marjorie sensed that she'd do well wherever she went.

'It's not as bad as it seems,' Marjorie had tried to explain. 'It's only five miles north of Edderton, which is a lovely little village set by the Firth. From the lodge, on a fine day you can see the Cnoc Muigh Bhlaraidh and the Struie Mountains. And just think, we'll have picnics in the forest in summer. That will be fun.'

Sensing her grandparents' fears, Lana had clung to Marjorie and climbed on her lap.

'It's going to be wonderful, Lana. There's a huge garden. Paddywonks will love it.'

'Heavens, he'll be bringing mud all over the house,' Mum exclaimed. 'We'll have to tie him up.'

'No! Never!' Lana shrieked. 'No one's going to tie up Paddywonks.' She jumped down and flung her arms around the dog, who endured the pushing and squeezing with a resigned air.

'And there's stables so you could have a pony.'

'And who's going to look after it?' Dad grumbled. 'Don't think you're adding a horse to our responsibilities. Nor another child. There'll be no more dumping, my girl.'

Then Marjorie noticed her daughter's rapt expression. She was a strange child, with a wide face, wiry hair, dark eyes that were large and set wide apart, a sallow skin and an impish expression. Her nose was small and tilted, her lips naturally red, her smile generous, and right now she was gazing out of the window murmuring: 'A pony. Oh . . . My own pony.'

'But you'd have to feed him and look after him,' Marjorie warned her.

'What if you fall out with Hamish and we get flung out?' Mum chipped in.

'Oh, Mum. It isn't going to be like that. It's for life.'

'How do you know he'll want us wandering round the place? He won't like us and we'll feel uncomfortable.'

'No, he's not like that, Dad, and he will like you.'

'Then how come he hasn't been to see us?'

A good question. If only Hamish had met her family, but his usual response to her pleas was: 'after the wedding'. She was learning that Hamish wasn't quite as easy to manipulate as she had imagined.

'It's like this,' she had tried to explain. 'I won't be able to afford to run two homes, and if Lana stays here I'll never see her, so that's out, but if I take her to Scotland when will you ever see her? It has to be like this.'

Dad had transfixed her with his pebble-hard stare.

'Give it a go for a year, please,' she had begged. 'If you're not happy I'll make another plan. Promise! I think you'll love it and we'll all be together.'

'That's the worst part.' Dad had delivered his verdict scathingly before returning to his newspaper to sulk.

Her wedding was an event she hoped to forget as soon as possible. Her family and a few friends had gathered at Marylebone Register Office, a gloomly and intensely impersonal setting. The dust on the shelves gave Lana violent hay fever, and she sneezed until her nose bled, so they made her lie on her back on a bench while they waited. Lana had labelled Hamish her enemy and as soon as she stood up she kicked him hard on his shins. Dad had responded with a swift backhand and her nose had started bleeding again.

'Now you've seen us, do you want to call it off?' she

had challenged Hamish against a backdrop of Lana's wails, Dad's cursing and Barbara's placatory cooing.

'Do you?' Hamish had retorted, his eyes hard as agate.

'Well, no.'

'Then don't talk such rot.'

He had not spoken to her for the rest of the ceremony, other than murmuring 'I do', which had been directed towards the registrar, not her.

After the ceremony, the family had squeezed into a taxi, while Barbara, Garth and David had followed with Joe and Véronique in Joe's car.

Lana, who was overwrought at the imagined threat of losing her mother, had vomited into Hamish's lap. Dad was doing his best to ignore Hamish. Clearly he didn't like him, and Mum was so flustered she hardly knew what she was doing.

Other than greeting her parents, Hamish had not spoken to them, but once he started, there was no stopping him: 'Life as Lana knew it has been destroyed.' Unbelievably he had grabbed the soiled and smelly child and put her on his lap, hugging her close. 'She doesn't know what's coming next. I didn't think. I should have taken her to see Inveraird. The trouble is, I hate the place.' He sighed.

'It's silly of us to think that we own our children, or that they belong to us. Lana is an individual entrusted to our care during her formative years. She is her own person, and she always has been, when she had other parents and other lives. She's an old soul in a young body, feeling her way. She's here to learn, as we all are. Hitting her won't teach her anything. I don't believe in smacking children. This morning she's scared because she thinks she's losing her mother and she's not at all sure she likes me. I blame myself.'

There was a long and horrible silence.

'Well, that's a good Christian philosophy,' Mum had muttered eventually, trying to counteract Dad's visible contempt.

'I'm not a Christian, Mrs Hardy,' Hamish had explained. 'I'm Zen Buddhist, like my mother. She was Japanese, you see.'

'Japanese?' Mum squeaked. 'Well I never,' she added faintly. 'Fancy that!'

Dad's eyes sought Marjorie's. There was murder in them.

'He's as nutty as a fruitcake,' Mum had hissed as they piled out of the taxi. Adding: 'But nice nutty, if you know what I mean.'

'No, I don't,' Marjorie had replied coldly. She did her best to ignore her mother. She and Barbara bathed Lana and put her to bed while the others tossed off the drinks and gobbled the snacks she had prepared, and shortly afterwards they had all left.

Chapter 50

——— ———

Switching her mind off her parents, Marjorie glanced up at the sky. With luck they'd have a lovely day. As she drove, she calculated her worth, something she did often lately. Unbelievably, on paper she was worth well over a million. She was short of ready cash, but the bank had given her a bridging loan and she had taken a mortgage on her London flat.

By early August, her split with Joe had been legalised. He had reluctantly taken over the trade publications and Garth had been left with the task of pulling the sales team under his wing. He'd coped, much to his surprise.

Joe had raised half the cash he owed her and they had met at her lawyer's to terminate their partnership. To Marjorie it had been an appalling day. She would never forget Joe's white face and shocked eyes, or the way his hands shook. Her guilt deepened when she learned that he had set up a trust fund for Lana three years earlier and that he was currently paying in five per cent of all taxable profits from his inventions. Lana would get the money when she was twenty-one, but she could borrow from it to finance her education if necessary.

It had taken all Marjorie's resolve not to break down. She shivered as she remembered Joe's words:

'You're damn lucky I couldn't raise all the cash now,

so you'll have something to fall back on in a year's time when you've blown this lot.' His mouth taut and eyes glittering with hurt, he had gripped her arm. 'Revenge is not a creed to build your life on, Marjorie. Don't say I didn't warn you, but remember, it's not too late to back out. Give up this insane marriage.'

She was spoiling for a fight. 'You're totally wrong, and look who's talking. You married for glamour.' She sensed his genuine concern and this brought her to tears. Suddenly she was in his arms.

'I never wanted to fight with you, Joe, but everything's changed now that you've married that French tart.'

'Hey there. Steady on. Do I insult your drunken Jap?' he'd growled.

She'd tried to laugh, but it was a poor effort. Grim-faced, they had signed the papers, shaken hands with each other and the lawyer, promised to keep in touch, and gone their separate ways. And then, unable to see for the tears in her eyes, she had tripped on the kerb outside her lawyer's offices and hurt her shin.

It still ached now, she brooded, reaching down to touch the scab. There was another ache somewhere deeper inside, but she was doing her best to ignore it.

She'd reached her destination at last. She parked and gazed anxiously through the iron gate. From a distance Inveraird Lodge looked truly stately with no hint of decay or neglect. Hamish should have been here with her. Why was he so strange? She had longed for him to help her renovate the house, but all her pleading and cajoling had been ineffective.

'Not until you've finished,' he'd insisted with that funny, bleak look in his eyes, which showed he'd switched right off her – his form of protection. 'Don't be surprised if you find me impotent. That hellhole knocks the stuffing out of me.'

He was flying to the Alps. He'd walked out with her farewell message ringing in his ears: 'I hope your bloody balls freeze.'

Would she be happy with Hamish? Wistful and unexpectedly longing for love, she stood at the gate nervously twisting her intrusive wedding ring. Then she realised that she was holding up the convoy.

She shivered and unlocked the rusty gate. Why worry? she reflected as she pushed at the heavy iron bars. She was not running after happiness, she reminded herself sternly. What would be the point? It was last seen sitting on a train in Dover Station one cold and misty dawn.

Whipping out her notebook she wrote: 'remote control for gate'. Then she drove up to the lodge.

'Brace yourself, Inveraird Lodge,' she called as she unlocked the front door. 'For you, life will never be the same again.' Then she laughed aloud and as her laugh echoed around the empty hall, it sounded hard and scary.

By afternoon, visibility was down to three metres and everyone was wearing cotton masks and goggles, but the cleaners were sneezing and coughing all the same. Part of the trouble was that the builders were stripping old wallpaper in some of the rooms, but they assured her the job was almost done. Wearing flat sandals, jeans, a T-shirt and an old sweater, with her hair tied up in a scarf, Marjorie stood in the foyer gazing with pleasure at the fine mosaic floor which was rapidly emerging as the scrubbing machine slowly conquered the dirt. The cleaning supervisor shouted something at her.

'What?' The noise pollution was as bad as the dust.

He cupped his hands round his mouth and bellowed in her ear. 'This floor's ruined six brushes so far.'

'I'm not surprised.' Taking his elbow, she propelled him outside where they could talk. Birds were circling and darting into the trees, upset by the noise and so many people.

'You must get the cottage cleaned quickly. My family are arriving with their furniture soon.'

They set off through the wood with Marjorie leading the way. She was quaking as she fumbled with the keys.

'You look pale, love,' the supervisor sympathised.

'I forced my family to come here and I haven't seen inside yet. It really is important to get this house looking good.'

'When are they coming?'

'Soon, and goodness knows what we'll find in there.' She wondered why she was unburdening her fears on a stranger.

'Okay, love. I get the message. Top priority!'

'Ah! This is the key.' The door swung open and they stepped inside.

Apart from the dirt and the dust that rose around them as they walked, and the cobwebs and the beetles scuttling over the floor, and the broken windows and torn curtains, and soot that had fallen down the chimney, the place looked . . . ? She tried to think of a reasonably cheerful description, but failed. It was very dark, painted in chocolate brown and beige, with dark beamed ceilings and a dirty cement floor.

'Does that convoy out there include a chimney sweep?'

'No!' She bit her lip. She'd forgotten that.

'Well, you better get one over here before we clean up. We should have remembered that up at the big house. No point letting soot fall all over a clean house every time the wind blows, is there?'

'Thanks.' She fumbled for her notebook. Groaning inwardly, she gazed around. The ground floor was mostly taken up with one very large room, and the staircase led off the northern wall. She half closed her eyes and imagined a variety of decors, but suddenly saw it as it could be, with white walls, a tiled floor and the ceiling sanded to light wood. There and then she decided to install underfloor heating.

When she saw the kitchen, she gasped with dismay. What a dump! The only thing she could leave here would be the four walls, but then she changed her mind. One of them must go to let some light in. If only she had more time, but Mum and Dad had rented out their house and there was nothing they could do about that now.

She felt a hand on her shoulder, startling her back to the present. 'Cheer up, ma'am. "Every long journey starts with one small step." From Mao Tse-tung, I think. I'm not a communist, but that's my favourite expression. It helps in a business like mine.'

'Yes.' She felt close to despair.

Upstairs was a mess of shoddy old dark and peeling wallpaper, a genuine antique bath with ball and claw feet, and a maze of tarnished green copper pipes.

'Oh God, Oh God . . .'

It was back to the telephone to summon a new assault team.

*   *   *

At tea-time Marjorie grabbed a sandwich and a paper mug of coffee from the canteen and sat on the floor in the pantry planning how she would like the shelves placed.

The supervisor poked his head round the door. 'I've been looking all over for you. There's a funny-looking bloke outside making a mess of your stonework. You better come and have a look.'

'Now what?' Her body felt like a lead weight while her knees had turned to rubber.

There was a van outside, and a man operating a hand-held scrubbing machine that also pumped out white goo. He looked endearingly familiar.

'Joe,' she yelled. 'Oh, Joe!' She was about to fling her arms around him when he backed off rapidly, raising his hands to fend her off.

'Some other time, Marjorie. Is that really you under all that soot? Thought you were the chimney sweep.' Then he grinned at her and it was like old times.

'It's like this. I'm looking for a really filthy stately home. Something like this place. I'm prepared to give it a free clean in return for the rights to take pictures, before-and-after style, to use for advertising, particularly in the States.'

'Thank you, Joe, I'm truly happy. Don't think I've fallen for that silly story, but I accept your assistance. How long will it take?' she added anxiously.

'For ever! There's hundreds of years of dirt stuck on this stonework.'

'I guessed slate grey was its natural colour.'

'Nah! This is lovely stuff. Look here, sort of pinky-white with sparkling crystals. Lovely, isn't it?' he enthused, showing her a circle where he'd worked on the stone.

She gasped. 'It's beautiful, Joe. And I found something else – the hall floor. Come and have a look.'

'Where's Hamish?'

'Climbing in the Alps. I wanted to get this place fixed up and he didn't want any part of it. After all, we have to live somewhere.'

'So where's he been living?'

'Bumming off friends for years.'

'You do realise that you're chucking your money away, don't you?'

'No, Joe. This is for real. I'll be here a long time. You'll see.'

She led him round the house, proudly explaining her plans, but Joe was examining the furniture with a predatory eye.

'Old,' he muttered. 'Very old. There's a lot of good stuff hidden between the junk. The trouble is, you don't know which is what, and you might chuck something out that's worth a fortune. Tell you what, I know a reputable antique restorer. I'll get him here to quote you on fixing the broken bits. He can value everything, and tell which pieces are worth mending. Phone working?'

'Yes. It's about the only thing that is. I had it reconnected last week.'

'I'll give him a ring.' He took out a tissue and fastidiously wiped the receiver.

'And there's another thing, Joe. D'you remember telling me about your industrial investigator? The bloke who found out who John Erskine was really working for?'

'What about him?' Joe always jumped on the defensive first, then calmed down later when he perceived that there was no threat to him.

'Can you give me his number? I have a job for him.'

'He doesn't take anyone without a recommendation.'

'Then recommend me. Make an appointment. I know you can.'

'Sure you know what you're doing?'

Marjorie suppressed a surge of irritation. So they were back to Big Daddy again. To Joe she would always be that helpless Dover schoolgirl who'd been done out of her commission. 'Joe, trust me,' she fumed. 'I'm so glad you came,' she added to make amends. 'You'll never know how glad.'

'Oh yes I would, looking at this lot.'

'No, that's not why.'

'Now don't get sloppy on me, Marj. You can't wipe out five years as if they never happened. I found that out as soon as you'd left. We're bonded. I'll settle for sister, if that's okay with you. Now let's talk about the business. I fancy you need a bit of help.'

'Suits me.' It was funny how the rooms seemed to have brightened, the job lightened and she felt a little less vulnerable. Humming to herself, she went off to get a cup of coffee and a sandwich for Joe.

Chapter 51

Perfect, Marjorie decided. Her parents' cottage was just as she had dreamed it would be, and it was finished on time, except for the kitchen where the tile plaster was still drying.

She went upstairs to gloat at Lana's room with its farmyard wallpaper and blue voile curtains. This was where Lana would stay when she was away on business, and her daughter would sleep here for the next few weeks – or would it be months? – until the lodge was completed.

She hurried through the wood, noting the changes. The leaves were turning red and gold, there was a sharp, misty tang to the air, and the shrubs were thick with berries: bird cherries, wild plum, hawthorne, elderberries and juniper.

Hurrying through the open door into the hall, she saw her new maid humming and polishing. The cleaning team had departed with their brooms and vacuums, leaving behind Zola, a vaguely dissatisfied girl from Jamaica who had difficulty relating to her peers because she was brain-damaged and slightly deaf. Work was her opium – she gobbled it like the birds were gobbling berries in the wood. She liked being here and she had volunteered to stay on. Marjorie was grateful.

The table was drenched with polish. 'Won't shine,

ma'am,' Zola grumbled. She was about to shake the
bottle over it when Marjorie reached forward to mop
up the surplus with a paper towel. She rubbed hard.

'Elbow grease is what you need here, Zola. There's
no substitute for it. Just watch me.'

'My own opinion exactly,' she heard behind her.

Marjorie spun around, but by then she had already
made a mental assessment of the voice: female, elderly,
a well-educated Scot. She was not prepared for the
tatty fur, the gnarled old hands covered in rings and
the ravaged face.

'Please come in,' Marjorie said. 'I'm Marjorie Cameron.
I won't offer to shake hands with you, since I'm covered
in polish. What must I look like?'

'You look like a determined young woman who's not
afraid of a bit of work,' the old lady said. 'I am Beatrice
Cameron, one of your husband's many great-aunts. I'm
looking for Hamish.'

'Hamish is away, but maybe I can help you.'

'Well, you aren't short of great-aunts, Marjorie, my
dear. I'll tell you that now,' the old lady said as she
hobbled inside, clubbing the tiles with her stick. 'We are
like a small army and I am here on behalf of many others
because of the rumours we've heard. They say you're
lavishing borrowed money on Hamish's ruined home.'

Her words were scathing and her shrewd old eyes
missed nothing, Marjorie noticed.

'No, not ruined, just run down,' she said. 'I'll show
you round if you like.'

When she had proudly shown off the mosaic tiles, the
beautiful restored wood, the new wallpaper, the mended
oak panelling in the library and the stonework which
was emerging satisfactorily from its century-old coat of

grime, she realised that she was not getting through to Aunt Beatrice at all. Quite the contrary. Now the old lady was clearly furious.

'Did Hamish give you permission to waste money on all this vanity, my dear?' she asked sternly. 'You must know that most of us live off our Glenaird dividends and precious little has been paid out for some years. We are suffering, so how could you spend so much money?' She looked exasperated.

Marjorie's first impulse was to take umbrage, but then she thought how frail and thin the poor old woman was. No doubt she had been deprived. Besides, she would soon be facing a room full of shareholders just like this old lady, and she needed to get them on her side.

'Come with me. I'll tell you all about it over a cup of tea, or coffee if you like. I hope you're not too proud to sit in the kitchen. It's the only room that's finished. I took my mother's advice,' she said, taking Aunt Beatrice by the arm. She was like a bird – so light, so fragile – but there was nothing fragile about her mind. 'Mother told me to get the bedroom and the kitchen done first. Once you can sleep and eat in comfort you can cope with everything else.'

'Admirable,' the old lady snarled, her expression as hostile as ever. Even the warm and gleaming kitchen did nothing to melt the iron in her eyes.

'Mrs Cameron, I have taken a bond on my London flat and sold my share of one of the businesses I was involved in, and I am investing this cash in Hamish's home and business, rather like a dowry. First I'm restoring and cleaning a very lovely home,' she confided. 'It has been badly treated. Then Hamish and I intend to get the distillery back on its feet.'

'I'm afraid you're too late for that,' Aunt Beatrice snapped. 'We, that is the shareholders, are about to sell out to Glentirran, and there's nothing you can do about it. Family shareholders are getting together at a meeting soon to try to bargain for a better price from Glentirran. Shares are rock bottom right now. You probably know that.'

Marjorie tried to regain her composure as she placed a cup of coffee and some biscuits in front of the woman.

'So when is this meeting?'

'Next Thursday.'

Marjorie felt the blood draining from her face, but she tried to hide her dismay. She was ruined. How could she possibly canvass the shareholders in time?

Aunt Beatrice opened a file and flicked through it. 'Here you are.' She offered Marjorie a small printed invitation.

'Who called the meeting?' Marjorie demanded. 'I wasn't informed of it.'

'Why should you be?'

'Because I'm a shareholder.'

'It's a private family meeting.'

'I'm family, too.' She gave Beatrice what she hoped was a warm smile.

'Yes, dear, but if you marry quietly and tell no one, you can't expect the rest of us to know, can you? Here's a copy of Glentirran's offer.'

'Neither Hamish nor I will be selling our shares, Mrs Cameron. You can tell that to the others. I'll be taking over the marketing of the company very shortly and I shall be dismissing John Erskine just as soon as I am in a position to do so.'

'Without the shareholders' support, there's very little

you can do, Marjorie.' The old woman's beady eyes looked haughty and offended.

'Nevertheless, I shall come to the meeting and when I prove to shareholders that John Erskine is Glentirran's man, and that he has been systematically and deliberately reducing the dividends that have been paid out, I am sure they will support us. I shall try to convince them that we can offer a better deal in the long run.'

'You can start with me,' Beatrice said.

'Well, I would have liked more time, but here goes,' Marjorie said nervously.

For the next fifteen minutes she outlined the plans she and Joe had compiled: a five-year, ten-year and fifteen-year programme that would make Glenaird Distillery a high profit earner, while providing a minimum dividend even during the first few years.

'Let's face it, the first five years will be tough,' she said, coming to the end of her presentation.

'My dear, your plan entails massive bank borrowing. No bank in the world will back you with this big a facility. You don't have enough collateral.'

'One merchant bank has agreed,' Marjorie told the surprised woman.

'Which one?'

'The Dover bank we've used since we began with a small publication four years ago. My business partner has just made a fortune with one of his inventions, and the publishing company is doing well, so they trust us.'

She really cares, Beatrice decided, watching Marjorie as she outlined her plans. But caring isn't enough. Does she have the stamina and the toughness and is she streetwise? Beatrice Cameron, Callum's widow and chairman of Grampian Bank, had made it her business to study Marjorie's background. She knew how well she had done, but how much of that was due to her ex-partner, Joe Segal? Splashing her money around on a home that did not belong to her was a sign of foolhardiness.

She pursed her lips as she watched the young girl's fingers gripping the table as if her life were at stake. Could she really run the marketing? And what about Hamish? There was nothing wrong with the boy's brains, he'd done well at school, but he could not stop running from life. Sometimes it takes a woman to bring out the strength in a man, she mused.

Was it fair to shareholders to give Hamish another chance? The old woman sighed and wished she were younger. She would give them a little time, she decided, but not much.

She could not help remembering how she had once been forced to take up the business reins on her husband's behalf. In those days it was not done for women to go into business, and she had hidden behind her husband for years. She had become his implacable will and his shrewdness, but he had provided the front. Would this young woman have done the same? There was strength there, and intelligence, and courage, but would that be enough?

'On behalf of our family shareholders, I can promise to defer the meeting for one month for you to get your plans into writing. We shall expect Hamish to be there. Marjorie, listen to me, you'll need more than empty promises to swing the voters. Bring something concrete to the meeting.'

The old woman stood up and thumped her way back to the porch where she shook hands gravely.

'Oh, by the way,' she called as she reached her car. 'Hurry up and produce an heir. That's very important.'

'I'm not a bloody milk cow,' Marjorie muttered to herself, smiling sweetly as she waved goodbye.

Chapter 52

Marjorie felt like a wrung-out rag after Beatrice Cameron's visit. She was sitting disconsolately on the top step of the porch, deep in thought, when she saw a car coming up the driveway. Mum and Dad! Her stomach lurched. Please God they would love it here.

Moments later the doors burst open and Paddy leaped out. He raced to the nearest bush to put up his leg, too intent on his emergency to greet her.

'Mummy!' Lana raced out and flung herself at her mother. Marjorie hugged her child and whirled her round. Then she put her on her feet and stroked back the wiry black curls that had been sticking on her damp forehead. A lump came in her throat as she studied her child. She loved her so. At last they would be able to be together most of the time.

Mum looked harassed as she pulled herself out of the car, sighing. Her blue dress was crumpled and soiled, her face was pink and moist, and her eyes looked puffy. 'That cat's fair driven me crazy,' she moaned.

Watching her made Marjorie feel even guiltier. She could hear the cat yowling somewhere in the back. Taking Lana's hand, she hurried to the car and lifted down the heavy basket, which rocked and wobbled. 'There, there, Tibby. Calm down. We'll lock him in your scullery for a day. There are plenty of rats around to keep him amused.'

'Oh dear me! What a journey!' Liz wiped her swollen red face with a large handkerchief. 'It was so hot. Lana was restless. She was good little girl, bless her heart, but it's too long for a child to sit cooped up like that. Poor old Paddywonks. Look at him!'

The dog, deep in concentration, was wobbling on his three legs while the stream went on and on.

'I told you we should have stopped,' Lana giggled. 'I expect that bush will die. Where does he keep it all? The longest pee ever.' She began giggling, skipping around, touching the flowers, and then she raced into the grass and threw herself amongst the poppies.

Dad was climbing stiffly out of the car. 'Is this it? Are we here?' He looked shocked and tired and even a little dazed, Marjorie decided, watching him carefully. He was one of life's walking wounded and she intended to look after him. It was strange to think that there were so many men, all over England, who had done more than men should be asked to do, and who, after the war, had put it out of their minds. But it was festering deep down, waiting to surface years later. Would he put down roots and be happy? A sudden wave of love made her long to hug him, but they were not a demonstrative family and this would embarrass Dad.

'This is it! Inveraird Lodge.' Marjorie smiled anxiously. 'What a mess it's been, but things are slowly coming right.'

'And where shall we stay?' Dad asked softly.

'Would you like to see your house first before I take you touring round this place?'

'Whatever you like.' Dad was determined to be non-committal and give nothing away. He looked as if he were about to be shot and her heart went out to him. She knew how he hated to be beholden to anyone.

'Righty-ho! Now let's decide. The driveway loops round the back of the stables to your cottage, or there's a short cut that way.' She pointed to the north-east. 'Through that little wood right to your front door. So . . . *Would you like to take a walk?*' She clowned a bit. Anything for a laugh.

'I'm sure we'd like to stretch our legs.' Mum glanced anxiously at Dad, before turning to the driver Dad had hired together with his car. 'What exactly are your plans?' she asked. 'Are you going straight back? You're very welcome to stay the night. That's so, isn't it, Marjorie?'

'No, no, but thanks, Mrs Hardy. I'll be staying over-night with friends in Inverness, so I'll be off as soon as we've unpacked the boot,' he told her.

Marjorie directed him to the road that led around the back of the lodge to the cottage.

'Well, here's a rum state of affairs,' Dad grumbled, pulling sweethearts off his trousers. 'Ruddy great posh home with a field in front of it?'

'I think it was a lawn once. I haven't tackled the garden yet. Haven't had time.'

'Well, I could take care of the lawn.' Dad's voice was strangely wobbly. 'Got a lawn mower, have you?'

Marjorie was about to sign a contract with a local gardening firm, but there and then she changed her mind. It was something to do with the longing in Dad's eyes.

'Could you? That would be wonderful. I'll get a lawn

mower tomorrow. Or better still you choose one. What
about those fancy things you sit on?'

'They cost too much.'

'Well, maybe not. Let's see.'

'How come Hamish is so broke if he's got all this
land?' Dad asked.

'It's entailed in a family trust. No part of it can
be sold, mortgaged, or disposed of in any way at all,
but death duties, rates and taxes keep him permanently in debt. That is apart from his lack of business
expertise.'

'Don't you go rushing in, Marjorie,' Mum nagged.
'Fools rush in where angels fear to tread. You don't know
the business, you're a stranger and if the distillery folds,
you certainly don't want to be held responsible. You can
keep this place going with your magazine earnings. Close
up part of the house and live in a small bit. That's my
advice.'

Mum's negative view on life, and her self-supportive
clichés, always prodded Marjorie to a state of irritation.
Mum did not know that she had sold her publishing
interests.

'Yes, Mum.' She tried not to sound exasperated.

Mum sighed. 'You be careful, my girl. You don't know
nothing about their world.'

Even less does poor Hamish know, she wanted to
retort, but resisted.

They had reached the overgrown roses. Dad stood
gazing at them with a strange expression on his face,
part wonder that there had been so many, part anger
that they had been so neglected, part longing to get his
hands on them.

'Look at that, a Pascali, and a Minnie Pearl, and a

Handel if I'm not mistaken. They've run wild, but maybe it's not too late to save them.'

Lana shrieked from the wood and they dashed forward. 'A fox, a fox, I saw a fox and it stood there! Right there! It stared at me. Paddywonks has gone after it. Save it, save it!'

'He won't catch it, don't worry.' Marjorie took her hand.

'There's lots of squirrels,' Lana squealed. 'I love squirrels.'

'And lots of birds,' Liz put in. 'Just listen to all that birdsong.'

'I heard a nightingale singing his head off last night. It was beautiful, but so lonely. I'm glad you're here.'

'Isn't Hamish with you?'

'No.' She frowned, unwilling to show how ashamed of him she was. He shouldn't have run away, but he had. 'He's climbing in the Alps.'

'What! On your honeymoon?'

'The problem is, he wanted to go away somewhere and I wanted to get stuck in with the work.'

'Well, Marjorie dear, now you're a married woman you can't always do exactly what you want to do, can you? I mean, not when it involves the two of you. He's entitled to a honeymoon. After all, he married you.'

'Yes, you're probaby right, Mum.'

She wasn't going to worry her family with news of the precarious state of Hamish's finances, and the absolute need to be in Britain, particularly now, when Joe was buying up every Glenaird share he could get on her behalf.

The moment they stepped into the cottage Marjorie

knew it was going to be all right. Mum was speechless, wandering around admiring the flowers, the views and the marvellous cupboard space.

'I'm sorry it's not quite ready, Mum.'

'You've spent a fortune on this place, I can see that. What if you fall out of love? Had you considered that?' Mum was sweating with the unaccustomed effort of taking a stand.

'I'm not in love.'

'More fool you, my girl. What's marriage without love? I don't care how rich and successful you are, marriage involves intimacy. There'll come those times you'll have to nurse him, and do those special things for him. The trick of living well is to hang on to something meaningful. Then it makes the ups and downs meaningless. You may find you have to wash his shirts, darn his socks or nurse him when he's sick. These simple chores are unendurable if you don't love your husband. It puts you down too much. Love's the answer. Then even silly jobs take on the utmost significance.'

It was the longest speech Mum had ever given. 'I shan't be darning any socks,' Marjorie answered briskly.

'So what do rich people do for each other?'

'Nothing, I hope. I have a maid.'

'Then I'm glad I'm poor.'

'Oh, Mum, don't nag so.'

Dad followed them around in silence, but when he gazed out of the bedroom window he was suddenly rooted to the spot.

'What's that?' He pointed southwards.

'What? Where? Oh, that,' she murmured with feigned carelessness. Dad's ambition had always been to have a duck pond. 'It's a lake. There's ducks and things.'

'Neighbour's?'

'No. Hamish's.'

'Can we go there?'

'Why not? I generally feed the ducks around sunset. There's a bin of corn in a shack behind the trees. I'd considered buying a swan. What do you think?'

'Two swans,' Dad said. 'That's if they aren't too expensive. Look here, Marjorie, I'm going to ask Hamish for a job. I'll be your gardener in return for the rent. I won't want no pay. Naturally so. No point in you being proud about these things. Being a gardener's better than being unemployed. It's something I know a lot about and I'll enjoy it. I'll have this place shipshape in no time at all. I might even make it pay a bit. There's money in cut flowers if you've got the space and the water. You'll see.'

'I know you will, Dad,' she answered softly. 'And there's an old overgrown vegetable garden over that way. Could you keep us supplied with fresh salad and vegetables? You know how expensive these things are.'

'Could I? You wait, my girl. And you won't have to wait too long neither.'

'Well then.' Marjorie exhaled a deep sigh which she'd been storing up for the past month. 'Well, then . . .'

Chapter 53

The day after her parents arrived, Marjorie set off early to visit the many family shareholders within driving distance. She had to find out for herself which way they would vote at the coming meeting, and if possible sway them to support her. The three calls she had made so far had been crushingly unsuccessful. It was almost noon and she was tired and depressed, for she had been the butt of so much ill will and aggression. She sighed as she drew up in front of 10 Riverside Drive, and glanced at her list.

Mrs Lucy Cameron, a widow, lived alone in a shabby bungalow. She opened the door and glared at Marjorie, her eyes and anger magnified by thick lenses, as she came right out with her grudges. 'I know who you are and what you've come about and you needn't waste your time here.' She hugged her cardigan around her, maybe for protection since it was too warm to be cold. Watching her, Marjorie guessed that she felt lost without her husband and found it hard to take a stand.

'No offence taken, Mrs Cameron. I'm pleased to meet you. Quite apart from business, I've also come to introduce myself. It may seem a little unusual, but I wanted to meet Hamish's family.'

'Family? Huh! I've never set eyes on him, and that's

the truth. But still,' she added as inbred good manners overcame her hostility. 'Come in, lass, perhaps you'd like a cup of tea?'

'Thanks. What a relief! I've been driving around for hours.'

The woman led the way inside, walking slowly on crippled legs. Marjorie could almost smell the loneliness and poverty in the bleak living room. Oh, Hamish. You should be here. So should John Erskine, Marjorie reflected bitterly.

She sipped her tea and mulled over her sales pitch while chatting inconsequentially with her hostess. She had been unsuccessful on her previous calls, although she had explained at length about their rosy future expectations. She had graphs, brochures, statistics and forecasts of future whisky prices, in a full-colour brochure, together with the latest issue of *Leadership* depicting Hamish clinging to a rocky peak and smiling confidently at shareholders and readers.

This hadn't worked so far and she had wasted three calls – three valuable shareholders who would vote against her at the meeting. She needed something new. Instinctively she felt that an emotional appeal would be better than financial explanations.

'Mrs Cameron, you've hung on to your shares through the bad years and I'm wondering why you never sold them?' she asked tentatively.

The woman twisted her cup nervously. 'Because he was a Cameron, as you know.' She gestured towards the mantelpiece where a faded picture of a man in a captain's uniform had pride of place. 'He always felt that Glenaird whisky would make good eventually. He used to tell me that when the industry resurrected itself from World War Two and the post-war years, you folks would build up the finest distillery in Scotland and we'd have a good income.' Her mouth turned down bitterly. 'He put all his demob and compensation pay and our savings into buying these shares, quite apart from what he inherited.'

Marjorie sipped her tea slowly as Mrs Cameron's story poured out, then made her appeal.

'The truth is, my husband and I have decided to make a comeback and build up the company, for the sake of the shareholders who have been robbed, and that includes Hamish, too. Let me explain what's been happening . . .'

She did, at length, and when she walked out she had the woman's proxy signed and sealed and witnessed by a neighbouring policeman.

By evening Marjorie felt bloated with cups of tea and slabs of fruitcake, but despite her efforts she only had voting power on another three per cent of family-owned shares. She longed to go home, but she had an appointment with Joe's spy first thing in the morning, and Garth wanted to see her, so she was flying to London on the late flight and staying the night at her London flat. She felt depressed as she parked her car at Inverness airport. Belatedly she realised that only a miracle could save them.

Derek Olivier turned out to be quite the opposite to what Marjorie had expected. He operated from an exclusive address in Conduit Street. Commercial Intelligence Investigations, read the discreet sign on the door. Olivier might have been an ageing lawyer or a banker with his dark suit, conservative tie, grey and white striped shirt and sleek brown hair. Only his eyes gave him away – they were young eyes of a remarkable blue shade, translucent like ice crystals, and glinting with fun and a yen for adventure.

Marjorie came to the point speedily. 'My husband is the chairman of Glenaird whisky,' she explained. 'We are currently fighting for the company's survival against a takeover bid. It is you who alerted us to the fact that John Erskine has one foot in the enemy's camp and . . .'

'Relax, Mrs Cameron. How about tea? Take your time, please. If you're in a hurry, come back later.'

She refused tea, and explained about the need to pull a rabbit out of the hat, and how she longed to discover more details about Glentirran's underhand tactics.

'You see, Mr Olivier, I intend to use Glentirran's methods to make sure that I know exactly what they are doing in future: expansion plans, marketing and investments. I need to know their strengths and their weaknesses.'

'You are assuming that you will survive this envisaged takeover.'

'Yes.' She took a deep breath and looked away. 'We don't have any choice really. We must succeed.'

He smiled, but there was a shrewdly assessing look in his eyes. 'I have a good deal of background information which was of no interest to Mr Segal. He tells me that the Glenaird shares were purchased on your behalf.'

'Yes.'

'Well, that's what friends are for, I suppose.'

She ignored his probing, wondering how much Joe had told him.

'Hamish Cameron seems to have turned his back on his mother's side of the family. As far as I am concerned, that is Glentirran's greatest weakness, and your husband's greatest strength.'

'What is? I don't understand.' A jolt of excitement dried her mouth. She licked her lips nervously. She had assumed that the Hong Kong trading company was long since defunct.

'I'm talking about your husband's Eastern connections. Simon, his late father, merged the Inver-Asian Trading Company, in Hong Kong, with his brother-in-law's Korean outfit, based all over the place, but lately mainly in Singapore.' He laughed deprecatingly. 'He moves as the wind and tax benefits dictate. Yoshi Tohara, your husband's uncle, plays things very close to the cuff. It's hard to pin down exactly what they're worth, but it's rumoured Tohara is very rich indeed. Presumably your husband owns half of the whole. He's unlikely to see much of past profits, but he could call in their help to bail him out of trouble. After all, they owe him, although they will deny this. I didn't pursue this area, mainly because Joe wasn't interested.'

'Pursue it quickly,' she crowed. 'We only have a month.'

'Well, how's this for starters,' Olivier replied smugly. He produced a file from the cabinet and laid it reverently on the desk.

As Marjorie went through the papers with him, the print blurred in front of her eyes. Was this the miracle she needed so badly?

Chapter 54

Hamish's nights were filled with images: a hard-headed woman standing at the reception desk hammering her fist on the counter, emerald eyes glinting with determination, Titian hair ablaze in the sunlight. Then there was that other woman, gentle as a deer, softly smiling as she hugged her child, eyes that were full of caring and sparkling with love. It was strange how her eyes changed, sometimes so flinty hard, and sometimes melting into infinite warmth and promise. That was Marjorie for you. He thought, too, about her beautiful breasts, and the way she slept, hair in a tangle, lashes fanning her cheeks. She looked so virginal yet so sensual.

He regretted his decision to run away from the shareholders' meeting, for Marjorie was bound to pick up the flak. There would be press reports, maybe journalists hanging around, papers to sign. He should have been there to help her.

The truth was, he couldn't face his wife. It was only a matter of days before he was flung out by Aunt Beatrice and Glentirran moved in, with Andrew and Ian at the helm.

It wasn't that he was a coward, Hamish rationalised. He was a fighter, but he wasn't a fool. He knew he could never expect to get the Scottish Camerons on his side.

Without their support he stood no chance of combating his uncle and cousin in their bid. Andrew, a true Scot, and a huge man with bull shoulders, smouldering blue eyes and a mop of sandy hair, was the sort of figure shareholders could look up to.

So while his future was being played out, he had opted for a long climb in the Alps, but as if to punish him, the expedition had been cursed from the start, one disaster following another. The wind had been bad, the weather foul, they had lost a man in an avalanche that nearly killed them all, and his team had voted to pack up and go home.

He didn't know how he was going to tell Marjorie that he'd lost the business. She was one of the world's winners, whereas he was a loser. He'd soon fall off the pedestal she'd made for him, and then what?

Hamish had left his car at Inverness airport, and by three p.m. he was speeding home, wondering what he would find there. Autumn mists drifted in valleys, leaves were turning gold, the hedgerows were full of crab apples and berries. Birds were swooping, circling and gathering restlessly as they prepared for their long southern migrations. Hamish hardly noticed. He was seeing Marjorie in his scruffy home, trying to cope with soot and dust sheets and rotten old furniture. How could he do that to her? He wondered if she'd missed him. Would she be waiting for him, or would she have packed up and gone back to London? He wouldn't blame her one little bit if she had.

His mouth was dry as he tried to open the gate, but it resisted all his efforts. Then he noticed a button and a voice box. That was new. He pushed the button.

'Hello,' he heard Lana call. 'Hello, hello, hello.' Another voice was calling in the background.

'Can you open the gate, Lana? It's me, Hamish.' Should he have said, Daddy?

'Go away. No one wants you here,' she called quite distinctly and cut him off.

Hamish sighed. Winning over Lana was one of his first priorities, but since she was there, Marjorie couldn't be far away. His heart pounding, he parked his car and climbed over the gate. Moments later he was jogging up the driveway.

As he rounded the bend to the front of the house, he stopped in wonder to gaze at the smooth lawn that sloped down to the lake. A child's tricycle lay on its side and further off he saw Mr Hardy on a mobile lawn mower that was ploughing into the long grass by the lake. A dog was loping along behind. He turned to the house and gaped at the scaffolding. He'd always hated that dirty grey stone. He walked up to the house and ran his finger over a clean patch. It was not grey at all, sort of pinky-white and quite lovely. Clearly Marjorie had been flinging her money around.

Rushing up the steps he threw open the door and yelled, 'Marjorie . . . Where are you?'

'My God!' He stood in a daze staring for a long time. The hall was clean and freshly painted, the floor took his breath away it was so exquisite, and the old paintings had been dusted and cleaned. They looked different. Maybe the walls had something to do with that – surely the colour had changed?

He wasn't quite sure what had happened in detail, only that a fairy godmother had waved her wand and transformed the lodge into a home. And the fairy godmother was Marjorie, of course. Who else could make this transformation in a matter of weeks?

There were so many changes, he noticed, many of them only half-completed. In a daze he walked to the kitchen, which was warm and homely, with a spotless marble floor, a long kitchen table that gleamed in the evening light, lacy curtains and copper pots hanging on the walls. The black Welsh dressers he'd always hated were now a light brown shade and the shelves were full of bright plates and cups and vases. Beyond the pantry and scullery was the gun room, but it looked as if it was being converted into a laundry room, with newly cemented walls still drying out.

Hamish jumped with shock when a dark-skinned woman hurried in wearing a green overall.

'You the master?' she asked, her face impassive.

'I'm Hamish Cameron.'

'I'm Zola.' She pointed to herself and grinned. 'You want some food?'

'No thanks. Where's Marjorie?'

'She's out. Lana is with the old madam.'

'And where's the old madam?' he asked, feeling bemused.

'Over by the cottage.'

He hurried down the steps and went across the lawn towards the mower. Were the family already living here? He knew Mr Hardy didn't like him and he felt appalled at being back in the familiar situation where he was not wanted in his own home. Lana's voice seemed to echo in his ear with a new urgency. 'Go away. No one wants you here.'

'Hello, sir.' He held out his hand to shake the older man's with a show of false heartiness.

'Hamish? Is that what I call you? We didn't expect you back for another week at least. Marjorie will be so pleased.'

'But where is she?'

'Working, of course. That's girl's always working at something or other. You'll get used to it, I expect. Look, I'm glad you're here.' He climbed off the mower. 'I want to have a talk, man to man, so to speak, without our bossy womenfolk around. But wait a minute. Oh dear me.'

He walked back and took the key out of the ignition. 'I have to remember to never leave the key there, and the same applies to you, if you should decide to cut the grass. Lana's got her eye on it. We caught her trying to start it yesterday. She's a regular daredevil and sly as they come. Just leave this key around and she'll be up here the moment we turn our backs.

'No, Hamish. It's like this.' His story poured out in a rush and Hamish realised he had rehearsed it many times. Their house in Dover had been let on a short lease when Marjorie had insisted they move. The truth was they were loving it here, but hating the idea of being in the way or unwanted. Hamish should just say the word and they'd be gone. They weren't folks for staying where they weren't wanted. Marjorie was headstrong and determined, but she had her faults and one of them was sweeping away other folks' desires. It wasn't that they were homeless, he mustn't think that, they had their house in Dover. She'd have sold that if she could, but they wouldn't let her. She was getting together all the cash she could lay her hands on to revamp the lodge and the distillery.

Oh God! Hamish cringed. How awful! She had spent a fortune on the lodge. As to the distillery, it was no longer his. Had she found out about the meeting yet? He felt like weeping. He'd pay her back every last penny out of the cash he'd be paid for his shares. The fact that he could do that made him feel a bit better. The old man seemed to have exhausted his explanations and Hamish was glad of this because he hated to see people suffering.

He clapped him on the shoulder. 'I'm so glad you're here.' He felt sad to see Mr Hardy hanging on his every word. 'It's too lonely for Marjorie when I'm away, and besides Lana needs all of us, and we need you for Lana . . . and for Marjorie. As for me, I get as lonely as the next man stuck out here. I'll be delighted to have company, too. The old houses were built for larger families. That's what they're all about.'

He broke off. 'I'm worried about Marjorie. I should never have left, only . . .' How could he possibly explain?

'Don't worry about Marjorie. She goes her own way. Come and have a drink with me at the cottage, Hamish. I daresay Mother will make some ham sandwiches. Do Buddhists eat ham?'

'I eat anything,' Hamish assured him.

Remembering how dull and horrible the cottage was, Hamish shuddered as he followed the old man through the wood, but once inside he saw that it had been transformed into a cosy home. Liz was ironing while Lana played with her bricks on the floor. The child was watching him intently.

'Are you going to be my daddy like they say?' she burst out, looking daggers at him.

'I'd like that if you want me to. But it's up to you. Wait a few days and see if you like me enough. Then choose.'

'Choose what?'

'What you'd like me to be.'

'What else could you be?' She wrinkled her forehead.

'I could be the dog brusher, or the duck feeder, or the car mender, or the window cleaner. You decide.'

'Would you smack me when I'm naughty?'

'No, never,' he promised.

'Would I be your 'dopted daughter or your real daughter?'

'My real daughter.'

'Then you can be my daddy, but you have to be all those other things, too.' She climbed on to his lap and ran her fingers through his hair and for the second time in his life, Hamish fell in love.

Chapter 55

Marjorie drove home feeling satisfied, but tired. It was almost nine and the land was suffused with the beautiful lingering Scottish twilight that transforms the landscape into a magical place of muted colours under an incandescent sky. As she turned into the last home stretch, a deer leapt across the road and bounded over the eight-foot boundary fence as if it were of trifling height. Then a brown hare stood rigid with fright, blinded by the beam, so she braked violently and switched off her lights until the startled creature bolted.

A sense of peace and calm sank into her, and a feeling of contentment. Her own home! She had lived there for only a month, yet she had never felt for any place so deeply and she was not alone in this. Seeing Dad so happy as he transformed the gardens was both a relief and a joy. She liked to watch him standing by the lake in the twilight, feeding his greedy ducks. Lana loved their wood with a passion, and it was rich with berries from rowan bushes and hawthorne. The gorse was still blooming, although it was late for gorse. She had seen wild cats and pine martens in the evenings. The fox had made its lair in a thicket, and she saw it often. There were red squirrels and hundreds of birds: woodpeckers, goldcrests, siskins, woodcocks, sparrowhawks, harriers and several owls.

Turning the last bend, she saw a car parked in the shadows under the tall oaks by the gate. She felt a glow of happiness as she realised that Hamish was back – but why had he left his car outside? The probable explanation set her smiling. She would drive it in later. She opened the gates and drove up to the house, loving everything she saw.

Parking in the garage, she hurried through the connecting door to the scullery. Zola was sitting yawning in the rocking chair.

'Why so late, Zola?'

Zola's eyes and mouth contorted into a smile of immense proportions. 'I was waiting for the master to come back from the old madam. He might not know where to sleep.'

'Not "the master". Please call him Mr Cameron. I'll tell him that I'm back. Good night, Zola.'

Taking a torch from the shelf in the scullery, she hurried across the lawn. Moving through the copse she saw two green eyes glinting. She stood still and saw the fox quite plainly. Then it was gone.

Reaching the cottage she could hardly suppress a feeling of anxiety. Was everything all right? Then she heard the sound of Lana's laughter and that at least was comforting.

The French windows were open and the room was brightly lit. She could sense the warm atmosphere as she loitered outside the window, enjoying the scent of lavender and newly cut grass. For a moment no one noticed her.

She smiled. Dad had put up a dartboard at one end of the room and Hamish was aiming his dart, while Lana, hanging from his back, giggled happily.

'Steady on, Lana. Freeze!' Hamish commanded. As his hand flicked forward, Lana jerked her legs and the dart went wide. She giggled more than ever.

'Put her down, Hamish,' Mum called nervously.

'She's my handicap,' Hamish explained patiently to his mother-in-law. 'I happen to be a dab hand at darts. She can stay till she's tired of hanging on. After that, I'll show you a thing or two, Mr Hardy.'

'Well, I don't doubt that,' Dad replied ponderously. 'But listen here, Hamish. Why don't you call me Dad?'

'Mummy, Mummy, Mummy,' came the excited shrieks as Lana slid to the floor. Marjorie bent down to hug her and for a few minutes she could only see tousled black ringlets. When at last she straightened up, she glanced across the room at Hamish. His eyes locked with hers. There was so much caring there.

For a moment she felt loved and secure. Then common sense swung back like a pendulum. Love was an illusion and as for secure – Hamish was incapable of looking after himself, let alone her. It was need, not love, that shone in his eyes, based on a longing to be accepted and a craving for a strong woman to help him face his shareholders and creditors.

She submitted when Hamish folded her in his arms, and smiled up at him, playing out her wifely role. 'Surprised?' she asked. 'Have you been inside the lodge? Did you like it? Were you home in time to see the garden?'

'Unbelievable,' Hamish murmured, looking guilty rather than pleased, she noticed. 'You must have a magic wand hidden somewhere.'

'The real question is,' she persisted gravely, 'do you like it?'

Hamish nodded and sat down at the table as naturally as if he'd been there all his life. He wolfed a pile of ham sandwiches Mum pushed towards him, washing them down with lager. Dad and he were quite at home with each other, she noticed. How strange that Hamish fitted into the family, while she never really had.

'Eat,' Hamish nagged. 'That's an order, wife. I bet you haven't eaten all day. Have you?'

Wife, she thought. How odd!

It was decided that Marjorie looked too tired to bath Lana and that Lana must continue to sleep with her grandparents until such time as the old house was properly heated.

While Mum put Lana to bed, Marjorie sat at the table and listened to the two men chatter as she gratefully sipped her Scotch on ice, feeling safely insulated from the sad, impoverished shareholders.

She listened dreamily as Dad outlined his latest problem to Hamish. The fox was taking the ducklings nightly. The silly creatures slept under the willow fronds on the sandy ledge by the lake. 'Fat lot of protection that gives them,' she heard. 'I have a dream of creating an island in the middle of the lake with willows on it, but that will take a while. Meantime the fox is as wily as can be. I've left Paddy down there, but it doesn't make a blind bit of difference to that crafty creature. That's why he's here, for the ducks,' Dad was grumbling.

'What about that old wooden jetty falling to bits by the boathouse?' Hamish suggested. 'It's long past repair. Why don't we turn it into a raft and tow it out to the centre? We could build some sort of a shelter on it. They'd soon get used to sleeping there.'

She became bored, and thought about the figures

that tumbled around in her head. How could she get the bank and the shareholders on her side? There was only a month until the meeting. After a while she felt Hamish tugging at her hand under the table and pushing it down on his penis, which was hard and bursting against his jeans.

Looking up with a guilty start, she saw that Mum was making tea.

'Where's Dad?' she whispered, flushing.

'He's taken Paddy to guard the ducks. I don't want tea, do you?'

'No.'

'Come on. Let's say goodnight to Lana and go. I'm longing for you.' He pushed her hand down harder and writhed his hips. 'I want you so badly,' he whispered.

'Me too,' she said automatically and then realised that it was the truth. 'Oh, Hamish, yes. I really do.'

Something stirred in Marjorie that night. It was partly a physical awakening, a widening of her boundaries of sensuality and fulfilment. There was also a sense of trust and merging which she had never experienced before. For the first time each portion of flesh, each hollow and cleft, was a place of exquisite pleasure, and there was that promise that there was more, much more to be explored, and that they had for ever. Then there was the knowledge that she was loved by a man who adored women. For Hamish there was no holding back, no sense of arrogance in his maleness, no shrinking from the female psyche. He loved, simply, entirely and tenderly, and he adored her body. But there was still more, an intellectual acceptance that what they shared was extraordinary and that they would treasure and nurture this gift of sharing and bonding. For Marjorie it was a night of wonder. She gave up her separateness and merged with Hamish and the pleasure he created.

At midnight he woke her again. When she felt his naked flesh against hers, she thrilled to his touch, but she was tired, so tired, too exhausted to move. She lay as if in a coma, compliant and inert, but inside her every pulse and nerve lay quivering in eager acceptance of the coming sensations.

Once again he wooed her with his tongue and finger-tips, with that careful probing, sensing and exploring for those hidden pleasure places, while deep down, the molten lava of her need was mounting, shifting, compressing, hotter and fiercer, until she was nothing more than a volcano heaved up out of the earth by its own unbearable pressure. As she came rushing towards her climax she screamed, erupting with red-hot spasms of ecstasy.

'Hamish, oh my love, oh my dear, oh Hamish, darling, I love you,' she sobbed out. Yet still a small part of her held back and remained inviolate. She would not share her inner core. That way led to disaster.

Chapter 56

Hamish lay sleeping on his back in bed. His head was slightly turned towards the open window, and the moon, lustrous and unashamed, explored his body, enhancing each contour, outlining the sinews and muscles, bathing his flesh with her lascivious light. His flared nostrils, the set of his jawline, the width of his cheeks and his high forehead showed power and resilience, but Hamish had turned away from his fellow men. His fitness and courage were lavished instead on unknown mountain peaks. God knew how many awesome battles he had fought and won, alone and unheralded, Marjorie reflected, watching him now.

He was ashamed of his genes, yet in them lay his extraordinary strength. Looking at him, she sensed that his talents and his resolve came from his Japanese mother. She sat up abruptly as an idea hit her. Reaching over, she shook Hamish until he woke.

'Hamish, listen to me,' she said urgently. 'If you can't hide it, flaunt it.'

'Marjorie, why aren't you sleeping?' he asked drowsily. He peered at his watch beside the bed. 'Good God! It's two a.m. Why do you feed me clichés in the middle of the night?'

'Please, Hamish. Tell me about your mother. It's important.'

He sighed. 'I will indulge your whims since we are newly married, but don't expect this state of affairs to last for ever, wife. I remember her so well,' he said dreamily. 'She was so gentle, so noble, and her manners were always impeccable. She was clever, make no mistake, but always feminine . . .'

'And your father was in partnership with her brother,' Marjorie interrupted impatiently.

He looked surprised that she should know. 'Is this a business conversation?'

'Yes, of course. What else? Why didn't you tell me about your mother's side of the family? It's important, Hamish.'

'Silly of me to think . . .' He broke off. Then he said abruptly, 'Is business that vital? Do you have to know?'

'Yes, we have to survive, Hamish.'

'My father merged the Inver-Asian Trading Company with the Tohara Trading Company owned by my uncle, Yoshi Tohara . . .'

'And where is Tohara?'

'Toharasan,' he corrected her.

'So where is he and where is your half-share of the profits? What happened to all your father's hard work? Surely you realise that they owe you?'

'Look here.' He sat up, scowling. 'If this is to be an all-night affair, I want some coffee.'

'Done!' She bent over and kissed his eyes and his forehead and the lovely sloping line of his cheeks. When he tried to grab her she scrambled out of bed.

Five minutes later they were side by side in bed, dunking biscuits in their coffee and watching the clouds race past the moon. Sitting there Marjorie felt a strange sense of oneness with Hamish. He was a warm and loyal man and very sexy. What if she had met him first?

'I have not heard from my uncle since I came to Scotland,' Hamish began.

'Well, I've checked and he's very rich and powerful. Furthermore, he owes you eighteen years of profits. Of course, he won't pay up. He'll say there weren't any, but he'll know he owes you and we'll work on his guilt. Tell me more.'

'Aunt Beatrice paid someone to try to get some cash out of Toharasan to reimburse the trust, but my uncle was hard to pin down. According to her, Toharasan refused to deal with the Camerons because they had been so rude to his sister. He claimed that my father was almost bankrupt when he died and that he bailed him out. Naturally he holds all the accounts. After the loan period was up, Aunt Beatrice bought the Glenaird shares from the bank. She owns them personally, so she has all the power and the minor family shareholders follow her lead.'

'Beatrice?' she queried, feeling shocked. 'Just how many Beatrice Camerons are there?'

'One, to my knowledge. She's stone rich and batty.'

'With beady blackbird eyes, and sparrow's bones reinforced with rings and things?'

'The same.'

'There's nothing batty about her. So how much equity does she own?' she asked with a quaver in her voice.

'Wrong tense,' he said, looking shame-faced. 'You see, darling, there was this meeting on the fourteenth . . .'

'No, there wasn't. Beatrice Cameron came to see me when you were away and I persuaded her to delay the meeting until the thirtieth of September, to give us

time.' Marjorie could hardly control her excitement.
'Hamish, listen to me. Problems are opportunities for
correction. Your problem, you think, is that you are not
one of them. You can't hide your Asian bit, so flaunt it.
Nothing ventured, nothing . . .'

'Give it a break, Marjorie. You sound just like your
mother.'

'All the same, they're not going to sell you down
the river.'

'One more cliché and it's rape for you, young lady,'
he warned.

'Hamish, we're going to win.' She watched his eyes
narrow with a sense of pain.

'So what if we win? We don't have the cash to see us
through.'

'All I'm worth is going into Glenaird and my bank's
prepared to back me. Of course, I'll expect shares for my
cash. Joe will help, too. We'll raise the working capital
somehow.'

'And you would do all this for me?' he asked incredulously.

Her guilt surged 'We're married, aren't we? It's for
both of us. We're going to become very rich one day.'

'Is that all you want?'

'No,' she said. 'Not nearly all. Hamish, I want you
to win.'

Long after Hamish was sleeping, Marjorie lay
scheming and worrying. The key lay in Singapore.
Tohara-what's-it must be persuaded to help them, and
there were dozens of ways to encourage him to do
this. If Glentirran wanted Glenaird so much, it was a
viable business. So possibly Toharasan could be tempted,
at a price.

But how could she market it to him? She had always relied on her strength and negotiating expertise, but she would be lost if she could not speak his language. There was no point in relying on Hamish. In the jungle called business he'd be more vulnerable than a baby deer. She had to have someone on her side who spoke their language. Perhaps Joe could think of something.

She curled up behind Hamish and he stirred. One hand fumbled behind him to grab hers and press it over his penis.

'Go to sleep. I have to think,' she whispered.

What if they gave Toharasan sole rights to all Glenaird whisky sales in the Far East? Or what if they went into partnership with him with half of the distillery's production? If he had the cash it might be worth his while to pay to put down stocks, or to pay for their expansion . . . ? What if . . . ?

Eventually she fell asleep.

Chapter 57

It was noon, a sultry, clouded, stuffy noon, but the ten top Tohara executives were looking immaculate in their expensive tropical suits as they chatted around an occasional table in Singapore's famous Raffles Hotel, drinking ice-cold beer. Above them gigantic punkahs made their exotic turns. Dark-skinned waiters in white overalls with red cummerbunds and fezzes to match hovered with trays of drinks. In the background someone was playing 'Pale Hands I Love' on the piano.

Marjorie was disappointed with the 'lion' city. She had expected something exciting and oriental. This extravaganza of high-rise luxury hotels, shops and office blocks with streets boasting names like Hollyhock Crescent and Springfield Lane offended her. Even this famous old hotel contrived to pretend that they were safely back in colonial days. It was funny how the English put their stamp on faraway places. She had yet to see a cricket match on a village green, but this would come, too, she felt sure.

If only they had had time to see the older parts of the city, but their hosts had whisked them from one expensive nightclub to the next, and most of the business meetings had taken place in the group's air-conditioned offices in a modern high-rise office tower, overlooking the picturesque harbour. They had been brought here for drinks only as a concession to her pleas to see something with atmosphere, but this wasn't quite what she had meant.

Yoshi Tohara, Hamish's uncle, was darker and shorter than Hamish, but otherwise they might have been father and son, she noticed, studying them both. Falteringly at first, but later with increasing efficiency, Hamish had remembered his childhood language, but in deference to her presence they sometimes spoke in English.

For three days Marjorie tried to assess whether her longed-for deal was materialising, but feedback from Hamish was agonisingly inadequate.

It was obvious that Toharasan was downgrading his success and insisting that there had been no profits, merely a slow uphill push towards expansion, but he could not diminish Hamish's future rights and at least on that point they were agreed. So be it for the time being, she decided. At the moment they wanted his uncle's goodwill and all his organisational ability. They needed him on their side, but with certain precautions.

One of those precautions, belatedly produced by Joe like a rabbit out of a hat, was about to land in Singapore. Marjorie could not wait to see if the famous oriental inscrutability would pass the test.

It was five days since Marjorie had called Joe and, in a long, impassioned plea for his assistance, outlined her plans and her incredible disadvantage in not speaking Japanese. It had not taken Joe long to find the person she needed: a newly qualified lawyer, Melanie Robinson, half-Japanese, half-British, who was setting up as a contract and business broker specialising in Far East trade. She was fluent in both languages, but domiciled and educated in London and she had agreed to act on behalf of Glenaird as their legal, marketing and financial advisor in the new whisky export company Marjorie envisaged, in partnership with Toharasan.

'Be prepared for a shock,' Joe had warned, 'but remember, this person is highly qualified. And Marjorie, for once, please trust me.'

What a strange thing to say. She had always trusted him.

Nevertheless, for a moment she almost flinched as Ms Melanie Robinson rose to greet them when they returned to Toharasan's offices. How could anyone so exquisite be the least bit intelligent? How could anyone so petite fight for their cause? How could anyone so immaculately groomed have time to do anything other than study her image in the mirror? As Melanie stood waiting to be introduced, absolutely at ease, the sunlight struck her face, illuminating the smooth contours. She might have walked off a fashion rostrum, despite thirty-six hours of travelling. Even Toharasan had a speculative, predatory look in his eyes as if he were wondering just how far he would be able to go.

Nowhere, Marjorie guessed with a glint of laughter. She could see that Ms Robinson was well able to look after herself. It was strange that the men obviously saw her so differently. She was introduced by Marjorie as the company's 'East-West relations consultant', but it was clear that 'watchdog' would be a better description.

There was a great deal of laughter and bowing as they moved to the boardroom. Hamish had Ms Robinson by the arm, but there was something strangely wooden about his gait. Then Marjorie realised that he was tense with anger, but he was trying to hide his feelings.

The men were hovering by the chairs, not knowing quite where to seat Ms Robinson, gazing questioningly at Hamish. He turned to her and now they could all see his shock and embarrassment. She had some explaining to do and she had been putting it off. Marjorie sighed and beckoned to Ms Robinson.

'I think you'd better sit next to me, please, Melanie.

'Gentlemen, it's like this. We face a crisis back home. The Cameron family are trying to force Hamish out of control of the distillery. They don't want someone who's half-Japanese taking over what has always been considered a Scottish heritage. Hamish is fighting back, and I'm with him in his fight. I'm with him, gentlemen, to the tune of one million pounds of my own cash. If we win, Hamish will run the plant, production, finance, admin, quality control, all those things. I will run marketing, that's my strength.

'We are here to establish an Eastern export company for Glenaird whisky. You are family and we'd rather keep it in the family, but . . .' She left the matter open to their imagination. 'I can't negotiate with you because I can't speak your language. Melanie Robinson is here to make up for my shortcomings. Melanie, would you translate, please.'

'Not necessary at all,' Toharasan muttered brusquely, his face a picture of glittering unease.

'Then if you will allow me, I'll outline our plan. Ms Robinson will be able to translate anything that is not clear to you.'

What she wanted was a three-million-dollar invest-ment in Glenaird, secured by their stocks of spirit maturing in the barrels. In return Glenaird would form a separate Eastern trading company, in partnership with Hamish's uncle. Her own cash would go into this export arm, rather than Glenaird, and she would hold fifty per cent of the shares. Toharasan's cash would keep Glenaird floating through the long years of no income until they were able to export malt whisky to the East. She began at the end, listing the profits that would accrue to bottling and marketing twelve-year-old whisky with their own brand name. Then she moved back in time to the interim period when they would market an inferior, cheaper blend from existing five-year-old stocks of spirit.

When she finished outlining her plans the meeting came to an abrupt end. Uncle Tom Cobley and all, as she privately called Toharasan and his stooges, wished to have a private family meeting with Hamish. Toharasan looked guilty as he showed the women to the lift.

'You must remember, Hamish left here when he was eight and he never wrote and never returned. You must forgive us for considering that he had turned his back on the East. We assumed that he was ashamed of his Japanese side.'

'Maybe he turned his back on unhappiness and memories of his bereavement,' Marjorie murmured with a soft smile, 'but never on his father's business. After all, it is his birthright. Where were you, Toharasan, when Hamish was alone and frightened and being victimised in a foreign land?'

With impeccable timing the lift door slid open and Marjorie and Ms Robinson stepped in, leaving Uncle Tom Cobley to squirm.

Chapter 58

———— ————

'You made me feel ashamed. How could you behave like this? You should have seen your face – you looked so hard, so set against them, so . . .' Hamish turned to her and she saw the appeal in his eyes. She, too, was suffering, for this was their first fight.

'So what?' she asked flatly.

'So obsessed with winning. Someone I didn't like.'

Marjorie grieved inwardly, but now was not the time to weaken. 'You didn't include me in your business discussions. You hardly bothered to translate or tell me what was happening.'

'That is the Japanese way.'

'Does your bloody Japanese way include wives investing their life savings in their husband's companies? I want to know what's going on. Why shouldn't I? I'm paying for it. Besides, this was my idea and I'm scared you won't pull it off.'

'Thanks! That showed very clearly.'

'Sorry, Hamish, but this deal is make or break for you. At times I suspect you don't care enough.'

'Calling in that watchdog of yours made it clear we don't trust them.'

'Good! I, for one, don't trust them. For eighteen years you haven't received a single balance sheet or one penny in profits, but from now on Melanie will keep tabs on them. She's highly qualified. They won't diddle you again.'

'They are family,' Hamish protested. 'Toharasan was almost in tears.'

'Remember this, Hamish. Words are cheap, but actions count. Let's see if they care enough to help you out of the shit. We're not asking for charity, since they're getting a damned good deal out of it. Trust is built on actions made over a period of time. If they want to be trusted, then let them start building trust now. You can give them that from me. Free!'

'How did you grow so tough, my Marjorie?' Hamish mourned.

'In a tough, hurtful school, Hamish.'

'Marjorie, dearest, I can't fight you. I love you.' He folded her in his arms and rocked her gently. Marjorie had to hang on to her steely resolve or she would have melted there and then. Plenty of time for melting when they were safely out of Singapore, she reminded herself. Right now she needed her wits about her.

Hamish still needed reassurance. 'Marjorie, have you thought carefully what would happen if this doesn't work? What if Beatrice sells out to Glentirran? You're in too deep already, and now there's this trip, and the Robinson woman's services which must cost a bomb. Why are you doing all this?'

'Because we're going to win the fight against Glentirran.'

'Sometimes I wonder how did I get so lucky as to have someone like you loving me? Then I think, if we fail, how shall I ever repay you?'

'We won't fail. Trust me.'

For a moment they stood side by side at the window,

arms around each other, watching the darkening bay. A
light flared and then another as the sampans lit their
lanterns. Soon the bay was blazing with light.

'It's so lovely,' Hamish murmured, hugging her closer.

Marjorie hardly noticed. She was imagining Robert's
face when he found he'd lost out. This is just the start,
Robert. From now on it's you versus me, she vowed.
Lana will get her birthright and you will regret the day
you dumped us both. Suddenly she felt very cold and
she shivered.

'What is it, darling? What's the matter?' Hamish
pressed his lips on hers, blotting out bitterness and
rejection.

'Hamish,' she whispered. 'I want to be loved. Please,
hold me, make love to me. I need you.'

How strange, she thought as he picked her up and carried her to the bed. She really did want him so badly.

Lana was grieving for her mother, anyone could see that.
It hurt Liz, for she could never understand the intensely
strong bond between Marjorie and Lana. Hadn't she
brought up her granddaughter as if she were her own
child?

'Where's Mummy?' Lana cried, glancing at Liz with
lost, frightened eyes. 'I want my mummy.'

'I told you. She's in Singapore. I showed you where
that is on the globe. Didn't Grandpa show you pictures
of the city? Mummy will be home soon and she'll bring
you a present if you're a good girl.'

There was a long silence. 'Why can't she phone me?
She always phones me.'

'I'm sure she will soon, but it costs a lot of money
from so far away. Be good and stop grizzling.'

'I'm not grizzling. I'm not. I'm not.'

Lana knew she was lying. She could taste the salty tears and her cheek itched where they kept on trickling down. She stuck her finger in her mouth and blinked hard, so she could see her picture book. She was aware that she was too old to cry. She was four and a half, almost grown up.

'Cheer up,' Gran said. 'Angela's coming to play this afternoon. Won't that be nice?'

Lana did not like Angela much – she was such a scare-baby – but she seemed to be the only prospect for play. 'How long before she comes?'

'Just after lunch. Won't be long.'

There were two sorts of time Lana recognised: now, and too-far-off-to-be-concerned-about. Mainly she lived in the here and now, which today seemed unbearable. She did not want to eat her lunch: lamb, green peas, mashed potatoes and gravy. For the past two months the cuddly white lambs had been leaping around the fields so trustingly, and everyone had said how lovely they were, but now they were eating them all the same. Grown-ups were funny. Lana didn't much like them, except for Mummy, who was the most wonderful Mummy anyone could ever have and the most beautiful woman in the world. Just thinking about her large green eyes and her mass of red curls made Lana want to cry.

Angela looked just like the rabbits she kept. Her eyes were nearly always bloodshot, her skin was pink and her hair was almost white. She was scared of spiders and bees and almost everything that crawled and she never wanted to do anything, so she wasn't much fun.

She was thin and smaller than Lana, although she had turned five a month back.

Mrs Rose, her grandmother, liked to have tea and play cards with Gran. They called it tea, but the fact was, they had a glass of beer each, or two, and nuts, while the children had cake and lemonade. Sometimes Grandpa joined them, but he didn't much like Mrs Rose, Lana had noticed, so he usually found a job that had to be done in the vegetable garden.

Today Angela was wearing a pink dress that her mum had knitted on her knitting machine. It looked horrible, with clumsy frills around the bottom. She kept smoothing it out with her long white fingers. She wore a pink slide in her straight blonde hair, and thin metal bracelets that rattled when she moved.

Angela liked to be pompous because she was older, but Lana had ways of getting her own back and playing Snap was one of them. Angela had never won.

Lana produced the Snap cards and saw Angela's eyes start to water. She was such a baby.

'I'll give you the big half. That gives you a better chance,' Lana told her.

Moments later she was yelling: 'Snap! Snap! Snap!' and giggling madly.

'Go and play on the kitchen table, and Lana, you don't have to scream so loudly. I don't hear Angela making such a noise.'

'That's because she never wins,' Lana retorted, and saw Angela's eyes glint with envy.

The two girls became bored, Lana of winning and Angela of losing.

'D'you want to go for a walk?' Lana suggested. 'We could see what Grandpa's doing.'

'Let's play on the swing. You can push me.'

'All right,' Lana agreed.

'You girls must put your coats on,' Gran called. Angela's coat was white and furry, but it was too short and too tight and it looked silly.

'They grow so fast,' Mrs Rose complained.

'Don't they just.'

Lana took her windbreaker off the low peg in the scullery, shrugged into it and stood impatiently by the door watching Mrs Rose fumbling with Angela's buttons. 'Don't get dirty,' she called as they rushed outside.

The door closed with a bang and the two girls stood uncertainly, looking towards the lake that was suddenly wreathed in shadowy mists. It was getting dark already. A strange hush seemed to have fallen around them: the wind had stopped and the birds were holding their breath. They could hear raindrops falling from the trees and the rhythmic thud of Grandpa's spade against the frozen earth. The noise stopped and Gramps came stamping by carrying a bag of corn, his breath a hoary cloud, his cheeks and nose bright red with cold. They could hear Paddy barking far away.

'I'm going to feed the ducks,' he called 'Coming?'

'No, it's dark down there,' Angela moaned.

Lana sighed inwardly. 'So get on the swing.'

The two of them were very quiet as they watched Gramps' figure moving into the shadows. The ducks were small white blobs moving towards him.

'Will they eat all that bagful?'

'Yes. They're greedy.'

'My gran said Mr Hardy might give us a duck for Sunday lunch.'

Lana stood very still, holding her breath, trying not

to breathe in case she screamed. He would not. Oh no, he would not. She would not let him.

'No,' she said, eventually, when she had her breathing under control. 'He won't give you one. We never eat them. They're our pets, you see. Besides, they're my dad's ducks, not Gramps'.'

Angela brushed imaginary dirt off the wooden seat with her hand and perched on it, clutching the iron chains. 'Push,' she commanded.

Lana pushed her gently, knowing how scared she was of almost everything.

'What d'you mean, your dad's? You don't have a dad. I heard my mum talking to *my* dad. She said you're lucky to be here, since you're adopted.'

'I know I'm adopted,' Lana said flatly. 'But I've still got a mum and dad.' Adopted was just a word that made her feel safe and special.

'Bet you don't know what adopted means.'

'I do, so there.'

'So what does it mean?'

Lana did not reply.

'I'll tell you what it means. It means you had no parents, so you were put in the orphanage. I know you used to be in the orphanage because Mum told me when we took our old clothes there,' her hateful voice went on dreamily. 'Those girls don't have much, you see, because they've got no one to look after them. I bet you've never even seen your real mum and dad, have you?'

Lana stood as if in a trance, pushing gently, her eyes fixed on the lake, as if help lay that way.

'Hamish is my real dad. He said so.'

'Silly! If Uncle Hamish were your real dad, your name would be Lana Cameron, but it's not, is it? Your mother's not your real mum at all. Just someone who looks after you.'

Lana began to push harder, forcing her arms to thrust forward with all her strength.

'Stop! That's high enough,' Angela squeaked.

Lana pushed harder, panting with the effort.

Angela gave a funny whooping sound. Her knuckles had turned white where she hung on to the chain.

The swing came back fast and when Lana caught hold of it, it swept her back off her feet, but she hung on, and when her feet hit the ground she ran forward, lashing her arms out, sending it flying.

Angela gave a high-pitched squeal and threw herself off the swing. She rolled in the damp mud while taking great gulping sobs. The swing swung over her head the first time, but as she climbed shakily to her knees and peered around, half-scared, half-furious, the swing swung back again and slammed into her forehead.

Her wails brought the two women racing from the cottage.

'Oh, my poor lamb, oh, my dear. What's happened?' Mrs Rose rocked her granddaughter in her arms and tried to examine her forehead, which was turning purplish.

'She pushed me too high, so I jumped off. She's horrid. I don't want to come here again,' Angela gasped between her sobs.

Lana kept her eyes fixed firmly on her shoes. Far worse than the fear of coming punishment was a cold, scary feeling deep inside. Mum wasn't her real mum. She felt bewildered. So who was her real mum and why hadn't she wanted her? Great scalding tears washed down her cheeks.

Gran sent her to bed without tea for a punishment,

but she didn't care. She tiptoed out of her room and onto the landing, to hear Mrs Rose say:

'You take on trouble when you take on one of those deprived children. You don't know who or what they really are. They've all been dumped for a reason; the flaw is there, in themselves or in their parents' genes. Normal folks don't abandon their kids. There's something wrong with those that do. You'll have trouble with her. You mark my words.'

Lana wasn't quite sure what it all meant, but she caught the general drift of things. Gran started to answer back, defending her, but she couldn't bear to listen.

She crept back into her room and closed the door. The room looked safe and reassuring. Nothing had changed, yet something had. It wasn't hers by right, it was a gift from Mum to her, just like Angela's furry coat would be given to one of the orphans soon, but it wouldn't really be hers.

She looked at her doll lying face down on the bed, her face a mess, her clothes on the floor. Retrieving the tiny garments, she dressed the doll carefully. Then she combed her hair and washed the smudges off her with a face flannel, before placing her carefully on the shelf where she would stay.

As she lay on the bed staring out of the window Lana seemed to sense the terrors of the night. She thought about the ducks who were prey to the fox and to greedy people like Mrs Rose, the squirrels and birds who might die of the cold or hunger this winter, the deer who were hunted down and shot for sport and the sweet little lambs who were killed and eaten. In some strange way, they and she seemed to be one.

Chapter 59

Robert the boy and Robert the man appeared to have no real connection, Rhoda thought, watching her stepson enjoying his porridge. The bashful shyness of the boy had long since disappeared, and with it had gone some vital spark of warmth, caring and reaching out to his fellow man. She remembered how the boy had always been groping for love, although she had not been able to give it to him. This man was inviolate and self-sufficient.

She was aware that Robert hated her, but she felt that there was no sense or rightness in his feelings. She had always done her best and God knows it had been hard in the beginning. She wasn't his real mother, that was her only crime. Thank goodness she was nothing like that silly, frail creature who had filled this wonderful home with junk and scruffy pets and allowed her children to run wild.

She had battled to bring order and a sense of worth to the castle and the family, no mean feat, but Robert was her failure. She eyed him critically, sitting there in his shorts and tattered T-shirt, his beard wild and tangled, his hair cut too short, and his eyes gleaming fiercely – especially when they looked at her. He was a real Scottish barbarian, who ate his porridge with salt instead of sugar. He was about to tackle a plate of eggs, bacon, black pudding and kidneys. Just the sight of him wolfing down the food made her feel queasy.

She was longing to light a cigarette, but Robert would not allow her to smoke in the dining room. She would have defied him, but she had something she had to confess, and this appeared to be her only opportunity. Nothing else could persuade her to endure the breakfast table in this house.

Lately Robert was so inaccessible. If it wasn't sport it was Greenpeace, or some wildlife project – he ran so many of them. They were all excuses to keep him away from taking up his responsibilities in the home, although she had to admit that the distillery was excellently run, albeit from a safe distance, through his many expert managers.

Robert could sense the tension and unease radiating from Rhoda. Whatever it was, it must be serious to get her out of bed at this time of the morning. How ugly she had become, he thought, trying to keep his gaze averted from her ravaged face. Her skin resembled a gravel patch and her eyes, anguished and liverish, were half-hidden by folds of skin.

She cleared her throat nervously. 'Robert, listen to me.' One wrinkled, bejewelled hand slid out to touch his, but he moved away.

'There are some damaging comments in today's papers concerning your failed efforts to take over Glenaird.'

'That's absurd,' he said, without looking up. 'I offered a rescue plan to Beatrice Cameron to save the distillery from being bought by British gin distillers. It was a perfectly reasonable offer. Beatrice was anxious to keep the distillery in Scottish hands.'

'And the plan failed. The Camerons fought back, but

it was the Japanese investment that saved them finally,' she persisted.

'Good for them. It was about time.'

'It wasn't quite as straightforward as you might think.'

Robert looked up sharply, scanning her face. She looked guilty and that surprised him. He could see little beads of moisture gathering on her skin. Her bloodshot eyes wavered anxiously towards their housekeeper, Mrs Thomson, who was hovering over their plates.

'If you have some explaining to do, I suggest you get on with it.' He glanced ostentatiously at his watch. 'Mrs Thomson, would you please fetch some more coffee?'

'It's like this,' Rhoda said when the woman had left the room. 'There was a family split because half of the Camerons wanted to get Hamish, the heir, out. Andrew Cameron, his uncle, appointed his friend, John Erskine, as the MD to soften shareholders with poor performance. Erskine reported directly to Andrew and to me.'

'The more I see of your Machiavellian business strategies, the more anxious I become to have you out of the plant,' Robert said disgustedly. 'Is there anything else you have to tell me?'

She shook her head.

'Then I'll be on my way.'

'No, wait! You don't understand. The press have got hold of the story and blown it up sky-high. There are allegations of foul play against us. The papers are full of it.'

'There's nothing we can do about that now. Do not involve our distillery with Andrew Cameron again. He's a man I particularly dislike. You've tarred our image with this devious scheme of yours.'

Rhoda left the room with an exclamation of annoyance.

Robert's appetite was gone. He pushed his food aside and drank his coffee. He detested all forms of intrigue and double-dealing. The human capacity for lying and cheating was what had driven him into the wilderness for most of his adult life. Nature was clean, straightforward and pure. The need to survive was a creed he understood. There was no malice or deceit. He made up his mind to speak to his lawyer about curbing Rhoda's intrusion into the running of the distillery. Father was failing fast. After he died, Rhoda would never set foot in Glentirran Distillers again.

He picked up the newspaper and glanced at the headlines of the finance section. Reading between the lines, it appeared that Cameron's new wife was the power behind the resurrected distillery. She was quoted as saying: 'History has always proved that right triumphs over wrong. Glentirran played dirty and they got what they deserved, but I advise them to hang on to their Glenaird shares. I predict they will receive better returns from their recent Glenaird outlay than from Glentirran. Our new Asian marketing division will be competing for Glentirran's US and Eastern markets, so they can watch out.'

Robert tossed the newspaper aside. The new Mrs Cameron sounded cheeky and audacious – much like Marjorie had been. A sudden stab of longing for what might have been left him feeling strangely bereft.

Chapter 60

Marjorie was ready early. She was wearing a pure silk backless Dior evening dress that clung to her figure, and large, blue-grey pearl earrings with a matching pearl pendant. She was holding her first formal dinner party for several business acquaintances, and Joe and Véronique were coming, too. They were staying the night and driving on to the Western Isles in the morning to spend a long weekend together. According to Joe they were going through a bad patch and the holiday was an attempt to talk things out, away from all distractions.

She hurried downstairs to read the newspaper before their guests arrived. 'Glenaird Distillers on takeover trail,' she read. She skimmed through the text with a glow of satisfaction.

Since they returned from Singapore six months before, with Tohara's signed agreement to form a joint marketing venture, fortune had favoured them, and so had the press. Toharasan had promised to invest a minimum of three million dollars over the next five years in their joint new venture, starting with one million this year.

Glenaird's Asian sales had gone much better than expected and Tohara was so pleased he was talking about another million-dollar cash infusion this year to increase production. Later, Inver-Asian would tackle expansion into the US. Less known and never publicised was their incredible battle to pay the interest on the bank loans, and their creative bid to run Glenaird on a shoestring until they started making money, which was at least five years in the future. This latest takeover of a small distillery in the Lowlands would enable them to produce a good blended Scotch whisky for Toharasan to sell.

She was startled back to the present by a ring from the gate's remote control. Good heavens, was it seven already? She glanced at her watch and saw that it was. She heard Lana race to answer it and scream with delight as she pressed the button and raced to the front door.

Moments later Joe's latest car, a silver-grey Rolls, drew up below the steps and Marjorie hurried down.

Joe stepped out and hugged Lana, whirling her around. Evidently this was a mistake. Véronique's face was rigid with temper when Marjorie opened her door, but Joe didn't notice. Lana would not let him go as she hugged him, giggling madly and digging her hands in his pockets looking for a present. Eventually he produced a battery cat that shook its head and mewed.

'Thanks, Joe. Very thoughtful of you,' Marjorie laughed, holding her hands over her ears.

As their visitors walked up the steps, their joint gloom preceded them like a cold aura. She kissed them both, but she could tell something was badly wrong.

'You look tremendous, Marjorie,' Joe said. 'I can see you're happy.' There was a touch of bitterness in his voice. She stepped back and frowned anxiously. He looked defeated – that was new. She made up her mind to see more of him. She should never have neglected him so. They met once a week in London – usually hasty lunchtime meetings – but that was not good enough, she decided.

Véronique was wearing a stunning creation of black muslin with sequins. She paused in the doorway of the living room and looked around disdainfully. 'It takes for ever to get settled, doesn't it?' she purred in her sexy Parisian accent.

'We're settled,' Marjorie said coolly.

From Véronique's expression Marjorie assumed that she was here under duress and she was suffering. Suddenly she saw their home through Véronique's eyes: their family room was vast by any standards, but Marjorie had brightened it with large, roomy settees, flowers, rugs and cushions. But there were books and magazines and newspapers on the tables, cat hairs on the sofa, and new designs for whisky labels spread out over the table. Damn! She'd forgotten to clear them away. Cushions and toys lay on the floor, while their newly adopted old tabby cat, Scarsie, so named by Lana because of his chewed ears and battlescars, was curled up in an easy chair. Lana's dolls littered the rug in front of the roaring fire.

'Where did that thing come from?' Joe pointed at the cat.

'Just pitched up. He got through a window to raid the larder, was caught red-handed, and now he won't go. Mum's none too happy because he fights with her Tibby.'

'Clever cat! A tough old tom by the look of it. Bet he's won a few fights. Did you have him nicked?'

''Fraid so. I couldn't stand the smell, but I had to wait until Hamish was away. He wasn't keen and he doesn't know,' she whispered, 'so don't say anything.'

'Lana looks well.'

'Yes. She and Hamish are great mates.' She turned to include Véronique. 'We love it here,' she told her. 'I forgot you hadn't been before. I feel ashamed. Of course, we're only home at weekends. We stay at my London flat in the week. The truth is, we never stop working.'

Véronique went over to the window and stared towards the lake. She looked bored and unhappy until she saw Hamish running up from the lake, naked except for the towel around his hips. A Greek statue could not have been more graceful, or more manly. Véronique was gazing at all that tanned flesh with the expression of a big cat just before it pounces. She leaned out of the window and waved.

Hamish smiled lazily and casually. 'Oh hi, Véronique, and you, Joe.' He paused under the window. 'A rather unexpected meeting.' Unbelievably he winked at Véronique. 'Nice to see you. I'll be down in a shake. I was kept late at the office and I just had to have a swim.' Then he sneaked a surreptitious glance at Véronique, who was smiling gently to herself. What exactly had passed between these two? Marjorie wondered. A bolt of jealousy hit home.

'What time are the others coming?' Hamish called.

'In half an hour. Hurry! Dinner's at eight-thirty.'

'Are you having drinks in there?'

'I thought the library, then we'll go into dinner.'

'Good thinking.' He bounded up the stairs.

Joe hadn't changed much, despite his millionaire status, Marjorie noticed. When he learned that she had bought a CD of Brian Ferneyhough's *Transit*, he put it on loudly and snarled at everyone who dared to speak to him. Hamish came in, took Véronique's arm and led her to a corner settee, where they sat whispering in a huddle, giggling occasionally, while Marjorie sat moodily suffering. Damn him! How he's changed, she thought. The hangdog look was entirely gone. He stood straight, and walked instead of shuffling, and felt at ease with women. Right there and then she lusted after him. She kept seeking his glance, longing for reassurance, but he was bent over the bitch.

When Greta, their new Swedish au pair appeared, Lana ran to Hamish, winding her arms around his neck. 'Save me from the wicked witch,' she screamed.

'Don't be rude, Lana,' Marjorie scolded.

'I'd watch out for her if I were you,' Joe warned teasingly as Greta led the child around to say goodnight. 'What a looker!'

'Is she? I hadn't noticed.'

'Oh, come on, Marjorie, who're you kidding? She belongs in Hollywood.'

Marjorie shivered. Why hadn't she noticed how lovely she was? And why was she so damned complacent about Hamish? She scanned Greta, noting the honey blonde hair, the huge baby blue eyes, the willowy figure. Exactly Joe's taste, but was it Hamish's? Suddenly every woman seemed a threat.

Their guests arrived on time, and Marjorie tried to stem her anxiety and perform her role of hostess perfectly. She had never before entertained twenty-four people at one sitting. Much to her surprise, she seemed to be succeeding. The local caterer had brought the food half an hour before their guests arrived. The hired waiters were standing around ready for action and the dining room looked divine with the long oak table, the flickering candlelight and the fire roaring in the hearth at the end of the room.

Greta joined them shortly afterwards and Joe rearranged the seating so that she would sit next to him.

What a nerve! Marjorie fumed, but she could hardly create a fuss in public. From then on Joe devoted himself to Greta.

Marjorie felt a sudden shaft of pity for Véronique, which she immediately quelled. After all, she'd been digging for gold and she'd found plenty of it. Joe's patented brick-cleaning goo was franchised throughout the world and he was coining it. Commodity broking had made him another fortune. They lived in a massive mansion backing on to the Thames, but they were seldom there. They had joined the jet set's rigid routine: skiing, the London season, grouse shooting, and attending all the best concerts throughout the world. When they were home, they entertained the people who mattered. How could he stand it? Looking at him carefully she realised that he couldn't.

They were halfway through the beef stroganoff, which was divine, when Greta glanced at the window and screamed. The guests turned as one to see Lana dangling by one hand from the scaffolding outside. Her pyjamas were torn, her face was scratched and she was trying not to let go.

Hamish moved so fast. It seemed like a split second before he was pushing up the window to grab Lana.

'You can let go. I've got you,' he said.

She let go, laughing nervously. For a moment no one spoke. Then Marjorie began to cry with relief. Moments later Lana's arms were round her neck as she tried to comfort her mother.

'I knew you'd catch me. You or Daddy,' she crowed triumphantly. 'She's always locking me in.' She shot an accusing glare in Greta's direction. 'I don't like that.'

'Who's she, the cat's mother?' Hamish asked.

Greta gathered her up. 'I'll take her back to bed,' she said, trying to disguise her fury.

'I'll read Lana a story,' Joe added, leaping to his feet. 'Back soon, but don't wait for us.'

No one did, which was just as well, Marjorie decided, since they must have read her every book in her room.

Their guests began leaving at eleven. When they had all gone, Joe returned looking shame-faced. There was no sign of Greta.

Véronique, who had refused coffee but drunk a great deal of cognac, threw herself into an armchair and burst into tears.

'This is not at all what I expected,' she complained between her sobs. 'Joe is obsessed with music and his shit inventions. There's no part of him that's left for me. How I envy you, Marjorie. Yes, me, an international beauty, a household face. Is that how you say it? Can you believe that I still envy *you*?'

I'm quite well-known myself and not exactly ugly, although sometimes I feel ugly, Marjorie argued to herself.

Joe stood up and turned the music up to blast levels to drown her sobs.

Marjorie turned it down. 'You've just taken four hours to get Lana to sleep – there's no point in waking her,' she pointed out.

Joe was eyeing Véronique with a curious expression on his face. He's dismissing her, Marjorie mused, watching him sidelong.

'I can't see this long weekend is getting us anywhere.

What do you say to calling it off? Let's get back to London and see my lawyer,' he suggested coldly.

Véronique's sobs became louder.

When they had retrieved their gear, Véronique paused in the hall looking tragic and misunderstood. 'Goodbye, Hamish,' she whispered. Then she remembered to nod to Marjorie. Seconds later they were gone.

'Off with the old and on with the new. Joe doesn't know when he's had enough punishment,' Hamish marvelled.

'What a disaster,' Marjorie fumed. 'Our first dinner party became absolute chaos.'

'The food was good.' Hamish tried to console her. 'But why does Lana keep doing these terribly dangerous tricks?'

He wound his arm around her and rocked her gently. 'It's as if she's testing us. Almost as if she wants to prove that we love her and we'll be there to rescue her. Joe must finish the job and remove the scaffolding. In the meantime we'll have to keep her away from it. I'll get bars up at her window first thing tomorrow and make sure to remove the key, so Greta can't lock her in. I don't want Lana to be locked in her room. How could Greta do that? I think you should let her go. She's not at all suitable.'

It struck her that Hamish, at least, was impervious to Greta's looks. 'I think you'll find she'll resign in the morning. If I'm not mistaken, she and Joe have other plans.'

Chapter 61

Derek Olivier was always on his guard when Marjorie Cameron arrived. She was clever, receptive and almost psychic in her perceptions, but prickly and quick to take a slight. If she suspected she were being put down, she would hit back hard before thinking. She was also one of the most beautiful women he had ever encountered. Her magnificent hair, her flawless pale skin and her huge green eyes would have made her a famous beauty in another era. Nowadays no one seemed to take the time to notice, Olivier lamented, except in pop and film stars. These gorgeous looks were wasted on Mrs Cameron, for she was obsessed with business.

She was dead on time, as usual, and dressed in a clinging bottle-green shantung shift dress with a matching green and black striped jacket which he guessed she had bought on one of her recent trips to the East. She had never thanked him for the information that had saved them, but of course she paid her bills promptly and he didn't come cheap, so perhaps she'd decided he did not need thanks as well.

He had always been puzzled by her excessive business zeal, so today he had a little game to play.

'Come and sit down, Mrs Cameron. Coffee?' He called his secretary. 'Well, your *bête noire*, Robert MacLaren,

seems to have a death wish,' he began jovially before
she had time to put up her guard. 'He went missing
in Venezuela. It seems that he was piloting a locally
hired aircraft from Margarita down to Solano, but it
disappeared . . .'

Mrs Cameron made a strange mewing noise and
collapsed into a chair. Her eyes closed, her face took
on a fine sheen of perspiration and then she slumped
forward, but by then Olivier had recovered his senses
enough to catch her. He called his secretary to bring a
glass of cold water.

Minutes later she was sipping the water and fighting
to pull herself together.

'As I was saying, he went missing, but he was found a
few hours ago. It seems he developed engine trouble near
a tributary of the Amazon and, with a rare stroke of luck,
found an airstrip beside an Indian village currently being
developed for the tourist trade. He was on a mission to
discuss ways of saving the Venezuelan forest. Perhaps
you know that he joined Greenpeace some time ago.'

Olivier watched his client with interest. So this was
more than merely business. He'd guessed as much. He
remembered the second time she came to see him.
Something about her manner had alerted his interest.

'I want a regular report on the personal activities of
the company chairman, Robert MacLaren,' she had told
him imperiously.

He had watched her studying her hands and trying
to look nonchalant. Then she had remembered to smile.
What a false smile it had been.

'Exactly how personal must these personal reports be?'
he had asked. 'I'm a business investigator. That's what I
do. I'm not a private detective. I normally consider that

anything not relevant to business would be outside my sphere.'

'Suit yourself,' she had snapped. 'Do what you can. We'll see how it goes. I would have considered it highly relevant for our business if, for instance, Mr MacLaren should marry the heiress to Selbies Gin, or have a heart attack, if you see what I mean.'

'I'll bear that in mind,' he had countered. 'By the way, his father died recently. It's Sir Robert nowadays, not Mr MacLaren. And these reports are for your eyes only, not your husband's, I assume.'

'Naturally, since I'm your client,' she had snarled, flushing deeply.

He had grinned at her and for some reason this had infuriated her. She had stood up, fumbling with her gloves, playing for time while she found a way to hit back.

'You may give yourself a fancy title, but where I come from, we call a spade a spade. What does it matter who or what you spy on, as long as you're paid?'

How dare she! He swallowed when he remembered how angry he had been. Since then he had forgiven her.

'Better? Good! As I was saying. Sir Robert seems to think he has his business sewn up. He had a couple of bad years at the beginning, but now it's running according to his plan. A good plan, I might add, and similar to yours. Whereas you hope to grab a major market share in the East, he's well established in the States. He's meeting his interest payments with his bank, and he has some good managers whom he trusts, so now he's able to devote himself to causes he considers to be more worthwhile

than business. He has the typical landed gentry view of
business, that it's a bit beneath him. For the past three
years he has devoted himself to ecological causes, mainly
abroad.'

'Good.' She smiled cautiously.

'Let's see now.' He riffled through his file.

'He's written a book on Amazon Indians which has
sold well, and a small volume of poetry that flopped.
Nowadays he's mainly writing for the *National Geographic Magazine*.

'Last spring he organised a twenty-four-hour watch
to guard osprey nests, and he headed up the team
that objected to the reintroduction of wolves into the
Highland forests . . .' He read a list of 'green' projects
Robert had organised.

'Now, Mrs Cameron, back to business. Here are the
exact advertising plans for Glentirran for the next season.
Quite a coup, don't you think? Bear them in mind when
planning your own campaign. You've time to let the
opposition look very foolish indeed, but whatever you
do, never mention your source.'

She shot him a scathing glance as she took the folder.
Then she swept out with a smile and a wave, looking
so light-hearted you could swear she had nothing more
serious on her mind than her next shopping expedition.

'If I were twenty years younger I'd win her myself,'
Olivier boasted foolishly to himself.

Marjorie was about to enter the restaurant when the sun
burst out and she stood there sunning herself, enjoying
the warmth and hoping that Hamish had arrived in
London by now. Perhaps he had. On impulse she went
in, asked to use the telephone and called home, but

there was no answer. When she called the London office, Hamish answered.

'Oh, hi. I'm glad you're here. I missed you.'

'I missed you, too. I arrived five minutes ago, but there's no one here. Everyone's at lunch.'

'I'm having lunch with Joe at the Good Earth in Knightsbridge. We've been there before, remember? Join us, why don't you?'

'Well, I don't know.'

'Please, Hamish.'

'Okay. Be there shortly. Order me something light.'

Joe looked prosperous. He was always one step ahead in the fashion stakes, but he still looked distinguished despite his long hair and swarthy complexion. Today he was wearing a bottle-green shirt and a fancy waistcoat. It suited him and he could carry it off, but she noticed he was gaining weight. He was beaming, and she sensed that he could not wait to tell her his news.

'Greta and I are getting married as soon as the divorce comes through. Cheers,' he said as the fruit juice arrived.

'Congratulations. And when will that be?' she asked. She wasn't surprised, she'd half expected this.

'Maybe next month.'

'Heavens, surely that's impossible, Joe.'

'We didn't marry in England, if you remember. I wouldn't be that daft.'

'You mean you were thinking about divorce when you married? No wonder it didn't last.'

'Being in love is not synonymous with being an idiot, although most times it seems like it.'

'And this time?'

'This time it's for real. Marjorie.' He reached forward

and grabbed her hand, his eyes shining. She'd never seen him look so happy. 'I want to ask a favour. Can we hold the reception at Inveraird? I'd really like that.'

'Of course you can, Joe.' She felt pleased that she could do something for Joe for once – he did so much for her. She began to plan. They were still very strapped for cash, so half of the lodge was closed up, although it was cleaned regularly. There was a huge ballroom which they had never used. She could tart it up in time. Suddenly she was full of plans she couldn't wait to put into action. It would look absolutely perfect and Lana, who had turned five in May, would make a lovely flowermaid. Greta could hardly refuse, and Lana would love it.

Joe spent the next ten minutes telling her how wise and capable Greta was. It didn't sound like the same Greta she had lived with for two months. Had she changed, or was she on her best behaviour?

Hamish walked in and she waved. 'Hi, sweetie,' she trilled happily, lifting her face for a kiss.

'You're looking fit, Hamish,' Joe said. 'Still climbing?'

'Not as often as I should. Too many attractions at home,' he teased, sitting beside Marjorie and squeezing her hand.

'Oh! Marjorie. I almost forgot this.' Joe produced a large envelope from under his chair. He took out the papers and spread them over the table.

'We can look at them later, Joe,' she stammered.

'Why not now?'

She sighed. A week ago she had asked Joe to commission his man in New York to find out all he could about Glentirran's US expansion plans and specifically the financial strength of the company's American distributors. She had not told Hamish, who was squeamish about underhand tactics.

'So soon,' she ventured. 'Your guy's a fast worker.'

'In this case it was too easy. He knows a girl who works there. Here's their next season's marketing strategy in detail. You pass it on to Hamish's uncle but don't let on who stole it for you.'

'Sure thing.' She was unable to look Hamish in the eyes.

'Hang on,' Hamish interrupted. 'Why is this necessary? Things are going well for us. There's plenty of market space for both companies.'

'We didn't start the war, Hamish. They did,' Marjorie pleaded, her voice trembling with the need to convince him that she was right. 'They tried to gobble you up, now we're going to gobble them up. It may take a few years, but one day we'll own Glentirran, I promise you. It's only a matter of time.'

He gave her a long, sad smile. 'My tiger wife! You have such a capacity for revenge and for protecting your own. But Marjorie, listen to me.' His hand slid over hers again and squeezed hard. 'It wasn't a personal vendetta on Glentirran's part. It's business. Admittedly Uncle Andrew's role was underhand, but it's still just business. Takeovers happen all the time. You don't have to feel wounded by it. Yet the look on your face then, well . . . all the sadness in the world seemed to be mirrored in your eyes. Remember, sweetie, keep emotions out of business.'

'Naturally.' She dredged up a smile. 'Ah!' She gave a sigh of relief as the waiter came to save her, carrying their prawn salad. 'I'm famished.'

Joe was watching her intently, a gleam of sly amusement in his slanting eyes. Puck-like, his mouth quivered into an enigmatic smile.

Hamish did not pursue the matter again and she assumed it would soon be safely forgotten.

Chapter 62

It was a beautiful autumn afternoon and they were nearing the end of the Highland Games, which had been held this year at the local sports club's playing fields. Smiling softly to herself, Marjorie watched the trials and the competition dancing with a deep glow of contentment. As she gazed at her daughter proudly, she could not resist a self-satisfied smirk. Lana was where she deserved to be, and exactly where Marjorie had intended she should be. Unbelievably, everything had worked out. Cash-strapped they might be, but the Camerons were going places. Everything they touched went well for them. Apart from her dreams inexplicably coming true, she had an added bonus: she was happy, deliriously, unexpectedly and undeservedly happy with Hamish.

Why? What is love? she wondered. Was it the joy of feasting her eyes on a man who was beautiful and strong and as sensitive as he was brave. Sometimes it seemed that she was caught up in a strange energy that had renewed her world and taken the blinkers off her eyes, making her see beauty in commonplace things she had never noticed before. Sometimes it seemed it was a fever that had taken root deep in her soul. Love was spilling out of her and it showed, she knew, for people smiled when they looked at her, and she loved each and every one of them. She had not married Hamish for love, yet she loved him and she felt deeply fulfilled.

And here they were, Hamish and she, so happy and so settled after one year together, and feeling exactly like a real family. Just look at Dad sitting there with Mum, both as proud as peacocks as they watched their granddaughter. And Lana, eyes sparkling, was showing off the swirl of her new Cameron kilt. Her daughter was longing to get her prize, for she had been judged the best Scottish dancer in the under-six category.

Reluctantly, Marjorie roused herself from her happy contemplation. Why was Judy Applethwaite, the post-mistress, looking so self-important as she pushed her way onto the stage and grabbed the microphone?

'Ladies and gentlemen, I have a surprise,' she began in her soft, lyrical Inverness accent. 'I have just caught sight of Sir Robert MacLaren, who's been making headlines lately for his tireless battle on behalf of the world's ecology.' She waited for the clapping to cease. 'Och, I canna believe our good fortune, for he's agreed to award the prizes and say a few words to the lads and lassies here today. This way, Sir Robert.'

Marjorie cursed under her breath. She felt she was going to scream. She couldn't sit here on the platform in full view of Robert. Fumbling in her bag, she found her sunglasses and put them on, then pulled the brim of her hat over her face.

She panicked as Robert pushed his way up towards them. In her mind's eye she was seeing his expression when he read out the name Lana Hardy, and saw those thick black curls rising from a pronounced widow's peak, and looked into those compelling brown eyes.

His eyes! And if Robert guessed, Hamish would find out.

Grabbing the list, she surreptitiously scribbled over Hardy, making it look like Darby. It would pass. Then she excused herself and slipped off the platform to hide behind her parents. Hamish looked surprised and then hurt as he gazed in her direction.

The prize-giving soon got under way. Billy Mackintosh, their storeman, tossed the caber the furthest, as usual, and some of their typists scored in the dancing.

Would it never end? Marjorie considered grabbing her daughter and going home, but how could she? Hamish had the car keys and although she kept beckoning he would not leave the platform.

God! Here it comes. There was a sudden hush as Robert tried to read the altered name. Then a voice, well known and once loved, called: 'Lana Darby.'

'That's not my name,' Lana called out, looking furious.

'Go, go . . .' Marjorie ducked down behind Dad and thrust her daughter forward. 'Go on. He means you. Hurry or he'll give it to someone else. Don't worry about your name.'

When she went bounding up the steps a gasp of admiration went around the crowd. She looked so pretty and vivacious in her kilt with the lace blouse and black waistcoat.

Marjorie watched her daughter whirling round, unable to control her glee, for she had practised for weeks with Hamish.

Robert, never one for bothering with protocol, picked her up, swung her round and gave her a long hug and a kiss on the cheek before handing her the prize, to the applause of the crowd.

At the sight of Robert's face and his brown eyes gleaming with fun, and his arms around his daughter, Marjorie almost burst into tears. She was poignantly reminded of how it could have been.

'Off you go then,' Robert suggested.

'You got my name all wrong.' Clearly Lana was in no hurry to leave the platform. 'It's not Darby at all.'

There were some gasps and a snigger. Robert looked surprised.

'I'm sorry,' he apologised. 'So what's your name?'

Marjorie could have screamed. 'Mum, get her back here,' she pleaded.

Mum called out: 'You come back here, my girl,' but as she stood up, she pushed her chair on Paddywonks' foot and the dog let out a howl of anguish. Lana came rushing back and Robert turned to the next prize-winner.

It was time for the pipe band. Suddenly Marjorie was staring wildly across the crowd at Robert. Had he seen them? *Had* he? And had Hamish noticed? The pipers came swinging around the field, the crowd thrilling to the sound of the music and the beat of the drums and marching feet.

Enough was enough. 'Mum, get Hamish, please. Tell him I'm sick. Tell him any damn thing. Please, bring him.'

She grabbed Lana's hand and pulled her across the grass to the car park.

'Why are we going?' Lana began to whine. 'Mummy, I don't want to go. What about the swings, Mummy? Can't I have an ice cream? You promised.'

The day was spoiled. Hamish looked grim as he joined them. Lana loved to walk between them, hanging on tightly, but today she was angry and she ran back to her grandparents.

Marjorie smiled nervously towards Dad and motioned that he should hurry. Even Paddywonks was sulking because his foot was sore.

'Hamish,' Marjorie exclaimed, taking his hand. 'I've fallen so deeply in love with you.'

His face registered astonishment. 'Of course.' He smiled at her, but it was a sad smile. 'I know that you love me, but it's not like you to be demonstrative. Why tell me today, of all days?'

'Why not?'

He squeezed her hand. 'More than when we met?'

'Oh, Hamish. So much more. Today I've discovered that it's you I love,' she blabbed and then stopped short, feeling frantic and foolish.

Now he was frowning and Marjorie tried to put things right.

'Although I loved you in the beginning. Now I understand what real love is,' she lied.

'Thank you,' he muttered, looking grimmer.

Oops! Now what had she done? She struggled to think of a way to make it sound better, but at that moment Lana came running back. They reached the car and the moment was lost. When they arrived home and she hurried up the steps she felt a familiar ache in her loins, that awful heaviness that meant a period was coming.

She wanted to burst into tears there and then. She had not yet fallen pregnant, although heaven knew they tried hard enough. Their sex was deeply satisfying for both of them and they seldom missed a night. So why had she not conceived? She longed to hold Hamish's baby in her arms. Then their happiness would be complete.

From the feel of things it was going to be a bad one, perhaps because of all the hard work she'd been obliged to do to organise the catering and help to get the marquee ready. Well, maybe next month, she told herself wearily.

A week later Marjorie visited a private gynaecologist in London. The stuffy waiting room was full of pregnant women and smelled of antiseptic. She dreaded the prospect of bringing Hamish here. After the examination she dressed and sat in a chair in front of the doctor, a tall, thin, plain woman with sympathetic eyes, which were her best feature.

'Tell me about your lifestyle,' Pat Mathieson suggested.

'It's pretty hectic.' Marjorie smiled at her, feeling reassured by her friendliness. 'I spend Monday to Friday in London. Friday afternoons we fly back to Inverness for the weekend. We make the most of our time there: riding, gardening, hiking, that sort of thing. We go dancing on Saturday nights in the local hotel. We have a few friends and stacks of acquaintances and sometimes we give parties or pop down to the village for a pub lunch with my parents. We always spend Saturday mornings in the distillery. I have a resident cleaner at home and my parents keep an eye on things.'

'And in the week?'

'Pretty punishing, but it's worth it. On Mondays, I take the early morning shuttle to Heathrow. Sometimes Hamish stays in Scotland, sometimes he comes with me. We have a London flat, and I have a char on Fridays, otherwise I do the cleaning myself. Most of my time is spent in Glenaird's marketing headquarters in Kensington, where I advise and keep an eye on things. When Hamish is with me I do the shopping at lunchtime and cook when I get home. I get so tired, I'm asleep when my head touches the pillow.'

'So then you don't make love?'

'Well,' she flushed. 'Hamish usually wakes me around five or six in the morning. After that, there's barely time to shower and rush off to work. There! You have my life in a nutshell.' The truth was she had played down her function in the Glenaird marketing company. She ran it, although she called in experts each time she came up against a problem. Joe was a great help, too. She knew she was working too hard, but she loved it.

'Apart from the hard work, you have quite a lot of tension, I presume?'

'That's an understatement, actually.'

'That's what I guessed. You see, there's nothing physically wrong with you, Mrs Cameron, but you're under a lot of stress. Try to do less, shift the load, rest a bit during the day, have more sleep. Wait a few more months. That's what I suggest. If you don't fall pregnant, come back in six months' time, or a year, and bring your husband for tests, too. You're a healthy woman and you already have one child, so I'd say you're worrying too soon.'

'You see, we have to have a male heir,' Marjorie confided. 'It may take a few babies before the right sex emerges, so it's time I fell pregnant.'

Dr Mathieson smiled sympathetically. 'I hope it will come right without our help, Mrs Cameron.'

Life's the damnedest thing, Marjorie decided, brushing away a stray tear with her knuckles as she waved for a taxi. When I feared being pregnant more than anything in the world, I got there with only one try. Now that I long to have a baby I can't make it happen.

Murphy's law, Mum would say. Her mum was a prey to superstition of all kinds. She lived her life in the shadow of an ever-watchful, all-seeing evil eye that waited to ensnare the unwary. Consequently, boasting was bound to lead to a downfall, pride was asking for trouble. If good fortune favoured you, it was best to keep quiet about it. Touch wood before taking anything for granted. Never, never count your chickens before the eggs hatched. On Sundays Mum prayed in church to a merciful God of love, but for the rest of the week she placated some more ancient and malevolent deity, a heritage of her Celtic genes, and she tried to keep her head down and out of sight. But what was there really?

'Come on, Marjorie, loosen up,' she muttered. 'Or are you planning to nip down to Stonehenge with a couple of live sacrifices?'

Chapter 63

A month later Joe's divorce was finalised. Greta and he were married in Inverness Register Office at four in the afternoon late in October, with only the Camerons attending. After the brief ceremony they drove back to Inveraird Lodge, where Joe's friends and business colleagues were already arriving. Thank goodness she'd thought to employ local youths to direct the traffic, Marjorie reflected as they threaded their way between cars to the lodge, straining to see in the gathering dusk.

Lana was jumping up and down in her frilly pink flowergirl dress, impatient to throw the dried rose petals provided by Dad. The ballroom looked beautiful, with masses of flowers. The floor had been polished until it gleamed, and carpet runners had been laid between the tables, which were clustered around the side of the room, leaving the centre open for dancing. And dance they did, between speeches and toasts and the five-course dinner. Mum had hired the part-time staff and she was supervising the catering and the waitresses.

'Mum, you could have made a fortune with your own catering business,' Marjorie told her when she popped into the kitchen. Mum was wearing a cocktail dress with a large overall on top. She'd had her hair permed and she looked pretty good.

'Not me, lass. Maybe I have the talent, but I lack the ambition. That's where you and I differ.'

'Go on with you.' Marjorie pondered over the 'lass'. Mum must have made some local friends to pick up that expression. 'You'll be joining us, won't you? You don't have to stay here all night, surely?'

'Aye, I'll be there soon enough.'

'You're looking bonnie,' Marjorie teased.

Mum wasn't listening. She was tasting the brandy sauce and frowning slightly. Marjorie hurried back to the ballroom.

Greta looked radiant in a white lace suit with a flared skirt and tight bodice. It shimmered with stitched-in pearls and enhanced her stately charm. Her blonde hair fell over her shoulders and her pale skin was adorned with the very expensive diamonds and pearls Joe had showered on her.

As the dancing pounded on, Marjorie became aware of someone staring at her. She looked round instinctively and gazed into Hamish's eyes. How strange he looked. He had been disconcertingly elusive the past few weeks.

Now he beckoned to her. 'Come and see the moon,' he called.

It was a clear night, crispy cool but not cold, yet clouds were gathering on the horizon. Leaves crackled underfoot, and there was a scent of damp earth and newly mown grass. The moon hung as if poised over the wood, larger than life, transforming the world into a strange, ethereal landscape.

Marjorie leaned against Hamish and wrapped her arms around his waist, resting her head on his chest. She shuddered and snuggled closer.

'What is it?' he asked her. 'What's wrong? You should be triumphant. You've been magnificently successful, as usual. I can see how hard you've worked.'

'True.'

'Everyone's having a wonderful time.'

'Of course!'

'So?'

'It's just that . . .' She sighed and brushed her lips over his cheek. 'Well, I wish that we had done this. I mean, the whole bit – orange blossom, bridesmaids, confetti, the works.' She felt unwilling to question him about his new, unwelcome remoteness.

'We could have. You didn't want a big wedding. I begged you, but you refused.'

'Yes, I did.' She frowned up at him, desperate for love. 'You see, in those days I wasn't romantic. You've changed me so much.'

'How come?' he asked, deceptively gently.

She spoke without thinking: 'Because I fell in love with you.'

'And in the beginning?' he asked softly.

Patiently she stroked his hand, wishing the night were over so they could go to bed and make love. 'In the beginning I didn't realise how much I would love you. You mean the world to me now.'

'So you didn't love me when you married me?' the soft voice persisted.

A strange shiver ran through her. 'I'm cold. Let's go back inside.'

'No.' His hand held her arm. It felt like a steel vice.

'We must go. We should be in there. Come, Hamish.'

'No. Stay. Why did you marry me, Marjorie?'

'Idiot.' She tried out a laugh and patted his cheek

maternally. 'For hundreds of reasons. For love,' she murmured, hating to lie, 'because you asked me to, because you needed me, because it was a challenge and I wanted you to win. And you won,' she added decisively. 'That means something, doesn't it? Now can I go?' Her voice was cool with apprehension as she wrenched her hand from his.

'You look afraid. What are you afraid of?'

He pulled her close, pressing her against him. For a few precious moments his cheek rested on her head, but then he sighed and pushed her away. Stepping back, he sat heavily on the top step and sat gazing over the lawn. She could see the hurt in his eyes.

Swiftly bending over him, she began to smother him with light kisses, on his cheek and his chin and his forehead. 'I love you, I love you, I love you,' she murmured.

'You used me,' he grieved with a sob in his voice. 'I've been puzzling over your actions, your obsession with destroying Glentirran. You see, Marjorie, your passion to win went beyond business strategy. So I did some checking. You married me to create the means to destroy Robert MacLaren. He is Lana's father, isn't he? And he dumped you both.'

She clutched him. She had feared this moment for so long, but now that it had arrived, the shame of being found out was as nothing to her anguish for Hamish and what he was suffering. He was the light of her life, he was everything to her.

'Hamish,' she implored him. 'Think of all we have built up. Think how I love you. Think how successful we've been. I made a promise to God once. It went something like this: "I don't love him as much as he loves me, but I'll give him all the love I have, and I'll look after him and I'll build up his home and his business and I'll make him happy. I'll never harm him, so help me God."'

'But now I am harmed. Can't you see that? I have to rewrite all those wonderful memories of love scenes with the knowledge that I was not loved, merely used. That you opened your legs to grab Glenaird, the only means to attack Robert.'

'No, that's not true.' She was crying now. 'It was never for revenge. It was to get back Lana's heritage. Can't you understand? I always lusted after you. I loved you in my own way. You taught me to love more deeply. That's all.'

He turned and smiled, such a sad smile, and now she could see that his cheeks were glistening with tears. She couldn't bear it. 'I love you,' she mourned.

'I know you do. Now . . .'

'Why can't we be grateful for the present?' she cried, interrupting him.

There was no answer.

Looking beyond him she saw a glint of dark water and moonbeams glittering on willow fronds as they swayed in the soft breeze. Hamish's world was as cold as the moon's. Aloof and uncompromising, he saw the world in tones of pristine white and deepest black, good and evil. She must be a saint or Satan and she had fallen off her pedestal.

He sighed. 'I can't bear the pain of the way you tricked me. You led me to believe that it was all for love. I was amazed. To think that a beautiful, clever girl like you could fall for me. And more than that, you threw all that you had into saving my business. What a gamble to take. I was awed by your love and loyalty and your courage. And all the time . . .

'I've been watching you, Marjorie. You have a knack of manipulating people. I've seen you with Lana. Why do you and your parents bring up Lana in the fiction that she's adopted?'

'Surely you understand,' she argued. 'Lana doesn't need the stigma of being illegitimate. Anyway, my parents *did* adopt her and they invented the story that she is the child of distant relatives who emigrated. It's better for everyone this way.'

'No, Marjorie, it's not. You must tell her the truth. Do you manipulate yourself, too? Or can you be straight and honest with yourself? Did you convince yourself that you loved me? Or did you grasp your chance with both hands, knowing exactly what you were doing?'

'I couldn't resist you. Remember? Please, Hamish, stop punishing yourself and me. It was fate.'

'Not fate, you.'

'It all worked out, didn't it?'

'Yes, your plan worked out wonderfully well. And you got a bonus for your hard work. You fell in love.'

'So . . . ? Doesn't that mean something to you?' she cried out.

'No! You're the best, Marjorie. I never had an inkling of what was going on. I was sure that you loved me, but you were using me. Then, in the restaurant last month, Joe's eyes told me the truth. He looked so sad and embarrassed as his eyes scanned my face to find out if I knew. Then there was your absurd behaviour at the Highland Games. That's when I started checking. Well, it's all yours. You sold yourself to get it. You deserve it. I want to be alone to think.'

A palpable dread seemed to be falling over her like a shroud. As if in a dream she returned to the reception. While she danced and chatted and beamed at everyone her mind was in a turmoil. Everyone had fights sometimes. It wasn't important. So why did it feel as if she'd fallen into a black hole?

The wind was getting up. Glancing through the window, she could see that clouds were obscuring the moon. She excused herself again and ran outside. The first raindrops spattered against her face as she reached the wood. 'Hamish, Hamish,' she called. The trees groaned and the wind surged and buffeted her and the rain drove her back to the house. She took the back stairs to their bedroom, but it was empty. She wanted to curl up under the blankets and stay there until Hamish returned, but how could she? 'The past is the past,' she muttered. Eventually she dried herself and went back to the party, where she spent most of the night watching out for Hamish.

Hamish was halfway to Inverness, speeding along the dark road. He'd changed into casual gear and his climbing equipment was stowed in the boot. He had to get away from *her*. The male in him was utterly squashed. His marriage had become a business strategy. She was different from what she had seemed. He had thought she was the only person in the whole wide world who only wanted to give, and never to take. How wrong he had been.

All his life the rest of the family had wanted what he had. With Marjorie he had imagined that it was different. By then he had nothing worth having – a near-bankrupt distillery, a ruined stately home – but it had been something worthwhile after all, a tool with which to attack her enemy. And she had sharpened and honed that tool to a fine and brilliant point. How patient she was. How strong-willed and determined.

Her final pleading had hurt him. If he stayed she would force him to forget, force him to love her, force him to accept that it was not the least important how they began. She had that power over him, and right now he wanted to be free of her influence. There was only one place to find peace, and that was high up on some snowy glacier, far from the grabbing hands and grasping minds of men and women. Only when he was at one with the snow and ice and the thrilling clarity of the sky, could he feel truly free.

Marjorie went through the next five days in blind agony, giving up work to remain close to the telephone. Hamish would be missing her. Of course he would. He would call soon. So she comforted herself every hour, but she could not shake off a feeling of dread.

Finally, a police inspector called from Inverness. He tried to break the news tactfully, but failed dismally. Hamish had fallen to his death climbing a Swiss glacier. Marjorie must make the necessary arrangements to have the body identified and flown home for burial.

Chapter 64

The service was over at last, but Marjorie had heard very little of it. Instead her ears were ringing with Hamish's voice: 'You were the best, Marjorie, really the best. I was so sure that you loved me, but you were using me all the way. It's all yours. You sold yourself to get it and you deserve it.'

Emerging into the sunlight she paused, thinking that his words would remain with her for ever. She stood there blinking defensively, unable to take a step forward, locked into the past.

Five days ago, Marjorie had flown to Switzerland to identify Hamish's body. She had been taken to the mortuary by a young and very raw policeman. The long drawer had slid out of the freezer and the shroud had been pulled back. When she had seen his torn and battered face, she had cried out, longing to smooth away the wounds and bury the past with future promises. She had yearned to give way to grief, clutch the body she still loved so much and never let go, but such behaviour was out of the question.

'Is this the body of Hamish Callum Tohara Cameron?' the policeman had asked in French.

Frozen with grief and guilt and the sheer impossibility of all this happening, she had stood there, trying to force her frozen lips to move. Oh, Hamish, what have you done? What have I done?

It was the awful finality of it that was unbearable. There had been no goodbye. If only he could return for five minutes, so they could have it out, perhaps then she could bear their separation.

Marjorie was still standing outside the church alone in her despair when she felt Mum take her arm. Barbara, who had flown up to help out for a while, flanked her other side. Together they walked towards the cemetery where Hamish's grave stood gaping open.

Lana was pale and fretful, and when she began to cry Mum offered to take her home, and that was some small mercy. Lana's grief increased Marjorie's guilt.

What did it mean, ashes to ashes, dust to dust? she pondered woodenly as the coffin was lowered into the ground. Was Hamish's spirit in existence somewhere else in time and space? Could he see her? Did he care? A kaleidoscope of images raced through her mind: Hamish standing in reception offering her coffee; Hamish's eyes glowing with love when she promised to marry him; Hamish playing darts with Dad with Lana perched on his shoulders. Was that when she had fallen in love? She could feel tears pouring down her cheeks and she scuffed them away with her fist.

Time had gone crazy. Every second seemed to last an eternity, but her mind was racing faster than the speed of light, thinking hundreds of thoughts each second. The fact was, they were all the same, but expressed in different ways: had he lost his footing, or had he thrown himself from the ledge? Why wasn't he roped? She would never know and this would be her lifelong punishment.

Someone touched her hand briefly and looking up she

saw a glitter of brown eyes through heavy black veiling. 'My dear, I am very, very sorry,' she heard.

'Thank you, Aunt Beatrice,' Marjorie whispered. The old woman trudged off towards her car. There was nothing else to be said.

John Erskine was standing at the edge of the crowd, flanked by Uncle Andrew and his son, Ian. 'The three stooges,' she whispered to Barbara. 'I wish they had stayed away.'

As the coffin was lowered, tears began to stream down her cheeks again. Through watery vistas she saw a large shadow looming on her right side, and a heavy arm came round her shoulders.

'I'm so sorry, Marjorie,' she heard.

Blinking hard, she looked up into Uncle Andrew's pale blue eyes, and unbelievably his face was wreathed with concern. Perhaps he was kinder than they had imagined. She smiled gratefully.

'Hamish liked to live dangerously. If the climbing hadn't got him, the booze would have,' he exclaimed in a booming voice that echoed round the graveside.

'That's a vicious lie,' she stammered. 'He didn't drink. Not any more.'

He shrugged. 'Well, Marjorie. I'm sorry to hassle you at a time like this, but how soon can you remove your personal effects from Inveraird Lodge and the distillery?'

'What do you mean?' As she gazed up into those amused blue eyes, suddenly she knew exactly what he meant. He laughed and the unaccustomed effort produced a twitch in his neck.

'Surely you realise that I am the legitimate heir. Don't leave it too long, dear. I'd hate to involve you in litigation after such a sad loss.' He waved his hand towards the grave, which was being rapidly filled with earth.

'No,' she cried out. Impossible! Insane! But she knew it was the truth. How could she give up all that she had created? Her life's savings had been invested in the lodge and the distillery. All that she owned. Vaguely she realised that Dad was pushing Andrew away from her.

'You bastard! Fuck off, or I'll bust your nose,' she heard Dad shout in a sudden regression to dockyard days. 'Get out of here . . . go on, get out. You're not wanted round these parts.'

So many emotions were whirling in her mind: embarrassment, anger, guilt and the warm feeling that Dad was on her side. He cared! Then fear set in: had Dad heard what Andrew had said? She felt herself falling and heard Barbara scream. Her world was spinning and darkening. She felt so cold. So strange. Perhaps she was dying, too. She hoped she was.

She woke at home, clutching Dad's hand.

'Oh dear! Oh dear.' She closed her eyes to hide her tears as all her sorrow welled up.

'Be brave, that's my girl,' Dad murmured. 'We love you and we'll help you get over this tragedy. Keep your mind on that.'

She whispered, 'Dad, oh Dad.' She felt a lump in her throat so large she could hardly breathe. She looked up into Dad's eyes and searched for signs of reproof or a hint of anger, but there was only caring.

'We're not a family for showing our feelings,' Dad admitted in a husky voice, 'but just as long as you know we're right behind you, Marj. Hamish was a good man and we'll all mourn him, but you've still got Lana and us. You're not alone. Remember that, my girl.'

She closed her eyes as Dad squeezed her hand. She could not remember him ever doing that before. Dad cared. The tears began to trickle down her cheeks.

'What's money? Money isn't important. You can't lie there for days, giving up, because you've lost out. You're being absurd.'

Joe's voice!

Marjorie tried to block her ears. She kept her eyes tightly shut, knowing that she was too frightened to face reality. She was afraid of what she might do. Kill Andrew, or wreck the house. How long had she been lying in bed? She could not remember, for her days had become one long, agonising blur.

Joe, a multi-millionaire despite the punishing divorce settlement with Véronique, went on at length about money being of little concern. He was getting through to her and her reaction was pure rage.

'It's not the money,' she screamed, sitting up suddenly. 'For God's sake! It's not the money.'

'I'm glad to see you can sit up. Then what is it?'

'It's Hamish!' Speaking his name brought on a fresh flood of tears. Her face and eyes were so inflamed that it hurt to cry. She wished she could stop.

'At least you've got your priorities in order.'

Joe had become insufferably pompous! Looking back, she realised that it had come about imperceptibly. She really hadn't noticed. There was a prim set to his pursed lips, the expression in his eyes was complacent, and he was putting on weight.

'Do my parents know about the terms of the trust?'

she asked him. 'Have you told them we have to get out?'

'No. Stop worrying about things that are unimportant.'

'My life's savings are in the distillery and this home. And it's my parents' home, too,' she retorted hotly. 'Dad loves his market garden and his ducks. I've just spent a fortune, all borrowed, putting in irrigation. Besides, he's not been well lately, this blow will affect his health.'

'So we're back to money again?'

She stared at him, noting the lines under his eyes. He looked so stern and hard. 'I told you, it's not because of the money. It's because it's our home. You don't understand. You never have. Go away. Leave me alone.'

But there was also the overdraft she had run up in doing more than she should have on the lodge, the swimming pool, Hamish's billiard room. Childlike, she pulled the pillow over her head, but nothing helped.

'No! I want you to get it straight in your mind exactly what it is you are grieving about.'

'Hamish,' she sobbed.

'So could we forget the stately home, Dad's market garden and all your money that's gone into the distillery? Because Marjorie, it's only money. That's the very last thing to grieve about. As for your life's savings, you're only twenty-five – doesn't that tell you something?'

'Go away,' she wailed.

'Marjorie, listen to me. This is something I know. We aren't bodies with spirits, we're spirits in bodies and when the body dies, the spirit moves on. Love survives death. Hamish still exists and he still loves you, and now at last he understands you. Nothing stops you from loving him as much as ever you did.'

'I wish you'd shut up, Joe,' she muttered, hating him at that moment. 'Honestly, you're getting on my nerves.'

'Life is like a river,' he went on, while she pulled the blankets over her head. 'The art of living is to flow with the current, not to hang on to anything, learning to take what comes, knowing there will always be both joy and grief and nothing lasts for ever. Change is the only sure thing in life.

'Marjorie, listen. A year ago you set in motion a series of events based on revenge and lies and deceit. Bad motives! Naturally they have boomeranged back to you. There's such a thing as karmic compensation and retribution and the scales are perfectly adjusted. No one loses through sacrifice and no one gains through selfishness. Despite your disastrous motives, you learned to love. Be thankful for that grace.'

'D'you think you're so special?' she shrieked. 'You dumped one wife for another because she was better-looking.'

'And I fear she's about to dump me. I've discovered she had a lover before I met her, and now she's seeing him again. He's younger and handsomer and they plan to live happily on my money.'

'Well, I could say it serves you right, but the truth is, it was predictable,' she muttered.

'There's no need to be a bitch. I came to suggest that you take a short break with Barbara. She's still here, by the way. Drives me batty. She won't go until you recover, she says. Right now she's making tea. Take Lana, too. She doesn't look well. In the meantime, I'll get some top lawyers on to salvaging whatever they can. Andrew Cameron can't take Inver-Asian; it has nothing to do with him. If I work fast I'll be able to transfer more Glenaird assets into that company. I'll make sure your investment in the distillery is backed by debenture shares so you won't lose out too badly. Give me your power of attorney and buzz off.'

Marjorie lay turning over his suggestion. 'Now you're talking sense,' she told him. 'I'll have a holiday here at home. I love this place and it's my last chance to enjoy it. Besides, you might need me, but I'll ask Barbara to stay on. And I would be grateful if you would help me. Thank you, Joe. I know you mean well. It's just that nothing really helps at present.'

How could she tell Joe the truth: that she was utterly lost in the hell of despising herself?

Chapter 65

Barbara wanted to help Marjorie so much, but making cups of tea was the only gesture her friend would accept, so she made tea all the time. Swirling the bags around the mugs, she remembered belatedly that Joe had left that morning, but she had made for three. Damn!

'Zola,' Barbara called from the kitchen. 'We're running out of things. I'll go shopping later if you'll write down what we need.'

If she could only stop worrying. She'd been due to start a new job three days ago, but she was reluctant to leave Marjorie until she recovered a little. She'd tried explaining this to her future boss when she'd called him in Torquay, but he was none too pleased with her. Tough! So she'd find another job.

Carrying the mugs to Marjorie's bedroom, she found her on her knees packing duvets into a tin trunk. She was shocked anew at Marjorie's appearance. Marjorie had lost so much weight her clothes looked like other people's cast-offs, and the only relief from the pallor of her face were the deep black shadows under her eyes. She suffered from migraine headaches and constant nausea. She looked so crushed and sad, yet she stubbornly refused the helping hand Barbara was thrusting at her.

'You have to put this loss behind you, Marjorie,'

Barbara began hesitantly, passing the mug to her. 'You're not the first woman to be widowed young. You still have your life to lead. You owe it to Lana to make an effort and pull yourself together. I know it seems a terrible thing to say, but everyone tells me that time heals even the saddest loss.'

Marjorie looked away and sipped her tea. Barbara meant well, but how could she explain to her friend that while she was longing for Hamish physically and emotionally, she felt half-crazed with guilt and self-recrimination? She had used Hamish, and when he had found out, the shock had driven him to his death. Whichever way she looked at it, accident or suicide, Hamish had died because of her actions. She would never forgive herself. Grief swept through her, leaving a sense of loneliness. There was yet another loss, but she could not face up to that right now.

'I think you're wrong to leave your home in such a hurry, love,' Barbara went on. 'You might regret it later. Stay put until you feel better.'

Marjorie was tempted to confide at least some of her problems, for Barbara's sake as much as for her own. Barbara felt rejected and she was trying so hard to help. But what if she told Mum and Dad? Joe was still trying to persuade the trustees to separate the cottage from the lodge so that her parents would be able to stay on, but in the meantime, it was pointless to worry them for nothing.

'First of all, none of this must go back to my parents,' she began tentatively. 'You see, Barbara, it's more complicated than you realise. In the beginning I didn't love Hamish as he deserved to be loved. I used him. I knew what I was doing, too. All my life I'd longed to give Lana the life she deserved as Robert's daughter. It's her birthright, you must see that. Hamish offered what Robert had taken away.' She sighed and pressed another pillowcase into the trunk, before crouching back on her heels.

'Hamish fell in love with me and I . . .' Her voice faltered. 'I used him,' she said, squaring her shoulders and glaring defiantly at Barbara. 'Glenaird gave me the means to fight Robert and I grabbed the chance with both hands, but I felt it was a fair bargain. I saved Hamish from losing the distillery. I put every penny I had into this home and the business, over a million pounds, and I reconciled him with his uncle, Toharasan. But then I fell in love with him, so deeply. Honest to God I did. I was so happy and secure and I let my defences down, and like a fool I admitted that I had fallen in love with him.'

'Oops!' Barbara said.

'I knew you'd understand. He was furious and hurt and we had a fight. He said he'd have to rewrite all his memories. So he ran away to the mountains, as he'd always done as a child, and he fell. Or . . . well, who knows? Either way I know that I'm responsible for his death.'

'No, you're wrong, love. No one can make any other human being do anything they don't want to do. He could have caused a scene, asked for a divorce, got another woman, or simply stayed away for a month to punish you. That's probably what he had in mind,' Barbara went on, longing to comfort her friend.

'But there's worse to come,' Marjorie whispered. 'In a way I feel that Robert is responsible, too. Now he has even more to answer for. Do you know why I'm suffering so? It's not only the grief of losing Hamish, although that's terrible. It's not my guilt, although that's unbearable, too. It's the knowledge that I've lost the distillery, which was the only means I had to destroy Robert and grab Glentirran for Lana. That's what's killing me.'

'Oh Marjorie! I'm so sorry.' Barbara did not know why Marjorie had to lose the distillery, but guessed it was best not to question her further. It would all come out when Marjorie was ready. 'You must try to let go of your hatred. It's not Robert you're destroying, it's yourself.'

Marjorie shrugged. 'I've told you now and that's that. I don't want to talk about it again.'

She looked so defeated, Barbara wanted to cry for her.

After this Marjorie became even more introverted. She hovered near the telephone most of the time and Barbara could not prise her out of the house. Constant messages from Joe Segal didn't seem to be helping matters much either, in Barbara's opinion.

'I have to keep in touch with Joe,' Marjorie explained. 'The position is fluid. The trustees are making certain allowances, but not much. The trust was set up in England and according to Joe, that's better for us. We don't have much time and I think my parents will have to move out, but I must be sure before I tell them.'

This was the closest Marjorie had come to unburdening herself about her financial position, but Barbara sensed her fears.

The next few days passed slowly, while Marjorie wandered in the garden under overcast skies and walked sadly around the house. Christmas loomed, and to Barbara's mind it looked like being the worst ever.

On the third Friday of December the two women woke to find the lodge covered in snow. As Marjorie looked out of the window, a glimmer of past joy penetrated her defences. How lovely it was. Leaving Lana in Barbara's care, she went for a long walk in the woods and round the lake, digging into the past, trying to make sense of it all. How was it possible to love two different men so passionately? Her memories of Robert were so real she felt she could reach out to touch him. She could see his dark, glowing eyes, his black burnished hair, his teasing smile. Later she had learned to love Hamish, but in the end she had lost them both. Recently, she had found herself gripped by a deep anger against Hamish. How could he do this to both of them? He had ruined her life. Images and memories faded, but strangely her hatred for Robert burned as fiercely as ever. It was hate that was giving her strength, she knew.

At that moment it occurred to Marjorie that hate and evil were synonymous and that she had fallen under the spell of evil. She sensed that it was a strangely subtle force that had invaded her mind. She was like a chameleon that had wandered into a black bog, so that she was turning black, as black as the bog, as black as night, as black as the hatred she nurtured. She saw that now as clearly as if she were watching her own life on a cinema screen. What was evil? she wondered. Was it the absence of goodness or love? Or was it a force of energy that could zoom into the minds of those who were defenceless because they were bereft of love? And did evil look after its own?

Suddenly she knew with certainty that she would not lose the distillery and she walked back filled with a sense of fatalism. 'So be it,' she murmured.

'Oh, there you are.'

Barbara's face was a picture of relief and irritation. 'I've looked everywhere for you. We were due at your mum's half an hour ago. Dinner, remember? Joe arrived a while back.'

Mum had tried hard, with curried mutton and rhubarb tart and cream, both Marjorie's favourites, but she picked at the food and could not join in the conversation. She kept staring into space while Barbara struggled to keep the conversation going.

Joe took Marjorie aside and whispered in her ear. 'It's no go, sorry. I tried my best. Andrew wants the cottage. You have two months. I suppose you'd better tell them.'

'Yes. Thanks for all you've done, Joe.'

'Well, for the rest I haven't done badly. Tell you later.'

On impulse, Marjorie turned and saw that Barbara was gazing sympathetically at her. Kindness was wrapped around her friend like a warm cloak on a winter's day, and watching her, Marjorie felt naked and ashamed. She shuddered violently.

Dad leaped up and slammed the window shut.

'Well, my girl,' he said softly. 'This time round you're enduring a terrible pregnancy. How much longer will it be before you are delivered?'

There was a strange hiatus as everyone stared at her face.

'Are you all right, love?' Mum called out. 'You've turned as pale as death.'

But I'm not pregnant, she wanted to say, but could not find the words. She looked around at their shocked faces, feeling puzzled. Was that what they thought? Surely they understood that it was grief that had laid her low? Hadn't she had a period only the other day – when was it? Days before Joe's wedding. No, it was two weeks before. But that was ages ago, in October, wasn't it? Two weeks before Hamish died. She turned to Joe and their eyes met. He cocked an eyebrow, watching her quizzically.

'Idiot!' he muttered, but she could see his laughter starting up.

She began to giggle. Softly at first, but then her voice became louder and her laughter harsher. Of course her unborn child would be a boy. She was saved, as she had sensed she would be, but in such an unexpected manner. She spread her hands protectively over her belly, feeling thankful that her child had been conceived with love.

Part 4 – Lana
June 1990 – April 1995

——— ———

Chapter 66

Marjorie replaced the receiver with a gesture of annoyance. So where was Alasdair? Almost simultaneously she heard her son calling from outside her office window.

'Oh, Alasdair. You're in trouble, my boy.'

The sight of him made her catch her breath. He was beautiful and taller than most boys of eleven, with a strange self-possession about him. His features were a real family mix: Mum's heart-shaped face and her smile, Dad's wide cheekbones, and Hamish's beautiful oriental eyes – although his were light amber. He had Hamish's strangely introverted, obsessive character, too.

Yes, he was altogether special, but far from angelic, Marjorie reflected, frowning at him. He was naughty, headstrong and canny, but he was kind and caring, too, particularly where animals were involved. And he was every bit as obstinate as that decrepit, starving donkey he had tethered to the pillar at the bottom of their steps.

'You stole it.' She leaned out of the window and pointed her finger. 'The police called. The gypsies intend to lay a charge. You're in trouble, my boy.'

He shrugged and stared at her, stony-faced, and her heart lurched. He gets away with murder, she mused, but only because of those eyes.

'They have no right . . .' he began, clenching his

fists. 'Life is above law. How can life be owned? Life belongs to itself,' he muttered, gesturing towards the donkey.

'Maybe one day you'll be able to change the law, but in the meantime that donkey belongs to the gypsies and back to them it will go. Double quick, my boy.'

'Look at it. Just look at it, Mum. Then hand it back to them, if you can. Can you?'

Feeling that she was on trial and resenting this, Marjorie walked outside, blinking in the early June sunshine. She gazed sadly at the mangy beast who stood with tail and head drooping, ribs jutting out and coat half gone.

'Don't you dare let him near Lana's mare. She'll catch something.' Damn! The words had slipped out and it was too late to back down now.

'And don't give him too much feed because his stomach's probably shrivelled. He could die. Little and often and put him to graze on the lawn. You got that?'

'He's a she and I'm not an idiot.'

At that moment a raggedy bunch of half-drunk men came swaying and cursing down the driveway. Marjorie felt intimidated, but she knew she would cope as soon as she lost her temper. It was only a matter of time.

'You left the gate open?' she grumbled at her son.

'Sorry.'

'You'd better go and take that thing with you.'

'No!' he argued, standing his ground.

When one of the men tried to grab the donkey's halter, the beast whipped round and got in a hefty kick. She's not as beaten as she looks, Marjorie fancied, feeling a certain bond with her.

As they loomed too close, well into her private space,

she stood her ground, almost gagging at the stench of stale beer, sweat and tobacco.

Alasdair pushed in front of her, the donkey's lead clenched in his hand. 'This donkey has been impounded,' he pronounced solemnly. 'I advise you not to touch it. Inspectors from the police and the RSPCA are on the way.'

'Hey, fuck off, boy, or I'll give you a hiding,' one of them jeered. 'Who're you kidding?'

For a moment Marjorie feared they were going to strike her son and she grabbed hold of his shoulders, pulling him back against her. The gypsies hung back uncertainly, unwilling to push her.

'Look here, ma'am, hand over the donkey and we'll say no more.'

Marjorie hesitated. Perhaps the RSPCA should confiscate the donkey, she decided. She would let the beast go, and call them. She grabbed Alasdair's arm to pull him away, but he shook her off roughly and hung on to the halter, shooting her a look of utter contempt. She quailed.

'How much do you want for it?' Marjorie blurted out.

The eldest of the bunch, with a dirty mass of iron grey beard and shrewd brown eyes, was quick to size up her weakness. 'Five hundred pounds or *he* gets charged with theft,' he shouted, pointing at Alasdair.

The deal was quickly settled, but Marjorie knew she had sunk in Alasdair's estimation.

'That was real dumb, Mum,' he muttered as they departed, singing jovially.

'I wasn't paying for her. It was to keep you out of trouble. You'll work in the garden to pay me back,' she snarled. She spent her life trying to hang on to the shreds of parental authority. The problem was she wanted his love more than she wanted him disciplined. She'd never had that trouble with Lana.

'What's her name?' she asked, anxious to mend their bruised friendship.

'*Daisy*,' he muttered, as the donkey took a large mouthful of her double marguerites. 'I don't care what you say, I'm calling the RSPCA. There's plenty more donkeys in just as bad a state where this one came from.'

'What a shame,' she exclaimed, meaning it, but hoping that they would not all land up eating her flowers.

At that moment the telephone rang. 'You'd best call the vet first,' she called over her shoulder as she hurried to the library.

'Mrs Cameron?' It was a familiar voice, but she couldn't immediately place it.

'Speaking.'

'Hugh Ross here.'

Lana's headmaster! Now what? she wondered anxiously.

'It's about Lana's studies,' Ross explained when he had finished his lengthy preamble. 'It's important that I talk to you at once.'

'But Lana's always top in everything. I can't believe she isn't working.'

'Oh yes, she's working all right. That's why I want to see you.' There was a note of derision in his voice.

'I'm leaving for the States tomorrow,' she told him. 'Perhaps when I return . . .'

'Mrs Cameron, I would not bother you if it weren't extremely important.'

'Oh my! Very well. Tomorrow morning. How about ten?'

She replaced the receiver muttering: 'What on earth?'

Lana was clever and it showed in her work, but she was also a rebel, a headstrong, self-willed, hard-headed child who was frequently in conflict with her teachers. Marjorie smiled indulgently as she remembered the time Lana had carried her drunken school friends one by one up six flights to bed, and told the matron they had food poisoning. Matron had believed her until the doctor arrived to diagnose alcoholic poisoning.

And there was the unfortunate episode when matron had hit her and she had struck back, resulting in the poor woman slipping and spraining her ankle.

Until now, there had never been complaints about her studies, for her work was always close to perfect. Feeling apprehensive, Marjorie called her secretary at the distillery and asked her to change her flights.

The ringing went on and on. Eventually Marjorie surfaced and her hand groped for the alarm switch. As her mind cleared she remembered that she had to be at Lana's school by ten, which meant leaving home by six-thirty. Hurrying to the bathroom, she subjected herself to her morning scan, examining her pale skin dispassionately, noting the tiny cracks running from her nose to each side of her mouth. Laughter lines, they called them, but she didn't remember laughing for some time. Her skin was still youthful and mainly unblemished, if you overlooked the tiny crow's-feet at the corners of her eyes.

She was thirty-six, but she knew that she looked younger, perhaps because she had been living in an emotional vacuum since Hamish had died, eleven years ago. She had never grown beyond that point, never truly loving, or living, since then. To the outside world she was the brave widow who had put grief aside to cope with running the distillery while being both mother and father to her fatherless children.

The truth, as Marjorie saw it, was less palatable. She had become addicted to her own particular narcotic, which was business. Like all addicts she had to have more and more shots: of success, of revenge, of coups. Remove her opiate and she went cold turkey, so holidays with the children became close to intolerable unless there was a fax handy.

In the evenings she called sales executives in Hong Kong or America and put in a few hours of solid planning. The sun never set on Glenaird sales offices; there was always someone to bully or manipulate.

Yet there was one person whom she could not manipulate and that was Lana, although she knew that her daughter adored her and was always open to reason. She had brought Lana up to question authority and think for herself. Sometimes she wondered if she had overdone it.

Goodness, she was dawdling. She hurriedly dressed, drank the coffee Zola brought and joined Mr Jenkins, their driver, in the courtyard. Because of her American trip, Alasdair had moved in with her parents last night.

As they parked outside the cottage, Marjorie noticed that the front door was open. Angus, their cross Labrador–Irish wolfhound, who had replaced Paddy, was sitting outside, sniffing the morning air and gazing towards the lake and the ducks.

'I won't be a minute.' She walked to the doorway and lingered there, filled with strange longings, stroking the dog's head, inhaling the warmth, the smell of breakfast and the homeliness of the living room. There were marigolds in a vase on the table, and a bunch of mint in a glass jug on the windowsill. A younger, fluffier Tibby was sitting at the stove watching Mum cooking and waiting for his titbits.

Alasdair was eating breakfast. His plate was piled with eggs, bacon, sausage, kidneys and liver. She had never seen such an appetite. She watched him, loving him, but not wanting to play the doting mother, which always embarrassed her son.

'I'm off. Bye everyone,' she called.

Alasdair looked round and grinned. He ran to her and gave her a hard, quick hug.

'Bye, Mum. Give Lana hell. Tell her to work.'

'You're a fine one to talk,' Liz murmured. 'You look smart,' she went on, turning towards her daughter. 'Is that the new French number?'

Marjorie nodded and smoothed her Chanel suit. 'How's Dad?'

'He seems better.'

'But you will get the doctor, won't you?'

'I suppose so.' She shrugged. 'He'll be furious.'

'I'd best hurry or Mr Jenkins will be late to fetch Alasdair for school.'

'I'll die of misery if I miss prayers,' he muttered, smirking.

She looked back, smiling, but he was engrossed in his breakfast. Will he ever guess how much I love him? she wondered. And should he?

Chapter 67

——— ———

Marjorie could not banish the butterflies in her stomach as she was shown into the headmaster's study. How absurd! She wanted to laugh at herself. She still reacted fearfully to school authority, exactly as she had years ago. This was one of her many hang-ups which she had been determined Lana would never experience.

The headmaster, white-haired and raw-skinned, with shrewd blue eyes, shook hands, smiling briefly. According to Lana this was his 'parents' face'. The true Hugh Ross was both remote and unfriendly, Lana insisted, and Marjorie was inclined to believe her.

'Thank you for your prompt attention to this problem,' he began.

As if I had any choice, Marjorie reflected, watching him retrieve a folder from his filing cabinet. Poor Lana, she commiserated. There lay all her faults, documented and filed for posterity, but did it mention that she was outrageously brave, a staunch friend or a bitter enemy, or her cheerful nature, or the way she coped with almost any setback?

He opened it and sighed ominously and again Marjorie's stomach lurched.

'So tell me the worst. What has she done?' she blurted out.

Ross looked up, and spread his hands in a helpless gesture. 'Mrs Cameron, this is the first time I have ever had to complain of such a problem. The fact is, Lana works too hard. She is too conscientious. Would you like some coffee?'

Marjorie nodded grimly as a woman walked in carrying a tray. So I delayed an important trip and ten appointments to hear that my daughter works hard? She struggled to bite back her annoyance.

'Naturally she will be awarded the prize for the most hard-working girl in the school,' he said softly, as if sensing her anger. 'As usual she is top in almost everything. I was concerned that she was obliged to add Japanese to her very tough curriculum, but I hear that she is excelling in that, too.'

'Not obliged,' Marjorie murmured. 'It was merely a suggestion.'

'She can't carry on like this, Mrs Cameron,' he insisted. 'She works all hours. Eventually we were forced to switch off her lights at the mains. So she took to spending most of the night in the toilet, until we found out. Three nights ago she was found on the toilet floor, having fallen asleep over her Japanese studies, *of all things*,' he added distastefully. 'Naturally she has caught a bad cold.'

Marjorie helped herself to sugar and stirred slowly, using the pause to summon her self-control and ignore the implied criticism in the headmaster's tone.

'I hoped you might enlighten me as to why your daughter is so determined to excel and so terrified of failure.'

'Perhaps because she belongs to a family of achievers,' she offered, feeling resentful and unfairly burdened by this revelation of Lana's ambition.

'Or perhaps because she feels she doesn't belong? She is adopted, isn't she?'

A bolt of fear brought bile to her mouth. 'That's irrelevant,' Marjorie snapped. 'She's my only daughter and spoiled silly.'

'Perhaps that has merely added to her burden.'

'What burden? What are you talking about?' Marjorie hung on to her temper and tried not to snarl.

'Her burden of guilt.'

'How ridiculous. I love Lana and she is absolutely free to run her life as she feels best.' She made an effort to unclench her fists as she lapsed into sullen silence.

'Mrs Cameron, have you any idea what it must be like to be seventeen years old, and brought up in the lap of luxury by a doting mother, who is also a business magnate, and to know that sheer chance made all this happen? Surely you understand her guilt. She can't afford to fail you, Mrs Cameron. She owes you too much.'

'That's a wicked lie.' Marjorie was fast losing her self-control. 'Lana is not like that. She's clever, witty, streetwise – all those things. She never gives a fig about being adopted. Why should she? What's the difference, after all? She practically runs the family.'

'At seventeen? Was she ever a child?'

'Of course she was! Though I suppose she did sort of take over bringing up Alasdair. I was always working. I . . . we . . . didn't have any choice. Of course, my mother was always there for the children.'

'I understand.' He sighed softly. 'Mrs Cameron, I took the liberty of asking a psychiatrist to talk to your daughter. Did you know that Lana has fanciful dreams of what her real mother might be like? I'll read this to you. Please note that in the absence of knowing what her natural parents are like, she has created what she considers to be ideal mother material. Are you with me?'

Marjorie nodded weakly, filled with a sense of unreality as Ross opened his file and cleared his throat. She wanted to burst out laughing. How absurd! Insane really! Yet to Lana it was real enough. Once again a bolt of fear raced through her, leaving her shuddering. What had she done to her beloved daughter?

'This is Lana talking,' he began. '"When I was young, I used to visualise my mother as being exactly like the good fairy in my Cinderella picture book. She had sparkling blue eyes and blonde hair and she was soft and gentle. She had all the time in the world to listen to my problems. She liked to go on picnics and spend time with us. Now that I'm older I realise that she was only a dream person, but I know that my real mother is somewhere out there and one day I shall find her. I know she'll be a gentle person, not businesslike at all, but perhaps she'll run a nursery, or work in a hospital. Perhaps she's a nun and working with poor children."'

'Stop it!' Marjorie commanded, fumbling in her handbag for a tissue. 'It's impertinent to read out confidences like these.' She blew her nose vigorously 'Too bad if I don't match up to her expectations. I can clearly remember wishing my mother were the Queen. One doesn't always get exactly what one wants in life.' She stood up, ready for flight.

'Please sit down, Mrs Cameron. I'm not trying to criticise your lifestyle, I'm merely attempting to enlist your aid in helping Lana. I want you to explain clearly to her the nature of your *unconditional* love. That it doesn't matter if she succeeds or fails.'

'She knows that,' Marjorie snapped, sinking back into

her chair. 'After all the years she's been here, you still don't understand her. Don't you understand, no one can make Lana do a damn thing that she doesn't want to do? I certainly can't. She knows I love her unconditionally. After all, I love Alasdair and he never works, except at sport. You're missing the point entirely.'

'Which is?' he asked quietly.

'That she loves me desperately and she wants to take some of the workload off me as soon as she can. She's longing to take over.'

'She refers to Alasdair as your "*real*" child. Did you know that? Not once, but several times.' He was flicking the pages and making curious little marks with his pencil. Probably an occupational disease, she fancied. He couldn't stop ticking things.

'I think she's longing to repay you, Mrs Cameron. She's carrying a huge millstone of gratitude on her shoulders. If it weren't for you she might be in the orphanage right now . . .'

'No, stop! Lana knows nothing about an orphanage. How could she?' She realised she was shouting and she tried to lower her voice. 'All she knows is that her parents, who were our relatives, emigrated, and that I, with my parents' back-up, adopted her. You see,' she mumbled, 'once, years back, she wanted to know why her family name was the same as mine, and who her father was, and Mum explained it all to her.'

Marjorie broke off, remembering that she had ducked out, leaving it to Mum to explain. Exactly what had Mum told her? 'She was only six at the time, I think. I'm sure she's forgotten about it. She's my *real* daughter. That's all there is to it.'

She cringed as she felt tears running down her cheeks.

'Mrs Cameron, try not to distress yourself. No one could have done more for this little girl than you . . .'

Oh, dear God!

'But listen to this . . .' He was riffling through the file again. That damned file should be burned.

'"Sometimes I wonder what might have happened if my mum hadn't given me a home. It makes me feel quite scared. I get nightmares worrying about it. That's why I have to show her that I appreciate all that she has done. I have to pay her back."'

'Oh God! Stop! Please stop. I can't bear it.'

'I think it would be in your daughter's interest to allow her to find her natural parents.'

'Her what? Good heavens, no.' Marjorie felt sick with guilt. 'I absolutely forbid it. I am all the mother she will ever need. This matter must be dropped at once. I had no idea, but I shall speak to Lana.' She stood up once more.

'I'm sorry, but I must go. I have another appointment,' she lied. She had intended to stay and see Lana, but now all she wanted was to get out of there. This was one problem she did not have the courage to tackle.

As she left the school she wondered if Lana had seen her. If her daughter was suffering so much from this innocent deceit, then how much more would she suffer if she ever found out the truth?

Chapter 68

Mum was sitting in her favourite rocking chair in the kitchen, stroking Tibby, who lay on her lap purring and extending his claws in rhythmic spasms. They could hear the clop, clop, clop of Dad's spade in the vegetable patch beyond the cottage, for at eleven p.m. it was still light enough to work. A slight breeze swayed the curtains, discreet and unobtrusive, and her mother's glance was warning Marjorie to be discreet, too, like the night, for Marjorie's love was acceptable only in small doses. Intimacies were frowned upon in the Hardy family.

Marjorie had never really understood her mother. At fifty-nine she was still handsome, her dark hair flecked with grey, her figure trim, for she never gave way to temptation. Everything about her showed moderation and restraint. She could not abide excesses of any type in others. Not even love.

'I don't know what to do, Mum, really I don't,' Marjorie repeated, understanding that her problem was unwelcome, but needing help. 'I had no idea Lana felt this way. Shall I tell her the truth? The trouble is, things have changed. The awful slur of having an illegitimate child has almost gone. She'll wonder what I was worrying about. I mean, how can she understand what it was like in those days?'

'Let sleeping dogs lie. That's what I say,' Liz answered. 'Nowadays they make too much of hang-ups and traumas. The world's gone crazy. There's right and there's wrong and there's such a thing as discipline. You might have abandoned Lana to be adopted. Other people in your situation did, but you didn't, so why should you be penalised now? It's only a small thing, really, Marjorie, it's not important at all. Don't meet trouble halfway!'

'Yet I understand how she feels about wanting to know about her genes,' Marjorie persisted. 'Of course she's me. Me and Robert. Two hard-headed achievers, but she doesn't know that.'

'That's where your problem lies, my girl,' Mum said softly, fingering her pearl necklace with her long fingers while her other hand kept on stroking. 'Once she found out she was your . . . well, your love child, she'd want to know who her father was. Then she'd want to meet him. He dumped you, so he's hardly likely to want her. She'd get hurt.'

'Yes,' Marjorie murmured.

'She's grown up now. I'm going to give her a good talking to,' Liz said crossly. 'You can't have everything you want in life. Not even the Queen gets that. Most girls of her age would love to have what she has. What she hasn't got, won't hurt her.'

'Maybe you're right.' Marjorie longed to have her mother's clear-cut vision of the rightness of things. Mother cut through doubts and guilt like a sharp knife through butter. She had never known the agony of wondering what was best, or right.

'Well, Mum, I'm sure I can shelve the problem for a couple of years. I'll stall for time. By then she'll be working and far too busy to worry about things like this.

In the meantime, maybe I should spend more time with her and Alasdair.'

'How lovely to have a picnic. Do let's go. And why not today? It's such a perfect day,' Marjorie told her astonished children at breakfast on the first long weekend Lana was home from school. It was early July, the weather was perfect and there seemed little likelihood of rain.

'A picnic,' they chorused, looking astonished and not very pleased. Lana, in particular, seemed wary, forewarned. Her eyes, still larger than life and too expressive for her own good, were clouded with doubt. Looking at her now, Marjorie realised that her early fears had been groundless. Lana's looks were all and more than she had ever hoped for: a face that was still square, but not unpleasingly so, delicate features, thick brows under a wide forehead and topped with a mass of black curls rising from a pronounced widow's peak. She had never told her daughter that she was beautiful, not wishing her to become vain.

'That's what other families do, isn't it?' Marjorie responded gaily.

'Other people don't have a lake and a boat and a maid to bring the food down to them,' Alasdair muttered.

'Or their own wood with a summerhouse in it,' Lana added, entering into the spirit of their shared mutiny.

'Or a Gran who makes the best food in Scotland,' Alasdair pointed out, always the family's realist.

'And they don't fly to Spain or France or Corsica when they feel like it, as we do. And maybe they live in apartments and feel an awful need to get out,' Lana improvised. 'Ugh! How grim.'

Marjorie shot a quick, suspicious glance at her. Had she been lying to the psychiatrist? 'I remember having the most wonderful picnics on the cliffs with your Aunt Barbara,' she lied. Although on second thoughts she could remember an occasion when Barbara and she had missed school and taken their sandwiches up on the cliffs. It had been fun, but cold.

'We are going to have fun,' Marjorie promised. 'Zola is packing a picnic hamper. We leave at ten.'

'Zola?' they chorused in horror.

'I'd better check it out,' Lana said breathlessly, and before Marjorie could stop her she had rushed off to the kitchen. That was Lana for you. Did she feel like the family servant? Marjorie hurried after her.

'You're not the servant here, Lana. I'll do it myself.'

Lana crumpled onto a chair and buried her face in her hands, which was most unlike her.

'What is it? What have I said?' Marjorie cried, wrapping her arms around her daughter's sullen shoulders.

'You! It's you! You guard your territory so jealously. You want to be the only woman of the house and I must stay a child. You don't even trust me to check the picnic hamper. You won't let me grow up.'

'Good God!' Marjorie collapsed on a kitchen chair in shock.

'Lana, listen to me,' she persisted as Lana determinedly unpacked the hamper and began checking the items. 'It's only that I believe you do too much for all of us. Truly! I feel I should lighten your load. You know that I love you, don't you? I mean *unconditionally*. You understand what unconditionally means, don't you?'

'Give over, Mum. How old do you think I am? Ten?'

Marjorie gave up. 'See you at the car at nine. Okay?'
Feeling hopelessly inadequate to cope, she went off to
finish paying her accounts and then to gather her hat
and walking shoes. She thrust them into a big bag and
carted it down to the hall.

'Bet you forgot the water for Angus,' Alasdair yelled,
sprawling on the rug by the open door and making no
move to do anything.

'Angus must stay and guard the house.'

'I'm not going without him,' Alasdair said moodily.

'You want him to go in my car?'

'Did you think he'd run behind?'

Oh God! She went to look for a towel for Angus to
sit on, regretting that she'd given Mr Jenkins the old
Rover for his weekend off. Only her new Jaguar, which
she loved, was left to them.

As soon as they set off the dog started yelping with
excitement. Nothing they did could shut him up. His
yelping was high-pitched and incessant. On and on,
Marjorie drove, taking the road northwards, looking
for a likely spot, but nothing looked quite as she had
planned.

An hour later, when the dog threw up, she decided
any spot would do. She parked under a tree and they
set off across the moors. She had imagined willows, a
stream, a grassy field, but never mind.

She and Alasdair carried the basket and Lana humped
the groundsheet. Big black bog flies buzzed them as their
feet sunk into the marshy ground and a curious smell rose
all about them.

Soon Marjorie was sweating and her arm ached. They
came across lonely spruce and she put down the basket
in its shade.

'Isn't this fun?' she said lightly.

'I'm hungry,' Alasdair replied.

Lana was too busy to talk. She had taken over, as she was wont to do, spreading the tablecloth on the ground, putting out plates, knives and forks and glasses, and Marjorie noticed she had added a bottle of wine. Well, why not?

'Cheers,' she said a few minutes later when Lana handed her a glass.

'Why can't I have some wine?' Alasdair moaned.

'You can. Pour him some, dear.'

He drained it in a gulp and helped himself to some more.

The flies had become frantic at the sight of all this food. They took chances, zooming down in close formation, dive-bombing the food, while all three of them took swipes and missed.

Alasdair aped around, pretending to be a wine taster. Then he was a greedy gourmet, grabbing a little of everything and wolfing it down. Suddenly a bog fly zoomed onto his salami sandwich just as he was taking a large gulp.

'I swallowed it! I swallowed a fly,' he yelped.

'Of course you'll die,' Lana sang.

She began to sing the song loudly to drown the sound of Alasdair trying to throw up behind the tree.

'There was an old woman who swallowed a fly . . .'

'What an adventure,' Marjorie enthused bravely as she helped herself to salad.

'At least we're a family for once,' Lana said ominously.

Marjorie's temper surged at this blow below the belt. 'I'm sure I look the part of the ugly stepmother,' she blurted out and then wished she could cut off her tongue.

Lana gazed at her warily, with dawning horror in her eyes. 'So that's why we had a picnic,' she said flatly.

'I'd rather do fifty lines than go through this again,' Alasdair added, unaware of the tension as he rejoined them.

'I thought sessions with a psychiatrist were totally sacrosanct,' Lana snarled.

Marjorie quailed before her daughter's fury. 'I'm sorry, dear. So did I. But in this case, he is the school psychiatrist and in your own interests . . .'

Suddenly Lana flung her arms around Marjorie and hugged her. 'There, there, Mum. Don't fret. You've got to try to understand me. I love you more than anyone in the whole world, I always will. Even when I get married, you'll still be number one. *Always!* But somewhere out there is the woman who gave birth to me. Gran once told me she's a distant relative of ours, but you've lost touch with her. I have to find out who she is and why she abandoned me. Probably when I find her, I'll simply give her a piece of my mind and leave her. But I must know what she's like. You have to understand that.

'You took a chance adopting someone, Mum,' she went on, when Marjorie did not reply. She twisted to wave the flies off her ham sandwich. 'I never would. Do you know how important genes are? We learned about it in biology. Ninety per cent of one's make-up is inherited. *She* might be a murderess. I have to know what sort of genes I've got. Mum, listen to me. You've always given me whatever I wanted, haven't you? Help me find my roots. It's so important to me.'

Marjorie tried to hold back her tears. 'You're too

young,' she said, wiping her cheeks dry with muddy fingers. 'I swear I'll help you when you're twenty-one. In the meantime, I can assure you there are no congenital defects in either family. Both of your parents are hard-working, well thought-of people. You've got to be content with that, at least for the time being.'

'Just how wonderful can they be since they abandoned their child?' Lana muttered.

That was her cue, wasn't it? Now was the time to confess everything. Suddenly they heard a gunshot, followed a second later by another, quite close to them. They sat in stunned silence while three more shots rang out.

'Where's Angus?' Alasdair cried, the fly forgotten.

'Angus,' he yelled, and whistled furiously. 'Come boy, come.' There were more shots, closer this time.

'He must have chased the sheep,' Lana said ominously. 'They'll shoot him. They have the right, you know.'

Forgetting the meal, the three of them rushed towards the sound of the shots, calling and whistling. Angus shot out of some bushes, shaking like a fox in a chase, his eyes rolling. He was covered in blood and mud.

'Oh my God,' Marjorie yelped, grabbing the dog. Lana screamed.

'Shut up, you two. Oh God! Women! It's not his blood, I tell you,' Alasdair shouted. 'It's something else's blood. He's been after the sheep. Let's run for it. The road's that way.'

Abandoning their picnic, the three of them fled through shin-deep oozing mire towards where they thought the road and the car lay, but soon they were lost. They had stumbled into enemy territory, bog flies' territory, and it was war. At last they reached the road, but between them and it, was a wire fence with a roll of barbed wire lying on the outside of it.

'Come on, it's easy. Don't be sissies,' Alasdair said grimly. He climbed up and jumped over the wire, the force of his fall rolling him down the bank to a ditch by the roadside. Somehow Angus managed to squeeze through the roll of barbed wire, yelping like crazy until he was free.

Lana climbed up the wire fence, hung on to the post and then threw herself forward. 'Ouch! she yelled as she landed. She sat up rubbing her knee.

'Are you all right, Lana?'

'Yes, I'm all right, Mum. Come on,' she urged.

Marjorie remained clinging to the fence post, wobbling on the second highest wire. How could she possibly leap over that?

A shot came close behind her.

Suddenly Alasdair was running back towards her, his face contorted, his eyes wide with fear. 'Mum, if they catch us, the police'll shoot Angus. He killed a sheep, so come on,' he begged.

It was her or Angus. Who was she to hesitate? She flung herself over the fence and fell.

Horrified, she saw that she was falling face first onto the barbed wire, but suddenly Lana sprang forward and threw herself onto the coil, and Marjorie fell heavily on her daughter.

'Oh, heavens, Lana. Why did you do that?' She scrambled to her feet and tried to extricate Lana from the wire. Why ask, she wondered, since she knew? She helped her daughter to her feet, found a tissue to stem the bleeding cuts and led her back along the road towards where they thought the car lay.

'If anyone stops us along the road, we'll say we were taking a walk,' Alasdair said grimly.

'Yes, of course, we look as if we were enjoying a walk,' Lana said, indicating the black and smelly mud that coated them up to their thighs, their torn clothes, Marjorie's shocked, white face and the blood over Lana and Angus.

Suddenly they began to laugh, and Marjorie was so relieved to hear her children's laughter, she burst into song:

'There was a young boy who swallowed a fly . . .'

'What a dumb guy to swallow a fly,' Lana trilled.

'He's sure to die,' they heard Alasdair's high-pitched soprano.

They improvised until they reached the car, then drove straight to the doctor's house, where Lana was stitched up and injected for tetanus.

Lana didn't mention her roots again and Marjorie hoped that the problem had been shelved for a few years.

Chapter 69

The bad news struck home without prior warning, as bad news has a habit of doing, and it came in the manner of a three-pronged fork. After three blows had struck, Liz Hardy felt a certain mournful satisfaction. Her superstitious beliefs never failed her, which was just as well, for they were the only control she had over a capricious fate.

First Lana had run over the cat. She was reversing out of the garage in the old Rover, which Marjorie had agreed she could use, more fool her (goodness, how she spoiled these children), when Tibby came running after her.

Lana was inconsolable. She screamed and nursed the writhing cat and later buried it in the wood. Alasdair made a cross for the grave. Sometimes Lana could be so adult, and then she could turn into a child at a moment's notice, Liz had noticed. It was bewildering to say the least. After that, Lana had come into the kitchen, taken the scissors from the hook on the wall, and cut her driving licence into little pieces. It had been her pride and joy.

'I'll never drive again, Gran,' she cried sadly, her face swollen with grief. 'Tibby trusted me and she was such a lovely cat. I've never seen such a clever cat. Oh dear. Oh dear. If only I'd been more careful.'

Liz had learned the hard way. She loved cats, but

had found it safe never to lavish her affection on any particular cat. However, what with Lana's grief and Alasdair's contempt of his sister for being so careless, she dared not suggest replacing Tibby yet.

The second calamity made the first one pale into insignificance and it was quite breath-taking in its implications, Liz knew. Old Aunt Beatrice died.

The news came at breakfast when both children were staying with her, partly because it was the holidays, but also because Marjorie was in New York.

The telephone rang and Liz picked it up unsuspectingly.

A strange voice asked to speak to Marjorie Cameron, but when Liz explained that she was in New York he introduced himself as the manager of Grampian Bank.

'I'm sorry to tell you that Mrs Beatrice Cameron died in her sleep last night. Your daughter has been appointed chairman of the bank until her son comes of age. We need her here urgently and we need to fix the date of the funeral. And then, of course, there's the house and the effects, all of which goes to Alasdair Cameron, your grandson. I'd be obliged if you would contact your daughter and ask her to return as soon as possible.'

Liz replaced the receiver thoughtfully. Not before time, she considered, since Aunt Beatrice had been almost ninety-five years old, and almost as shrivelled as an Egyptian mummy.

'Mind you,' she told the children. 'She was still in full possession of her wits right up to the last time we saw her. You have to take your hat off to her,' she added. Dad, who was drinking his tea, actually put aside his newspaper.

'She had her head screwed on the right way,' he

agreed. 'You'll have to call Marjorie. She must be here for the funeral.'

Liz had a moment of misgiving. Two disasters so far! How could she tell Marjorie to fly home when the third disaster was hanging over their heads? Dread stiffened her limbs and suddenly her fingers were all thumbs. She sent the marmalade pot skimming over the table to the floor. Moments later, she and the children were gathering pieces of sticky china from all over the place. Could this be the third disaster? No! It was only a silly accident. So what next?

She gazed speculatively at Alasdair, who was now a millionaire banker, although he did not know this yet. Liz sighed. She hoped it would not go to his head. Beatrice Cameron, for all her wealth and power, was now nothing more than fodder for worms. Death was the final leveller. So what was the point in getting all puffed up with power and strutting around arrogantly? What are we really? Worm fodder in the making. It was as well to remember that since life didn't last very long. Accepting death was the hardest part of living, she reflected. You sort of pretended that it never happened.

'Oh dear,' she muttered to Dad. 'I suppose I'll have to call Marjorie home, but goodness knows what'll happen next.'

Liz was filled with dread at the prospect of her daughter flying back on the first flight she could get, and maybe on one of those lax foreign airlines, when the third calamity had not yet struck home. She couldn't bring herself to make the call.

When they had washed the dishes, a family chore, Dad humped a few bags of soil into the rowing boat and set off for the middle of the lake. Slowly but surely, his island was being eroded around the shoreline.

It was some time before they heard his yells from the island.

'Something must be wrong,' Alasdair warned. 'Listen! He's calling for help.' In next to no time the boy had ripped off his shirt and he was surging across the lake. Alasdair could swim better than Dad ever had, Liz noticed, frowning as she watched Dad. Why was he lying in the mud? Lana followed hard behind and Liz watched them half lift Dad into the boat.

Dad had slipped a disc manhandling the sacks. She could see he was in agony, although he was trying not to alarm the children, but he could hardly move without groaning with pain. Mr Jenkins, their driver, was off, so Lana had to drive Dad to the doctor. It was lucky that she'd remembered to retrieve the pieces of Lana's licence out of the bin and stick them back together, Liz decided.

Later, when Dad was in bed and the children had gone down to the RSPCA depot to see if they had a stray tabby kitten, Liz felt a sense of peace. 'Disasters come in threes,' she told Dad without any doubt in her voice. 'It could have been a lot worse. Now we can rest easy for a while.'

She went calmly downstairs to call Marjorie.

Chapter 70

New York was like another home to Marjorie. She loved the space, the skyscrapers that combined power with grace, and the sheer symmetry of the parallel and vertical lines. Walking in Manhattan never failed to give her a high. You could pace the streets of London for ever, and never be more than one lonely unit amongst a nation of introverts, but here in New York she immediately felt at one with the people rushing by and with the throbbing pulse of this vibrant city.

Her usual suite on the fifty-fourth floor of the tower block of the Helmsley Hotel never failed to thrill her. The suite overlooked the west and north sides of the city. Marjorie always made an effort to arrive before sunset. From this height, watching the sun, a huge, blood-red globe, sink into the violet shadows over the Hudson River was a magnificent experience. Far below she could see the beautiful domes and spires of St Patrick's cathedral. There was a large crowd gathered around it, looking ant-sized from here, but even at this height she could catch their voices: 'Crack down on crack; crack down on crack,' the people chanted in unison.

It was only here in America that Marjorie truly felt democracy in action. Elsewhere people paid lip service to it, or voted for it. Here they felt it, lived it, expressed it, ate, slept and drank it. Through them she caught a glimpse of what it should be like. Here each citizen made his own decisions about the nation's best direction and went out and voiced his intentions loud and clear. She had never met this sense of joint and several caring and responsibility anywhere else in the world. She loved it.

At last she tore herself away from the window because the porter was waiting. What did they call them here? Bellboys, she remembered. She admired the bowl of fresh roses on the table, and the fruit and bottle of French wine on the sideboard and a card saying: 'Welcome back. Glad to have you here in New York again. Enjoy your stay.'

The darnedest thing was, she believed them. She believed the bellboy when he grinned and chanted: 'Have a good day, Mrs Cameron.' And the housekeeper who called to assure her that they had not forgotten her allergy to feathers, and how pleasant it was to talk to her again. Had she had a good trip?

Maybe one day she would live in New York. It was a cherished dream that had little chance of fulfilment, but sometimes at night when she was alone in her vast, empty lodge, she would visualise the throbbing streets as they were at that moment, and the sunset from the tower suite. This never failed to make her feel absolutely great.

She smiled at herself as she realised that she was already mentally shifting gear into American expressions.

There was a message on the sideboard: '*Urgent. Please call Mr Yoshi Tohara who is waiting at his office. He must see you at once.*'

She had flown to New York to see Yoshi, so why did he have to see her now? She had a date. Unbeknown to

the family, she had a lover in New York, which she felt
was far enough away from home for her secret never to
reach them.

He was twenty-nine years old, a brash, arrogant,
go-getting man of Italian descent, and he was an ardent
and imaginative lover and very handsome in a traditional
Roman way. His name was Carlo Losapio and he was
Glenaird's American distributor, a vast contract for such
a young man, but he was good, she had to admit that. She
sighed and picked up the telephone to call Yoshi.

Inver-Asian maintained a sales office in Fifth Avenue,
which was a mere five minutes' walk away. Even after
a late night meeting, Marjorie loved to walk back alone,
and despite all the warnings she had received, she had
found it safe and the streets always thronged with
people.

Today the humidity made it almost impossible to
hurry. The streets were half-empty. Everyone who
could, had taken off for cooler, hilly areas for their
August holidays. It was strange to see so many empty
parking places. This was not the best time to visit New
York, but Yoshi's summons could not be ignored. She
had never known him to fly over at this time of the
year, either.

She swung into the imposing foyer, took the elevator
to the seventh floor and pushed open the swing glass
doors to the Inver-Asian reception area.

She stood there for a moment looking around and
thinking, perhaps Yoshi had been right. They had fought
long and hard over the decor. She had wanted something
light and Japanese – Joe had left her with a penchant for
wide open spaces – but Yoshi had been adamant.

'Japan doesn't make good whisky,' he had reminded her.

So the chairs were upholstered in the Mackintosh hunting tartan. 'Why Mackintosh?' she had asked him, feeling perplexed.

'Because it is the only harmonious tartan I could find,' he had laughed. She had to admit that the faded autumn colours against the light green carpets and beige curtains looked really good. On the walls were some first-class paintings of Scottish hunting scenes and lochs. Naturally a Scottish receptionist sat behind the desk, and of course she was young and blonde, with blue eyes and a tall, willowy figure.

'Go right in, Mrs Cameron,' she told her, in a soft, well-modulated Inverness accent.

Yoshi's office was quite different: white and beige with little in it. Like Joe, he spoiled himself with space, perhaps because his homeland was so crowded.

Yoshi stood up and bowed Japanese-style. Then he shook hands, English-style, and hugged her, planting a kiss on either cheek, French-style.

'What a greeting, Yoshi,' she said, laughing.

'Real international, huh? This way I can't go wrong. Now Marjorie, sit down and have a drink. I can only offer you sake.'

'I don't want to drink too much.'

'Why not? You're so English when you're tipsy. You always make me laugh.' He poured her a small glass and then one for himself, which he knocked back in a gulp, expecting her to do the same, so she did, but only once. When he refilled her glass, she reminded herself to sip at it.

'I remember you telling me of your English lessons. "I

like ice cream." That was how it went, yes? I, too, have been suffering, but you will note that nowadays I have no problem at all with my "r"s and "l"s.'

He leaned back and burst out laughing, but it wasn't all that funny and Marjorie heard warning bells in the back of her head. He was softening her up. For what? She liked and trusted Yoshi. Over the years he had become a distant family guardian. Did he have bad news for her?

Yoshi had a curiously soft voice, and each syllable was pronounced sensuously, as if he were caressing the English language. The net result was incredibly sexy. Long ago, a year after she was widowed, his resemblance to Hamish had led her to make a fool of herself one night after a long, romantic dinner. They had landed up in bed, and Yoshi had been the most expert and accomplished lover, sending her to heights of physical pleasure she had never known before or since.

'Yoshi,' she had murmured afterwards. 'You're fantastic. You're the best.'

'I make special effort,' he had replied with a straight face. 'I sense I fuck for Japan.' Then he had burst out laughing.

It hadn't taken either of them long to realise that her attraction to him was merely an effort to remember Hamish. Yoshi had pulled out of the affair, gently but inexorably, and they had developed a caring friendship.

'You're softening me up for the kill, Yoshi. I know you too well,' she complained now. 'Out with it.'

'Let me refill your glass first. Drink up, for old times' sake. You know you've become even lovelier, Marjorie. Here's to you, the sexiest woman in the world. I still dream about you.'

It was then that she realised the blow was going to

affect her womanly self-esteem. Yoshi was trying to make her feel good. 'What's he done?' she muttered.

'You're psychic. I'm sure of that. Okay, Marjorie, this is where you have to take the blow on the cheek . . .'

'Chin,' she corrected him. 'Take it on the chin, not take it on the cheek.'

'Either way . . . you've been taken, Marjorie. It was sensible of you to choose a lover who was far from your home territory, but your choice was faulty. Losapio must be dumped, at once.'

'I presume you have a good reason for saying that,' she countered.

'Of course. He's two-timing you, both in business and in his personal life.'

'Why are you spying on me?'

His black eyes became opaque and remote and he looked away.

'Don't sulk, Yoshi. How else could you have known?'

'I was about to tell you,' he muttered a trifle coldly.

Marjorie leaned back, sipped her sake and digested this information. Something hurt badly. What was it? She wasn't in love with Carlo, although she often lusted after him. Was it the business angle that was causing the hurt?

'First the business,' she sighed.

Yoshi laughed. 'I knew you'd choose that one first. Okay, Losapio is under-capitalised and his cash flow position is desperate. Like all greedy men, he is dishonest. Despite his signed agreement with you not to carry competitive lines, he's formed an entirely separate company and he has persuaded Glentirran's sales manager to appoint him as their main distributor in the States. Losapio lied to them about his connection with you, I'm sure. Otherwise Glentirran would have backed off fast.

'As you know, Glentirran's former distributors, Amix, ran a very conservative show, refusing to get into any fast expansion plans, but since the proprietor died, management has been looking around for a more go-getting outfit. Losapio has promised them the earth.

'Losapio needs a massive cash injection and he's going to put the touch on you later tonight. He figures that as a woman pushing forty, you might be desperate enough to pay him, to keep him.'

'How on earth do you know all this?' She tried to disguise her hurt.

'He's screwing a compatriot of mine. As a matter of fact, he has asked her to marry him. She works for me and he is under the foolish impression that she is giving him information. Of course, she gives him the information I tell her to.

'Cheer up,' Yoshi added. 'I have a lovely plan for him. Long-term, but highly satisfying. Tonight I want you to tell him that you cannot raise the cash because most of the company shares are in trust for your children, which is the truth. Tell him you have great influence with me and send him to me. Then dump him fast.'

Marjorie began to laugh. Perhaps it was the sake, or the news, or Yoshi's Machiavellian plans, but soon her laughter became almost hysterical.

'He will be waiting for you when you get back, Marjorie. He will ask you for money and he will be very convincing. To help you to be strong, here are some photographs.'

He flung an envelope across the desk. Her faithful lover, who begged her to marry him on every trip, was entwined with a luscious sloe-eyed siren. For the first time she noticed how narrow his shoulders were – and his backside was getting flabby, she noted. So much for Losapio. Briefly she mourned his fawn's eyes, his jet-black hair and perfect Roman profile.

She pushed back the envelope. 'How did you get them?'

'She arranged it.' He got up and pushed the envelope into the shredding machine. 'The past is the past. How about dinner?'

'Not today, Yoshi. Maybe tomorrow. I'll be in touch.'

She walked back slowly, steeling herself to feel nothing, condemning Carlo to the realms of 'what was'. It was strange how his youth had made her forget her looming forties.

By the time the call came through from Mum about the death of poor Aunt Beatrice, Losapio was history.

Chapter 71

——— ———

They walked down the aisle as a tight-knit family group, each of them feeling glad that it was almost over. The service had been tedious, with four eulogies and a long sermon. Now they were moving towards the door where they would shake hands with the mourners. As Marjorie took up her position she could not help remembering her last meeting with Aunt Beatrice.

'You kept all the promises you made to shareholders, Marjorie,' the old woman had recalled. 'You stuck to your ten-year plan and you always paid your interest fees on time. I can only guess at how hard it must have been at times.'

'True,' she had murmured. 'To be honest, Aunt Beatrice, it's only recently that we started to see the light at the end of the long tunnel. It's been . . .' She had broken off to do a quick calculation. 'Eleven years? No, twelve years' hard grind. But it's been worth it.'

'Well done.' The old woman had reached forward to pat her hand. 'Now listen to me, Marjorie. I've made it my business to keep *au fait* with your private affairs. I hope you will forgive me.'

Marjorie had murmured something trite, remembering the first time she had met Beatrice. She had battled to keep her tongue between her teeth and not tell the old lady to mind her own business. This same scene had been repeated often enough, and here she was doing it again, right at the very end. Suddenly, without any doubt at all, she realised that Aunt Beatrice was about to die. Thank goodness she can't read my mind, she had mused, feeling sad.

'Most of your Inver-Asian shares are in a family trust which you created, and Lana has the major share. You, on the other hand, have next to nothing. Why is that?'

'I have never felt that Glenaird belongs to me. Besides, I have two children, Aunt Beatrice: one of them is a millionaire, and I don't want the other one to be a pauper. As for me, I have enough.'

'Yes, I guessed as much.'

Beatrice had smiled, her hard bird eyes softening. Watching her, Marjorie had felt quite touched.

'My dear, I am leaving my shares in Grampian Bank and my home to your son, Alasdair. He is so like his grandfather, a man I admired so much. And besides, I have no children and he is the obvious choice. On my death, you will be appointed chairman of the board until Alasdair reaches twenty-five,' the precise voice went on. 'Even then he won't be fully in control for many years. There are other directors, the most important one being Mark Baxter, our lawyer, and I shall appoint another director – if he agrees, your friend, Joe Segal, in whom I have the greatest faith. He has created a trust fund for Lana, I believe.'

'How did you learn about that?' Marjorie had asked, smiling.

'I have my sources.' The old woman had looked smug.

'You don't have to have these sources,' Marjorie had

argued, putting one hand over Beatrice's gnarled fingers in a rare show of affection. 'You only have to ask.'

'Listen to me, I am tired,' she had told Marjorie, holding up one hand to silence her. 'I, too, am leaving something for Lana in the form of a trust. The rest of my wealth and the bank goes to Alasdair. So you, my dear, will have enormous power, but very little personal wealth. Use the power wisely.'

The old woman's words rang in Marjorie's ears as she watched the coffin being carried outside.

Rhoda MacLaren sniffed derisively as she watched the Cameron family standing in a stiff, straight line by the church door, exchanging a few words with the mourners as they shook hands and filed by. Just look at their long faces! Anyone would think they cared about old Beatrice Cameron, but the truth was, they must have been waiting for her to die for years, and she'd taken her time. That gawky boy, standing well back from the crowd, was a millionaire many times over now, she'd heard. He looked uncomfortable in his dark grey suit, fidgeting with his hands and running a finger round the collar of his shirt.

A tall girl standing beside the boy caught her attention. There was something familiar about her, but she couldn't think why. She puzzled over this. A real go-getter, Rhoda sensed, envying her youth, and the extraordinary intensity of her large brown eyes. Oh, to be young! In her day, being young was a misfortune to be dispensed with as soon as possible, but nowadays youth was everything, she brooded bitterly. Clearly the girl was one of that new breed of youngsters, a citizen of Europe, at home in most capital cities, and her clothes reflected her personality.

Rhoda was quick to spot the dark grey MaxMara skirt, the Escada blouse, and Charles Jourdan court shoes. She was obviously spoiled. What else could you expect from the nouveau riche?

She was moving up towards Mrs Cameron, who was surrounded by officials from the bank. Rhoda had never met the woman, but knew her as an ancient enemy. It was she who had saved Glenaird and turned the tables on poor Andrew Cameron. She'd never set eyes on her, never wanted to. Rhoda had heard Mrs Cameron came from nothing, but there was no denying her business skills.

She strained up on tiptoe, trying to get a good look at her, but the woman was surrounded with people and she was wearing a hat with a thick black veil.

Rhoda sighed with impatience, longing to get out of there. She'd do anything for a cigarette. Tension was stiffening her limbs and making her skin crawl. She felt so overlooked. She had expected something a little better. Admittedly, they had reserved a pew for her, but no one had come to greet her. She might have been invisible for all the attention she drew. She felt slighted and almost insulted.

Someone should have accompanied her down the aisle. She was so tired of always being alone. Damn Robert, she fumed. Once again he was away on one of his silly expeditions, this time to launch a scheme to save the howling monkeys in Belize. It was all an escape. He detested her.

At last she had reached the head of the queue. She stepped forward, smiled sadly and appropriately, and held out her hand.

Mrs Cameron made no move to shake her hand,

but lifted her veil, and Rhoda found herself gazing straight into the well-remembered, emerald-green eyes of Robert's Dover trollop.

Rhoda gasped and rocked on her feet. How was this possible? For a moment she felt dazed and slightly unreal. Her mouth opened, but no sound came. Was she hallucinating? Or perhaps this was someone she'd met at a charity function? But then she noticed that damned unruly red hair curling round the edges of her black hat. She was still beautiful, her skin still white and flawless, but nowadays her make-up was flawless, too. She was poised and groomed and perfectly dressed.

'So we meet again, Lady MacLaren. And again on such a sad occasion,' the apparition from the past was saying. 'It seems to me we're reaching the last round. Now it's just you and me.'

But it couldn't be her – the voice was all wrong. Rhoda murmured something almost inaudible and staggered outside. For a few moments she was blinded by sunlight and suddenly she saw Marjorie Hardy, yes, that was her name, standing in the doorway of her home, and she heard her silly voice saying: 'Your cruelty will bounce back on you. It always does.'

Was that why . . . ? Had she been slowly planning . . . ?

Rhoda missed her footing and felt herself falling. Moments later she sprawled on the ground. She looked up, feeling a sharp pain in her knee, but that was nothing compared with her humiliation. People ran to pick her up.

'It's nothing, I assure you,' she repeated as they oohed over her bloodied knee and torn stocking. Feeling utterly foolish and very old, she was half-supported to her car. She knew she had made a fool of herself and that the dreadful Mrs Cameron had seen. Rhoda had certainly read the message in her green eyes. It was of the utmost hatred.

Sitting in her car as they moved slowly in convoy down the main street of the village, Rhoda reviewed the past. She had wronged the girl, she knew, but she had been acting in the best interests of the family. A woman like that could never have . . . But she had, hadn't she? She had entered their world and won through and now she was a force to be reckoned with. Rhoda felt shaken to the core by the encounter.

Chapter 72

Bart Shaw, Robert's auditor, had taken on more offices over the past twenty years and he had prospered. His company now occupied one entire wing, but his own room was unchanged. It always seemed adequate, except on the rare occasions when Robert came, and then it shrank. Robert seemed to exude waves of energy. Bart, who was balding and losing weight, felt dwarfed by Robert's presence on the other side of his desk, for he was a huge man, looking as if he belonged out of doors. He dominated the space, making everything look fragile and impermanent.

'Ah, Robert,' Bart greeted him. 'I'm glad to see you. Every time you go off to one of these savage places I can't help wondering if you will ever return.'

'If you had got to know the Indians, as I have, you'd find they're a gentle people; kind, too, with a good sense of humour,' Robert chided him.

'The noble savage and all that, eh? I think modern Africa has knocked that theory into a cocked hat.'

Robert smiled enigmatically, unwilling to be pulled into a racial argument. He knew Bart's views.

'Well, Robert, I think congratulations are in order. How about a drink? Growth is up six per cent, profits four per cent, and you have achieved a significant percentage of the top end of the US whisky market. Your new labels are outstanding.'

The labels were spread over Bart's desk and they showed the Glentirran crest in bottle-green on gold, with the words 'seventeen-year-old pure malt' discreetly printed under the crest.

As Robert sat gazing at his latest achievement, he was remembering how much sacrifice had gone into holding back part of their production. It had been so bad for so long. After he took over, they had lived in poverty for five years until the first malt became sufficiently matured to be sold. The staff had been on low salaries and double workload, but he had compensated them with company shares and they were all pleased with their long-term gains.

Only in 1978 had he begun to sell their malt to bring in income. Meanwhile the overdraft had soared. Each year since, they had put aside at least a third of the matured spirit for a few more years. It had cost them, but it had been worth it. Now they had their entire stock coming off yearly in twelve- and seventeen-year-old spirit. Market research showed they were the whisky most in favour in the States and they tied with Glenaird in Britain.

Bart poured out two glasses of the new bottle of Glentirran he had been sent as a gift, and for a while the two of them reminisced.

Eventually Bart brought the conversation back to business. 'There's another matter: Beatrice Cameron died.'

'Yes, I know. I was in Belize or I would have attended the funeral. Did you go?'

'No, but Lady MacLaren did.'

'That's good. So what's the problem?'

'Grampian. It's a privately owned bank and Hamish

Cameron's son, Alasdair, has inherited it, lock, stock and barrel.'

'I'm aware of that,' Robert replied, trying to quell his irritation. 'We've banked with Grampian for five generations. There was some marriage link way back.'

'Alasdair Cameron is only eleven, so his mother has been appointed acting chairman of the bank.'

'That's not relevant. The bank's management is first class and will probably remain unchanged. I have no cause to complain and I don't think you have, Bart.'

Bart sighed. 'Listen, Robert. I wouldn't have brought this up, but your stepmother has been badgering me. She told me a strange story about Mrs Cameron, the chairman, having a personal grudge against you. It's something to do with the failed takeover bid on Glenaird back in 1977.'

There was a long silence as Robert digested this.

'Beatrice Cameron ran that outfit like Genghis Khan,' Bart went on mournfully.

'And she was very good at it,' Robert said, 'but now she's dead, the more's the pity, but she was almost ninety-five, so this was inevitable. I can't see that we have a problem. I don't suppose there is a grudge either. Water under the bridge. The only hiccup I can envisage is the Glenaird connection, but what the hell? Our credit's good, and if they refused to finance us when we needed finance, we'd simply move our business elsewhere.'

'If you say so,' Bart agreed. 'Let's move on.' He refilled Robert's glass.

'Now sit down and listen, Robert. Regarding your missing daughter, the law as it stands regarding the rights of fathers of illegitimate offspring is flawed. Quite simply the law hasn't kept up with technology. It's still based on the old days when only the mother knew who the father of her child was, and she didn't always.' He laughed at his own joke. 'Nowadays we can determine fatherhood without any shadow of a doubt and therefore it's high time natural fathers had some rights over their offspring. It's a difficult, delicate subject all round, but it will come. In the meantime, as the natural father of a child put up for adoption in 1973, you have no rights at all, not even to knowing where your child is.'

'We've been through this enough times,' Robert interrupted.

'Yes, but listen. I have a better idea. I do believe that the convent would bend the rules if they felt that it was in the best interests of the child. Now I've an idea.'

He paused as he took out a folder and leafed through it. He grinned triumphantly at Robert. 'What if I contact the Mother Superior, telling her that we wish to establish a family trust for Marjorie Hardy's firstborn child. We won't claim that it's your child, because that's where we've been failing so far, but there's nothing to stop us from establishing a trust for whomever we like.'

'Good thinking, Batman.'

'I think we can be sure that they would take steps to discover where the child is. And Robert, consider, even if this information were never made available to you, I reckon your daughter will contact you herself when she reaches the right age to come into her inheritance. She probably doesn't know that you are her father, but this will show her. With your permission, I'll set up the trust now, and from then on it's merely a waiting game.'

'Of course.' Robert sighed. 'This is the best idea you've come up with yet, so go ahead.'

'I want you to sign all these relevant papers now, Robert, then I won't have nightmares about anyone contesting your will should you disappear into the unknown on your next trip, never to return. Nothing and no one can touch a trust if it's properly set up.'

Robert spent the next ten minutes signing papers. When he had finished, he had a sinking feeling that he was being foolish. His daughter was lost to him for ever, he told himself, and it was high time he came to terms with reality.

Chapter 73

Who was she? But who was she really? Lana was tormented because she could not get to grips with herself. While her friends were reaching into adulthood, playing with flirting and lust, seeking and finding their sexual power, searching for love, Lana shrank into the darkness of her self-doubts. How could she reach out to another human being when she did not know what she could offer? How could she love another if she could not love herself? And how could she love herself if she did not know who or what she was?

She was like a transplanted tree that remains in shock, fails to put its roots down, and slowly withers.

Why had her natural mother abandoned her? Something inside her prevented her from blaming this unknown woman. She had been dumped because of some hidden defect and it lay deep inside her like the San Andreas fault, waiting to move and destroy her world. It might not show, but it was there. Who knew what faulty genes she carried in her body – perhaps madness, or some incurable disease? She began to feel like a walking time bomb. She took herself to a private doctor and had everything possible tested, but no one could find anything wrong with her.

Was her mother a prostitute? That was her very worst

imagining. When boys ogled her, she imagined that she looked like a whore. If one tried to date her, she felt insulted. Clearly they had scented her wayward genes, true and sure as sniffer dogs. They slobbered around, sensing, longing, pretending to like her, but that was a lie, since there was nothing to like.

Her best friend, a Spanish girl from Barcelona, took her out to lunch one day and spoke long and earnestly to her. 'The boys are saying you must be weird. They say you don't like boys.' She gulped her wine to cover her embarrassment. 'They even asked if you'd made advances to me. I've told them you have to study, you don't have time to have fun, but Lana, can't you bend a little, give a little? Would it be so bad to come dancing with me tonight? There's a really good crowd coming. You'll like them.'

Lana shook her head. 'You see, I have to do well in the exams,' she explained. 'It's important to me. Mother has just been made a Dame by the Queen. Can you imagine? She's Dame Marjorie now. I can't get over it. It's because of her contribution to the British export market. Mother works all the time. She has far too much to do and I have to help her as soon as I can. As a matter of fact, I'm longing to join her world. It's the only way I can bond with her. With a family like mine it's important that I do well. You must see that?'

'But Lana, you always do well, you know you do. There's more to life than work. And why are you so obsessed with your mother? Everyone has one, but quite honestly, they're usually a pain in the butt. You've put yours on a pedestal. I wonder why? You have your own life to live. You're not living, only working.'

Lana shook her head.

'All work and no play makes Lana a dull girl,' her friend ventured.

She meant well, but from then on Lana avoided her. She added 'lesbian' to the nightmare list of possible flaws.

How lucky she was that her mum had adopted her, and given her a family and a brother, a gran, a grandpa and a home. If she worked day and night, all her life, she could not do enough for her. Not nearly enough. But there was anger, too. Why had she been rejected? Why did she have to feel like a spare part in the family, never good enough to be one of them?

She decided to read law, hoping that it was the best background she could have to help Mum in the business, and Alasdair, too, when he inherited the business. There was a university in Buckingham, she learned, where she could gain her law degree in two years, so she went there. It was close to London, so she spent some weekends with Joe, who was a lonely person since his second divorce and always pleased to see her.

When she arrived at Buckingham University in January, the ground was covered with frost and snow, the trees were bare and ugly, and she was always cold.

Inexorably spring came and there was something incredibly painful about it: all those nests, and young birds being fed, and the lambs frolicking around their mothers. It hurt, but she wasn't sure why, except that she felt excluded, so she threw herself into her studies, using anger as a form of energy.

Summer came and she found herself surrounded by the beautiful greens of English fields and meadows, flowering hedgerows, and birds who were lazy and filled with joy. Her anger at her rejection became

larger than she was and brought her skin out in a
rush of spots. She came home for the holidays to
find the moors alive with harebells, purple and rosy
heather, and blazing gorse bushes, so she shrank back
into herself and her books. It was too much, too much
altogether. How could she bear it? She was nature's
reject.

She remembered how happy she had been before she
realised what 'adopted' meant and how Angela's visit had
destroyed her sense of worth. Still later, her security had
been dealt an even tougher blow. She had been jealous
of Mother's new baby, so one morning she had pushed
the pram into the lake, not meaning to harm the baby,
but just to spoil his beautiful clothes. Gramps had raced
in to rescue him and carried him home screaming and
covered in mud.

Gran had been pale and shaking with fright. 'If I were
you, my girl, I'd try to be good and put your jealous
temper aside,' Gran had told her, her eyes wide with
shock. 'Touch Alasdair again and back you go to the
orphanage, quick as you can wink.'

She'd never been naughty again.

Her second and last year at University passed as quickly
as the first. Joe took her to Spain for the Easter break.
She had wanted to swot, but Joe would not let her.
He drove her out into the sun, coaxing her to swim,
cycle, snorkle and paddle-ski. He bought an inflatable
dinghy and on calm days they skimmed along the coast
getting drenched with water, screaming as the ice-cold
spray hit their sun-hot bodies. Her skin became deeply
tanned, her hair sun-streaked, her eyes sparkled and she
laughed a lot.

Uncle Joe was fun to be with, but it was more than that – she sensed that they had a bond. He was real family, not because she'd been brought into the family, but because he liked her for herself.

Chapter 74

Despite his inventions and his music, Joe was a lonely man. He waited impatiently for Lana's next holiday, hoping that she would join him for at least a part of it. He agonised over where they should go, one night even resorting to sticking a pin in an atlas with his eyes closed. It pinpointed the Great Barrier Reef, but his fear of sharks disposed of that idea.

Finally he chose the Seychelles and hired a trimaran, a skipper, and crew. The latter consisted of the skipper's black girlfriend, who also did the cooking, he discovered when he arrived two days before Lana to check out the arrangements. The yacht was berthed in the yacht club basin in Victoria, the main city of the main island, Mahé.

Two days later, Joe was waiting at Victoria's airport to meet the flight from Mauritius which was due at seven p.m. The plane was six hours late. When Lana emerged through customs Joe saw with a jolt that she was in a state of shock. Her eyes were wide and staring, her face white, her lips drawn into a taut line. She looked like an alien amongst the chattering, happy throngs. She flung herself at him, complaining that she found the heat and the waiting around intolerable, and that she was in a state of exhaustion.

'I can see that. God, just look at you! You obviously need this holiday badly,' he told her.

She wound her arms around his neck.

'Uncle Joe, I've failed my exams,' she confided. 'I'm so angry. I can't believe I could let myself down like this.'

Her story poured out. She had suffered from exam nerves because it was her finals. Unable to sleep or eat for days beforehand, she had stumbled in to write the paper like a zombie. 'I didn't understand the questions. I was in shock. I don't remember what I wrote. Probably gibberish,' she told him. She hung on to her composure until they were in the taxi and then she fell into his arms and burst into tears.

Slowly Lana recovered from her misery. The warm winds soothed her, and she spent hours sleeping in the sun, or swimming off the islands with Joe. They snorkelled and explored the islands by day, then moved on to the next one by night. Magical days, Joe thought, watching Lana return to the happy child she once was.

On the second last day, they put into Mahé, paid off the crew and booked into a French-owned hotel overlooking a sheltered cove. Here Joe put through a call to Buckingham while Lana was snorkelling in the bay. She'd achieved an upper second and gained her LLB. Stupid girl! he exulted. Everyone knew she'd done well except Lana herself. He swam out to give her the news.

Lana went wild with joy. She leapt on him, pulling him under the water. They rolled and played like seals and emerged spluttering and laughing.

On their last night Joe took her to a seaside shellfish restaurant where Lana drank too much ice-cold Portuguese wine while extracting the last shreds of flesh from the claws of her lobster.

'Uncle Joe, thank you,' she said simply.

'For what? It's I who should thank you. I've never had such a good holiday.'

'It's not only the holiday I'm talking about, it's you. You really feel for me because you like me.'

He frowned at her, sensing her probing. 'I always have done, ever since you were crawling around in rompers,' he recalled, choosing his words carefully. 'You see, I never had a daughter, Lana. You are a daughter to me.

'Long ago, when your mother and I were working together, there was a vague possibility that you might really be my daughter – I mean legally. I became very fond of you and those feelings have never changed.'

He waved to the waiter and ordered another bottle of wine. Filling her glass, he sat back and studied her. The holidays had done her good. She was a different person from the tense young woman who had stumbled into the airport a month back. But she was still hurting, he sensed, despite her joy at her exam results.

Her eyes looked over-large, a fawn's eyes, and so troubled.

'Lana, please, tell me what's eating away at you. I know there's something very wrong. Don't hurry. We have all night.'

'Is that why you invited me for a holiday? Did Mother talk to you?' She was instantly on the defensive.

'No. I was lonely and I miss you. It's no good my having an adopted daughter if I never see her.'

'If you say that word *adopted* again you'll have this wine flung over you.' She scowled and bit back her tears. Suddenly, it seemed, the evening was ruined.

'Ah. So you've answered my question,' Joe retorted. 'Can you talk about it, or is it too hurtful?'

'I suppose I can. Mother says she knows who my real mother is,' she muttered. 'She won't tell me. At least, not until I'm twenty-one, but I can't wait that long. I feel sort of lost in limbo. I can't go forward.'

Joe sighed. 'This revelation might upset your mother very much,' he said. 'Don't you love her enough to give up this search?'

'No. Of course I love Mum, but this has nothing to do with my feelings for her. It's an inner compulsion. It's out of my control. I have to find my roots so that I can grow. I feel stunted.'

'Are you aware that you will inherit most of the Western-held half of Inver-Asian? It won't be a case of helping Mum and your brother in the business. You will own just as much as Alasdair, your mum took care of that. You come into your shares when you reach twenty-five. Isn't Marjorie a strong enough root for you?'

Lana took a great gulp of wine. She sat in silence for a while considering this shocking news. 'Of course, Mum would do that,' she answered eventually. 'It's just like her. She's so kind, but can't you see – this just increases my sense of guilt.'

'Why should you feel guilty?'

'Because I'm the cuckoo in the nest. I shouldn't be there at all. You must see that, Uncle Joe.'

'Oh God!' Joe turned white.

Lana had noticed Joe's discomfort creeping up, but now he looked as if he were in shock. His dark face seemed pallid, his wise old eyes, so large and handsome, were flinching as if she had struck him. She hadn't wanted to hurt him because she loved him so much.

Sometimes she wished he weren't her uncle, so she

could marry him, she loved him so. How old was he? She quickly calculated. Seven years older than Mum, she'd heard. That made him forty-six. Well, he looked his age, but at the same time he was the type that always looked young – a young spirit trapped in an older body. She studied him carefully. He'd lost ten pounds at least on the holiday and he was lean and lithe and very strong. His hair was shoulder-length, his face long and pointed, his nose sharp and straight, his eyes huge and glowing. Wherever they went people stared at him. Everyone thought he was someone important, which of course he was.

She always felt safe with Joe, yet now, watching him cautiously, she began to feel distinctly uneasy. Why? What was he afraid of? There was something about the adoption that frightened him. What terrible knowledge were they conspiring to keep from her?

'Lana, you must finish your law practice year and then ask your mother to tell you who you are. Be very straightforward with her. Talk to her like you've talked to me,' Joe told her.

'And if she fobs me off, like she always does?'

There was a long, uneasy silence.

'You must help me, Uncle Joe,' she murmured. She stared long and hard, imploring him to understand her pain.

'Well, I think you have a right to know,' he admitted eventually, but she could see that he felt bad about his decision. 'I can see how important it is to you. You simply check the birth certificate at the central register, get someone else to do it for you, but you must give your mother a chance to tell you first. Why not wait until you are twenty-one? Please, Lana.'

She considered his suggestion in silence.

'Now listen,' he went on, 'when you reach twenty-one next year, you'll come into a trust fund which I've set up for you. It will provide you with a small income for life, no matter what you decide to do. This might make you feel freer. Maybe you won't want to go into the family business.'

'Oh, but I will. Of course I will.' She gave a loud hiccup and giggled. 'I'm not drunk, promise. I can't wait to help Mother. After all she's done for me, it's the least I can do.'

'What with my trust and your mother's Inver-Asian trust, you'll be a very rich woman. Isn't that enough? Do you really have to find your roots too?'

'Uncle Joe, listen to me.' She reached out and held his hand. 'If I had to give everything I'll ever own to find my parents, I would do that.'

'Then it's just as well everything's tied up in a trust, isn't it?' Uncle Joe teased, smiling sadly. 'Come on, young lady. You're tipsy and I'm taking you back to bed.'

Walking silently along the beach to their hotel, Lana felt that she had spoiled the evening. Joe seemed to be torn in two with his divided loyalties to her and to her mother. Whatever it is, it must be very bad, she decided.

Chapter 75

———— ————

Her son's love affair with the distillery had begun when he was eleven, Marjorie remembered. Since then Alasdair's passion to learn the art of making good whisky had caused him to spend most of his holidays working at Glenaird. Jim Rutherford, their famous blender, was slowly teaching Alasdair his skills.

Marjorie understood a little of her son's fascination. After Hamish's death she had moved the marketing office from London to the distillery itself, so that she could spend more time with the children, and over the years she had learned to love the smell of the smoke from the peat fuel as it drifted gently upwards through the wire mesh floor to dry out the barley. Even now, she mused, as she walked towards the malting house, even at this very early process, the smell was subtly reminiscent of the matured Glenaird whisky. It was something to do with their own particular natural peat and pure, soft spring water.

She found Alasdair sweating as he shovelled peat fuel into the furnace. Although it was early November he was wearing only a T-shirt and shorts and his gumboots. How fit he looked. The muscles of his shoulders were rippling and Marjorie could not help thinking complacently that he was a handsome boy, with his wide-open, amber-brown eyes that so often seemed to be glowing with affection, but could sometimes be so cool and distant. His soft brown hair, damp with sweat, was falling forward over his forehead. His cheeks glowed and his skin was still fresh and clear. His soft voice was Hamish's entirely, but his temper was hers. Sometimes he looked like a lamb, with his quietness and his reserve, but let him see cruelty or injustice and he changed into an avenging Viking. Today he was relaxed, enjoying his work, and above him the smoke drifted gently through the mesh floor where the germinating barley lay drying out.

'Aren't you cold?' she called.

Alasdair looked up and pulled a face. 'While stocking a furnace? Is that a serious question?'

'He's got a rare talent, this boy of yours,' Jim called out to her. 'He's going to make the world's best whisky, I'm telling you now.'

She waved happily at Alasdair and Jim as she hurried past the huge, swan-necked copper stills and on to the first warehouse where five thousand casks of malt spirit were silently maturing in their oak casks. However mechanised the equipment became, the final quality was heavily dependent upon men's skills. Jim, in particular, had to judge the precise moment at which to separate the 'middle cut', the precious best quality alcohol which would be used to make whisky. She could not help worrying, because Jim was well past retirement age.

She continued towards the office block, passing several of their new, heavily secured warehouses. Here lay their most significant capital investment: right now there was over three million pound's worth of Scotch maturing in their many warehouses while the soft Scottish air mellowed the spirit. Three years was the legal minimum period, but at Glenaird they had reached a state where most of their stock matured for thirteen years.

As Marjorie walked her breath was condensing, her fingers were tingling – and her feet had been numb for the past hour. She decided to buy some better fur-lined boots as soon as she had the time.

She spent the next hour with the auditor. All his news was good. They were almost through when her secretary announced that Yoshi was calling from the States. She looked at her watch. Ten a.m.! It must be important for Yoshi to call at this hour.

Yoshi came straight to the point as usual. 'Marjorie, some time back I made a decision to prop up our mutual friend, a certain Carlo Losapio, whom you may remember.'

She could hear the laughter in his voice.

'Unfortunately, it was a flawed decision on my part. He has not returned the trust I placed in him, and I have had to pressurise him for a very considerable amount of cash. Are you following me?'

'Of course.'

'When I learned that he was heavily into South American wines, which have not done well in the States, I had to pull the rug. Silly man,' he enthused. 'He should never have listened to his girlfriend. Now he's bankrupt.'

She tried not to remember Carlo in bed, closing her mind to regret.

'The point is,' Yoshi was saying, 'the timing of this disaster was most unfortunate for our competitors, Glentirran whisky. You see, Carlo had recently received their New Year's stocks, a very considerable quantity in bottles and barrels, all of which have been seized by the liquidators.'

Suddenly her mouth dried. A sword thrust pierced her midriff. All these years, she pondered. So long a wait, but this was it. She had always known it would happen, but the hows and whens had been unclear. Now the time was ripe: she had the power and fate had delivered her enemy into her grasp.

'You must understand, Marjorie, that Glentirran now find themselves in a difficult position. Losapio owed them over six million dollars. Furthermore, sixty-five per cent of their year's production was shipped to the States. They will need a great deal of cash to establish themselves with new distributors, and of course to offset this terrible financial loss. Speaking as a banker, I would say they represent a bad risk. I must advise you to curtail their overdraft at once. You might offer a plan to bail them out. I suggest something along the lines of the deal they offered Glenaird in 1977.'

Marjorie found she had difficulty breathing. There was a tight band around her chest and a lump in her throat was making it hard to talk.

'Are you listening, Marjorie?'

'Of course.'

'Strike now while they are incapacitated by cash flow problems. Even if you can't achieve a takeover bid, keep them cash-strapped while I move in and win their markets. If need be, can you ship out four times the normal quantity?'

'Not entirely in thirteen-year-old malt, but in blends and eight-year-old, yes,' she suggested thoughtfully.

'Yoshi, well done.'

Her hands were still tingling and shaking five minutes

later when she picked up the receiver and called the bank's manager, James Littlewood.

'James, it's Marjorie here. I've just had the most disquietening news. One of our major clients is in financial difficulties. Actually, it's Glentirran and they're in very deep trouble.'

'I don't think it could be that bad, Mrs Cameron,' Littlewood demurred in his best Sunday school manner. 'They run a tight outfit, very stable. It's their distributor that is in trouble.'

'Believe me, it's worse than that. They will be requesting considerable funds, but we can't take that kind of risk. As it is, we have to cut back their standing facility. Please review the account, itemise their security in detail, and let me know the exact extent of their borrowings. Oh, yes, and make sure the overdraft goes no higher than it is now. Expect me at three this afternoon.'

It was a while before she managed to pull herself together. Strange, she reflected, holding her hand out and watching how it shook. Good news is as bad a shock to the system as a disaster. Her triumph was a physical force that raced through her blood like a tab of Ecstasy, heightening colours and sounds, making her tingle and shiver. She felt as if she and the world had been tossed into a giant blender, to make one whole and totally fabulous mixture.

———— ━━━ ————

Chapter 76

Just one fatal error had brought him to the very lip of disaster. Robert's face showed no trace of his grief as he gazed at the papers spread before him, but across the desk, Bart's haggard expression reflected his own feelings. He was all but ruined.

For twenty years they had built a skyscraper upon one hairline crack in their foundations. The truth was, at the time he had been wet behind the ears, just out of Dover College, in love and in a hurry to get back to Dover. So he had hocked all that he and his family owned to the bank, as one job lot of security, so to speak. In return they had given him all the cash he needed for expansion over the next twenty years.

Why had he pledged his entire wealth and possessions in one bundle? That was his error. He could not unbundle it, at least not fast enough. He needed much more cash now, but Grampian Bank would not give it to him. He could not go, cap in hand, to another bank. He had nothing to offer for security because Grampian had the lot. But who would have guessed how things would change and that their own bank, like a guardian angel all these years, would turn into the enemy?

'All this . . .' Robert gestured towards the lists of his very considerable assets scattered over Bart's desk, 'must be worth more than what we owe. I'm not insolvent. You and I both know that.'

'True,' Bart said mournfully. 'But they won't release the pledge of your total assets unless we significantly reduce the overdraft. They have the right to do this and they know you don't have this amount of cash because you have recently increased warehousing facilities, pending the expected increase in American sales.

'They also know that the assets pledged are worth far more than the book value of them, or as they have valued them.

'They point out quite rightly that they aren't in the business of selling breeding stock, second-hand planes and cars, warehouses or whisky in barrels. Of course, they could never touch that part of your assets that belongs to the trust and neither can you. That is just another drawback for you. They know all this. They've chosen their time very well indeed, Robert. They want Glentirran.

'Quite honestly, I can't see a way out of this, except through a lengthy court case to get back your pledges, which would take us far too long. Time is what you don't have right now. You don't have the ready cash to meet overheads for more than three months, because they've clamped down on your facility. Clearly they are using the bank to benefit their distillery and wipe out their principal opposition. It's quite simple. Apart from the distillery, they also want your US market share.

'You have two choices,' Bart explained uncomfortably. 'On the one hand, you can sell the whisky in the barrels to one of the Lowlands blenders. This will keep you going for a while. You can even slowly expand again over the next few years, but make no mistake, this will put you back twenty years or more, back to where your father put the business. Let's face it, both financially and from the stock position, it would take you years to get into a strong enough position to make a new assault on the American market. By then Glenaird would be so strongly entrenched you'd have to fight for every one per cent gain.

'The second, and better, deal is to merge. They know that, of course. They will have the majority vote, so basically you'll be out, but it protects shareholders to a certain extent. Glenaird have always paid good yields. Some might say that the merge makes sound economic sense.'

'I need time,' Robert said. 'You must buy this time for me. Go and see them. It's better that I don't go there. Point out that if I put the business into voluntary liquidation, they'll get nothing. Lie to them. Tell them they must cover us for two months – wages, rent, basic overheads – while we put the deal they're offering to shareholders to vote on.

'Meanwhile, maybe we'll hit on a way out,' he concluded sadly.

He did not intend to tell Bart yet that Glentirran belonged to his daughter and by God she would have it, when he found her. She was his only heir.

'By the way,' Bart said, as if reading his thoughts. 'This might not be a good time to broach the subject, but the Mother Superior of the convent in Wales has agreed to pass on to your natural daughter news of the trust we're setting up.'

'That's exactly why we must resist defeat,' Robert said slowly. 'I have someone to fight for. You must see that, Bart.'

*   *   *

Marjorie stared out of the window of her office at Glenaird Distillers and gazed at the snowflakes swirling past. She knew that her visitor had been waiting to see her for almost thirty minutes, but she was in no hurry to let her in. She was waiting for her daughter to leave. The meeting would be private, but later she would share this exquisite triumph with Lana.

She leaned back, closed her eyes and experienced a sudden vivid recall of a similar scene twenty-one years ago, on just as bitter a day. She had been cold and lost and she had gone to Robert's home to beg for kindness for her unborn child. She had been dismissed without kindness, and now this same woman was waiting to see her, and she, too, would beg, but in vain. Fate had completed its full circle.

That unborn child was now her closest companion. Lana was working as her assistant for a few months before returning to University for post-graduate studies. She was a quick learner. Already she knew more about Glenaird's marketing strategy than anyone else in the organisation.

Marjorie looked up and frowned. Lana was taking an extraordinarily long time to leave her office. She noticed for the first time how pale and tired her daughter looked.

Perhaps I push her too hard, she considered, but she's getting the best training any young woman could have. She's tough, she can take it. She felt proud as she watched Lana gather her things together. She was all that Marjorie would have loved to have been at her age: self-assured, poised and cultured. One look at her said 'top drawer'. Besides all this, she had an amazing flair for business.

'Wait a minute, darling,' she called. 'Come over here and see these business reports. I must be honest, I leaked the story to the press. You'll find out that the media can be a very valuable business tool if properly used. Never neglect to make friends out of journalists and editors.'

'*Glenaird's bid to salvage Glentirran could save shareholders' investments*,' was the headline. 'Go on, read it, Lana.'

Lana read on, conscious of Marjorie leaning over her. She could sense her mother's tension and her joy. She had never seen her quite so excited.

'Very good,' she said, stepping back to study her mother closely. 'What exactly is the reason for your extreme joy, Mum?' she asked. 'What's going on?'

Mother was smiling triumphantly. 'It's far more than business, darling,' she gloated. 'It comes under the category of revenge. I shall tell you everything very soon. Promise!

'This long fight has much more to do with you than you realise. I can't tell you more now, but soon I'll tell you everything.' She stepped forward and hugged her tightly. Lana could not remember her ever doing that in the office. She kept emotions for home. Curiosity was killing her.

'I've ordered two coffees for you, Mother, but why can't I be present?'

'Be patient, Lana. You'll understand soon. This is the finale, and it's been a long time coming.'

Mother began to pace the office from the window to her desk and back again. Stranger and stranger! On impulse, Lana went back to her desk, half-opened her top drawer and switched on her tape recorder. Moments later she was hurrying to the canteen for a late breakfast.

Chapter 77

As Rhoda MacLaren was led towards Glenaird's executive suite by a young Scottish clerk, she glanced myopically around her, fired with curiosity. She was passing through a maze of offices, but at last they approached a double door which the clerk pushed open. Rhoda hovered in the doorway and sniffed haughtily. The office was so spacious it seemed ostentatious. Did Mrs Cameron think she was the queen? But wasn't she a dame nowadays? Yes, that's right, Rhoda remembered. No doubt this accounted for her delusions of grandeur.

The entire west wall was a huge double-glazed window overlooking the park; the floor was of embossed beige marble tiles and she could feel the gentle warmth rising from the floor. One good blue Chinese carpet lay in front of the window. The furniture was stark and modern and of light wood, the desk large and completely uncluttered. Mrs Cameron was standing in front of a very costly Turner painting. She looked as expensive. Now she was clearly recognisable. Yes, it was her! Robert's whore! There was no mistake this time.

She was much thinner than Rhoda remembered, and beautifully dressed in an emerald green blouse and a black suit, with small emerald earrings and a matching bracelet. She was poised, well-groomed and looked years younger than her real age. She must be at least forty, Rhoda calculated.

'How pleasant to see you again, Lady MacLaren,' Mrs Cameron said, in the manner of old friends. 'Would you like some coffee?'

She picked up the silver coffee pot and poured into the delicate bone china cups. 'Winter is so cold this year. I thank heavens I had the good sense to put in underfloor heating. If you're too warm, please say so and I'll take your jacket.'

She smiled, looking as cool and self-possessed as if they had nothing better to do than pass the time of day.

'You must stop this absurd personal vendetta, my dear,' Rhoda began as she had planned. 'At least take the trouble to discover who your real enemy is. Not Robert, Mrs Cameron, I assure you. Me! I am your enemy. I never liked you, I'll be honest about it. A marriage between you and Robert would have been disastrous, but he is blameless.'

'Whatever are you talking about, Lady MacLaren? Vendetta? Enemies?'

'You know perfectly well what I'm talking about. You have brought Glentirran to the brink of ruin, or so you think. You are wrong to use the bank's resources for your personal vendetta. This will bounce back on you. Folk around here have long memories. If you try to ruin us, other Scottish investors will move their assets away. Do you want to ruin your son's heritage?'

'Lady MacLaren,' the bitch responded, with a sugar-sweet smile, 'your company has suffered a most unfortunate loss. In our opinion your distillery no longer provides a good risk to offset your excessive borrowings.'

'Do you really think I am taken in by you? Listen to me, Mrs Cameron, the MacLarens have dealt with Grampian Bank for six generations. How could someone like you possibly understand how these matters are conducted? It's a question of honour. After six generations of goodwill, you don't pull the rug from under one of your best and oldest clients simply because they have suffered a temporary misfortune. Have you any idea what people are saying about you, behind your back? That you are using poor Beatrice Cameron's assets for your own unscrupulous ends.'

'Lady MacLaren, let me put my cards on the table,' Marjorie said. 'All these years I've fought for my daughter's birthright. It's in my grasp. It's a matter of days, or weeks at the outside. I am going to tell her who her father is when I give her back her rightful inheritance – Glentirran. That has always been my plan.'

Rhoda flinched with shock. Suddenly she remembered the young dark girl at the funeral. Of course she had reminded her of someone – Robert! Clearly she was his daughter. So Mrs Cameron had never put the child up for adoption. She had lied.

Rhoda could feel her temper rising and she regretted this. She had to be in control, but the joy of telling this arrogant woman exactly who and what she had been was a temptation she was not sure she could resist.

'Why did you come, Lady MacLaren?' the bitch was saying. 'To let off steam? Was this confession time? Or was there something specific that you wanted to ask me?'

Rhoda made one more monumental effort to control

her spite. 'Why punish Robert because of what I did?' There, now she had said it.

'I'm not punishing Sir Robert. Grampian Bank has foreclosed because Glentirran do not offer a reasonable business risk, in their opinion. You have suffered a bad loss through your US distributors. However, Glenaird are offering to bail you out. Accept our terms or the bank will put you into liquidation. As from this moment your personal account is closed, Lady MacLaren. Good day to you.'

Rhoda stood up, open-mouthed with indignation.

'Beatrice Cameron would turn in her grave,' she spluttered. 'You act as if the bank were your own, but you got where you are on your back. You failed with Robert, but that didn't daunt you, did it?' Her voice was rising as her temper soared. 'If you ruin me socially, you'll never get Glentirran for your daughter, I promise you that. Not even a part of it. I'll put it into liquidation first, and I do have that power because I, too, am a creditor. If you don't cover me for the season, I'll see the business is destroyed. No one will benefit and least of all your daughter.'

Rhoda tried to pull herself together. She watched the younger woman for signs of weakening. She could not help remembering how vulnerable she had been twenty-one years ago: eyes brimming with tears, cheeks white with shock, lips trembling with indignation. How she longed to make those gloating cat's eyes flinch. Yet the woman had turned pale and Rhoda sensed that her bluff was working.

Or was it bluff? Rhoda had no idea how far her spite would take her if her social year was ruined by this common upstart. She had so many events planned, but the highlight of the season was her invitation to multi-millionaire William Palmer-Oppenheimer, owner of the South American Palmer hotel chain, and his heiress daughter, Maria, who would stay at Tirran Lodge for ten days. A party had been planned to welcome their arrival and she intended it to be the society highlight of the year. The ballroom would be packed to overflowing with guests whose names read like the *Who's Who* of the international set. Four members of the Royal family had already agreed to come. Rhoda was hoping to encourage a romance between Robert and Maria – he had stayed with the family in Rio de Janeiro many times, and Rhoda knew she had a willing ally in Maria.

Rhoda watched the hateful Cameron woman toy with her pen as she weakened. 'I suggest you let the bank have a list of your other assets. Then perhaps they could extend your facility to cover your social commitments for a few months.'

Triumph flared. She had found her enemy's weakness – her daughter.

'Let me show you out,' the slut said. Rhoda felt a firm grip on her elbow, guiding her to the door. She hovered in the doorway. 'You have become a cruel and greedy woman, Mrs Cameron, but we are far from beaten yet.' She tried to stop her voice from quivering.

'They were my words twenty-one years ago when I begged you for mercy. Do you remember, Lady MacLaren?'

The slut smiled cruelly and closed the door in Rhoda's face.

Mother had given her half an hour off to have a break. Lana could not remember her doing so before, and this, in itself, was suspect. Just what was Mother up to this time? She sighed and gave her hair a last comb through.

Hurrying to the office, she saw an old woman poised in the doorway, Mother holding her elbow. Heavens! She was almost pushing her out. Lana paused and held her breath. Even from a distance she could sense the antagonism between the two women. She had seen the visitor before, but where? Then she remembered: she was Lady MacLaren and she had fallen down the steps at Aunt Beatrice's funeral. Suddenly, Lana could not wait to play back the tape.

_____ _____

Chapter 78

Marjorie returned from the cloakroom to find Lana crouched over her desk. She jumped up with a clatter and backed against the wall.

'Goodness, Lana, I thought you were having breakfast. You look so pale. What is it? What's the matter?'

'Nothing.'

The girl seemed to crumple, her shoulders sagging and her head hanging forward. Then she turned and rushed out. Marjorie heard her footsteps clattering down the corridor.

Work wasn't the place for family drama, Marjorie reminded herself. Whatever the problem, it would have to wait until they were home tonight. But she couldn't help feeling alarmed. Some sixth sense told her that Lana had been getting back on that old worryhorse of hers again: her roots.

'Hold on, my darling,' she muttered. 'We're within weeks of winning, and then I'll tell you everything you want to know. You'll be so happy, so soon. We'll have such a celebration. It's taken twenty years to be able to give you back what's rightfully yours, and it will be worth every week of it.'

As Lana raced out of the office building she felt confused.

One moment she was walking on air because Mother was real – a real, natural mother. It stood to reason that her mother would never abandon her. She felt thrilled to know who her real mother was at last. This was the happiest day of her life. So why did she feel so sad?

Unbelievably she burst into tears right in the middle of the courtyard. Fumbling for a tissue and her sunglasses, she hurried on, not really caring where she was going.

No one had abandoned her after all, least of all her mother, who was a wonderful person and incapable of doing such a wicked thing. She could not think straight, at all. Was she in shock, she wondered? The strangest memories kept exploding into her mind as if they were happening in the here and now. In all of them she saw herself bending over backwards to help everyone. She had reared Alasdair like surrogate mother. Why? Because he was Mother's *real* child.

But so was she! Something seemed to lift from her mind and the sensation was so moving, it might have been a physical burden that slid silently from her shoulders to the ground. And as the burden fell away, anger rushed in to replace it. How dared they deny her that vital sense of belonging! Mother should have told her the truth. A surge of bitterness brought bile to her mouth. Never before, in thought or words, had she criticised her mother. Now she felt overwhelmed by her anger.

She slipped and realised that she was wandering along the riverbank. Unaware of the cold, she sat on a grassy mound trying to sort out her muddled emotions. Clearly Mother was flawed. She wasn't a guardian angel after all. Suddenly Lana felt a terrible sense of loss. Sobbing, she smothered her face with her hands.

Eventually she heard an old lady calling to her from

the road. 'Can I help you?' her voice wavered. 'You'll catch your death, lass, sitting there in winter without a coat and all. Look, it's starting to rain. Come back up here.'

'No. Leave me alone,' she muttered, wondering how long she had sat there. The woman hovered for a while, then eventually left.

Dispensing with tears, Lana got up and walked on. She had to keep moving. She felt betrayed by someone she had loved and trusted, and sick with humiliation at the memory of all that gratitude she had lavished on this hard-hearted, crooked family. It was Mother who was most to blame. The more she thought about her monumental con, the more she despised her. All because she was ashamed of having a love child! Everyone else could suffer, as long as Mother looked good. She strode on through the rain, losing all sense of time and place.

The old woman called the police, Lana learned later, who found her and took her home, but by then she had a raging fever. She lay in bed for three weeks, unable to breathe properly, half-heartedly fighting pneumonia, while her temperature shot up and up, but her rage blazed even higher. With it came a need to hit back. Ignoring the family's best efforts to cheer her, she plotted her revenge, confiding only in Alasdair.

Once she had a plan she could not wait to get better.

Lana was like a young, half-broken colt with the bit between its teeth, frantic and in full flight. It was her third day out of the house and in the past two days she had accomplished so much she could hardly believe it. She had just spent the morning in the editorial offices of the local newspaper. There she had struck the first blow against bloody Mother who had repudiated her. She had declared war publicly; there was no turning back now.

Driving the car seemed to give vent to her fury. She skidded round the corner and for a moment that seemed to last for ever she lost control. The car veered off the road and smashed its way over holes and clumps of grass, narrowly missing the ditch, as Lana wrestled with the steering wheel. At last she swung back onto the tarmac and took a deep breath.

'That was close,' she muttered breathlessly. She wanted to slow down, but she could not. The car and she were one and she was running wild.

Twenty minutes later she reached Inveraird and swung into the driveway. Alasdair was swimming in the lake.

It was typical of him to swim in this freezing weather, she thought. She waved him to the bank and scowled as he climbed out of the water. He had a rare vitality that seemed to surround him like an aura. She always felt more alive with Alasdair. He was almost a man, she realised, watching him surreptitiously. His legs were long and lithe, his shoulders sinewy. He was going to become a very good-looking boy, she sensed, but so pig-headed. Would he help her? God knew how many times she'd been out on a limb for him.

'Alasdair, you *must* help me,' she said, with heavy emphasis. 'We've always stood together and now I need you. Mother's trying to ruin my father by withdrawing his overdraft facility, just when he's hard hit. I can't let her win. Not this time, Alasdair. Only you can help me. I've never before asked you for anything, but now I'm begging you.'

The hint of desperation in her voice took Alasdair by surprise. Her wide open brown eyes were sending a complex message which he struggled to interpret: there was a sense of excitement, as well as her blazing appeal. He grabbed his towel, flung it over his shoulders and tried to control his shivering.

'Mother's using the bank's power to play out her private vendetta,' she rushed on. 'All my life she's made me feel like a cuckoo in the nest and now she wants to grab my inheritance and hand it back to me – as her gift to me. But it's mine and my father's. Not hers.'

Alasdair tried with all the sensibility of his fourteen years to delve back to the roots of the problem. 'But as it turned out, this cuckoo in the nest thing was only a feeling on your part. It wasn't true. You were never adopted, so what's the big deal? I don't see why you should feel like that now. You've got as much coming to you as I have. We share the same mother, different fathers. How is it different for me than for you?'

'Well, if you can't see the difference there's something wrong with you,' she replied sulkily.

Alasdair sat down on a rock with his back to a bush, trying to shelter from the wind. His teeth were chattering and he was becoming numb with cold, but Lana did not notice, she was too obsessed with her own problems.

'All right, so I know now,' she retorted, 'but knowing and feeling is not the same at all. You could never possibly understand what it's like to be adopted, to feel such an outsider, to know that your home and family just happened by chance. Knowing that it wasn't like that after all, doesn't change how I feel inside.

'Now, at last, I've found roots. Real roots! Oh, Alasdair, I want them so badly. I shall force my father to accept me as his heir, I don't care how much it costs in legal fees.'

She crouched beside him and wrapped her arms around his waist. 'Please try and understand how I feel, Alasdair. All my life Mother prevented me from having any sense of belonging.'

'That was wrong of her,' Alasdair said, feeling traitorous, but knowing he spoke the truth. 'But Lana, don't keep saying the same thing in different words.'

'Well, then, say you'll help me. And listen to me. This is what we must do.' She explained in detail.

I'm not going to do that, Alasdair thought, when he'd heard her out. It would be madness to take sides, and disloyal, too. After all, I love them both equally. Besides, how could we go to the bank and try to pre-empt Mother's decision? She's the chairman and she's pretty smart. She'd laugh at us. All the same, Lana has never let me down.

'Okay. I'll do it on one condition: Uncle Joe must be told.'

'All right,' she agreed. 'Please hurry. I'll get Jenkins to drive us and he can bring you back. You can drop me at the airport, I'm going on to Edinburgh. I intend to confront my father with my demands. Tonight's the night of his big social do – perfect timing for the press report. You can't believe how busy I've been. Come on, Alasdair. Hurry up and get ready. I'm going to grab a few things.'

'What am I supposed to tell Mother when she gets back?'

'Tell her . . . ? Oh, tell her whatever you like.'

'Lana, you don't even know this man,' Alasdair argued, trying to make her see sense. 'Mum brought you up. She's done everything she can for us. Don't do anything you'll regret . . .'

But Lana wasn't listening. She was already racing back to the house.

'Women,' he muttered.

Chapter 79

The two calls came almost simultaneously around three p.m. and as luck would have it, Joe was practising the flute, a new craze of his. He turned off the CD player reluctantly and picked up his cell phone. The first call was from James Littlewood, bank manager at Grampian. Joe could hear from his voice that they had an emergency.

'I'm very concerned, Joe.' Littlewood came straight to the point. 'I'd like you to get up here right away. We have a problem which is so delicate it could do the bank and the distillery incredible damage, and wreck the family. I can't tell you how disturbed I am, particularly since I had always considered the Camerons to be a really united family.'

'What's the problem?' Joe asked.

'You probably know that Glentirran's overdraft has been curtailed on Mrs Cameron's orders, mainly because the company is in financial difficulties, or so it seems. Now since young Alasdair's a minor, his opinion counts for less than nothing, even though he owns the bank. He's been here with Lana, his sister, and they've jointly accused their mother of using the bank as a lever in a personal vendetta against Glentirran.'

Joe frowned and tried to ignore a sinking feeling in his stomach.

'I can't believe that the children would take such a hard-headed attitude against Mrs Cameron,' Littlewood went on, his words pouring out in a hurry. 'They want to call the directors together for an emergency board meeting to discuss the bank's decision to curtail credit facilities to Glentirran. Even worse, Lana claims that Sir Robert is her father. Did you know that? It's the first I've heard of all this.'

Joe sighed. 'Naturally it's confidential,' he said.

'Not any more. Lana's fighting to save her inheritance, or so she says, and the methods she's using are hardly commendable. She's been to the press with her story and her accusations.'

'Oh my God!' She'd learned how to fight dirty from her mother, Joe mused, but he kept his ideas to himself.

'The point is, this scandal will hammer the bank and Glenaird. To say nothing of Glentirran. I'm asking you to get up here right away wearing two hats – bank director and family friend.

'By the way,' Littlewood went on, 'I tried to contact the newspaper and stop the report, but they were particularly offensive. It'll be all over Scotland by tomorrow morning, and I do mean the whole bit. Lana's told it to them like a soap opera, highlighting her search for her roots against her mother's wishes, and finally zooming in to the whisky vendetta. She's opened a real can of worms, I'm telling you. God knows what we're going to do.'

'I'll see you at nine-thirty tomorrow morning,' Joe said.

It was only a moment later when the phone rang again. It was Lana.

'Littlewood's already been on to me, Lana,' Joe said,

trying to hide some of his anger. 'You can't expect help from me if you damage your mother. You're way out of line. Family squabbles should be kept private. It was unforgivable of you to go to the press. After this there's no hope of a reconciliation. Your mother will never forgive you. I'll see you at the bank at nine-thirty tomorrow morning. I'm not prepared to see you privately. I can't tell you how hurt and disappointed I am.'

Lana slammed down the receiver, but not before he heard a loud sob.

He sighed and riffled through his cupboard for some casual gear. How was he to cope with a family rebellion, particularly when Marjorie was so obviously to blame? Should he call her? No, he'd rather fly up there and have it out with her face to face. He was extremely fond of all of them, although Lana was his special ward. He'd have to do what he could.

First things first!

He called the newspaper's editor and threatened him with litigation if Lana Hardy's story was published. The call took twenty minutes, and by the end of it the editor had promised to fax the story to Sir Robert and Marjorie for their comments. That, at least, bought some time.

Joe felt like a man who, having warned the population of a threatened avalanche for years, was called in to help the injured after his many warnings had gone unheeded.

All afternoon, Marjorie had been trying to cope with a sense of rejection. Lana had driven home to see Alasdair, leaving without saying either hello or goodbye. Since then, she had disappeared.

Efforts to discover her whereabouts through Alasdair

had proved futile. He had belatedly remembered a date with friends and left in a hurry with Jenkins, Mum told her. Later he had called to tell Liz he was staying the night with his friend's family.

Why had he called Liz and not her? Why were both her children avoiding her? And why had Lana been so secretive and hostile while recuperating in bed? Come to that, why had she been sitting in the rain on the riverbank in the first place? In the past month she had tried repeatedly to get through to Lana, but with no success.

Marjorie could not throw off a strange sense of foreboding. Lana had been so openly antagonistic lately. Marjorie missed her daughter badly, but what could she do? Perhaps it was just part of the painful process of growing up.

At six p.m. she decided to counter her depression by spoiling herself. She filled the bath with perfumed bubbles and steaming hot water, placed a Scotch and ice beside her and tried to relax as she soaked luxuriously and read a novel. The night was bitterly cold, but she replenished the bath with gushes of steaming water. Despite this, she could not relax enough to concentrate on the story.

Eventually she put her book aside and lay analysing the possible reasons for her rejection, without success. By the time she got out of the bath, she was cold, and even more fearful. Wrapping herself in her warm velvet dressing gown she went downstairs to make some tea.

Passing the library she heard the fax working. She switched on the light in her office and bent over the desk. The letterhead was from the local newspaper. Strange! Switching on the desk lamp, she bent over the machine.

Madam, we are intending to publish this article in tomorrow's evening edition. The information came in the form of a personal interview with your daughter, Lana Hardy. If there are any comments you would like to make, would you kindly fax them through to us at the above number, to arrive not later than midnight, for possible inclusion.

Marjorie could hardly turn the paper, she was so distraught. Heart pounding with dread, she read on.

Dame Marjorie Cameron, chairman of Glenaird Distillers and Grampian Bank, won the latest round in the fight between her son Alasdair's distillery and their competitors, Glentirran Distillers, by knocking her opponent for six with a clampdown on credit and overdraft facilities.

The blow was struck at the precise moment when Glentirran were laid low following the collapse of their US distributors, Losapio Holdings Inc.

Five million dollars' worth of Glentirran 12-year-old malt was seized from the customs by the company's New York liquidators. It will be auctioned for the benefit of creditors. The final dividend could be as little as five cents to the dollar.

This latest fiasco could bring the fourteen-year-old whisky war between two close competitors to a rapid conclusion. Glentirran, currently the leading brand in the US, are unlikely to recover from the loss of both their whisky and their distributor, particularly since Grampian Bank have seen fit to withdraw their borrowing facility.

No doubt, Glenaird's export arm, Inver-Asian,

with its network of sales offices in the States and Japan, will move fast to capture Glentirran's traditional markets.

It is rumoured that only a miracle can save Glentirran now. But Lana Cameron, 20, who claims to be the love child of Dame Marjorie Cameron and Sir Robert MacLaren, chairman of Glentirran, is searching for that miracle in a last-ditch stand to save her father's business. She hopes to sell forward maturing stocks of whisky in the barrels stored in Glentirran warehouses in the Highlands. She claims that a well-known London-based commodity broker will be assisting her.

In the meantime, vital questions are being asked in financial circles.

First, isn't it time that the authorities passed legislation preventing banks from using their power to annihilate competitive companies to those in which management have an interest?

Second, should a bank's power be used for a personal vendetta? Ethical considerations apart, the implications for future client relationships are far-reaching.

Grampian Bank manager Mr James Littlewood confirmed that the bank's proprietor, Alasdair Cameron, aged 14, had 'voiced his concern' at his mother's handling of the so-called 'whisky war'.

Is Grampian Bank acting in bad faith? Are Glentirran being softened up for a takeover bid? And even more important, if the bank is prepared to use its power to wipe out Dame Cameron's competitors, then who will be next? Perhaps she has as yet unknown interests in building, or shipbuilding, or retail trading? If so, the bank's investors might well be on their guard.

Lastly, one has to ask if this is the type of morality we look for in an old-established Scottish bank.

Marjorie pulled the paper from the fax and flung it into the bin. She had to get out of there. She was panting as she ran outside and collapsed on the front steps.

I am cursed, she thought. Robert abandoned me, Hamish, too, and now my children. How could they turn against me? All that I did was for them. How can they be so cruel?

The moon rose, an owl called from the wood, the wind came gusting through the trees, but Marjorie was oblivious. She sat staring at the dark lake, filled with a sense of emptiness.

Chapter 80

——— ———

Frantic with haste, Lana had hitched a lift to Edinburgh in a friend's private jet, and hired a car at the airport after she had changed her clothes in the toilet. But now she was caught up in a long convoy of cars moving frustratingly slowly towards Tirran Lodge.

She was feeling scared and confused, unable to get to grips with her warring emotions. There was so much guilt. In particular, she regretted quarrelling with Uncle Joe. She could not remember him ever having taken Mother's side against her and this worried her. Was he right? Was she way out of line?

Switching her mind off Uncle Joe, she was over-come with envy of all these people who shared her father's world. Why didn't she? Why had she been rejected and excluded from his life? She was going to see him for the first time and far from being happy, she could not remember ever feeling so tearful, or so angry.

By now she knew almost all there was to know about this eccentric man. She'd spent hours in the newspaper library, and she'd talked to people who knew him, but this would be the first time she set eyes on him. It was hard to come to grips with reality. Sir Robert MacLaren, explorer, ecologist, animal rights' activist and regular contributor to the *National Geographic Magazine*, was her father.

How come he cared so much about the ecology and howling monkeys if he didn't give two hoots about his own daughter? She intended to confront him with this, although she wasn't sure what she would do or say when she came face to face with him. She would play it by ear.

'Don't make too big a fool of yourself, Lana,' she muttered, as her stomach quailed with fear.

Lana gasped when she caught sight of Tirran Lodge. It was an old castle, huge, graceful and very grand. Here were real roots, old money, ancestors, the whole bit – enough to satisfy her lifetime of searching, she reckoned. She had to admit that lately she'd been obsessed with genealogy. As she drove closer, the butterflies in her stomach went quietly crazy while her hands were slippery on the steering wheel.

She knew that the planned celebration would continue late into the night, that Shirley Bassey was to be singing and that a magnificent meal would be followed by a display by the Edinburgh Pipe Band. Scottish dancing would thrill the guests until midnight, followed by a ball, which was expected to last until dawn. All this had been reported extensively in the press and Lana had eagerly read every word of it.

She had bullied a titled friend from law school, who hobnobbed with the social set, to hand over her invitation, then she had lashed out on a new dress, a stunning black Valentino creation with a beaded halter neck. Her mop of curly black hair had been pushed up into a chignon and wrapped in a string of pearls. She knew she looked good and this gave her confidence.

When she reached the gate, she saw that a crowd had gathered, hoping to catch sight of famous visitors. They peered into her car, trying to place her, and turned away disappointed.

She was shown to a parking lot on a side lawn and moments later she was tripping over the grass towards the main hall, pulling Mum's black mohair cloak closer around her. A sudden whiff of Mum's perfume caught her off-guard. She stumbled and almost burst into tears. Absurd, she told herself crossly. She had burned her bridges. Then suddenly, without any doubt at all, she realised that Mum would be hurting badly. Had the newspaper contacted her? Did Mum guess where she was, or why?

Marjorie had pulled herself together sufficiently to compose her reply to the fax from the newspaper. Still in her dressing gown she gave one final check to her reply, reading from the word processor screen. The crux of her message was contained in one paragraph:

> Yes, it is because I am chairman of Glenaird whisky that I advised the bank to foreclose on Glentirran. I do wear two hats and I readily accept this point. It is my experience in the whisky industry which has given me sufficient expertise to realise just how dangerous Glentirran's position is. Whatever they do now, they will never manage to hold on to their present US market share. They could not appoint a new distributor and get stocks over to America in time. They will lose a part at least and maybe a large proportion of their market share to their competition. In so doing, they become a much

smaller and less powerful company, they will have to borrow heavily and it will take them years to recoup their losses, let alone future borrowings. And yes, Glenaird did offer to buy the majority of their shares. It is the better option for them under the circumstances.

And Lana? What was she supposed to say about her daughter?

She thought for a few moments and then she typed: 'In response to all personal matters erroneously reported in your proposed article, I have no comment. You will be hearing from my lawyers regarding this matter.'

She was interrupted by the telephone. It was Littlewood at the bank. As usual, he came straight to the point: 'Marjorie, there's a board meeting at nine-thirty tomorrow morning. Joe Segal is flying up from London this evening, I believe.'

So that's where Joe was, she thought wearily. She'd been trying to call him for the past hour.

'You have my very sincere sympathy over this family crisis, and we shall all be behind you to give you whatever assistance we can,' James was saying. 'I suggest you call the newspaper's editor and . . .'

'I've done all I can in that direction,' she interrupted him.

'Good. Now, listen. The various managers and I have held an emergency session here for the past few hours and our final conclusion is that you were quite right. Glentirran no longer provide a viable risk for the type of funding they will be needing. We intend to stick by your decision and if necessary we'll back our policy with statements to the press.'

'Yes,' she said dully. 'Thank you for letting me know.'

'See you tomorrow morning.'

'Oh, no . . . No, James . . . Listen! I'm resigning as chairman of the bank and the distillery as of now. I shall fax my intentions through to you this evening. I am sure Joe Segal will help out until you find someone suitable to replace me.'

'No, Marjorie. Don't do anything in a hurry. I can imagine how you must be feeling, but . . .'

She replaced the receiver, cutting out further arguments. She had to think.

The foyer and the huge ballroom were packed with people. Lana wandered around gazing at the walls, which were at least a yard thick, loving the old, flagged floors worn concave with centuries of use and the heavy portraits of family ancestors around the walls.

Her stomach lurched when she found herself standing close to Sir Robert MacLaren. He looked bemused as he sipped his drink and stood talking to a girl who faced him at eye-level. Lana guessed that she must be Maria, the guest of honour. She was almost as tall as her six-foot-six father who was hovering in the background, bending down apologetically like a wilting flower, as if ashamed of his height, his wealth and his nondescript appearance. Lana had heard the gossip. Maria, at thirty-one, had designs on Sir Robert, aided and abetted by his step-mother, Rhoda. The thought of her father marrying was almost more than she could bear.

She sipped her drink and studied him surreptitiously. He was a huge man and he wore a kilt well. She had seen enough photographs of him to know exactly what he looked like, but now she realised that no photograph could ever do justice to him. With his mass of wiry black hair, fierce dark eyes, strong features and athletic build, he could have been an ancient Scottish warrior chief. There was a surge of magnetic energy emanating from him that made him seem larger than life. Although he appeared to be sunk into a grave, almost lamb-like quietness, you could still sense the force and power in the man. His big, dark, brilliant eyes seemed to have a life of their own. They scanned the chattering guests with a kind of amused tolerance. His air of tense, quiet alertness must come from years spent exploring the wilds, she decided. For some reason the sight of him, his powerful intensity, and his stubborn inflexibility, made her want to cry.

How could Mother have got the better of such a man in business? But Mother was clever, too, wasn't she? She had been so patient and cunning, plotting her revenge, manipulating Hamish and everyone connected with Glenaird and the bank. Even Alasdair had been drawn into Mother's war.

A moment of self-knowledge hit her like a revelation. Her roots lay in these two obstinate, brilliant, unforgiving, exceptional parents of hers. Their genes were her genes, their blood ran in her veins, she had their brains and their guile, and she was a match for both of them.

First and foremost, she wanted her father. Dimly, in her sad-happy, muddled state, she knew that she wanted his love above all else. After that she would set about saving him from Mother.

Lana moved on, not wishing to draw attention to herself. She had no plans as yet, merely a longing to find out more about this man, to touch his desk, to see where he worked, to wander into his bedroom and see how he lived. She would mingle with the guests until Shirley Bassey took the stage and then she would find her way around.

The waiting was agonising. Time had shifted gear to dead slow and Lana was too uptight to eat anything.

When at last Shirley Bassey let rip with 'Big Spender', Lana left the ballroom and crept down the passage. There was no one looking, so she opened the first door she came to and went inside.

It was a very large room, a strange mixture of old and new, with hundreds of leather-bound books. One entire wall was taken up with the bottom half of a larger-than-life stone engraving of a knight in armour seated on a magnificent stallion, but the top half was lost above the ceiling. She guessed that somewhere upstairs the rider's torso and his stallion's head were sprouting from the floor.

Family portraits kept her wandering around the room. She found herself gazing at the portrait of a young woman who could have been herself. She gasped and stood entranced, her arms tingling with goose pimples. Fiona MacLaren, she read, 1862–1900, African explorer and missionary. The likeness was amazing.

She walked around the room, studying the photographs of Father at school. Dover College! That figured, she thought with a smile. A moment of second sight told her that his bedroom would be up above the study, where the top half of the warring knight would be found. She crept outside and crossed the huge hall, thrilling to the music and feeling unafraid as she mounted the circular marble staircase.

As she pushed open the door, she felt as if she'd entered a holy place. She stood smelling the strange male fragrance of the man, loving it. It was his room, she knew by the photographs on the dressing table and the clothes.

She was sitting on the bed, smoothing her hands over the mohair rug in the MacLaren tartan, when the door crashed open and a security man stood blocking any escape. Moments later he caught hold of her elbow and thrust her roughly towards a chair. Now two more uniformed men were moving in on her. She watched them, feeling bemused. Nothing mattered. She had seen her father. He was all that she had longed for and so much more besides.

Chapter 81

Could there be anything in the world as painful as the contempt of one's own children? Marjorie was crouched over her desk, her head in her hands, trying to make sense of her world, and longing to find where she had gone wrong.

Why had they turned against her? All those years, all that struggle had been for them. Now there was nothing left.

Memories of Lana plagued her: her excitement when she saw the fox, sitting astride her first horse, her grief when Paddywonks died. She had always turned to her mother for comfort. And why not? She could not help remembering the time Lana had flung herself onto barbed wire to cushion her fall. Lana had always adored her. Now the hurt had become physical pain in her stomach.

'I've won back Glentirran,' she reminded herself, speaking aloud. 'It's only a matter of days now. It was all for Lana. But she's taken his side. Why?

'How did Lana find out about her father? She fights dirty, but that's the only way she knows: tooth and nail, just as she learned from me. I should be proud of her.'

Marjorie groped in the bin for the crumpled fax from the newspaper. What had they said about Lana?

'. . . *searching for that miracle in a last-ditch stand to save her father . . .*'

'Crazy,' she murmured. 'There is no miracle, Lana. You're too late.' In the past three weeks Yoshi had moved fast to grab Glentirran's US outlets, and in the face of bad press reports all Glentirran's creditors were clamouring for their cash. Last week their auditor had begged Littlewood for credit to pay their wages.

Jumping up from her desk she began to pace the office, muttering to herself.

'Of course I'll win. Lana hasn't the resources, or the power, or the experience, and in particular she doesn't have the time. The trap has been a long time closing, but it's about to snap shut and there's nothing anyone can do about it. I'll beat her father into the ground. Then I'll hand her Glentirran on a plate.' She laughed mirthlessly. 'She'll get her inheritance, as I always intended, but from me.'

But that didn't make sense. Her motives were suspect. As the real reason became apparent, Marjorie wondered at the sense of denial she'd clung to all these years. The real truth, which she was forced to accept, was as unwelcome as a cold shower and equally shocking.

So it wasn't only for Lana. I've been obsessed with revenge for years and I didn't care who got hurt. I conned them all: Joe, Hamish, my children and finally myself. I kidded myself I was doing it all for Lana.

Walking to the window, she stared up at the night sky. 'If I win,' she whispered, 'will she learn to hate, like I did?'

A spark of outrage dried her mouth. She took a deep breath and screamed: 'No!'

'I am being punished,' she told herself, harking back

to Sunday School teaching. But the answer came from within herself: *No one is punished. Like attracts like and I attracted hatred and revenge.*

One thought penetrated her confusion like a beacon through fog on a treacherous night: *Lana must win! I love her too much to let her lose.*

She returned to her desk and sat plotting, as she had done so often in the past when she faced opposition. This time she had to outwit her Machiavellian self. It took a while, but eventually she stood up, feeling stiff and cold, and opened the walk-in safe where she kept the family trust papers and certificates. Lana would be a millionare when she turned twenty-five. She had only to alter the dates to twenty.

It did not take long to sign the papers and initial the changes, after which she wrote a message to Lana:

'I suggest you use your shares as collateral for Glentirran's borrowings. The bank must accept them. It won't take too long for Glentirran to recover if you merge Glentirran's export marketing drive with Glenaird's, while keeping separate labels. Good luck. I love you.'

She put the papers into a large envelope labelled *Express hand delivery to Lana Hardy*, and placed it in the 'out' basket for her messenger to collect when he called in the morning.

There was one more job to do. She wrote two covering messages for Joe and Littlewood and faxed them.

When the telephone rang, she picked up the receiver out of habit and instantly regretted doing so.

'Marjorie.' It was Joe's voice. 'I'm flying up tonight. I was just leaving when your fax came through.'

'I have nothing to add . . .' Marjorie began coldly.

'No. Don't hang up. Listen to me. Lana has been

indulging in wishful thinking. For starters, I'm certainly not marketing Glentirran malt in the barrels against Glenaird. Likewise, she hasn't yet met her father . . .'

'What?' Marjorie went ice-cold.

'She's flown to Edinburgh to confront him tonight. She's intending to threaten litigation to force him to recognise her as his legitimate heir. Evidently there was a similar case recently and she learned about it in law school. Alasdair called me half an hour ago and told me all this. He's staying with friends, but he's worried about her. He doesn't know how she'll handle rejection after waiting this long to find her roots.'

'Oh God . . .'

'It's not them against you, Marjorie, as you might have thought. It's Lana against both of you.'

'No! God help her.' At that moment she vividly recalled her own humiliation at Rhoda's hands. 'I must find her,' she said. 'Thanks, Joe.'

She ran upstairs to change. Ten minutes later she was in her car, speeding down the driveway, through the gates and on towards Inverness Airport. She had to find Lana and give her the share certificates. Robert didn't want her as a baby, why should he want her now? But Lana wasn't there to beg. She alone could save her father. This time it was altogether different.

There was no moon and a ground mist had reduced visibility to a few yards. She swore as she braked to sixty mph to negotiate the bends. She knew she was taking chances. Her hands became numb from gripping the steering wheel.

Five miles from Inverness she caught sight of a moving shape somewhere in the shadows of the trees zooming in on her. Twisting to the right, she saw the glitter of an eye, teeth bared in panic, antlers that seemed to rear up to the sky. It was beautiful and it was on a collision course.

'God . . .' she muttered. Even in her split second of panic a thought registered: she had done enough harm for one lifetime. She swerved violently to the left, away from the galloping creature, her foot hard down on the brakes. She saw the graceful beast surge past as she swung into a skid. She was dimly aware of hooves galloping away, of a deafening crash, a pain in her throat and a massive crack that seemed to come from within her head. Then she was falling, tumbling . . .

She was walking over Dover cliffs with Robert. She flung herself down in the long dry grass, and as he lay over her, she watched the prism of light fall like a halo around his tangled black hair.

Mum was leaning over the cot at the convent, lifting Lana. 'You're coming home, my love,' she was whispering as she wrapped the shawl around the baby. 'About time too, if you ask me.'

Hamish was clinging to the rocks, trying to hide his shyness as he grinned at her across the camera. Hamish, dearest Hamish. I loved you so much, but I was the fool who would not accept it.

Fleeting images! Then came snatches of other times. Ancient days! So she had been there, too.

The images passed, leaving her dazed. It was like stirring a crystal-clear pond until the sediment rose around her, all the debris of past mistakes. *But who was the stirrer?* That was her question.

She thought: I have evolved through millions of lifetimes, but who am I? She could see the body of Marjorie Hardy flung half out of the open door.

Then a great surge of love washed through her. She found she was drifting through time and space, no longer linked with her old self, but part of a living, dynamic energy-force, a force of intense love.

Chapter 82

It was ten p.m. when Rhoda MacLaren squared up to her stepson in his study, her eyes glittering like a fighting cock.

'I demand that you treat our guests with respect.' Her voice came out like a squawk and she made an effort to calm her temper.

'*Your* guests, Rhoda.'

She screwed up her eyes to see him more carefully. Oh how she disliked that unyielding expression, his face set into a sombre effigy. There was no reaching him when he looked like that.

'Can't you understand the mess we're in?'

'Probably better than you do, Rhoda.'

'So what are you doing about it?'

'Well, I'm certainly not marrying for money. God forbid!'

'It would be a good exchange.' She tried to convey some of her enthusiasm for this plan of hers. 'She gets a title, you get a fortune. We need an heir. Surely you realise that.'

Robert glared at her.

She tried again. 'She adores you. Everyone expects you to propose tonight.'

'Why? Because you've persistently thrown her at me?'

She was losing her nerve, despite her determination.

'I warned you before, Rhoda,' Robert went on in his quiet, deceptively gentle voice. 'I doubt I'll ever marry, but if I do, it sure as hell won't be for money. Now might be a good time to tell you that I have no intention of accepting Glenaird's offer, however much it might benefit shareholders. We shall tighten our belts and slowly rebuild.'

His words seemed to drain her. 'That would take for ever,' she grumbled. 'We'll be poor again – maybe for twenty years. I'll be dead by then. You're cutting off your nose to spite your face, you always have done.'

'Not really. The point is, Glentirran is the family's distillery and I intend to hang on to it . . .' He paused as he heard a knock on the door. Their butler walked in.

'Excuse me, sir, I'm sorry to intrude. Something's come up that needs your urgent attention.'

Robert stared at him in surprise. Mr Benjamin's normal inscrutability had given way to blatant curiosity.

'We caught this young lady in your bedroom, sir. We were about to call the police, but then we thought we'd do better to speak to you first. She's very agitated, sir, and she seems to be under some delusion.'

'Bring her in,' Robert said.

'I'm here, and I'm not under any delusion '

Wow! Robert thought as the young woman strode into his office. She was intensely lovely with her dark, dramatic looks and large, angry eyes. And what a dress! There was a strong sense of melodrama all about her. Clearly she was caught up in her role of avenging angel, but then, he thought forgivingly, she was so very, very young. He wondered who she was.

She shook off the security guards' hands. 'I'm a lawyer

and I'm warning you to tell your thugs to keep their hands off me or I'll sue. And I'll win,' she added. Despite her scowl, Robert felt that she was on the edge of breaking down.

'Don't I know you? I can't think where I've seen you before, yet I seem to know you well. Perhaps you've acted on TV?' Placing his hands on the young woman's shoulders, he twisted her round to face him, scanning her face and her eyes.

'You should know me, but you don't. The fault is entirely yours.'

What did she mean? Robert's heart missed a beat. He tried to tell himself that this was yet another red herring. God knows he'd had enough of them over the past years, but hope kept rising like rain clouds over drought-stricken plains.

'I've brought a tape recorder,' she was saying as she fumbled in her bag. He noticed that her hands were shaking badly. 'I want you to hear a certain conversation and then we'll see if you want to call the police.'

She turned to Rhoda. 'You can probably guess what's on this tape, Lady MacLaren. It's a conversation between you and my mother, Mrs Cameron, recorded yesterday at Grampian Bank.'

Robert frowned at the girl. 'Wait a minute. Are you saying your mother is Mrs Cameron? If you're here about the takeover, it's no and that's final.'

And what had Rhoda been doing at Grampian Bank? He scanned her face for signs of guilt. Yes, it was written all over her. Was she in a conspiracy against him?

The young woman bent over the desk to operate the tape recorder and the next moment he heard a voice that was vaguely familiar. It changed to high-pitched gabble

as the girl pushed fast forward. Moments later Robert
was struggling to keep his composure, while his mind
reeled in confusion at what he heard.

*'Lady MacLaren, let me put my cards on the table. All
these years I've fought for my daughter's birthright. It's in
my grasp. It's a matter of days, or weeks at the outside. I
am going to tell her who her father is when I give her back
her rightful inheritance Glentirran. That has always been
my plan.'*

What the hell? He'd never met Mrs Cameron. He
turned to the girl. 'What was your mother's name before
marriage?' His voice was too hoarse. He cleared his throat
and said the whole thing again.

'Majorie Hardy,' she said defiantly.

'And you are?'

'Lana Hardy.'

Robert was too stunned to react. He stood as if rooted
to the ground, mouth open foolishly, his thoughts racing:
of course she was his daughter. She was the image of
him. So she had not been adopted after all. He felt a
great sadness sinking into him at those wasted years
when he should have been there for her. Suddenly he
realised how badly he needed a family. And Marjorie
was the famous Dame Marjorie, his implacable enemy
who had brought his company to ruin. The whole absurd
so-called 'whisky war' began to make sense at last.

His eyes turned uncertainly to Rhoda. Had she always
known   ?

'Then there's this bit,' the girl muttered. She turned
her back on him, but her shoulders were shaking as she
bent over the tape recorder. Robert strode across the
room and switched it off.

'Maybe later, but not now. My dear child, if you're

Marjorie Hardy's daughter, then you're my daughter. There's no question about it. I was told you'd been adopted. My lawyers have been searching for you for years.'

The young woman stepped back from him and tilted her chin defiantly. 'I intend to sue for my rights as your legitimate heir. I'll probably win.'

Robert tried to read her expression through a mist of tears. 'My dear, I've been looking for you for a very long time,' he said. 'You don't have to sue anyone. Silly girl! You only had to come.'

Pulling his daughter into his arms, Robert rocked her backwards and forwards, remembering Marjorie and how much he had once loved her. He had never been able to forgive her for giving away his child. And now it seemed she never had.

Chapter 83

So her aloof, elusive stepson had feelings after all, Rhoda thought, watching him wonderingly. Lana, too, had adoration beaming from her eyes. They did not need Maria and her fortune after all. Here was their salvation. Rhoda knew how much Marjorie adored and spoiled her daughter. She would never fight against her. With luck their cash-flow problem would evaporate into thin air.

At the same time, it was the mother who controlled the purse strings. Rhoda sensed there was something she must do to bring about a reconciliation. Turning to Robert, she said: 'I have a letter . . . I kept it hidden for over twenty years. I was afraid to destroy it, or to give it to you, but it's been on my conscience. At the time I thought I was protecting you.' She sniffed and fumbled for a tissue. 'How can you ever forgive me?'

She watched Robert flush with distaste. She knew how much he hated emotional scenes – that was his Achilles heel – and she had always used his weakness to her advantage.

Belatedly, she realised that the security men and the butler were still there. That would mean the entire staff would know within the hour, and one or more of them would leak the story to the newspapers. Damn! 'Please leave,' she told them sternly.

At that moment the fax rang and began to print out a message.

'This can't be true,' Robert muttered as he scanned the message from the newspaper. 'Unforgivable! Lana, how could you do this to your mother?'

Watching Robert fast losing his temper with her as the newspaper's story curled over the machine, Lana knew she was out of her depth. Her script wasn't working. She felt like a pendulum swinging from ecstasy to blind panic. She had expected war, or derision, or a slanging match, or any damned thing other than instant acceptance, instant love. Now look at him! Lana decided that there might be disadvantages in having a father after all. His brows were knitted and his eyes, so caring seconds ago, were coldly furious.

'Was it necessary to air our private business in the newspaper? I can't believe that you could do this to your mother, or to me,' he muttered.

'She told me I was adopted. All my life I've felt deprived. I hate her for that.'

'Deprived?' He laughed curtly. 'Oh, you fool, Lana. You have a lot of learning ahead of you. Listen to the tape, but this time *hear* what your mother is saying.'

'I know it off by heart,' she shouted, close to tears. She shrugged angrily and turned away, but her father grabbed her arms and pushed her back to the tape recorder.

'Play it!' It wasn't a request.

Her eyes pricking with tears, she fumbled with the switches and once again they listened to her mother's voice.

'"*All these years . . .*"' Robert growled. 'Can't you understand how she loves you? Don't you realise that

she thought she'd failed you because I – like a fool –
told her she wasn't good enough for our family? And I
have no doubt Rhoda told her that, too. So she thought
we'd repudiate you as well. All her life she's battled to
get you back where she felt you ought to be. She thought
she was alone.'

Father's rich voice filled the room with his compelling
argument. His very reasonableness was like a douse of
cold water. Lana tried to change tack.

'Now that I've found you, all you care about is her.'
It sounded petty even to her. She felt ashamed as she
pulled away from him and stood by the desk frowning.

'You're right, of course,' she faltered. She thought
hard about her mother and how much she loved her,
seeing her image in her mind's eye, longing to be with
her. 'Oh Mum. What have I done?' she whispered. She
felt suddenly cold, and slightly nauseous. Something was
wrong. She had a terrible sensation of impending doom.
Then her head began to hurt badly and she was filled
with a heavy grief which was not of her making. She had
always had an intuitive link with her mother. Something
bad was happening to Mother.

'Never mind all this,' she burst out. 'It can wait, can't
it? Something's terribly wrong. How can I get back to
Inverness? Now, at once?'

'I'll fly you there,' her father said.

Later, Lana was never able to get to grips with the
exact sequence of events of that terrible night. Images
remained to haunt her for months: Mum's car wrapped
around the tree and the blood on the seat. The long, scary
drive to Casualty. Joe's face, so shocked and white, as he
sat outside the operating theatre.

Lana waited, obsessed with guilt, her face a mask of pain, until the doctor came to explain that it was mainly concussion and shock and that her mother had been stitched up and hopefully would regain consciousness soon. They could wait.

Then a social worker came and handed Lana Mother's bag and an envelope addressed to her, which the ambulancemen had found on the back seat of the wrecked car. Lana opened the envelope with shaking fingers.

'Wake up, Mother. Wake up! Please, Mother, *please*. I love you,' the voice kept repeating in her ears.

Familiar perfume enveloped the woman lying prone in the hospital bed. She wrinkled her nose. Chanel No. 5, Lana's favourite. She could feel her daughter's hot breath and her wiry hair tickling her face. 'Talk to me, Mum.' No one could ignore Lana's authoritative tone.

Marjorie opened her eyes with passive obedience and saw her daughter's brooding anxiety turn to relief. How haggard Lana looked, but her eyes gleamed with warmth as she forced a smile. 'Thank God!' she whispered.

Oh, how her head ached. Marjorie put her hand up and felt the bandages. What was this? But then she remembered and with remembrance came a flash of foolish remorse. She should have been more careful. Closing her eyes, she tried to slip back into merciful sleep, but her daughter had other ideas.

'Mother! Talk to me,' she commanded fiercely.

'I'm all right, Lana. Really I am. How long have I been here?'

'A day and a half.' Her daughter was willing her to stay awake, her brown eyes glaring at her, her unruly black hair falling forward over her face. 'Listen to me,' she urged fiercely. 'I *love* you. Alasdair will be here soon. He *loves* you, too. I was wrong. Unforgivable!' She spoke slowly and clearly, flagellating herself with every word.

'It's all right, Lana,' Marjorie whispered.

Lana reached forward and touched the bandages lightly. Tears were trickling down her cheeks. 'Listen, Mother. I want you to know that I forgive you for everything. I should have said that before. I'm sorry.'

Lana had always felt responsible for everything that went wrong. She apologised for accidents, bad films and even bad weather. She carried the world on her shoulders. But '*I forgive you*'? Marjorie puzzled over this.

Forgive me for what? For working like a dog so that I could afford to spoil you, and make no mistake you're utterly spoiled? For sending you to the best school and university money could buy? For making sure you had every single advantage I never had? Or for keeping quiet when you turned against me? Jesus, that hurt! And the worst pain of all was your public declaration of war.

All she said was: 'I'm so tired, dear.'

'Are you listening, Mother? I forgive you.'

'Go on, Marjorie, be brave, say it,' a small voice whispered.

'Forgive me for what?' Oops! That came out a little too harshly. Now is not the time for a confrontation.

'For letting me believe I was adopted. I feel it's important for you to know that I have completely forgiven you.'

Marjorie sat up feeling mystified, anger surging despite her best intentions. 'Oh!' she gasped with pain and sank back on the pillows.

'Heavens, Lana, how can you possibly understand the

pressures of that time? It wasn't like now. People have
different values nowadays. Besides, who cares if you're
adopted?'

'And I forgive you for working all hours, and never
being home with us.'

'You had Granny.'

'I wanted *you*.' Inexplicably Lana's eyes filled with
tears.

'Lana, listen to me and stop crying. I had this dream.
I longed to win back your heritage. To put you back
where you belonged and to strike a blow for my own
self-esteem, too. I was once branded second-class and it
hurt . . .'

'I know, Dad told me. I understand you so much better
now. And then when I read your note . . .' She broke off,
looking overwhelmed. 'Well, what can I say? Thank you,
that's all. Of course, I'll do what you suggested. I realise
now that you were doing your best for me.

'Father made me see it straight. He's gone now, but
he was here all night. The day before yesterday Rhoda
gave him the letter you once wrote telling him you were
pregnant. He only found out much later, you see. He
went to the convent and they told him I'd been adopted.
His lawyer's been trying to trace me ever since. Weird,
isn't it? We had nothing to do but talk all night and now
I feel as if I've known him all my life.'

Marjorie kept her face turned to the window and
tried to focus her attention on the scene outside. There
was a tall, leafy tree where a speckled bird was singing
its heart out. She tried to smother her mixed feelings
of grief, regret and rage. Now was not the time for
self-indulgence, not with Lana sitting there fired with
the importance of what she had done. How was she to

know that every word was like a dagger in her heart? She was so young.

And I forgive you, too, Marjorie thought, but she was too wise to say so.

'I think I'd like to sleep now,' she begged.

'Just as long as you know that I love you. We all do. You do believe me, don't you? By the way, Father wants to know if he can come and see you.'

Marjorie managed to hang on to some semblance of normality until Lana left, then she buried her face in the pillow and let her tears flow.

Chapter 84

It was noon when Mum arrived. She'd taken a lot of trouble with her appearance, Marjorie could see, but she looked anxious and confused, as if she could not make up her mind what attitude to strike: compassion or censure.

'You didn't need to come, Mum,' Marjorie said, feeling guilty. 'I'm all right. I'll be home soon.'

'The matron said tomorrow.' Mum stared around stonily. 'Look, I brought you a couple of books to read,' she faltered, 'and other things.' She pointed to Marjorie's packed leather bag she had brought with her.

Mum could never get to grips with emotional problems. Instead she began to talk about the vegetable garden and the prices they were getting, avoiding the subject that was uppermost in their minds.

'Don't worry about Lana and me,' Marjorie interrupted her. 'It's all sorted out.'

'Well, if you say so, Marjorie. I must say, this is a rum do, all our private problems trotted out in the press for everyone to read. We took so much trouble to tell everyone Lana was adopted, and it's not as if we were lying. We did adopt her. You've spoiled that girl, no mistake. Dad gave her a piece of his mind and so did I. If it were me I wouldn't forgive her so quickly. Don't

pretend you weren't hurt, haring off in the middle of
the night like that and wrapping your car around a tree.
Of course, it had to be the Jaguar. It's insured, is it?'

'Yes. Don't fret. I love you, Mum,' Marjorie said. 'I
really do. I'm sorry I worried you.'

Liz dabbed her eyes with a tissue. 'I don't know why
you do. We've always thought we were a drain on you,
seeing as how you've done so well and . . . well . . . what
have we ever amounted to? Dad worries about that a lot.'

'Oh, Mum! I'd swap everything for a man who loved
me. You lead good lives. You love each other, so what
sort of a yardstick are you talking about – money?'

'That Robert of yours has been around.' Mum's voice
became calmer once she'd changed the subject. 'I thought
you might like to know that. He told us he's moved into
his house in Keith so that he can be near in case we
need him.'

Mum's sniff was eloquent. 'We've got on all right
without him all these years. I expect he wants to keep
out of his house because his stepmother's moving to
France and taking all her furniture with her. According
to him there won't be much left.

'He had the cheek to thank me for bringing up *his*
daughter so well. I gave him a mouthful. "She's our
daughter," I told him. "Don't you forget it!" Typical
nob! Thinks the world revolves around him. Not like
Hamish. Dad adored Hamish. Well, we all did . . .'
Her voice trailed off, but she pulled herself out of
despondency with a quick laugh.

'Funny how transparent men are. Robert brought me
flowers. I ask you! A huge bowl of irises. He's trying to
get you back. But remember, Marjorie, he let you down
before, so I wouldn't trust him again if I were you. I

almost brought the flowers to you, but then I thought they'd only be wasted. I put them in your bedroom. They'll be there when you get home.'

'Thank you, Mum.' Marjorie reached out and took her mother's hand, but her mother pulled hers away. Then she put it back again, which surprised Marjorie.

'We've never been a demonstrative family, have we, Marj?' Mum said, turning pink with embarrassment. 'I see these other people, well, you know the sort I mean, and they're always hugging each other. That Mrs Turnbull down in the village is always kissed by her daughters. I can't help wishing I'd brought you up like that.'

'You did fine, Mum.' Marjorie sat up and gasped at the sudden, shooting pain in her head. Mum grabbed her bag, ready for instant flight. 'I'll call the nurse.'

'No, please.' She put her arm around her mother's shoulders and hugged her, kissing her cheek. Mum smelt of perfume and soap, a nice, familiar scent.

'The press have been hanging around by the score,' Mum told Marjorie. 'They've got their job to do, I suppose. We ignore them. As for Lana – when she phoned me to tell me what you've done for her I could have cried. As soon as you're better she's flying to the States to plan the joint marketing with Yoshi Tohara. Robert agrees; since she's his heir he says it stands to reason to merge her two inheritances. I don't know how we'll live with her now she's got her hands on her shares. She was bossy enough before. I hope you won't live to regret what you've done.'

'I won't, Mum. I'll be here if she needs me and she'll have Yoshi and Robert. Later there'll be Alasdair, too. She can't go too far wrong.'

'Well, you seem okay, so I'll be off. I can't stand hospitals and there's never anything much to say. Just the smell of them turns my stomach. Dad's sorry he couldn't make it. He had to get the soil prepared for a new load of potatoes.'

'Of course,' Marjorie said quickly. 'Remember to give him my love.'

'I brought Alasdair with me. He's waiting outside. I didn't bring him in just in case you were poorly. Don't keep him too long, I'm taking him back to school. Oh, and this is from Robert.' She dropped an envelope on Marjorie's knees.

Alasdair was all feet and hands, his face puzzled and humble, unsure what to say.

'Alasdair, I love you,' she said firmly. 'I shall never, ever drive so carelessly again. Please forgive me.'

'Mum, I'm so sorry. I should never have . . .'

'Yes, you should have. I was wrong. We'll talk about it one day, when you're older. But in the meantime . . .'

'Oh, Mum.' Alasdair flung himself on the bed. His voice was breaking and the few sobs that escaped were high and low and very hoarse.

'There's just one good thing came out of this,' he said. 'At least I know you're human. I've never known you to be really silly before.'

She reached down and took her son's hand. 'I was just overworked. I've resigned and now I'm due for a long holiday. I'll be home soon. Give me a hug and off you go to school.'

When he had gone, she opened the envelope with trembling fingers. She gasped when her own letter, written twenty-one years ago, fell out.

'Dearest Marjorie,' she read. 'I have recorded the events and my own interpretation of them, as faithfully as I can recall. This is sent merely to shed light on a shadowy period in our lives. I can never forgive myself for not understanding or trusting you. Regards, Robert. (P.S. I won't insult you by using the word *love*. You know how to love, but I don't think I have any true understanding of it, although I used to think I did.)'

The rest was only history although she reread it many times. Eventually she fell asleep. She woke much later to find the room filled with tulips, daffodils, hothouse roses and violets, and all were from the same person. That was Lana for you, full of excesses. Clearly, she'd bought the florist's shop.

Chapter 85

It was four p.m. on the following day when Marjorie decided to discharge herself with or without the hospital's approval. She had unfinished business to attend to. She dressed and thrust her belongings into the bag Mum had brought, called home to Mr Jenkins, their driver, and then dialled Robert's number in Keith.

'I'll fetch you. I don't want you driving all this way when you're getting over concussion.'

A rather authoritarian statement, she thought critically. Despite herself, she thrilled to the sound of his voice. She had forgotten that it was deep and throaty and full of sensual promise, and it brought back so many memories. But that was then, and this was now, twenty-one years on, she reminded herself sternly.

'My driver is fetching me. I'd like to come,' she replied firmly. 'If it's not too inconvenient, that is. There's something that needs to be said.'

It was dark when she arrived at five. Robert was standing in the doorway of a small, pretty cottage. When he saw her car he hurried towards her in that funny loping walk that was uniquely his. He hadn't changed all that much, she thought. Hardly at all. Maybe he'd thickened out a bit. A little sterner perhaps.

'You really haven't changed,' he contended formally as she stepped out of the car.

You stole my line, she wanted to say, but instead she managed a weak 'Hello, Robert' and that was all.

His eyes, so brimming with love and compassion, propelled her into the past. She made an effort to pull herself together, shivering. What am I doing here? I must leave. This man has the power to make me quiver. Ridiculous! I'm not a teenager.

She began to babble on about feeling that she had changed, in fact feeling a hundred years old sometimes, but other times still only twenty. Help! Where was her carefully rehearsed speech? Why was she acting like an idiot?

'Let your driver go. I'll take you wherever you want,' he muttered.

Can I have that in writing? she longed to say. She decided to try out a nervous smile.

'Thank you, Mr Jenkins,' she ventured. 'Please go home. Tell Mum I'm with a friend in Keith.'

'Yes, ma'am,' he responded, a strange glint in his eyes.

'Let's go inside,' Robert said. He gripped her elbow and pulled her towards him. The old chemistry flared and she cursed herself for longing to pull him even closer. All that passed between us is ancient history. Remember that, you fool.

She caught a whiff of his aftershave and it smelled exactly as she remembered. Surely he hadn't been using the same aftershave for all these years?

She stepped into a pleasant chintzy room with a beamed ceiling and a log fire burning in the hearth.

'Let's have it. Let it all out,' Robert began before they had even sat down.

She felt disconcerted by his haste. I came to tell you that you're an arrogant, bigoted, class-ridden, introverted, distrustful idiot and that I have a sneaking feeling that I still love you. That would be near the truth, but she merely said: 'I'm concerned about Lana being torn in two. I've come to say that we must bury our bitterness and our differences for her sake. Our feud is getting like the Hundred Years' War, and just as boring. Who knows, one day we might become friends.'

'I'd hoped we might manage a glimmer of friendship tonight.'

She could hardly believe he had said that. She wanted to answer, but she could not. The long silence was painful.

'Love thine enemy,' Robert muttered. 'You'd do any thing for Lana, wouldn't you? I want to congratulate you. You did a wonderful job . . .'

'In bringing up your daughter? Forget it! Mum told me about your gaffe. Don't thank me, Robert. It would be an insult.'

'True! She's a very clever and strong-willed young woman and utterly spoiled by you, if you don't mind my saying so. Thank heavens you had your mother to balance things a bit.

'And thank you for not giving her away,' he went on, gazing fiercely at her. 'I have only one gripe left,' he added, ignoring her squeak of protest. 'Did you have to deny me my daughter for twenty years?'

She stood still, shuddering. How had she possibly hoped she could avoid this question? 'I'm cold.'

'Come and sit close to the fire.' He pulled her chair forward. 'Let's have a drink. What'll it be?'

'A sherry.'

'Coward!'

Despite her anxiety she smiled faintly.

'Of course the question still stands,' he said.

What could she say?

'Ask yourself, Robert. What made you believe Rhoda when you could have trusted me?' She shuddered again. 'How was I to know that Rhoda stole my letter? It was you I came to see.'

'If you had trusted me, you would have persisted until you found me.'

'If you had trusted me, you would never have believed Rhoda.'

'If we had both trusted . . .'

'Stop it!' Her words came out like a scream. She stood up in an abrupt, angry movement and began pacing the small room. 'Don't do this to us, Robert. There's no point. Besides, you have to understand that later, when I was married to Hamish, I didn't want him to know about you and me. Finally he did and he . . .' She almost choked on the words. 'He was very hurt. He went climbing and he never came back.'

'He found out that you married him in order to fight me?'

'Stop it,' she exclaimed sharply.

'But you loved him?'

'Yes, but love came too late. I'll never forgive myself.'

'Why not? You'd been badly hurt. You were hitting back the only way you could.'

'Oh God,' she whispered. 'I don't want to remember.'

'When you look at Lana you must see me. And yet you love her so passionately. Doesn't that tell you something?'

She stared at him long and hard until the silence

became embarrassing. How could she answer his question truthfully without ensnaring herself?

He's using the silence like I used to when I was selling advertising space. I used to sit back and let them sweat it out. Finally they said yes, if only to break the silence.

'What are you trying to sell me?' she asked.

'Sell you?' he echoed, frowning. Then he worked it out.

'Myself,' he replied without hesitating.

She felt stunned.

'It's strange,' she began, trying to lighten the atmosphere. 'Lana's never met you, but she has your mannerisms, your way of speaking and thinking. Remember how you used to push your hair up really hard, sort of tug at it, when you were exasperated? She does that. And so many other things. It's really weird. In a way it was as if you were with us.'

'And that made you love her even more. I don't know if we can go back in time, but I'd like to try. If you think there's a glimmer of a chance, why don't you stay for a few days? I guess your parents can look after Alasdair. We could stock up tomorrow and go out to eat tonight. There's a very nice inn within walking distance where they make a most delicious rabbit pie.'

'Idiot!' She smiled despite herself.

'Will you stay?' His fingers dug into her shoulder, and his eyes sent a message – one that she had not expected.

She shook her head. 'I made a mistake coming here. I'm sorry. I have too many grudges,' she whispered.

'Look here, Marjorie,' he retorted, looking so sad she could almost cry for him, 'since we're talking about grudges, you won the whisky war, but your hands aren't clean by any means. You changed your mind because of Lana, which showed me that you have your priorities in the right order, but I know your Yoshi Tohara was involved in Carlo's bankruptcy.'

'I didn't come here to talk about business. I'm finished with all that.' She felt guilty and resentful.

'Marjorie,' he whispered softly. 'We can trade grudge for grudge and part enemies, or we can reach out for what we once had, and . . . Oh Marjorie. Don't cry, my darling. Don't fight it. All you have to do is meet me halfway. I want my family back so badly.'

He bent over and kissed her throat and her lips. Looking up into his brown eyes glowing with love she remembered how it had been during their brief, poignant affair.

'It was always so sad,' she murmured, unable to see through her tears. 'The damn days kept getting less and our misery kept getting stronger.'

'Lately I've been thinking a good deal about the past, trying to find a reason for all that happened to us,' Robert said. 'I think I was afraid of the power you had over me. I was afraid to love.'

'And I felt unlovable. A losing combination.' She laughed harshly. 'Neither of us have changed, Robert.'

'I think you're wrong. I think we've both learned to trust. You could at least stay for dinner, if nothing else.'

He's so like me, she considered. That's how I used to operate. He got a 'no' from me, but he won't give up. Instead he's pushing in the thin edge of the wedge. I'd be a fool to stay for dinner. In next to no time I'd be signing on the dotted line.

So why was she saying: 'Oh yes? Dinner would be fine. I'm really hungry. As long as it's not veal.'

'Or pork.'

'Or rabbit.'

'Or *pâté de foie gras*. They make a very good *Darnes de Saumon Grillées au Beurre*. We could move on from there. Unlike last time, we're both free.'

'Perhaps,' she said. 'But I'm keeping my options open.'

'Being the woman that you are, I would expect nothing less.'

They walked to the inn and sat in a corner, oblivious to the world, and it seemed as if the years apart were fading into insignificance. She felt herself warming to him, enjoying his sense of humour as he tried to ease the awkwardness for both of them. Soon she was laughing. The past was over and done with.

That night they made love trustingly, like two friends, happy in their shared sensuality. Afterwards Marjorie lay close up against Robert, listening to his rhythmic breathing, feeling fulfilled and content. 'I forgive you, Marjorie Hardy,' she whispered. 'I'm even getting to trust you. You've turned into someone I like after all.'

Epilogue

———— ◆ ————

Marjorie was planting lavender seedlings around the terrace when she heard voices. Looking up, she saw Joe and Alasdair dressed in their white gear racing down the steps.

'Hello there,' she called. 'It's a lovely day for a work-out.'

Nowadays, by popular vote, most of the grass had been left to grow wild for the birds and rabbits, but the family had their portion, too, a wide strip of mowed lawn below the terrace, and there the two of them began their warming-up exercises. Joe, a black belt, had been teaching Alasdair judo for the past three months and they both took it very seriously indeed.

Marjorie watched them, loving them, and then she looked beyond them to the gardens and the lake and the wood. How lovely it was. She'd be sorry to leave, but she was moving into Tirran Lodge soon. Mum and Dad would act as caretakers until Alasdair needed the home.

A family of grouse raced through the long grass, blackbirds and rooks were tending their nests, the trees were flaunting their fresh green leaves and the field was full of white blossom: daisies, sorrel and anemones. The world was resurrected.

A strange feeling of longing swept through her. She shivered and sat on a step, hugging her arms around her knees. She wanted to join in, be a part of the morning and not be herself at all. But who and what was she?

She tried to pull herself together by watching Joe and Alasdair as they moved around each other, falling, rising, tumbling, twisting. Joe kept laughing at Alasdair, who kept losing. Lately Joe was more content with himself.

The advantage of being unemployed, she thought, is spending time with my family. But then the word 'unemployed', with all its horrid implications, made her feel uneasy. She could not help remembering that awful day when it seemed that there was no career of any account open to her, and she with a family to support. For a long while she was lost in her memories of the good times and the bad.

'What is it? What are you thinking?'

Joe hurried over, mopping his face with a towel, and sent Alasdair to fetch lemonade from the kitchen.

'I'm scared because I'm so happy, Joe. Everything's going so well for Robert and me, I'm afraid it will all be snatched away.'

'So, enjoy it while it lasts. Don't hang on. Accept life as it comes. That's the true meaning of happiness.'

'Oh, don't lecture me, Joe. It's nice to see you relax and have fun for once. I wonder why you enjoy judo so much. It's not just because you like teaching Alasdair, is it? You love tumbling around. You're a kid at heart.'

'Maybe,' he said thoughtfully. 'You could put it that way, but you'd be only partly right. The secret of life is to be found in judo. You learn to flow with change, but use it subtly.'

'Don't talk to me about the secret of life! I remember

telling Mum years back that life's like playing Snakes and Ladders. Since then events have only reinforced my views. Just when you're getting along fine, happy or rich, you get zapped back into the mire – undeserved and unexpected.'

Joe's face lit up with missionary zeal and she groaned inwardly. Here we go again . . .

'But look at it this way,' he was saying. 'What if those *zaps* represent the external world, or *life*, while your so-called long climb up the ladder is your *fight* against life. What if you grasp hold of those zaps and use their energy as your energy, just as I use Alasdair's strength to sweep him over my shoulder. You'd be at one with life and your ego would disappear. That's what judo and life are all about.'

'I'm afraid you've lost me,' she said.

'Doesn't matter. I'm thirsty. Ah! Come on, Alasdair.'

Her son walked out slowly, balancing the tray on his head. At fourteen he was tall and graceful.

'You'll drop it,' she grumbled.

'Zola taught me how.' He handed down the tray and crouched beside her. She slid her arm around him, pulling his sweat-drenched body against hers. His face was flushed, his hair wet and clinging to his forehead, and his eyes were sparkling with youth and joy. Hamish's eyes. He's going to be strong and athletic like his father, she thought fondly.

Alasdair drained his glass, gave her a quick hug and jumped up. 'I'm going for a swim, Mum. Coming, Joe?'

'No. Definitely not. I prefer a hot shower.'

Alasdair laughed and moments later he was racing through the long grass towards the lake.

'You never learned to flow, Marjorie,' Joe was saying mournfully. 'You've been very stubborn, like a beetle caught in a flood, clinging to your old ladder, half-drowning yourself in the process.' He looked at her fondly. 'I would really like to see you happy, Marjorie. You, of all people, deserve that.'

'I would like to become more spiritual,' she said shyly. 'You see, when I smashed the car I had a strange experience. Well, never mind that . . . If only I knew how to start.'

'Start by forgetting about spirituality. Forget dogma and rules. Don't get entangled with other people's ideas or labels. Find your own truth by living and really loving.'

'How?'

'By loving every moment with as much passion as you gave Robert and Hamish, and then more. Lavish it on all life. Meditate. Take each moment and live it with wonder. Live life the same way as you listen to music, with wonder and joy for every moment. Be free.'

He stood up and she watched him saunter up the steps. He had thickened out and there was a smattering of grey in his dark hair, but he was still strikingly handsome, with his sombre dark looks and his Pharoah's eyes. One of these days some new woman would get her hooks into him, Marjorie guessed, and he'd kick his way out of her female trap by shedding another few millions.

'Love the moment!' Joe had said. She gazed over the lawn, trying to get to grips with the moment, but it eluded her. It seemed to be retreating faster than she could chase it.

She shrugged and laughed. Who cared? She was feeling content. She stood up. She must plant the lavender seedlings before Robert arrived for lunch or they would wilt. It was just the day for it, warm and moist.

She began to dig up little portions of earth, smoothing the soil reverently, loving the feel of it. A ladybird fell onto her hand and she held it up, remembering an old childhood rhyme. 'Ladybird, ladybird fly away home,' she chanted, feeling heady with love. With a whirl of wings it soared towards the sun.

Hamilton Court
Ashbe Place
Outback bar